WEEP

THE IRISH EPIDEMIC

EOIN BRADY

CONTENTS

For Officer Pete Meegan of The NYPD.
Proof that dreams are realised through dedication and hard graft.

1

SO LONG SOLENE

"Storm Peggy will make landfall later this week. A red weather warning is in place along the west coast counties of Ireland. Expect power outages and interruptions to flights. People are advised to avoid unnecessary journeys and to stay indoors."

Fin could barely hear the news over the bitter wind whistling like static between his ears and headphones. He struggled up a long, steep hill. It felt like for every foot he managed to pedal, his bike was blown back two. Eyes stinging, tears streaming down his face. His knuckles were white with the effort of keeping the bike steady on the road. Leaning lower over the handlebars did nothing to reduce drag. He could see the humour in it; his headstone would read 'Killed by Peggy'. *New Year's resolution: get fit.* Old faithful, it had been the chosen resolution for the past five years.

He considered turning around and heading back, putting the wind behind him and letting it blow him down the hill to the Quay Hotel. Only a few rooms were occupied this close to Christmas. Given the circumstances, the management would not begrudge him staying. *Explaining why I need a suite might be difficult, but not as hard as telling Solene I won't be home for the last few hours we have this year.* He pushed on.

Winter-bald trees swayed, creaked and threatened to break over the wall surrounding Westport House. Storm-shed branches and a large broken bough obstructed the road into town. Household bins skittered between parked cars in front of dormant homes. A few windshields were cracked. Alarms rang out, shrieking to be heard above Peggy. His only solace in the storm was knowing that tomorrow would be a quiet day at work. *Who smiles on a rainy day? Somebody in the hotel trade.*

Reaching the peak of the hill, his legs were given a brief reprieve as he coasted down the other side. Ambulance and garda lights lit up the Castlebar road in the distance. A sudden downpour of rain trapped him in a sheltered cobblestone alleyway near his apartment. With no sign of it passing, he relented and hurried through the last stretch. Drenched to the skin he made a mental note to add 'get a car' to his list of resolutions. He punched the code in to get through to the gated courtyard above the town centre car park. Nothing happened: the door remained locked. *If the power went out, I'll have to go the whole way back to work.* It took two further attempts before the door stubbornly opened. It always faulted during rain. He carried the bike up the stairs. Small streams gushed out of the moss-muffled gutters.

His efforts to enter the house quietly were ruined when the wind caught the door and blew it out of his grip, knocking it against the wall. It left a deep dent in the plaster. *Well that's the house deposit gone.* On the table, a solitary candle sputtering above a shrinking puddle of wax went out. Water pooled around his feet in the time it took him to lock the door. In a few squeaky strides he was in the bathroom. He threw his jacket and uniform into the tub. Soggy socks and dripping shoes went in too for good measure.

Solene sat up in bed. When she was sure it was Fin and not a murderer, her head fell back onto her pillow. "Hi," she stifled a yawn. "It sounds horrible out there."

"There's a bit of a breeze alright." The air in the room was so warm it nearly shimmered. He knocked the heater off and undressed before chasing three cats off of his side of the bed, hissing to hurry them. He smiled when Solene glared to let her know it was meant in jest, but there was only so many times he could come home to a cat's ass on his pillow without hissing and meaning it. They plopped down off the bed and curled up in their baskets.

Solene moved across the bed. "I warmed it up for you."

He crawled in beside her. She gasped and wedged a pillow between their bodies. "If you even think of putting your hands on me, you'll be in the spare room."

"I have no idea what you're talking about." He drew his cold hands back to his side of the pillow.

Curled up behind her he quickly thawed as his eyes grew heavy. The red light of the electrical alarm clock showed a quarter to five in the morning. He turned the face away, disgusted at himself for adding up how few hours he had before it would ring.

"How was work, baby?" Solene asked.

"It was dead. The storm isn't due to hit fully until this evening, but it already feels like the end of the world out there, and we're only getting the hem of Peggy's skirt."

Solene scoffed. "I don't know how they decide to name these storms. I mean if they called it Storm Death Wish, you'd have fewer gobshites cycling home in it."

"I couldn't get through to any taxis. I'd say my tires only touched the ground twice on my way home," Fin said.

"I doubt that," she squeezed the flab of his stomach playfully.

"Warn me before you do that so I can suck my gut in. Wouldn't have been able to drive that road, there's enough downed branches out there to feed a fire for a month."

"We don't have a fireplace, babe."

"If you left that radiator on any longer we would have."

"Shh. Try to sleep, I have to be up soon."

"There's not a hope that you'll be flying if that weather keeps up." Fin broke the blanket border, and nestled up against her, one arm draped around her body to hold her hand. No storm would ever keep him from falling asleep next to her. "It wouldn't be the worst thing in the world, us spending the holidays together for once."

Solene turned to kiss him. "You're the one that wanted to work over Christmas, and I'm not spending it in an empty hotel. My grandparents don't have many Christmases left you know, I would still like them to meet their great grandchildren."

Fin started snoring loudly.

"Love you," she said. "Now go to sleep."

One of the cats started meowing until one of Fin's pillows startled it at high speed. Fin closed his eyes and listened to the storm, while the slowing rhythm of Solene's deep breathing lulled him.

He only noticed the quiet, encroaching footsteps when it was too late. Wide-eyed, he woke with a jolt. He tried to sit up, but a weight above the blanket pinned him down. There was a head next to his, breathing deeply against his neck. Lips dragged across his skin before teeth bit down hard, a tongue wetting the flesh. Fin went cross-eyed, an itch forming in the back of his throat.

"Get off me." He tried to push Solene off, but the futile and insincere effort only made her laugh.

The noise of the storm was a constant comfort. Warmth wrapped him completely. He laughed until he felt the fur on the hood of her winter jacket, reminding him that this was a goodbye kiss. He made to rise.

"Shh, stay." She kissed him. "Stay." She rolled off him and lay on the bed for a while. "I'm going to miss you."

"I'm going to enjoy having a reasonable electricity bill this month."

"You'll be living in the hotel, there's no way of telling which one of us is the cause. Anyway, stop giving out when I'm halfway out the door," she said.

"Our relationship is based around arguing, love. What would we talk about if I couldn't give out about the cats?"

"Exactly the reason why I'm keeping them. I've left your Christmas presents upstairs. Let me know what you think when you open them."

"You're not getting yours until we do our own Christmas after you get back." He was failing to keep his eyes open.

"I still think you forgot to get me anything. Let me see even the edge of wrapping paper and I'll believe you."

"And spoil the mystery?" Fin said.

"Hardly."

"I meant the mystery of whether I remembered or not. It's still dark out, what time is it?"

"Just gone past half seven."

Fin groaned.

"So you won't be walking me to the bus then?" She let

him suffer in silence for a few seconds before smiling, releasing him from having to get out of bed for a few more hours.

Heavy raindrops pelted against the window. Sluggish beads of water trickled down the glass. "Great, my hair's going to frizz."

Fin wrapped his arms around her, dragging her into the blanket. "You could stay you know. Tell your family you missed your flight. Or you went to the wrong airport. They mixed up the aviation fuel line with the lavatory pipe and they don't want to risk flying. Any of those excuses would do. Your granny would believe all of those."

"I miss them, Fin. Don't try to put this on me, you're the one turning down the invitation to spend the holidays with us."

"What if the flights are cancelled? It would take a fairly ballsy pilot, or one with a bad gambling streak, to fly in that weather."

"We'll stay with mam's friends in Dublin and then leave on the next available flight."

Her smell made her coming absence more painful. "I don't speak French and I'd feel too much like I was intruding. How would you like to spend your holiday as an unpaid translator?"

"Another unpaid position to add to my resumé when you're involved. Along with unpaid house cleaner and unpaid chef."

"I'll make dinner if you stay."

She laughed. "That's a point towards me leaving, not staying. I have to go, I'll miss my bus."

He held on tighter to her for a few seconds longer. She did not argue over it. "Have a lovely Christmas. I can't wait to see you when you're home."

"This is the last one we spend apart," she said.

He wrapped his pinky finger around hers. "Promise."

She lay beside him, curling back into the shape of his body and rubbed his head. He fell asleep.

* * *

When he woke it was still raining and she was gone. It was just after three in the afternoon. *She should be landing soon.* He was less enthusiastic about returning to work and wondered if he could chance calling in sick. On the verge of falling back to sleep, a gentle weight on the bottom of the bed startled him. As soon as he heard purring, he kicked out and listened to the patter of little paws retreating up the stairs. There would be no bare asses on his pillow, at least for as long as he was in charge of the house. He threw the blanket off and got up.

Solene took most of the shower products with her. *I don't know how I'm going to survive without the coconut-scented body wash.* He had only vague memories of her leaving, tip-toeing around the room, putting her makeup in her suitcase. Packing quietly so as not to wake him. Her use of the hair dryer ruining all her effort. Shushing the cats whenever one of them mewled, causing them to meow back in some weird conversation. Inevitably, one of them always clawed at his toes if a foot ever slipped out beneath the covers, which often happened. He was thinking about using the argument that either they go, or he would, but there were three of them, four if you counted Solene, against him. He would lose the vote.

Coming back from his shower, the cats had taken up their usual place on his pillow. He took the towel off and chased them without fear of reprisal from Solene. He only stopped when he caught sight of his neighbours in the apartment across the street watching him. There was no need to dry off, the heat of his embarrassment boiled the excess water away.

Solene had left the upstairs heater on, out of forgetfulness rather than a thoughtful gesture. Drawing the venetian blinds he saw a line of red tail lights creeping up the Castlebar road, leaving Westport. Last minute shoppers and people heading home to their families. Suddenly, the extra money for holiday work was poor recompense for missing out on spending time with his own family and Solene.

The countertops and kitchen table were full of wrapped packages and little letters in Solene's neat handwriting. *No wonder she was up so early.* The amount of effort she put into presents far surpassed his.

The first letter he picked up read: 'I hate the thought of you being alone for Christmas, so I've tried to make the house as cozy as possible. From what I could tell this is nice coffee. If you don't have an anxiety disorder before drinking it, then you probably will after you've had a few cups. I hope you enjoy it. There are plenty of things to pair it with; there's a new game for you by the PlayStation, or a new snowy peak to add to your mountainous pile of unread books.

'I miss you. Please don't just eat sweets while I'm away. I did a healthy shop. The fridge is packed with good food. If I come back and find you've put on an extra roll of pudge, then our New Year's resolutions will be much tougher. Picture us getting up early to go to the gym together tougher.'

Big words from a woman that hasn't seen a sunrise since I've known her. He could smell the coffee through the wrapping. He put the kettle on and sent her a text while it boiled. 'Got your gifts. Thank you, I love them. The coffee looks thick as tar and smells delicious. The books and games will help kill time until I get to see you again. It's not Christmas without you. I'm feeling it now. Miss you.'

She posted a short video clip on Facebook of her wheeling a suitcase through Dublin over three hours ago. 'Are the planes still going so? I don't envy you that flight if they are,' he commented.

The smell of brewing coffee wafted through the apartment. Two large mugs went a long way to waking him up. He ignored her comments about getting fatter while rifling through a selection box for breakfast, there were more empty wrappers than full ones. Already it was starting to get dark outside. He set an alarm on his phone in case he fell asleep.

The afternoon news reports showed the damage caused by the weather and the eye of the storm was still over the Atlantic. He unwrapped the new game Solene bought him and stuck it on. He had a few more hours to himself before work.

2

CHEEKY PINTS

If only time went as fast at work as it does in front of the television. Just as he was really getting into the game, he had to leave. He dressed in a creased shirt, the only one that did not smell of half a week's use. Already running late, he did not stop to find a tie in the wash basket.

The cats mewled until they were fed and purred into their bowls. Fin left his bike, the wind outside was treacherous; he had planned on walking in, but found one taxi, idling in town. "I didn't think anybody would be running tonight." His jacket was still damp from the morning.

"I was about to call it a day before you showed up. Half my house are sick, so I'm trying to avoid them as much as possible. All I seem to be doing today is ferrying people back and forth from the hospital, so if I didn't catch what my kids have, I've definitely gotten something. Where are we heading?"

"The Quay Hotel, please."

Fin felt the force of the wind when it pushed the car. The driver peered over the steering wheel up at the dangerously swaying branches hanging over the road. They did not come across another car the entire trip. On the radio, the presenter dedicated a song to a caller who complained about being bedridden.

"Terrible time to get sick," Fin said, to fill the silence between them.

"Happens every year, doesn't it? I reckon if I even hear the word 'holiday', my body temperature starts rising. Seems to be a bad flu going around though. Hospital seemed fairly busy."

The taxi stopped outside the hotel, a long, four-storey building. The front doors were braced shut against the storm. Spray lashed up from waves that washed over the pier. The windshield wipers were on the highest setting, but they were woefully inefficient. Fin paid while the driver cursed about what the salt water was going to do to his car.

"Will you be around in the morning? I'll be leaving about seven."

"I'll be up, give me a bell." The taxi driver handed him a business card.

"Well, best of luck with the patients at home." Fin left him a tip and ran into the hotel.

Christmas music played in the empty lobby. He knew the order of the next nine songs. It's all he listened to at work for the last two months. The veteran staff members swore the festive album had not been updated in over a decade. In a few more hours, when the management had long gone home and the majority of guests still awake were too drunk to care, he would have an audiobook playing over the speakers.

Cereal boxes wrapped in festive paper nestled beneath two real fir trees. Every night he clogged the hoover with their needles. The staff behind the reception desk looked miserable.

"How's it going, lads?" Fin asked.

They visibly cheered up when he arrived because they could now go home.

"Evening, Fin. I've been dying of thirst since I arrived this morning. I'll raise a pint for you at the Christmas party tonight," Rebecca said. She took off a pair of brown reindeer antlers and gave them to him. He dropped them in the recycling bin.

He unplugged his fully charged work radio and clipped it to his belt. There was a relaxed atmosphere in the building as the last few business hours wound down. At the end of each shift, all incidents of note were written down for the nightporter. There were too few people in house for there to be any complaints or special requests. When he opened the log book, 'Merry Christmas' was written under tonight's date. Beneath that he read that a bus tour of Americans, that were not due to leave until the following day, had already left. He would not have to spend an hour bringing their bags out to the bus in the morning, nor listen to their complaints that appliances were broken. Nine times out of ten, he went up and showed them exactly why they were wrong.

"Most of the guests left during the day," Rebecca said. "Worried the weather will get worse."

"Nobody wants to stick around and witness the full wrath of Peggy. How are you getting home later tonight? I'm pretty sure Achill Island will have washed away before morning," Fin said.

"I'm staying with Ciara. Oh, and the country music act in the bar is cancelled. The golden oldie group that booked it rescheduled for after the holiday."

"No scone zombies or country music, it really is starting to feel like Christmas."

"George and Ciara are on the late shift behind the bar. They must have asked about twenty times in the last hour if they can close up early, but Andrew has them on for the full shift."

"Easy money," Fin said. "Plus they save by not buying a heap of drink at the staff party." He did not add that he was glad they were forced to stay; he always welcomed the company on the long, lonely nights. Solene had not replied to any of his messages, he expected all the travel would mean she would not stay up late texting him.

Bartenders were on the late shift to keep the residents' bar open. Once they kicked out the stragglers, he would suggest Ciara and George stay on for a few pints, their own little staff party.

Andrew stuck his head out from the back office. "Fin, you're only in? Come here to me."

A bank of monitors showed the camera feeds from across the hotel; as many eyes were on staff as the guests. Everything that happened outside of the rooms and toilets was captured and stored here. It took Fin several months to discover all of the camera blindspots.

"Where's your tie?"

"I overheard a guest saying he forgot his while he was on his way out into town, I gave him mine. Don't worry, I'll bill the hotel for it."

Andrew raised an eyebrow. Fin barely kept a straight face, Andrew broke first and smiled. "I'll make sure to order you a few clip on ones after the break. I just need to run through a few last minute things before I can put this place behind me – for a few days at least." Andrew brought him through to the bar to make himself an espresso. The waiting staff still on the floor tried to look busy in his presence. He knew the impact he had and often revelled in causing them

13

discomfort, musing that it's harder to look busy than actually be busy. Fin caught a grin at the corner of his mouth, the corner out of view of the other staff.

"The most important thing is this: the hotel is closed. Don't let a soul in through the main door, no maintenance or deliveries." He swayed where he stood. Small beads of sweat bubbled up on his forehead. He wiped his face with a napkin. "Typical, my body waits until I'm off before getting sick."

"Seems to be a lot of it going around," Fin said. "Don't bother with beer when you're out tonight. Hot whiskeys will do the trick. Kill it before it kills you."

"That's not a bad idea actually. Right, I'll just run over the alarms with you, you know the rest. You're here for the sake of insurance, if something happens, we need a body on site. Think of this as a paid holiday."

"Oh I am, don't worry about that."

Darren, the restaurant manager, leaned out over the pass, switching off the heating lamps. "Make us a coffee if you're having one, boss."

Andrew stuck a mug under the spout and steaming coffee poured out. The kitchen was still full of activity. Usually when Fin started his shift, they were all at home. Porters scrubbed the cookers and fridges, while the hostesses used their phone cameras to apply makeup.

"I won't see you at the party," Darren said. "I'm heading off straight after this. Enjoy the holidays. Fin, what wine do you drink?"

"Red," he said, resisting the urge to say 'any.'

"Merlot?"

He nodded.

"I'll leave a few bottles of it out for you. Don't burn the place down."

"There's less of a chance of that happening if you don't give him the wine," Andrew said. "If it does happen, try and make it look like an accident." Andrew passed him the coffee. His hand was shaking.

"You don't look well, Andy."

"Are you offering to stay on finish my shift for me?"

In response Darren pulled the metal shutters down with a bang. The last couple in the restaurant looked towards them and awkwardly gathered their things to head to the bar. Before they made it to the counter, two waiters rushed in and cleared the table, then made for the kitchen and freedom.

Darren came out with three bottles of red and left them under the till. "Have a good one buddy." He went to deal with the last bits of clean-up.

"Help yourself to a few pints from the bar, but make sure to record them as waste," Andrew said in the face of Darren's generosity.

Once Fin signed off on everything, Andrew took off his tie and almost became a different person. "I've been craving a pint all week. You're not a Mayo man yourself, what has you staying down here instead of heading home to your family?" he asked Fin.

"Money. There's no way Santa was going to be able to compete with triple pay over the holidays. Looking to do a bit of travel next year with my girlfriend. This will be her Christmas surprise."

"Well you're saving me from doing it. Though my kids will miss having the pool to themselves." He shook Fin's hand and left.

When he heard the car engine start up, Fin drenched his hand in antibacterial sanitiser; whatever Andrew was coming down with, he could do without. He followed him out to the car park at the back of the hotel and locked the gates. *No more arrivals for the rest of the year.* He started his nightly routine, beginning with a walkabout, checking every lock and closing over the fire doors.

The staff did not stay long after Andrew left. Apart from the bar, the rest of the hotel was empty before midnight. He blew out all the candles on the tables in the lobby, reorganised the chairs and got the hoovering out of the way. He roughly estimated that if he lined up the amount of carpet he had hoovered during his employment, it would reach the moon and back.

The door from the bar opened, interrupting his audiobook. "Fin, call a hospital and let them know there's one coming in immediately," Ciara said. Her hand was wrapped in a dish cloth. When she opened it, he saw that her finger was covered in blood, flowing from a shallow cut. Glass shards glistened in the dim lobby light.

"Hospital's all the way in Castlebar, it'll be the morgue you'll need by the time an ambulance gets here."

"It would be livelier than the bar is tonight anyway. Would you mind bandaging me up? I'm already feeling a bit queasy. I can't stand the sight of blood."

"Of course." He brought her into the back office and took out the first aid kit. Ciara sat down and laid her hand flat on the table, pointedly looking in the opposite direction.

"All joking aside, it's pretty bad," he found the tweezers and steadied himself before rooting at her injury.

He used a wet wipe to dab off the smaller fragments of glass that had not broken the skin. "How did you manage this?"

"That gobshite George keeps putting the glass washer on the highest setting. Temperature's hot enough to reshape

16

them. One exploded in my hand when I was putting it away."

"And you said your night was boring."

"Yes, I often use cutting myself to feel something as a gauge of how an average day of work is going."

He cleaned the wound, wiped antiseptic cream on her hand and put a colourful child's plaster on her finger for good measure. "I think you'll live to work another day."

"Doctor, your bedside manner is atrocious. Is that how you give bad news to all your patients?"

"Here, no role play until after hours."

She swatted his shoulder with her good hand. "No end to the excitement of a nightporter, eh?"

"Yeah, you could write a book about my adventures here after hours."

"Oh I am, it's erotica – fictional."

"Feck off. Are there many left in the bar?"

"A few. Not enough to stay open. If each of them orders two more drinks, it might just cover the cost of keeping us here this long. Can't leave though, Andrew said he'd be watching the cameras from his phone."

"Next time he starts on about that, just mention something about privacy laws and watch how quickly he turns red."

Ciara thanked him and went back to the bar. Fin watched the security camera screens. There was no sound, but he only had to look at George to see that he was sorry. Ciara was laying it on hard. Fin laughed.

A young couple having a hushed argument drove the other guests out of the bar to bed. Fin wished them a good night and crossed his fingers that none of them would ask him for anything. After the lift doors closed, he snuck into the bar. George and Ciara cleaned while pretending that they did not hear the bickering. Fin turned the music down so it was barely audible, the universal bartender code for 'Go away.' If they refused the hint, he would start putting chairs on tables around them and turn the lights up full, that always seemed to do the trick.

While he made a pot of tea, the woman stormed off. The man nursed his pint, looked at his reflection in the mirror behind the bar and shook his head. His eyes were bloodshot and he was sweating. "Can I get the same again, please?" he said.

"Are you sure you're okay for another?" George asked. "You look a bit worse for wear."

"This is only my third one of the day." He took a closer look at himself in the mirror and used his sleeve to mop his brow. "Actually, forget the pint. Will you make me a hot toddy with plenty of lemon and cloves? I'll take it up to my room."

Fin could not detect slurring in his voice. He did not envy the bar staff having to stand a few feet in front of customers that constantly coughed, spluttered and sneezed in their direction.

"Do you mind if I bring up a jug of ice water with me too? Seem to be coming down with a cold."

George made up the drink, while Ciara stirred the tea, using her crippled hand as an excuse for getting out of cleaning. "How are you feeling about staying here by yourself over the holidays?" she asked Fin.

"It's no different than any other night during the year, except I've no silly complaints to worry about. I'll do a walk around after the tea and then, when yous clock out I'll pour us a few pints."

Ciara put the pot down. "Get on with your walk then. I'll

pour this out. A waste, making tea when pints are an option."

The hallways were so quiet that he scuffed his feet on the thick carpet and cleared his throat, just to see how far the sound travelled. Usually, if he listened closely, he could hear the snores of sleeping guests, little squabbles and trysts. Fin turned all the lights off behind him and imagined the settling silence was like that inside a tomb. The building was warm and lifeless. It reeked of bleach in the back halls, where no guests ever saw the old peeling paint and threadbare carpets.

The ice machine hummed and knocked as it refilled. During his first few weeks on the job, that sound always made him hurry back to the safety of the front desk. Now he walked the corridors in the dark by memory. Systematically, he locked all the doors that would not open again until the new year. The hotel entered a brief slumber. For a little under two weeks it would be home to just one person.

The radio on his hip squawked into life, startling him. He didn't mind the guys prank calling him while he was on his rounds. Any company to make the shadows shrink away was welcome.

"Fin, will you come down for a minute, please?" George said. To his credit he actually sounded worried. If something happened with the freezers or kegs, then that was his quiet night over with.

"There's a man in the basement, he's near the drinks store. Can't understand a word out of him."

"Are you trying to say he got into the drinks store or he's a foreign chap?"

"I don't think he's currently on this planet, he must have taken something. I asked him politely to piss off a few times, but he didn't pay any heed to me. I didn't want to go near him by myself."

"Hang on, I'll be down to you now."

Ciara and George waited for him in the lobby, they watched the door to the staircase, the spine of the hotel that led workers to the basement and guests to their rooms.

"What are the both of you doing out here? Is the bar empty?" Fin asked.

"That chap left soon after you did," George said. "We flew through the cleaning and were about to stock the bar. I thought we were the only ones left, until I went down to the drinks store and found him down there," George laughed. "They'll have a good chuckle when they check the cameras, I jumped a foot in the air when I stumbled over him."

"I could hear him crying from up here a few minutes ago," Ciara said. "I'm not going down there without you. You're trained to deal with people like that."

"Essentially you're saying you'll watch."

"Enthusiastically."

The stairs leading up were well-lit. Innocuous hotel art, the visual representation of elevator music, covered the walls. A 'Staff Only' sign hung on a fire door downstairs that led into the labyrinth of hallways buried beneath the hotel. The clock-in machine, florist's fridge, and laundry room were all behind that door, along with enough stock to keep drink flowing through January. The maintenance room was buried far in the back. Fin went in first. The place was empty.

"I swear he was here..." A noise from the far end of the corridor stopped George.

Fin found the switches and turned the lights on. The weak fluorescent bulbs in the tunnel flickered, but were not bright enough for them to see much.

Ciara took out her phone and shined the camera torch into the darkness. Two legs lay motionless, sticking out between housekeeping carts. From his position, the owner of the legs was of no immediate danger to them. They leaned in to get a better look. Ciara's phone beeped, she was recording.

"Come on, put that away, You wouldn't like somebody watching you through a camera instead of helping you," Fin said. He broke the phone's line of sight with his hand. Sensing he sounded a bit harsh, he added. "Don't be giving George ideas, he'll have his phone charged, ready for when you get langered later. Plus, if this chap remembers you taking a video, one conversation with management will cause you a lot of trouble."

"Sorry, I meant nothing by it. Only had it on just in case he attacked you, I'd have proof." The man wore a crumpled, mud stained suit. His trousers soiled and torn. He smelled exactly as they expected he would by the sight of him.

"Are you okay, mate?" Fin asked.

Ciara shined her light in his face, his eyes were dilated and did not shrink. "Shouldn't they look like pin-pricks in bright light? He barely notices it. That can't be good. It's drugs. Has to be."

"Well at least he's breathing." Fin was trained to handle rowdy drunks, but it was never a skill he looked forward to using, though he was glad to have it.

"Somebody that far gone could probably do with a hospital bed," Ciara said.

"Are you a guest here?" Fin nudged the man's leg with his boot. His head lolled onto his chest and he started to weep. The three of them took a step back; the sobs were so unsettling, it rose every small hair across Fin's body. "I swear

I barely touched him. Did either of you serve him drink in this state?"

"If somebody comes into the bar and can't say their own name, I wouldn't give them anything stronger than sparkling water," George said.

Ciara kept the light on him, and slowly his pupils reacted. His hands shook violently. He moved like a man too cold to feel the outline of himself. Fingers dug into his temples, palms covered his eyes. He curled into himself like a dying spider.

"Here, calm down there." Ciara lowered the phone. "He's definitely on something. What did you take buddy? I've been in since six and I haven't seen him in the bar."

"This goes beyond my first aid training," George said. "What about doctor on call or an ambulance?"

"I'll go up and call one," Ciara said. "Yous bring him up to the lobby."

"Wait, why do we have to do the heavy lifting and you get to make the call?" George said.

"Weren't you only saying the other night you got your raise? Head barman. You're paid more, you do more."

The fire door slowly closed behind her, leaving them little light to work with. Fin moved the cloth trolleys away from the man. They were damp where he lay against them. Standing either side of him, together they managed to get him to his feet. His clothes were saturated. Fin wore latex gloves, George was barehanded. The man was pale. Sweat dripped from his face onto the dusty floor like a leaky faucet.

"The suit is stuck to him," George said. He made to go through the man's pockets for information, a room key or a wallet with his name on it.

"Wait, I've gloves," Fin said. A hotel room card was the

first thing out of his jacket pocket. "Looks like you're our problem, David Brosnan."

"He's on fire." George grunted under the dead weight of the man. "We won't be able to drag him up the stairs. Let's use the service elevator."

David's teeth started chattering. He convulsed, gasping and gulping down air and wept sporadically. Every time he stopped, he seemed to come to his senses enough to be surprised that he was crying. Fin kept looking at George for reassurance. Neither of them had dealt with anything like this before.

The man retched and threw up rancid bile. It splattered on the metal floor of the elevator and covered their shoes. George cursed and dropped him on the ground when the door dinged open. Unlocking the staff exit to the car park, he washed his shoes under a tap. The cool air was refreshing after the repressive dark heat below. It seemed to soothe David. The weather had worsened since he locked the gates behind Andrew. Wind whistled above the hotel. He heard snapping and the clanging of flag poles on the roof.

"Nobody ever thought to bring the flags down, did they?" Fin asked.

"I put liquid in glasses, I thought that was your job." When George walked back inside, his shoes squelched, but there was no more vomit.

"By the time I came in, if I went up on the roof, the wind would have thrown me clear over half the country."

George tutted and ran into the rain. He came back with the Irish tri-colour, crumpled and dirty. Half the green was torn and frayed. Shielding his eyes from the rain, he looked up. "Looks like Europe is next."

"Flags can be replaced. Now come in and help me."

Before they got David out of the kitchen, Ciara burst through the door. George still carried the sopping flag. "Look at this, a disgrace."

"Would you go away out of that," Ciara said. "This coming from the man that wouldn't know if it was green or orange that came first, if not for the flagpole."

"Feck off," George laughed. "What's the story, who's coming for him?"

They lowered David gently to the ground. He whimpered for water. Ciara filled a cup and handed it to him. She nodded her head for them to follow and lowered her voice when she spoke. "I can't get through to anybody."

"You have to press nine first on the phone if you want to call out of the hotel," Fin said.

"I know, sure I wait until I'm at work to call my cousin in New Zealand. Besides, the number for emergency services should go straight through. I tried the doctor on call, then the garda station and then the national numbers. Nothing worked."

"The storm could be messing with the signal," Fin suggested.

"It's a landline. But fair enough, cables could have been knocked down. That doesn't explain why I can't get through to anybody on my mobile." She took out her mobile, dialled 911 and held it between them. They hunched over with their ears close to it.

"I don't think it's ringing," George said.

"Anybody come in to the bar while we were away?" Fin said.

"Not a soul."

"Lock up then." He took off the gloves and washed his hands in the sink using plenty of antibacterial soap and scalding water. Then he took out his own phone and tried to ring. George did the same.

"I've got nothing," Fin said.

"I'm the same. That's weird. I still have bars of signal though." George rang Ciara's phone. After a few seconds it buzzed on her palm. "Why does my name come up as 'Do Not Answer'?"

"Because you only ever call me to cover your shift."

"Taxi driver that drove me to work earlier mentioned that all he was doing for the day was ferrying people out to the hospital in Castlebar. Whatever's doing the rounds will have people ringing in, clogging the lines. We'll keep trying," Fin said. He opened the internet on his phone. "We could email somebody."

"Tweet the police," George said. "Hashtag 911."

"None of us drive," Ciara said. "Otherwise I would have suggested we take him to Castlebar ourselves."

David coughed up yellow phlegm and spoke. "I'm okay." He sipped the water and slid across the floor to lean against a fridge, relishing the chill. He retched again, but there was nothing left to come up.

"Where am I?"

"The Quay Hotel, Westport," George said.

There seemed to be no strength left in his body. His arms limp by his side, his head was kept up by resting it on the door behind him. He did manage a shadow of a smile. "I know I'm in Westport. I wanted to know why I was in the kitchen and not my room."

Unless this brief sobriety was like the calm eye of a storm, Fin doubted David had any alcohol in his system. "Have you taken anything? I'm a nightporter and these two are bartenders, they'll likely be taking something when they clock out. It's okay to tell us. Or is it a case that you were supposed to take medication and just forgot to? We're trying to get help for you, but at the moment we're all you have."

David lifted his mug up off the floor with great effort and gulped the water down. His head was starting to sway, his eyes unfocusing. *We're going to lose him again soon.*

Ciara rummaged through the freezer and took out a bag of vacuum-packed monkfish. She wrapped it in a dish cloth and held it against David's forehead. The cool touch brought him back to his senses.

"Wait, what? You're trying to get me help? What?" The cloth shaded his eyes from the light and the tension in his body slackened.

"We found you in the basement," Ciara said. "This is as lucid as we've seen you."

"You're running a fever. There's a bug doing the rounds, you've likely just picked that up from travelling." George said. "We nearly called an ambulance for you."

"No! I'll be okay. I don't need help."

"You're okay. We couldn't get through to anybody. The lines are clogged."

What little colour was left in David's face drained away. He looked dangerously pale.

"Hey, wow!" Ciara backed away from him.

He followed the look of shock on their faces down to his hand. His fist was closed so tightly that his nails were starting to cut his palm. "I can't feel it." When he concentrated, his fingers loosened. "You can't get through to anybody?"

"Lines are full," George said. "Do you want me to get you something for your hand?"

Daivd was lost in his own thoughts. When he spoke again, his voice was distant. "No. Help me to my room. Wear gloves."

He drank as much water as they gave him and kept the cup when they helped him to his feet. He looked horrid, his skin a sickly rubbery pallor like a mannequin.

"Are you okay to head to bed?" Fin said.

He nodded and grimaced, his movement caused him pain. "I'm so sorry."

"No need for that. There's no harm done."

* * *

The elevator stopped on the third floor and they brought him to his room. Even though he was more lucid, he still needed both Fin and George to support him. Ciara tried his card every possible way but the door remained locked.

"Hold him," Fin said. "I spend half my nights recoding cards that were wiped by phones."

"Great design." Ciara put one of David's hands around her shoulder and held him up, while Fin tried his master key.

"Ah, here!" Ciara stepped away, letting George shoulder the weight. He cursed trying to keep him up. The man's legs buckled and he slumped down. His trousers had darkened and the warm, acrid smell of urine filled the hall.

"He pissed on me," Ciara used her sleeve to rub her trousers and squirmed at the thought of it. "I'm going to have a shower and get some clean clothes from the laundry."

Fin and George tried to keep from sniggering until the elevator doors closed behind her.

"Mate, you're lucky there's not a website that allows hotel staff to review customers, because you're hovering around a solid one star right now," George said.

The red lock light turned green and the room opened.

Fin hooked David around the arm and they unceremoniously dumped him on the bed. He crumpled in a heap, his limbs curled close to his core. With the blanket covering him, his shivers started to calm. The room was immaculate. All of his clothes were still inside a small suitcase. The only mess was on the table, where a large laptop hummed, connected to several harddrives. No empty beer bottles filled the waste bin. It was not unusual for Fin to see people sleepwalking through the corridors late at night. He put David's getting lost in the basement down to the high fever. It worried him and no amount of coaxing could get another word out of David.

They stayed with him until they were confident that the housekeepers would not find a corpse in the morning.

"Thanks for waiting with me," Fin closed the door gently behind them.

"Don't mention it, I'm still clocked in, that was a few extra pints for the holidays. Likely the staff party was cut short by the storm anyway."

* * *

Back in the kitchen they scrubbed themselves as clean as they possibly could. George scoured his arms. "That's scary. He looks fit enough, imagine what that could do to an elderly or sick person. I'll have to remind my nan to get a flu booster shot. Ciara must still be downstairs showering. You know she's annoyed when she overcomes the fear of being down in the basement alone."

"Do you think we should hide down there and scare her?" Fin asked.

"Yes, yes I do. But she would actually kill us if we did that to her tonight."

Fin squeezed a quarter of a bottle of disinfectant into his hand and passed the rest to George. "I'm dying for that drink now."

Together they finished off the last of the clean-up in the bar, placing the stools on top of the counter and putting chairs on top of tables. He would vacuum and wash the floors later when they were gone. Excitement over the quiet pint they planned to share was marred by Ciara's absence, but it did not stop George and Fin having a round in one of the few camera blind spots. They sat on the top floor in high backed chairs in front of long windows. Rain obscured their view of the street below.

"Are you sure you want to walk home in that?" Fin said. "There aren't any taxis."

"I wouldn't mind staying here with another drink and settling into a book. Listening to that downpour. I'll risk it though. If I stay then I'll have to be up early to leave before the morning manager gets in and I've no desire for that. Will you be okay with your man?"

"He'll be in the horrors tomorrow," Fin took a long drink of his ale. "I'll check on him throughout the night. Imagine I came across him after yous went home. I wouldn't have the blood pressure left to call an ambulance for myself."

George laughed. Headlights lit up the road below, a taxi pulled up outside and three people rushed into the hotel, jackets covering their heads. George finished his pint in two swallows and started for the stairs.

"George, have a wonderful Christmas. If you're about, come in for a cheeky pint."

"I'll take you up on that."

3

AFTER PARTY

Rebecca arrived at seven to relieve him. She never looked as happy to see him at the start of the day as she did by its end. She still looked drunk enough that a bouncer would think twice about granting her entry to a club.

"How's the head?" Fin asked. She was pale, clammy and downcast. She was saturated from the rain, the spines of her umbrella bent by the force of the wind. He was sure when her alarm went off, she wondered how much she really needed this job. "How many times did you hit the snooze button?"

She shook her head in response and went straight for the coffee machine. There were usually pain killers under the till; he found a nearly empty packet and handed it to her. She took them gratefully and put on two coffees.

"The town was absolutely mad last night. I remember most of the dinner and the pub, but nothing of the club and that's the problem," she cringed. "We all went out dancing, there wasn't one among us sober. I'm afraid to go online in case I did something stupid and somebody recorded it."

"Anything scandalous happen?"

"Nothing more salacious than usual – I hope."

"Did Ciara seem angry to you last night?"

"Don't get me started. I was supposed to stay with her. She never showed up and wouldn't answer her phone. I ended up spending the night in my car."

"That's not like her. She left without saying a word last night. And you're a big eejit. Why didn't you come back here? There's nothing but empty beds."

"There weren't any taxis. Once the pubs and clubs emptied, the streets were packed with people trying to call family members but nobody seemed to be getting through. I was too drunk to walk back here. So I waited in my car. I thought the cold was going to kill me. How was the night? Anything to report here?"

He took a sip of the coffee and felt it thaw away the drowsiness that had set in around three A.M. It seemed to bring a bit more life back into Rebecca. Recounting the night had her on the verge of angry tears. She turned on one of the heating lamps over the pass and stood beside it. Fin wrote a quick message to Ciara. 'Hope you're okay after last night.'

"Quiet here for the most part," he said. "Ciara and George found somebody asleep in the basement. Scared them half to death. He wet himself as we took him back to his room. Ciara got the brunt of it. Of course, George and I laughed at the situation, but we thought she was out of earshot. Could have been why she was pissy." Rebecca's look of utter disgust only made it funnier.

"I've been checking in on him throughout the night. He's still alive. We tried calling an ambulance but never got through to one. I think he's through the worst of it now, so there's no panic. I wrote his room and details down for you. Told him he could stay on a bit longer after checkout. He looked like he could have kissed me when I said that – had he the strength. It'll be a slow one for you I reckon."

"Just one more day. Thank God. You all set for staying here over the holiday?"

"I've free range of the beer taps and I'm getting paid while I inspect them."

Rebecca nodded at the cameras. "Just remember they're watching."

"They'll have a lovely shot of my pimply arse to use for my employee of the month photo."

Rebecca snorted. "Want me to call you a taxi?"

"Please." Fin fished out the card he took off the taxi driver who had dropped him to work. She went out to the reception desk. She sat down in the cushioned chair and let out a sigh of relief. She looked so bedraggled that if they needed to cast a receptionist for the hotel in *The Shining* she would get the job. She dialed the number.

"That's weird," Rebecca said. "There's not even a tone." She pressed each button on the speed dial menu but all the calls went unanswered. "Nothing. Storm must have damaged something."

Fin took one look at the lashing rain outside. "That's disappointing."

"Not worth the money to head out in that weather. How did you manage to drive here?"

"It felt like I was on a go-kart track, weaving between fallen branches and blown-over bins. Looks like you're walking."

He finished the rest of his coffee and left the mug in the sink for the kitchen porter. "Where's that welcoming smile?" He pretended to take the fake smile off his face and threw it to her, like somebody throwing a kiss to a lover. She made a show of catching it in the air and slapped it over her mouth.

When she removed her hand she was grinning maniacally. She folded her arms and rested her head to nap.

"Listen, I'll not see you again until next year, have a great holiday," Fin said.

She gave a muffled goodbye.

"Just remember, they're watching."

She raised her head off the desk and, bleary-eyed, started her day.

* * *

The rain caught him out in the open when he was only halfway home. He sheltered beneath a tree, waiting for the worst of it to pass. Few cars were on the road, most of the drivers tried to avoid splashing through puddles next to him, apart from one that sent a wave of murky water over him. The driver erratically mounted the footpath further down the road to avoid a branch. Low clouds whipped past the peak of Croagh Patrick, known locally as The Reek. The mountain watched over the tourist town, drawing people from around the world.

Out beyond Clew Bay, dark clouds tumbled from the sky in thick sheets of rain. The shower swallowed Clare Island and rushed with a hunger towards the mainland. The rumbles of thunder grumbled in the black mass. Fin pulled the chords of his hood tighter, held the rim against the wind and continued homeward at a faster pace.

His walk home in the early morning before most people were awake was one of the few pleasures of the job. When it felt like dominion of the world would be fought over by him, the milkman and the people in the newspaper delivery vans. The shop he stopped off in to buy the paper was still closed, the young clerk possibly out drinking during the night, starting his day a little later than usual. The newspapers were tightly corded. The image for the front-page story was of a hospital in Dublin, the A&E packed with people waiting to be seen. Fin wormed a paper out from the bundle and waved at the camera. He mouthed 'I'll drop in later to pay.' He only hoped that there was enough food at home to feed the cats.

By the time he reached his apartment the paper was useless, soaked right through to the agony aunt section. It was tearing apart in his hands. He lost count of the number of times he correctly entered the code into the door, but the lock was still engaged. It was just a matter of luck that he spotted a woman from his block leaving for work. She nearly closed the door on him, after noticing him sketchily eyeing up a route into the courtyard from the car park. Solene's cats wove around his legs the moment he entered the apartment. Despite their incessant meowing, the place still felt empty without her.

"How do you have so much to talk about?" he said, nudging them aside with his boot. They were irritable; Mooch tried to run between his legs and escape the moment the door opened. "I only need to keep you alive until she comes back. This will go easier on you all if you behave." It had not seemed like such a difficult task until he saw the full litter box.

They ignored the food he poured out for them. Solene had filled the press with twice as much as was needed. Fin only noticed how bushy their tails were when he turned the light on. They hid in their cosy spots. "I was only messing when I said all I have to do is keep you alive." A pang of worry blossomed at the thought that Solene might return and they would be sick, or worse. He knew that whatever happened to them, he would experience as well.

There was a note inside the fridge. 'So you don't starve to death while I'm away.' Each shelf was full of food. The cupboards too. All of it healthy, not much of it appealing. While breakfast sizzled on the pan and the coffee brewed, he checked his phone. No response from Ciara. Alongside the weather warnings, there were breaking news articles talking about several reported flu deaths. *Merry Christmas.* Without reading any of them, he sent a link of the article to his father. 'Have you gotten a flu jab this year? This is not me trying to call you old, I just want you to be able to enjoy the few years you have left.'

His response was swift and expected. 'Go away out of that, I'm not that old yet.'

'Last I checked there wasn't an age limit you had to reach before you could die of something.'

'Knowing my luck I'll get sick over the holidays. Happens every year. Are you free to call? It's taking too long to reply by text.'

Fin put his phone up to his ear. "Hey Dad, considering the speed you text at, I think you should consider getting a shot."

His father ignored the comment. "See there were a few deaths over the last few days. It's some respiratory infection, I think."

"Should we be worried that there are enough cases to make the news? I mean doesn't the flu claim a few people every year?"

"Aye it does but... I don't know, these people weren't all old, a few of them were young with no underlying health issues by the reports. Might be a case of a bad batch of drugs in Dublin, a few people from the same club were struck down with something."

"That doesn't make sense, there's a rake of people sick

here. Now, I'm going off of what a taxi driver told me." Fin stepped away from the pan to better hear the conversation.

"I went to check on your granny. They've stopped visitors going to retirement homes."

"Ah I wouldn't worry about that. They'd be afraid if they let a moist breeze in, the place would be empty by evening."

"She's fine, thanks for asking. She sends her love, mostly to Solene. Will you be all right down there? News is saying to avoid public places – bars, cafes, buses and hotels."

"That's easy enough to do with the storm. The hotel will be empty before I head in tonight and then I just relax until it opens again. Easy money."

"Have you heard from Solene yet? How was her flight?"

"Her first one was delayed and then cancelled. She's supposed to be getting one tonight. She filled the house with food and little notes for me before she left."

"You don't deserve that woman."

"I know."

A silence remained long enough between them to become awkward. "I don't like the thought of you down there by yourself," his father said.

"Well then think of how I'll be making more money in a week than I normally would in a month. That's what's getting me through it."

"The taxman will be delighted. Don't forget to bring your camera to work with you, that storm will be ravaging the west coast. I'd say you'll be glad there's four floors tonight when the first two are underwater."

"That's not a bad idea, there's a little snug on the top floor in front of a massive window. Perfect view of the bay and mountain from there. Pint and a book with the camera at the ready."

"It's well for some. Go on, I'll let you go. I've to do my

shopping. I leave it until the last minute, happens every year. Do you think you should get a booster shot, what with being around so many people?"

"If there's something going around, I already have it. If you're chatting with granny again, let her know I was asking after her."

"Listen, she's in the best place for her to be."

"It's terrifying to think that one day that'll be us lying in bed most of the day in a home, with all our time behind us."

"Awful maudlin for a man that's going to be living in a massive hotel alone for the next week. She'll be grand, though she won't appreciate having that conversation with you."

"What I was getting at was, you best get me a decent present this year or else we won't be putting you in a home, we'll find a field with a view and ditch you there."

"I changed your nappy enough, now it's your turn to change mine."

"Go on. Good luck."

"Love you."

The line went dead, the phone hung limp in his hand. He rarely heard his father say he loved him, it was something unspoken. *Things must be worse than he let on to warrant a 'Love you.'*

* * *

Light shone through the corners of the blackout blinds, but it was the noise of the shoppers rushing below his window that kept him tossing and turning in bed. He ran himself a bath, dug out a few of Solene's lavender bath bombs and candles from the press under the sink. He dropped two of them into the hot stream. He videoed the result and sent it to Solene with the caption 'it does not feel like home without you, but I'm getting by'.

Opening the book she had bought him, he lay down in the purple, pink and perfumed water. Music and rain drowned out the noise from the busy market street. After the water became too cool to be comfortable, he moved upstairs. Several hours later, with a lot less light in the world, he was frightened awake by the game controller slipping from his lap and loudly hitting the ground. The cats scattered, their little claws scraping on the tiles.

Several people in the car park beeped their horns. He looked through the blinds. The place was a mess; shoppers ran to escape the rain, cars sped off and it looked like a fight was about to start between three people over a cart full of food. Somebody pulled out without looking and broke the lights of a car already on the road. Neither of the drivers stopped to exchange details. He was glad he had decided to leave most of his Christmas shopping until the January sales. Solene loved surprises and the best way to keep her presents a surprise was to keep them a mystery to himself. Lying back on the couch, he hit the snooze button five times before getting ready.

* * *

No taxi would take him to the Quay, many of the numbers he rang went straight to voicemail. It was pitch dark when he set out on the long walk to work. His umbrella caught in the wind and broke the moment he opened it. A pity, it was an expensive one he had stolen from the hotel. It went into the first bin he came across. Christmas lights swung in arcs across the road. Rain pipes throbbed and gurgled, streams of water shot out across the paths and flowed down the tarmac. The gutters were full, little rivers nearly mounted the kerb. The storm would wash through town.

There was little relief from the sharp rain on the walk in. He was running late and fighting against the wind slowed him further. Nobody would mind that much on the last day. Leaning into the wind, it was a struggle to keep his footing. He had to cross the road to avoid the swaying trees on the grounds of Westport House. It was the first time he had seen the harbour so full of boats. They rattled and roared, banging against tires lining the pier wall. Even in the relative safety of the harbour they looked to be in danger of damage. He tasted salt from the spray in the air. It was too dark to see far, but he could hear waves crashing over the storm wall in the distance. He could only imagine what it must be like for the residents out on the islands in the bay.

When the electric doors of the hotel hummed open, he was greeted by an empty lobby and the same old Christmas songs. He stood under the heater until he could feel his cheeks again. Rebecca walked out from the back office behind the reception desk. Her hard expression softened only moderately when she saw that it was not a customer.

"What the hell are you still doing here?" he asked.

"Since you've left, hardly anyone has come to work. There was one lad in the kitchen to do the breakfast, but there was nobody to cook for. Two housekeepers were in for I'd say half an hour before they left too. Never said a word, they just ran out of the building."

"Are you serious? Ciara was supposed to be on this evening. Have you called Andrew?"

"I have. His number just rings out and that's only when I actually get connected to him. I've tried all the managers, duty managers, even the owners. Nobody is answering.

Some people can't make it in with the weather. That, I understand. Others are sick. I couldn't even reach you."

"Oh, I turn my phone off until I've to be in so that I can't be reached. Must have been a really good night then on the staff party to have so many absent. How's your hangover?"

"Head's still at me, but more from anger now than anything else. I was supposed to be at home hours ago. I don't even know if I'm allowed to close the bar but I had to because I can't be everywhere at once."

"You're not thinking of driving out to Achill Island in that, are you? It's the highest weather warning they can give. Trees, electricity and phone lines down everywhere. At least ten thousand homes are already without power," Fin said, parroting off the information he had heard on the radio. "Not even Teresa Mannion would head out to make a warning video in that. I've the back-up generators should it go down here, so I'll have plenty of ice for the odd gin and tonic and the fridges will keep the beer cold. Honestly, I don't think you should chance it. Sure there aren't street lights for most of the journey and it's an hour long, on a good day. Stay here, I'll set you up in the suite. I'd feel much better if you did."

"I was tempted to stay. Wasn't looking forward to the drive home even when it was still bright out." She rattled the keys in her pocket while she thought. "Okay, I'll stay, on the condition that I get room service."

"I'll get a porter right on that. I'm going to make myself a brew before my fingers fall off, do you fancy one?"

"Dying for a coffee but before we do, we have to put the storm barriers up over the windows."

Fin let go of the zip of his jacket just before he could pull it down. "Just the two of us? That's a four man job."

"We'll have to make do."

It took them the guts of half an hour to bring the thick, perforated metal sheets out of storage. They protected the windows from whatever the storm threw at them. Beyond the shelter of the hotel the wind nearly knocked them off their feet. They carefully leaned the shields close against the wall before locking them into place. A gust of wind got behind the sheet and it took every ounce of strength Fin had to keep it from flying off.

With the job finished, they locked themselves in the hotel. They shivered in front of the coffee machine, listening as it ground the beans before pouring steaming coffee into two mugs. The heat in his hand defrosted his fingers. Outside, the noise of the storm was so intense that they could barely hear each other speak, let alone their phones. Rebecca's face went white when she checked hers. She listened to a voicemail and played it back again on loud-speaker so Fin could hear.

"For the love of God will you pick up, Becca! There was an accident on the road to the island. If you're not hurt and I go looking for you, you'll be worse off than if you did crash." She tried calling back but the storm was interfering with the network signal. She sent a text instead.

"I told you," Fin said. "It's madness to head out in that weather. Only stupidity and necessity would make some-body attempt it."

Fin checked his phone. Above the Met Éireann weather service storm alert, there was a warning he had never seen before, a government-issued, health service notification. 'Suspected dangerous influenza outbreak.' Fin clicked on it and was directed to a website that suggested safety precautions.

Rebecca looked at his screen. "I got that one too. Avoid

crowds and other people. That's not hard for you, you work so late that half the staff have never even seen you."

"I don't remember ever getting something like this from the government before."

His internet connection was spotty, but a string of breaking news articles popped up on his screen.

"What do you think this is about?" Rebecca asked.

"Nothing good. Will you have a pint with me and we'll put the news on?"

"Sure."

4

BAD NEWS

The storm swallowed the world. Visibility was reduced to the orbs of light surrounding the street lamps. Heating remained on throughout the hotel, but Fin still felt a chill. They sat in the camera's blind spot on the top floor. Their little table was stacked with empty, suddy pint glasses, a bucket of melting ice, and the end of a bottle of gin. Sloppy sandwiches made from microwaved bacon and hot wok chicken went down a treat.

Rebecca downed the rest of her drink and mixed them another.

"That looks like it's more gin than tonic," Fin said. He kept drinking but still felt too sober.

The alcohol did little to make the news on the large function room television any easier to watch. His stomach heaved, an acidic taste lurking in the back of his throat. He sat forward, back arched, elbows resting on his knees. The volume was set to maximum, to be heard above the storm. Wind warped and battered the windows. Rain turned to hail; cold radiated from the dark glass. More cars than he expected on such a night went past on the road below.

"A few storm watchers, perhaps," Rebecca said.

"This storm is a killer, if you're stupid enough to let it get you. Your folks will be alright, won't they?" Fin asked.

"The island will still be there in the morning," Rebecca said. She poured a little more gin into her glass.

Neither of them spoke as the news developed. Usually the night would be full of reruns of the day's events, or pundits talking about politics and sports. Now, primetime reporters were still up, having not left their desks all day. An average story could be chewed over until there was nothing left to it, but the spread of this suspected new strain of influenza was developing at a rate the news teams could barely keep up with. As soon as they started talking about one breaking story, they had to move on to another, more striking incident.

They only saw the full scale of it when they went online. At first, it was a suspected bad batch of poorly prepared drugs going around Dublin. A hospital was inundated with young people from the same street of nightclubs. Brief glimpses of those infected showed them babbling, incoherent and nearly manic. All of them had elevated heart rates and an inability to speak from sore, restricted throats which caused them difficulty breathing. When enough cases appeared across different hospitals around the larger cities of the country, it was clear that this was not isolated. Old or young, the reports showed the disease did not differentiate between the healthy and the sick.

Rebecca inhaled sharply and showed Fin a video on her phone of a young woman strapped down on a gurney, wailing in agony, sweating profusely and begging for water.

"That doesn't look like the flu," Rebecca said. "It's everywhere. There's a suspected case of it down the road in Castlebar."

"Maybe the storm will stop it spreading," Fin said.

"That could be the case. Or, it's the reason we aren't seeing too many people in hospital – either the roads are impassable or phone and electricity lines are down and the emergency services are already too busy to answer all the calls."

They watched the television late into the night. There was no end to the reports, they kept coming in. Stories broke first on social media, then news networks tried to play catch-up, censoring the worst of the footage. People in different time zones started paying attention, watching in fascination to see what would happen when Ireland woke up to an apparent epidemic. Fin was about to call it a night when the first deaths were announced. Respiratory complications. Panic online was immediate and Fin's was dulled only slightly by the alcohol in his system.

Public health warnings were upgraded, the wording more severe in tone. Earlier suggestions now read like orders. Emergency councils were convened in Dublin; the Taoiseach and President were woken. Government alerts flashed up on his phone as frequently as if they were from a needy partner. It was declared a health emergency of international concern. Every station they switched to carried the story. Ports were closed, all planes across the country were grounded. *Solene, I hope you got out.* Football matches, concerts and all public events were cancelled. Authorities across the world started the hunt for similar outbreaks in their own countries. The pundits now specu-lated on the origin of the new disease, the likely candidate in their eyes being antibiotic-resistant bacteria, though a target growing in popularity online was anti-vaxxers.

"The one thing they've not said yet, is what it is. A flu? Ebola? Or something new?" Rebecca said.

Fin stopped surfing through the channels and switched back to the national news station, where already the pundits were dissecting a new story. "It has been confirmed that the disease is airborne. Ensure you isolate sick family members. Cover your face and eyes if possible while doing so. At this point health professionals are assuming it can be spread through saliva, whether it's a cough or a sneeze. Early symptoms are deceptively similar to the onset of a cold or flu. If you are concerned, avoid hospitals – those are quarantine zones. If you are showing signs of infection – sore throat, runny nose, normal flu maladies – then avoid going out in public. The government has established an online and phone service to reach out and let them know where you are. They will have people to you as soon as possible." The health official sat in silence behind the news desk. The interviewer was stunned, any words she tried to form came out as "eh."

Noises echoed through the empty hotel, setting Rebecca on edge. "I honestly don't know how you work here at night by yourself."

"It's not so bad. Usually the place is full of people sleeping – you're never really alone. The noises you hear are from pipes settling."

It was soon reported that the Irish Army was now involved. Fin was not sure if that put him at ease or just made the gravity of the situation more apparent. Despite the danger, cameras followed all manner of hospital staff as they arrived to help, a legion of medical personnel, but they were vastly outnumbered by the sick. Ambulance sirens blared like wailing banshees stuck in a quagmire; people drove family and friends to the hospital, abandoning cars, blocking the roads.

"People give out that the health service is stretched to breaking point on an average day," Rebecca said. "What madness would make somebody bring their loved ones to a place that's guaranteed to have the infection?"

"You're forgetting the storm. Maybe they don't have power, and they don't know what they're heading into."

Video footage leaked from inside a hospital A&E in Dublin. There were too many people, not nearly enough gurneys. People were crammed tightly together. Many lay on the ground, blocking the orderlies. Those that were not sick were part of an angry group, mobbing the reception desk for answers.

"Look at this," Rebecca turned her phone screen towards him. A switchboard from a call centre was lit up, the sound of ringing phones was deafening. "That's from one of the centres the government set up. The person who posted the video wrote that most of them are going unanswered. There's too many of them."

By early morning, enough people had died that the general consensus was: this is something entirely new. Hearing that did not shock Fin as much as when they announced that all public transport was suspended.

"I don't feel well," Fin said.

"That's because we've stayed up all night drinking."

An interview with a bereft mother with clear signs of infection set Fin to pacing. "The fever was so hot, it burned the soul out of my little girl."

Fin put the back of his hand against his forehead. He had no idea what a normal temperature was. "We could be sick. Think of the amount of people that have been through these doors in the last week."

"Shh." Rebecca looked around as a new expert came on.

"The actual cause of death in the cases we've studied is from pulmonary complications." The expert looked like she would say more, but cleared her throat and changed into something rote learned. "This microbe kills the host. It is something the body has no experience dealing with. The lungs – I have never witnessed anything like the damage this causes." The interview was cut and a different story took its place.

No station would show autopsy photos, but they, too, leaked online. Fin could have been shown the inside of a normal lung and still think it horrifying, but the infected organ was absolutely destroyed, filled with what looked like a pale, fuzzy fungus.

"It is spread through bodily fluids. Watch out for bites." The newscaster had no time to digest that information off-screen before reading it on the teleprompter. His reaction to it was emblematic of a nation of people only waking up.

"Did he say bites?" Rebecca asked.

There was no filter on the internet; videos and images were becoming more graphic. One short clip showed a man restrained at home, his palms bloody from clenching his fists so hard that his fingernails dug into his flesh. The undersheet on the bed was saturated with sweat, urine and smeared blood from the wounds. His cough sounded like his lungs were congested. The autopsy image came to Fin's mind.

"Incredibly short incubation period."

"...Ports closed."

"...Panic."

"...What is the government's response?"

"Travellers detained."

"Embassies across the world warn against traveling to Ireland."

48

Exhausted, Fin looked away from the screen.

"I can't get through to my Mam," Rebecca said. Her face was pale, her eyes red and puffy.

Fin swallowed the lump in his throat and walked a bit away from her, breathing shallowly through his nose. *What if we are infected?* "The storm is interfering with the connection. Or the networks cannot take the strain. Don't worry about your family, most of the country is still asleep at this hour. Plus, we're hearing about this in the big cities. Dublin, Galway and Belfast. Those have massive populations, it'll take a while for it to get out to Achill Island. Aren't there more sheep than people out there? Your folks are safe," Fin said.

"Oh my God, Fin, I wasn't thinking. Your family are in Dublin."

"Close, they're in Drogheda, between Dublin and Belfast. It's the biggest town in the country. You can see the hospital from our back garden." He saw Rebecca lift her hand to try and console him, but she lowered it awkwardly.

"And Solene?"

"She's fine." He said it in such a harsh tone that Rebecca did not question him. He dialled her number again but it went straight to voicemail.

Fin noticed the sleeve of Rebecca's arm was rolled up and the flesh was raw and bruising where she pinched. *You're not dreaming.*

"I'm not touching anything in that lobby. This whole hotel has to be riddled with germs," she said.

"It works quick enough that if we had it, we'd know by now. I don't think there'd be any question about it. I feel sick, but I think that's just from watching what's happening. How are you feeling?" Fin asked. He took a deep breath, just to see if he could feel anything growing in his lungs. Everything seemed fine.

She shrugged. Each time she swallowed, she seemed to be on the brink of vomiting.

"If it puts your mind at rest, there's a layer of dust half an inch thick on the function room bar. It hasn't been used in weeks. We could bring up some cots from storage and stay there," Fin said.

They checked behind the bar to see if it was a viable place to sleep. The function room was a large open space, with old carpet, worn in front of the stage. It was filled with stacks of chairs and folded tables.

"Am I being paranoid, wanting to stay in here?" Rebecca said.

"The news did not leave much room for anything other than paranoia."

The sound of a blaring car alarm drew their attention outside, its wail nearly lost in the wind. Squinting through the window, Fin could see a shadow moving on the road. He would have missed it had the person not stumbled beneath a street lamp. The true force of the storm could be seen as she struggled against it. Her clothes whipped in the wind, she stumbled and fell beside the car she set off.

"Should we help?" Rebecca said, just as the lights went on in the house where the car was parked.

When the front door opened, a warm glow spilled onto the street. The prone person just stared at the blinking indicator. A couple braced the door against the wind and motioned for the person to come inside. She stumbled towards them, tripped and fell over the front step. A man lifted her up as his partner closed the door behind them.

"Can you imagine having to deal with her in the middle of all this," Fin said.

Rebecca did not come away from the window. "Do you think they know about what's happening? The storm will have cut power to a lot of places."

"They had lights. Everybody has phones, the first thing they would've seen when they check their phones would have been the government messages. I'd say she's just drunk," Fin said. "I often see people stumbling home at all hours. The disease hasn't gotten this far."

Fin checked his phone throughout the night but had not received a message from his parents or sister. He imagined them curled up in their beds, warm and snug against the storm. *I'll let them sleep. No point in waking them. Let them have a few more hours of peace before they learn of this.* There was also the worry that if he woke them, they might go check on others. Torn over the decision, he thought it best to try. Tell them everything he saw online. Put enough fear in them, so they would barricade themselves in safety. When he checked his phone, he saw a voice message from Solene. The small hairs across his body stood on end. If he did not open it, she was still okay. *Things are fine. She just wants to know how the cats are getting on, that's all.*

Noticing the change in him, Rebecca looked at his screen. "Play it," she said.

Fin opened it before the screen could go dark from disuse. He wanted to let it hibernate, put it in his pocket and forget all about it, but he knew it would be harder to open after that.

The audio crackled, wind or static. Solene could barely be heard over all the noise behind her; horns blared and people shouted – she was in a crowd. Breathless from crying, she spoke his name. It sounded like there was a scuffle and she lost the phone. The microphone picked up the fall and continued recording for a few more seconds. It was muffled but he knew it was the sound of trampling feet.

Rebecca's expression confirmed it for him. "I don't think she was weeping. She could have just been crying."

"Yeah." He sat down and rang her number until his battery died.

5

LAST MINUTE SHOPPERS

"I need to go home," Rebecca said, breaking a long period of silence. Neither of them even tried to sleep, switching out alcohol for coffee at around daybreak. Both of them threw up in the guest bathroom. This caused an excruciatingly long hour of worry, wondering if they were infected or not. In the end, they put it down to seeing the video footage from the streets of Dublin.

"It's light enough out. The worst of the storm has passed us by. The roads won't be too bad. I can get there. Did you hear me? Fin?"

He started, his forehead slipping on the cold window where he leaned. His mouth was dry. "People are already outside. I've never seen so many cars on the road at this hour."

"I'm leaving, Fin. My family are probably worried, and I can't have them going out looking for me and coming to harm. It must be safer than here. What's your plan?"

"The buses and trains aren't running and I don't drive. I'm stuck here." The thought struck him hard.

"Come with me. We can take food from storage here and a few crates of water. We'll be in Achill within an hour, but we have to leave now, before the traffic gets bad. The roads will be tricky enough if the storm blocked them."

"You're drunk."

"We'll go slow. The gardaí won't be out stopping cars, not today."

"If we do this then not only will we both lose our jobs, but neither of us will have enough saved to deal with the lawsuit the owners will put on us," Fin said.

"They're welcome to. This isn't normal. Nobody's going to prison for taking a bit of food. If we don't take it, then others will. I don't want to leave you alone. Come with me, please."

"We're safe here, why not bring your family?"

"You've seen the news, they've advised people to stay away from public spaces."

"Exactly! They'll be too afraid to loot here – not that it'll come to that."

"We don't know if the infection is already in the hotel. You said it yourself, somebody was sick here recently."

Fin went pale. "I forgot all about him." He could still remember the heat radiating from him. *But he's gone.* "You're right. We found him in the basement and took him up the service elevator. That leaves the food down there out. It's mostly vending machine stuff."

"Good, I'm glad you're coming. Your family and Sol... They would be happier knowing you were on the island. It's perfect – there's only one bridge to the mainland and plenty of open space and a small population."

There was too much to take in. He was certain that David was infected. Solene was still not answering his calls.

He charged his phone and tried to contact his parents, but they too were silent. None of his friends responded to his messages. When Rebecca was out of earshot, he played back Solene's voicemail; he was not certain if the people shouting in the background were French or Irish. *Is she still in the country or has this spread already?*

Rebecca checked her pockets to make sure she had everything. Fin stopped, remembering his responsibilities in the apartment. "I have three cats at home, I can't just leave them."

Rebecca turned on him. "How can you not be taking this seriously?"

Her anger made him think that she would go ahead without him. The prospect of staying in the hotel terrified him. He imagined watching her drive away, leaving him alone with all those empty rooms. "Solene stocked our apartment with food before she left," he said, hoping that he could entice her enough to make a detour to his apartment. "I feed the cats and we bring all of that food with us. Are you sure your parents won't mind me staying?"

That softened her. She looked relieved. "I promise you, they won't mind. That sounds like a plan. Let's get some breakfast before we start packing. I need more coffee in me. I'm not sure I could walk straight, let alone drive."

"That's reassuring," Fin said.

Food sat uneasily in his stomach, and bile rose regularly to burn his throat, but he felt better after eating. His head pounded from the drink. His jacket was still damp from walking to work the previous night. They wrapped kitchen towels over their faces as makeshift masks. He caught sight of his reflection in the lobby window and wondered how so much changed in such a short time.

"Come on," Rebecca said through the open car window. The windscreen wipers were frantic, the heater in her car rattled.

He checked his jacket for the keys one last time. The jingle in his pocket was reassuring. With the car boot and back seats full of stolen supplies, Fin unlocked the gates. Rebecca pulled out onto the road, while Fin fumbled with the keys, locking the gates behind her. For a moment, he feared that she would drive off without him. Cameras watched and recorded everything they did. The guilt he felt leaving his post fizzled to nothing. He knew when this ended, nobody would care.

Inside the car was immaculately clean, the pungent air freshener compounding his hangover headache. As he watched the hotel shrink in the rear-view mirror, his thoughts raced to horrible places, like rabbits running down a snake-infested burrow. Rebecca slowed down outside the house where the couple had helped the woman in the night. The front door was open, the lights were still on, but nothing moved.

"Do you think she was infected?" Rebecca asked.

"I think kindness is likely to get you killed." It sounded stupid, but not far from true.

Rebecca weaved across both lanes to avoid downed branches and upturned rubbish bins. She drove carefully, sticking to five below the speed limit. Glancing in the mirror, Fin saw a line of cars speeding towards them. The lead car lay on the horn. A driver behind him sped up and changed lanes to overtake them. He did not see the oncoming truck. The car crumpled against the truck; the sudden sound of tearing, screeching metal nearly caused Rebecca to lose control of the car. The airbags in both vehicles blossomed. Horns blared behind them. Nobody stopped.

The truck driver crawled out of the passenger door. Aside from a limp and a bloodied face, he seemed okay. He walked away from the crash. Fin looked back at the truck driver and thought the driver was looking off towards town, not at his truck. Flashing blue lights lit up the surrounding houses. Rebecca cursed but the Garda car parted the traffic, ignored the accident and sped off towards the quay.

"What the hell's going on?"

Traffic already clogged the streets. Cars were packed with bags and worried faces.

"This was a bad idea," Rebecca said. She locked the doors and hunched over the steering wheel.

"Just relax, we'll be okay. Let's rest in my apartment for a few hours, until the drink wears off and the roads clear." He ran his finger over the buttons on the radio.

"Please don't, I can't listen to any more."

They did not need the radio. All he had to do was look at the panic in the people around him. Things were not getting better.

"Where do you think all of those people are going?" Fin asked.

"Home? A lot of them are down for the holidays. If I had the money I'd be looking to get on a plane and get out of here. I don't need to pay to park, do I?" Rebecca asked as they turned into the car park behind Fin's apartment. She picked up more speed there than on the roads around town.

"I honestly don't think the ticket inspector will be doing his rounds today."

"This is probably the best time for it. Nobody will be thinking of paying."

The storm had calmed in the last few hours, but the

weather warnings were still in effect. The sound of sharp hail hitting his hood reminded him of camping with his family, when the water ran down the thin tent fabric and they played board games. He felt safe and comfortable. *I should be home with them.*

No birds flew; they hid in the woods. The sky was dark, keeping the rising sun behind boiling, black clouds. Fin faltered at the electrical keypad to get up to his apartment. Every single person that lived in the block had to have touched that pad.

"What's the code? I'll do it!" Rebecca hissed acidly, nudging him out of the way.

Using a pocket tissue, he put the security code in and used the sleeve of his jacket to pull the door open. It did not budge. He put the code in four more times but the rain must have shorted the box. The street was filling up with people.

Fin picked up a flowerpot next to the estate agents and tossed it through the single-pane glass door. It shattered, making people stop and stare. He pulled his hood over his blushing face and hurried through the communal garden area to his apartment.

"Mooch? Flo? Poncho?" The patter of little paws quickened and the three of them peered around the landing when he entered. They shied away from Rebecca.

Once inside, Fin washed his hands with an abrasive nail brush until they stung. Then he sprayed the front door handle with bleach and let it rest there.

He plugged his phone in to charge and tried Solene's number once more but it did not connect. He tried his father, expecting the same result. He was not disappointed. *They're still asleep.*

"It's a lovely apartment," Rebecca said. She went through the rooms closing the blinds.

Fin fed the cats and brewed coffee. He gathered up all of Solene's little letters and sticky notes, while Rebecca went through the presses and fridge. He held Solene's jumper under his nose and breathed in her smell. *I miss you.*

"I thought you said this place was full of food?" Rebecca said.

"By our normal standard, it is. We do two shops a week. How many people keep enough food in their homes to last them more than seven days? The only reason there's so much pasta is because Solene knew if there were more than two ingredients, I wouldn't bother making it."

"You're nearly thirty and you don't know how to cook for yourself?"

"I'm twenty-five – do I look thirty?"

They drank their coffee while staring at the black screen of the television. Neither of them wanted to turn it on to see what new horrors were unfolding throughout the country. Fin lay on the couch, watching the morning quicken, trying to pretend that the world was okay. Mooch jumped onto his lap and nuzzled his arm for a scratch. "It's going to be fine," he said.

From his sitting room he was three storeys high; he could see over the rooftops of most of the other buildings. Traffic came to a standstill on the Castlebar Road. In the silence that grew between them, they could hear the distant horns. Even if they wanted to leave, now was not the right time. Too many people were on the streets. Tempers were too high.

"There can't be many left in Ireland that don't know about what's going on now," Rebecca said. "Not with all that commotion."

"You take my bed. The sheets are relatively clean, new

ones in the wardrobe if you don't want to chance it. Try to sleep off the drink," Fin said.

"What about you?"

"I'm going to stay up a little bit longer, I don't think I'd be able to settle. I want to make a few calls, see if people are okay. I'll sleep on the couch."

"The lines are only going to get worse as the day goes on – think of how many people are trying to reach loved ones."

"I know, but somebody has to get through, eventually."

Town only got busier as the day wore on. Noise from the car park drew his attention to the window. Lifting up one of the slats on the venetian blind, he watched one man strap a Christmas tree to the top of his car. *Does he just think the general madness happening around him is from last minute shoppers?* People pushed shopping carts full of food and supplies to their cars, leaving the empty carts in the middle of the path. Horns blared and anger flared as people shouted at each other, though at a distance. Some wore masks. One man was in a full-face respirator. *So many people ignoring the government warnings.* People were the danger now.

When his phone rang, he clipped his shin off the coffee table in his haste to answer it.

"Hello? Hello!"

"Fin, oh thank God! I thought the worst." His father sounded panicked and out of breath. He had never heard such worry in his voice before.

"Dad, are you okay? Are you driving?"

He let out a long breath in answer. "We're not really okay. It's mad here. There's not a bit of food on the shelves in any of the shops."

His heart sank. "Dad, they said not to go out in public." Fin wanted to shout down the phone, but that would only exacerbate things.

"You know how your mother is, I didn't bring her along with me because she'd likely be the one rioting." He left a pause for laughter, but there was none. "I was careful. I'm wrapped up and I have my face covered."

Fin thought back to one of the specialists on the news. She had stated that masks and such protective gear were dangerous because they created a false sense of security.

"You could bring the virus home on your clothes. Just go back to the house, please, dad. It's Christmas, the presses should be fully stocked with food."

"They are, but we can't wipe our arses with tinfoil, Fin."

"Go home, now. Do you hear me? Go home. You're a fool!" He lost control and roared down the phone. The bedroom door opened downstairs and Rebecca was with him in seconds. She was wearing Solene's dressing gown. The sight gave him pause and the faint smell of her perfume made him sick with worry.

He did not know how long his father had been trying to speak over him; his father's voice was calm, trying to reassure him. "I wasn't near anybody else. I went to the stores out in the countryside. I've a mask, gloves and antibacterial gel. Look, I'm going home now. You big girl's blouse," he added jokingly.

"This is not a game, Dad. You've only been watching the news. I don't think they can show a fraction of what's coming up online. Either there's too much to show or it's censored. This is a killer. Have you enough food to stay indoors? Maybe go to Grandad's. Pool your resources." Hiding from it would have been easier if he was alone, but he had to face the thought of his family and Solene out there, being in danger. "I wish I was with yous."

"Is it bad in Westport?"

Over the phone he heard car indicators click on and

hoped that his father was actually turning around to go home. "I stayed the night in the hotel, a colleague of mine was there too. We're going to try to get out to Achill Island. She said I could stay at hers. I'm in the house now. I've never seen so many people on the streets here. You'd swear the world was ending."

"Panic will do that. Everybody has the same idea. Go out, get food and squirrel away. The island should be safe. It's a relief to hear that you'll be okay. Don't worry about us. I've been trying to get through to you for hours."

Fin went to every window to make sure they were all closed. The alleyway at the back of the house was thronged. He saw people in the adjacent house packing in a hurry.

"I'll wait until tomorrow morning, when the streets are empty again. We're safe here. If I had just gotten my full driving licence and saved for a car, I could have driven back home before most of the country was awake. I messed up." He really felt the distance between them now. It was the first time he could remember feeling homesick; it had always only ever taken a train and a bus ride to be sitting at home, watching a movie with his family.

"Does it take the fear of getting a really bad cold to light a fire under you? Just keep that burning for when this ends and get your licence then." He was silent for a moment. "Do you want me to come and get you?"

It was tempting. "No, dad, I'm looking at the main road leaving town and it's gridlock."

A rushing ambulance forced cars onto the footpath to let it pass. Some cheeky driver pulled in behind it and others followed, making the traffic worse. "No, I'll be fine, I'll – I'll come back when it's safe. Promise me you'll go to the house, no detours."

"You're not my mother, stop giving me orders."

"If I have to ring granny and tell her to send you home, I'm not above it."

"You little prick," he said with affection. "Have you heard from Solene?"

"I can't reach her, she sent me a voicemail during the night. She was crying. I don't know if her flights were cancelled ahead of the storm. I've no idea where she is."

"You worry about yourself. I'll try to get in contact with her. If she made it to France then she should be okay. From what I've heard, it's localised here. The storm saw to that. She's a tender soul, might have been her worry for you that caused her to cry. Sure I was nearly blubbering before you picked up the phone. Right, I'm coming up to a Garda checkpoint. If they give me a ticket for being on my phone, your mother will kill me. I love you."

"Would you stop saying that, I know, and I love you too but each time you say it, it's like a headstone at the end of a conversation."

His dad laughed. "Alright you little bollox, go on. Stay safe. Keep me updated on what's happening down your end."

"Tell everyone I was asking for them."

His father sighed. "I should have built that cabin in the woods down in Kerry years ago."

"Yeah, your midlife crisis would have come in handy right about now."

Hearing his father's voice made him feel foolish for over-reacting; the familiar cadence and tone had been there after every success and failure throughout his life, and for most of the mundane morning breakfasts, too. It was real and normal, an anchor in the storm.

Tears dampened his face. He heard his bedroom door close softly. Rebecca had courteously left him when she realised all was as well as it could possibly be. Fin turned the PlayStation on; any form of escapism would do. Before the television came on, the sound of Rebecca's phone dialing out reached him in the sitting room. He turned the volume up and he tuned out.

6

_____

HOLD YOUR BREATH

The vacuous first moments after waking were all the crueller for how normal they were; in his own home, listening to the soundtrack of a paused game. Flo yawned, arching her back as she stretched. *What a horrible dream.* Sitting up, he rubbed the sleep from his eyes with the palms of his hands. It was the noise from outside that woke him. *Our next house is going to be in the countryside. I'm sick of town.*

Rebecca sat at the kitchen table. She barely looked up from her phone to greet him. Fin bit back a sob at the sight of her. *It's real.* "How long have you been up?"

"A few hours."

"You should have woken me."

"You needed the rest and we're in no rush, not anymore."

"What have I missed?"

"Roads in and out of Newport are blocked. We can go around, but I think we should cycle. I noticed two bikes downstairs. It'll take longer and we won't be able to bring as much food, but we'll get there today."

"Wait a minute. It's that bad? We have a car full of food

out there and we don't have panniers for the bikes. Solene has a basket on hers but that won't fit much."

"The Gardaí are closing down roads to stop the spread, but I think it's too late. Whatever this is, it's too fast. We might have a chance now against the cops, but we'll be trapped here once the army arrive. They've started shooting people that break quarantine in Dublin."

Fin lay back on the couch. He did not want to look at the dark depths beneath her eyes, or experience that penetrating stare, desperate for answers, terrified of what they might be. He lost all sense of comfort, kicking the blanket off himself. Relief came in the form of laughter. It was the casual way in which she said the army was killing people. He could not remember the last time he laughed so heartily, long and hard. It sounded alien, perverse and maddening. It was just a build-up to tears.

Rebecca sat on the armrest of the couch. Fin covered his eyes. He felt a reassuring hand on his leg, it said 'I'm here.' When he composed himself enough to look at the world again, Rebecca was grinning. It was so unsettling that it gave him a start. She pretended to peel the grin from her mouth and tossed it through the air to Fin. Arm achingly heavy, he raised it up and slowly closed his fingers around the grin. Working hospitality, you always had to look happy, and you passed it on to your colleagues after your shift ended. A fake smile, for the benefit of others. Acting out their usual work routine settled him enough to steady his breathing. "Do you mind if I save this for later?"

"Not at all," she said in a low, echoey voice.

Fin mimicked putting the smile in his pocket. "So we cycle. What about all the food?"

"We leave it in the boot. It's mostly dry goods, it'll keep. Somebody I know from home posted pictures of roads blocked by empty cars. Abandoned scrap yards, building like clots. Look out the window, Fin. Those cars on the way to Castlebar, they were there before you fell asleep. People have just started walking. I don't think we have a choice either."

"It'll be miserable in this weather," he said.

"We go along the Greenway cycle path. The fewer people around us, the better."

"Okay, I'll see what bags I have here."

Fin filled every plate and bowl in the house with kibble and wet food for the cats. He plugged the sinks and bathtub and filled them with water. By his estimate, he had a little over a week before he would have to come back and check on them. *It will be over by then.*

Rebecca boiled the kettle twice and filled a hot water bottle for each of them. She tucked one beneath her jumper, using her waistband to keep it in place. She gave the other one to Fin. "Trust me, it's bitterly cold outside and we don't have the right clothing. You'll thank me later."

The first glint of morning was still hours away when they left the apartment. The unrelenting rain would mask the sound of their bikes. Rebecca took Solene's weighty city cruiser; both of them carried bulging shopping bags over their handlebars. Fin lifted his light road bike down the stairs, stepping lightly over the broken glass that cracked like thin ice beneath his feet. Rebecca watched the bags and bike while he brought hers down.

They walked through the empty streets. Perhaps yesterday's madness was forgotten, washed away with the storm. Passing through a tight alleyway, they turned right onto the main street, then followed the river left. Fin stopped outside the church. The doors were open.

"Will you hold this, please?" Fin asked, handing her his bike.

"Hurry up," she whispered.

Holding his scarf tight over his mouth, he peeked through the doors. The aisle was full of burning candles. The air above them shimmered; it was warm and perfumed by the scented ones people brought from home. A few people kneeled in the pews. Somebody sneezed but nobody else seemed to care. He took his bike back.

"What did you see?" Rebecca asked.

"Desperation."

Signs outside the petrol station read 'pumps empty'. The first person they came across was a man trying to break into the shuttered shop, an empty petrol can by his feet. Fin signaled for Rebecca to get on her bike. They mounted and quickly and, as quietly as they could, they passed him. Caution was for nothing, the man was too focused on his task. They only made it halfway up a steep hill on the Newport Road. Fin had to walk the bike the rest of the way. Gasping down clean morning air, it took Fin longer than he was proud of to catch his breath.

Once at the brow of the hill, he mounted and coasted down the other side. *This was a stupid idea.* He wanted to say it but knew by the look on her face that she already thought the same. There was no better plan. Water shot off his rear tire and lashed his back. Though his jacket was waterproof, his pants were not and the rain soaked through to his skin. His fingers were brittle from the cold. Traffic lights hummed at a crossroad. He felt exposed beneath the harsh beams of LED streetlights. Newport was straight ahead. Fin had only taken the left road as far as Westport House and back to the quay before. That way would bring them to the hotel. In twenty minutes they could be back on the top floor in their snug with a cold pint. He nearly suggested it, but they were through town and the worst of it – he thought. *Nothing but a bit of pedalling between us and an island, away from all of this.*

They turned right, down a small lane with only a few houses separated by fields. Most of the bedrooms had lights turned on. Curtains were drawn back out of curiosity. Scared faces watched them cycle by, wondering if they, too, should do the same.

"There won't be a child going to sleep in this country without a nightlight the next few months," Fin said.

"Plenty of adults, too."

At the end of the road they reached the Greenway trail. It ended at Achill Island. There were no streetlights here and they did not risk using the lamps on their bikes. Fin's bike was light, the tires slender tubes. The front one punctured within ten minutes. Pedalling on the rim caused too much noise. There was no other choice but to walk. Fin lifted the back wheel of Rebecca's bike off the ground by the saddle so that the chain would not catch and rattle.

His breath frosted in the air, the cold left him numb, but the horizon was brightening. He strained his eyes to make out any sign of movement, not knowing what they would do if they came across somebody coming the other way.

Cars passed in the distance, but beyond that there was only the constant drip of rain and the crunch of gravel on the path. Beyond the tree cover, they were exposed, walking on a rise. The path was more puddle than stone; the ditches on either side of the route were brimming. Twice they had to stop to lift the bikes over downed trees. They stopped beneath a bridge; a tourist map showed the route out to Achill.

Rebecca shivered, her teeth chattering when she spoke. "We may leave the bikes behind. They're not mine, I feel bad suggesting it, but yours is broken and if we cycle, we draw too much attention. It's too cold to walk them and if we do run into somebody, we won't be able to hide before they spot us. We might have to go through fields when the path takes us too close to the road."

"This hugs the main road most of the way," Fin said. "I don't mind hiding the bikes, it's the food I'm worried about. We won't be able to take all of it with us."

"It's not important. We have the luxury of one worry at a time. Right now, it's getting to safety."

It was peaceful beneath the bridge. Ivy grew from gaps in the stonework and hung down like a curtain, shielding them from the long path ahead. A veil of rain fell on either side. Despite the mild comfort, if they were surprised here, the hills to the side of the path were far too steep and slippery to climb. There was no choice but to continue.

They lifted the bikes off the path and hid them behind bushes at the bottom of a disused field. It sickened Fin to leave so much food behind. Laden with a full shopping bag in each hand, they continued at a slower pace, stopping only to put the bags down for a brief reprieve.

"How long do you think before we get there?" Fin asked.

"Six hours, I reckon – by bike."

"Knowing that is going to make it feel much longer."

"Bet you're not giving out about the hot water bottle now, are you?"

The heat slightly scalded his skin, but the warmth was welcome. "I'd have turned back by now without it."

When cars approached on the adjacent road, they ducked out of sight. Their clothes were bright enough to stand out if they were caught moving in the open. Lying on the ground, he watched the car speed on the empty road.

"That idiot's going to crash," Rebecca said. "I can barely make those corners doing the speed limit."

"How is this spreading so quickly?" Fin asked.

"Motorways, trains. Westport is the end of the rail line, another in Galway. Every large town and city is connected, like one big body. It doesn't matter if the infection gets in through a cut on a finger, given enough time, it'll spread through the whole system. The blacktop outside every house in the country will take you anywhere on the island within a few hours."

Once the road was clear, they started walking again. Fin stopped to watch a small river, turbulent from the storm. The banks were overgrown, hidden by trees and bushes. Pathless places where people seldom tread, there was safety there. The river disappeared out of sight at the end of the field. Fin imagined sitting in a boat, letting the current take him; once he was around the corner he would be invisible to most. "What if we went by boat to the island?"

"Do you have one? Because I don't."

The latest car to pass announced itself a while before they saw it.

"They'll wake half the countryside if they don't lay off the horn," Rebecca said.

As it came into view, Fin noticed that the windshield was smashed, a spiderweb of cracks spread from an indent over the passenger side. It veered dangerously across the road. A few moments later, it became clear why. Fin was about to stand up when people appeared, sprinting after the car. None of them were dressed for the weather. Rebecca pulled him down into a puddle. The only thing between them was a wire fence and a marshy field. The runners were breathless and weeping.

The group of people quieted and slowed after the car

passed. Fin pulled his hood down, afraid that it deafened him to his surroundings. "We can't go on," he said. "What are they running from?"

Rebecca remained silent and watched. A light went on in a farmhouse across the road. A dog barked, causing the people on the street to wail and weep.

"What are they playing at?" Fin asked.

The front door opened and a white-haired woman in a night dress stood on the porch. Smoke was swept away as it poured out of the chimney pot. The group ran up her driveway. The woman stumbled and hurried back inside, slamming the door closed, leaving her dog outside. The labrador tried to chase the intruders away. It dodged out of reach of frenzied attempts to grab him. They were indifferent to the snarling and seemed not to feel its teeth when it bit them. One caught the dogs tail, keeping it still long enough for the others to fall on it. The pained yowls and loud whimpering did not last long.

Heat from the hot water bottle burned Fin's stomach. He could barely lift his head high enough to turn it, but he did to look at Rebecca. He mouthed 'We have to go back.'

She nodded vigorously. "Leave the bags."

Without a second thought, he left the food in the gutter. They crawled across the path, sharp stones tearing at their jackets. Once they reached a tall hedge that hid them from the road, they rose into a crouch and ran. *If we had the bikes we never would have seen them, they'd be behind us and who knows what in front.* It felt like they were running from the mouth of a triggered trap.

Terror set the pace; it was not one Fin could keep for long, but they were too vulnerable on the path to stop. Fin slowed to catch his breath, the back of his throat raw from gasping.

"We can't stop," Rebecca punctuated each worth with a pant. "The road curves round, it crosses the bridge over our path. We're too exposed here. If those –"

"What were they running from? They were crying – it wasn't normal the way they were acting."

"I don't think they were running from anything." Rebecca put her hands on her head, constantly checking the path behind them. "The car's windshield was buckled, did you see that? Like a person rolled over the bonnet. I think the driver was fleeing from them. The speed they were going, I take that road to and from work every day and I dread the bends they're coming into."

"A bad joke in poor taste," Fin said.

Rebecca latched on to that. It was the only reasonable excuse for those people to act in such a way. "Maybe, but they must have scared the life out of that woman and that driver could have killed one of them." She seemed less sure of herself. "What do we do? We could leave the path and head further across the fields. Be slow going, but we could make it."

The weather was worsening and the sight of those people acting so strangely unsettled him so much that he would not consider continuing. "We go back before it gets too busy. I don't want to blindly wander through fields and hope we're going in the right direction. We'll have a look at maps online and choose a better route. We'll leave again tonight."

Rebecca nodded. "What about that woman back there? Should we help her?"

"Whatever they're doing, I want no part of it. They're just acting the maggot, trying to scare people. Sure what could we do anyway?"

"I suppose."

They started off towards town. A stitch took root in Fin's side, and the pain became more intense the longer they jogged. The periphery of his vision blurred. When he noticed Rebecca slowing down for him, the ensuing embarrassment spurred him on a little faster.

Light on the path ahead forced them to hide in the bones of a hawthorn bush. They sank in the marshy ditch, water rising above their ankles. Pressed tightly together, Fin realised he completely forgot to put on deodorant before leaving the apartment. The warm tang of sweat wafted up to his nostrils. He turned red, grateful for the low light hiding his blush. He felt stupid for worrying about it; for all he knew, the smell could be Rebecca.

"It's not moving," she whispered. "Maybe a Garda checkpoint?"

"We'll be fine then, can tell them what we saw down the road."

Cautiously, they came out of hiding, keeping to the side of the path where they could melt into the verge if need be. As they got closer to the bend, they heard an engine idling. Coming around the corner, they saw the car that had sped past those people: it had come off the road near the bridge and slid down the steep verge. The axle was cracked, jutting out from beneath the car like a broken bone, digging into the soft earth. Oil glistened on the surface of the ditch water.

Rebecca instinctively started towards the crash, but Fin grabbed her arm. They stepped around it, trying to get a better view of those inside, through the fractured glass. A woman lay back awkwardly in the driver's seat, her pale face covered with little cuts, spouting blood, her breathing laboured. There was no way of telling if she was infected or not.

Fin took his phone out and dialled the emergency services, while Rebecca tried to coax her back into consciousness.

"I'm not getting anything," he took Rebecca's phone and tried calling again. "Nothing, it's not even ringing."

"Fin, she's alive. Hey, are you okay?"

The woman looked around her in a confused daze. When she saw them standing in front of her headlights, a look of absolute horror crossed her face. "Leave me alone!" The engine roared as she pushed the accelerator to the floor but the car chuckled and conked out.

Fin and Rebecca jumped to the side but the car did not move. In the brief silence that followed, Rebecca tried to calm her, but nothing she said reached her.

"Please just go away, leave me alone." She turned the headlights off, leaving them night blind.

"Come on," Fin said. "We'll keep trying on the phone."

When she stopped sounding the horn, they heard crying, but it did not come from inside the car. The world was silenced by the sound of weeping. Rebecca took his arm and ran, no longer worried about the noise they made. The horn blared, but only briefly. Fin wanted to look behind, he could sense something following them. Every nerve in his body was on end.

"We'll try for the hotel," he said.

"Most of the food is still in the car."

"I'm sure your folks are okay," Fin said because it was the thing to say. She nodded.

They walked on the muddy verge the closer they came to town, no longer speaking, for fear of making too much noise. They nearly made it to the end of the Greenway before they were attacked. If the man did not start crying, he would have had them. The weeping startled Rebecca into a run, Fin turned. He was in his late thirties, Fin would have guessed at a glance. There was little time for more than that before the man was on him.

The infection made him look worn out. Weeping was odd coming from a man his size. It sounded like he was in agony, but his face was blank and lacked any expression, like somebody sleeping with their eyes open. He came from the driveway of a house just off the path. His mouth held open by the dead weight of his slack jaw. Hands outstretched, he lurched forward. Fin reflexively fell backwards away from danger. He gained his feet, but was pulled back by the man yanking a strap on his pack. His other hand grabbed his jacket, but his fingers slipped off the slick, waterproof fabric. Fin wrestled to get the backpack off. The man bit into a strap; his front teeth were loose, one hung on by a nerve. The sight made Fin recoil, that injury should have had him howling in agony, but he did not seem to notice.

The man dropped the bag and threw himself on Fin, locking his arms around the back of his knees. They rolled into an overflowing ditch of swift, cold water. Fin kicked out and they came apart. The man lunged without a care for his own safety. He misjudged, the bottom of his jaw smacked against the gravel path, and his teeth snapped together with a sickening, porcelain clack. Fin put his foot and his full weight on the infected man's chest, keeping him beneath the water. He sensed no fear or change in the man's body. He did not struggle or writhe with more vigour than he had before being faced with drowning.

Fin held his head away from the blind reach of those hands. The palms were ruined, raw flesh torn so badly that he could see bone, fat and sinew beneath. Rebecca grabbed the arms. Together they struggled to hold him. Teeth clenched, spittle formed at the side of Fin's mouth as he fought against every impulse, to let go, to let him breathe. *I'm killing him.* He saw it in Rebecca's eyes. They were alone and on the verge of ending a life.

The noise of his thrashing was hidden by the rain. This man had made it through life, its hardships and pleasures, to this point. Family and friends would never know his last moments were spent choking on ditch water at the hands of two strangers. *There might be concessions for some crimes during the current panic, but murder is murder.*

They were united in their effort; they would kill a person before the day had started in earnest.

"How long does it take to drown?" Fin asked.

"Not this long. I don't know."

There was no reduction in the man's efforts or movements. Below the surface, Fin could see the tendons in the man's neck straining to rise, to bite them. Their struggle churned the water in the ditch until the chomping mouth disappeared in silt. Rebecca kicked her boot down through the water, where his head should have been.

Fin felt it connect. "Watch out for his teeth."

"Look at his hands, the nails are broken and his palms are destroyed. It's like on the news, he's infected."

He knew time passed slower than normal in dangerous situations, but this was taking far too long. They had enough time to come to their senses. Rebecca called his name as loud as she dared. She still struggled with the man's arms, the fingers clutched and clawed like eels around her jacketed arms. The ripples on the surface showed no sign of calming. He counted to ten. The moments between each count drew on. The man was not dying.

"We have to go," Rebecca said. "We're making too much noise."

He nodded in agreement.

"On three, let go and run."

As soon as she finished the countdown, Fin jumped onto the shore. Without his weight, the man floated to the surface. His mouth and nostrils were full of water. Rebecca pulled Fin along the path until he managed to keep pace. *One foot after the other.* Slowing enough to glance back, he saw arms scrambling at the edge of the path for purchase. Fin had no religion, but he prayed fervently for the locked doors and barred windows of the hotel. What he saw made no sense. He had never tried to drown somebody before, but it struck him as something that was hard to fail at so spectacularly. *It must happen faster in movies, they have limited screen time.*

They rounded the corner and were back on the quiet, lonesome lane that ended at the crossroad.

"Did he get you?" Rebecca asked.

Adrenaline coursing through his body, he doubted he would be able to tell. There was a dull pain in his wrist but that was from the fall. "I'm not stripping off to check here," he said. "We'll head back to mine. We don't know that the hotel is clean and all our food's in your car."

The traffic lights still hummed, oblivious to the state of the world. Town was busier. looking through windows, Fin could see people sitting in front of television screens, waiting for good news. Drenched, muddy and running, they left a lot of scared locals in their wake.

He shook so badly that he could not get the key into the door of his apartment. It was impossible to tell the infected from the panicked. Most were heading towards the train station, even though public transport was cancelled. *Are they walking to Dublin?*

When the key finally entered the lock, he nearly broke it

in his haste to be inside. He slammed the door behind them and locked it, letting out a wheezy, relieved laugh.

"Take your clothes off." Rebecca gave him no time to relax. She was right, even if they were not infected, both of them had likely taken something from contact with that man. They quickly undressed to their underwear. Fin poured antibacterial, mint-scented soap into their cupped hands. He considered bleach for a moment and poured some of that on too. Rebecca showered first, not waiting for the stream to heat up before getting in. Stepping out from beneath the shower, she gasped and wiped water from her eyes. "I couldn't hold my breath for as long as he did. Will you check my back for broken skin?" Steam rose from the shower, but she was shivering.

Fin scrutinised her pale, freckled shoulder. "Aside from a spot and a mole you should keep an eye on, you're okay." He was not sure if he saw tears in her eyes or if it was just water from the shower.

"Your turn."

Fin hid himself behind a large bath towel. He sucked in his gut and stopped, struck by the stupidity of it.

"What are you smiling at?" Rebecca asked.

"I was worried about my stomach hanging out, while you're checking me over in case of a lethal infection, when really I should be concerned about Solene walking in and catching us in the nip." He had his back to her; she was silent for too long. "What?"

"Oh, Fin."

7

ZOMBIES?

Fin rubbed condensation off the mirror and stared at his back. A large purple welt stained his shoulder.

"Is the skin broken? I can't see properly."

Rebecca was apprehensive at first but stepped out of the shower and checked more thoroughly. Her touch caused him to wince. "I don't think he scratched you."

He held onto the edge of the sink for support. Relief made him lightheaded. Each breath caught in his throat. "You nearly gave me a heart attack."

"I'm sorry Fin, I got a fright. It must have happened when he knocked you to the ground. It's just badly bruised."

He stood beneath the shower and felt invisible hands melt from his skin. "We nearly killed a man." He collapsed to his knees and vomited bile. He watched it disappear down the soap-stained drain while he caught his breath. "I don't know what came over me. He just came out of nowhere and wouldn't stop. He looked like he wasn't even there, like he was on something and could have woken up later without even the memory of killing us."

"There was nothing normal about that, he was rabid.

Those people on the road... That woman in the car was speeding to get away from them, she was in shock."

They locked themselves in the bedroom. The cats hid in the open wardrobe pawing at the sleeves of jumpers and trouser legs dancing on hangers as Fin rifled through Solene's clothes. He laid out comfy sweatpants, a tee-shirt and a warm winter jumper on the bed for Rebecca.

"I don't know how you feel about wearing other people's underwear," he said. "But there's a selection of jocks, socks and granny knickers in the drawer."

"Granny knickers?" Rebecca's eyebrows raised with her smile.

"Yeah, she took all the fancy ones with her – actually, should I be worried about that?"

She scoffed, sat up and hunkered over the side of the bed. Fin turned the heater on when he noticed her shivering. She sneezed, her nose red and running. She looked up at Fin, worried what his reaction would be. "I've been out in the open air in the middle of winter and I'm saturated. It's just a normal sneeze. You don't look much better. Once I'm warmed up, it'll be gone."

Fin could not hold his breath any longer. "I'll leave you to get dressed," he said quickly and rushed from the room. Gulping down air in the bathroom, he wiped his face with a damp towel. "I'll be upstairs, when you're ready," he said, loud enough for her to hear him through the closed door. The misted mirror returned only a blur of a reflection.

The kettle boiled and cooled three times before she left the room.

"I never thought I'd feel warm again," she said, taking the offered mug and sitting on the recliner. She wrapped herself in a blanket from the back of the couch, pulling her knees up to her chin. "Can we put the television on?"

"I avoided it until you were up. Didn't feel like watching it by myself."

Rebecca took the remote and threw it to him, not wanting to take the blame for what they saw.

"Can I finish my tea first?" he said.

"World's not going to be set to rights after a cup of tea."

"Yeah, but it's not a bad brew, is it?" He took a sip and scalded his tongue.

"I tried ringing my parents again when I was getting dressed. Nobody answered," Rebecca said.

"Don't think too much into it, mine didn't either for a long time," Fin said.

"They quarantined Castlebar, I checked online. Military are enforcing it. Other than emergency vehicles, they're not letting anybody through. People are being removed from their homes."

"It's the closest hospital aside from Galway. I doubt many people are heeding the news. They can't keep them away from care."

"They're trying to, at least. Those medical centres are open Petri dishes." Fin braced himself and turned the television on.

An advertisement for a new car played on the news channel. The price that flashed quickly at the end would have taken all of his annual wage and most of Solene's for two years. Following that, there were four different ads dedicated to selling a fragrant shampoo, perfume, sore throat lozenges and a cold and flu medication. *That's disgustingly cheeky.*

"It's kind of disturbing isn't it? The ads are taking much longer than they normally would," Fin said.

"Those are prime slots now. Think of how many people are tuning in to the news, millions of fresh views. News outlets are going to make a fortune, raking it in, so long as people are desperate for answers," Rebecca said.

"At least show something useful. Personally, I don't care if my hair smells of raspberries right now. It's a bit daft, imagine a few months from now and somebody's in the shower, they get a hint of raspberries and get instant negative associations and PTSD, bringing them right back to this night."

The ads ended and the news returned. To save the reporters from having to repeat themselves, a title card played before video footage; it warned of shocking and graphic content. The clip was filmed on a camera phone. It followed a man slowly walking along a motorway. The road was full of empty cars. Some engines were still running and doors open. The man cautiously approached a car that had mounted the verge, two people sat in the front seats. They watched him, but did not respond to his calls.

"We snuck around the army cordon," the camera man whispered. "This is what they're hiding." He had a Northern Irish accent.

The car shuddered and the engine cut out. The image shook as the person recording got a fright.

"Where did all the people from those other cars go?" Fin asked.

The man cursed, steeled himself and approached the car. A young couple stared back at him. The sound was muffled by the door but the microphone picked up the sound of their weeping. Sweat bubbled from their emotionless faces. The footage was paused and the reporter started talking over it.

"That quarantine zone is around Belfast," Rebecca said, reading the banner at the bottom of the screen.

Not wanting to hear any more casualty estimates, Fin

walked to the window to investigate a commotion in the car park. People queued at the bus stop across the street. "This will spread from sheer stupidity."

"We need a plan," Rebecca said. "We get to the hotel and hide. Then what?"

Fin filled the kettle and put it on again. "You're asking as if I have a clue about what's happening right now."

Rebecca gasped. *What now?* Fin had to force himself to turn and look at the television. A fresh reporter looked as haggard as if she had been on all night. She talked over aerial drone footage above Dublin City. Crowds ran between a frozen metal river of traffic. Military checkpoints were on O'Connell Street. Statues and snipers watched over the crowd with similar coldness. Soldiers panicked in the face of so many people running towards them. Some opened fire, spraying bullets into the crowd.

"What the hell are they..." Fin stopped. People climbed over dead and writhing bodies to avoid the gunfire. Some did not, standing defiant. They kept walking towards the soldiers only to be put down.

"They move like the man on the Greenway." Fin felt strangely disconnected from what he was watching. The drone was too high to capture faces.

"Do you think it's an antibiotic-resistant superbug? Or it might be one of those things that moves from animals to people. Remember the Ebola outbreak? That was all they showed on the news. There was genuine unease but that was a world away. How the hell did this happen in Ireland?"

"Your guess is as good as mine," Rebecca said. She was exhausted. "I don't remember seeing the military shooting civilians during the Ebola outbreak though."

The weatherman appeared on screen. He read the forecast from the teleprompter; storm warnings still in place. He grit his teeth at the effort of getting through what he had to say. When he finished, he just stared slack jawed at the camera. "Stacey..." It cut back to the main host before he could finish. A new reporter sat behind the desk, her earpiece dangled over her shoulder, her tie undone. When she spoke, she sounded like she was reading an essay in front of a class for the first time. "While fear of global pandemic rises, hospitals across the country are no longer able to cope with the infected. Emergency staff cannot continue to give care to the sheer volume of admissions. The government are set to release a document this afternoon on the methods for dealing with the infected. People are ordered to stay home, for their own safety. The following quarantine areas are in effect, enforced by the Irish Army."

She started naming off cities first and then towns.

"She should have just displayed an atlas of the country," Fin said. "There was a reason I avoided the news. It has crossed my mind that I've gone mad and this is a dream or hallucination."

"Well stop and let me off," Rebecca said. "Those stories broke on the internet hours ago. I'd like to imagine the news rooms are just playing catch-up, but there's no way they could filter through the amount of stuff coming in. It's a time capsule for what's actually happening. You come off the internet and look at the old stories on the news and almost get nostalgic for better times."

"Better than this?" Fin asked. "How's it spreading so fast?"

"Kindness. This has really brought the best of us to light. There was a call for help online and people answered. Taxi drivers waiving their fees, school buses collecting the sick, and carpools bringing people to hospitals," Rebecca said. "Think about it. Those that only had a cold, or a touch of paranoia, came into contact with those who were actually infected. It's not the flu, Fin, I don't know what it is but it isn't that. Can I see your phone?"

He unlocked it and handed it over. She gave it back with a video already playing. The view count was in the millions. It was from the waiting room of a Dublin hospital, filmed by a receptionist on her phone. The staff were hiding behind safety glass and security doors in reception. The A&E waiting room was packed with the sick, dying and the worried. Orderlies passed out face masks. Garda officers in green jackets stood by the doors, stopping others from coming in. They looked terrifying, like modern-day plague doctors, their faces completely covered.

"It spreads as if it were fire and we were fuel," Rebecca said.

The person taking the video was shaking, making it difficult to focus. She zoomed in on a woman lying on a gurney, fighting against the restraints. Muscles bulged and the veins in her neck stood out as she reached indiscriminately for those around her. Her skin pale, her right arm was broken, a dark bruise forming where the edge of the bone pressed against the skin like thick, syrupy cordial, slowly diluting. A nurse administered something and stepped back. It had no effect on the patient. Another nurse in the background blessed herself. An orderly pushed through the crowd, heading for the door. It was only then that Fin realised the officers were there to stop people leaving.

Covered bodies filled trolleys while the infected grew sicker on the floor. A body beneath a sheet sat up, the sheet bundled in his lap. The person operating the camera focused on his vacant stare, a peaceful, serene look of indifference. His skin was waxy, almost like a mannequin. When his partner saw him up, she broke down and started undoing his restraints. Her eyes were red, Fin was not sure if it was from crying or infection. She held him close, her face contorted with emotion and then confusion. She seemed only slightly surprised when he bit into her shoulder, until the pain set in. She screamed and tried desperately to push away but he appeared to have bitten down to the bone. He flailed back as if he had suffered a terrible spasm. Colour drained from her face as blood flowed down her front.

Chaos engulfed the room. The gardaí rushed over. The woman holding the camera ducked behind the reception desk. Two gunshots went off, the sound so loud it crackled over the mobile's speakers.

"Let us in!" People begged and banged on the bullet-proof glass.

Fin looked up at Rebecca. His lips remained a stark, thin line that kept his emotions in check; when it cracked, he was relieved it was with grief and not laughter.

The woman holding the camera composed herself and turned the lens on her face giving a panicked, last message to her family. When she saw how many thousands of people were watching her livestream, she asked for help, but the bounty of attention was meaningless.

She stood up and pointed the lens at the lobby. Bodies were trampled. Some people wept hysterically. There were two groups: people desperately trying to escape and those chasing them.

Fin lost track of time watching the video. For most of it, the receptionist hid beneath a table with her colleagues. When she braved looking out, infected watched her from the other side of the glass. Fingers found and slipped through the talking holes in the partition. One man kept hitting his head against the glass, like a bluebottle confused by a window. They were all weeping, but the audio seemed out of sync with the video, because none of their faces matched the sounds they made.

The woman could not stand under the docile scrutiny of so many infected and darted around the reception area. Beneath every desk other masked staff members hid. A few hissed at her to get down and not make a sound. But she was manic with terror. "We have to get out of here, they're going to get in. We're trapped!"

Before anybody could stop her, she pulled apart the barricade and opened the door wide enough to get through to the main hall. More bodies lined the corridor. It looked more like an exposé on a scandalously run abattoir than a national hospital.

She knocked into a glass door and pressed a keycard against the lock. The light turned from red to green. She slammed the door shut, hunkered down to catch her breath. The sound of hands slapping against glass startled her. Some of the survivors in the office followed her, they screamed to get through, but it was already too late for them. There was a scuffle. She dropped the phone and screamed.

"Will you put it off please," Rebecca said. "I don't want to hear the rest."

Fin exited from the video and saw scores more like it, his feed constantly updating. The highest viewed on the trending page was drone footage above the streets of Dublin. People ran in all directions. There were small pockets of fighting, where people could not escape crazed infected that attacked randomly and relentlessly.

The drone hovered above the River Liffey. Families and strangers held each other as they threaded water and watched the madness unfold on the streets. A fallen tower crane blocked the road to the port. People climbed through and over the wreckage. Videos came in from Cork, Dublin, Galway, Belfast. There seemed no end to the uploads.

Fin looked to Rebecca. He could not think, let alone speak. He lay his phone on the coffee table and turned the television off. Every sound made him flinch. Poncho's paws twitched as he dreamed in his basket.

"I think we should head back to the hotel. Less people, stronger doors. We have the height. It feels like we're surrounded here. Too many windows," Rebecca said. Mooch made her jump by landing on her lap. He walked around in circles before kneading his paws into the blanket and lying down to rest.

Fin's insides felt restricted, like a spring that kept winding beyond a critical breaking point. Poncho got a fright and ran for cover when Fin pushed his chair back and dashed to the sink to throw up. Afterwards, he sat on the cold kitchen floor. The taste of vomit kept his stomach from settling. He blew bile from his nose. Wrapping his arms around his legs, he lay his head on his knees and wept. "What's happening?"

Rebecca looked him dead in the eye. "Zombies."

8

UNEXPECTED GUESTS

After dinner, Fin washed the dishes, Rebecca dried. The work was done in silence, just like the meal, which had been a chore, something to be done while they waited for the crowds to thin. Fin started scrubbing the countertops when it was done, just to focus on anything other than reality. The bubbles in the sink burst like impermanent pearls as the water loudly slurped down the drain.

"I don't think I can do it, Rebecca. I doubt I'd even be able to make it far from the front door."

"I know."

"That wasn't what I was hoping to hear."

"Will we take it in turns, being the strong one?" She put the last plate away. "I can't bear the thought of being out there with them, but I don't feel safe here. Too many windows and we're in the middle of town. Best to be in the hotel. Even with all the food we took, there's still plenty there to do us. I don't think I can do it either, but I know I have to try. Just think of the pint we'll have when we get to the hotel."

"I could do with one before it."

The basil and thyme plants drooped in their pots from lack of water. He buried his nose in the leaves, then ran the pots beneath the tap. He opened the window and left them on the sill.

"What are you doing?" Rebecca asked.

"They'll die if I leave them. At least this way they'll get rain and a bit of sun."

"The temperature will kill them."

"I know, but now they have a chance."

When he looked up, he caught the eye of a couple in the apartment across the street. They waved, which was completely off-putting considering there had been an unspoken tradition of pretending the other was invisible. They drew the curtains and opened their window. Aside from the flickering glow of a television, they were in complete darkness.

The man checked the street before leaning out. Fin's mind began to race. *What if they ask for help? Did they hear us speaking about the hotel?* He felt ashamed of those thoughts.

"How's it going?" the man said. "Have yous been watching the news?"

The sink stopped Fin from leaning out too far. "There can't be many that don't know. Sorry, guys, we've been neighbours for nearly a year now and I still don't know your names. I'm Fin, this is my friend Rebecca."

"I'm Mel and this is Matthew. We used to make up stories for you and the other woman that lives with you. Jobs too."

"I can promise you the reality is more disappointing," Fin said.

"See Castlebar is under military curfew?" Mel said.

Rebecca came to the window. "It's quarantine. They think that the infection would have had a harder time spreading, if not for so many flocking to the hospital. Everyone had the notion that they could get vaccinated for the flu and would be safe."

"We were thinking of trying for it tomorrow," Mel seemed unphased.

"You can't see it, but from the other window in this apartment we've a clear view of the Castlebar Road. There must be a block further along because people have just abandoned their cars. You won't drive it."

"We could walk. Leave in the morning and get there before the crowds," Matthew said.

Rebecca pinched him out of view of the others, but she did not need to. He was not going to risk infection for familiar strangers.

"I wouldn't chance it, guys. The advice everywhere is to stay inside and avoid contact with others." He stressed that last part before they suggested joining up. "If you go to Castlebar, you're likely going to get sick. I don't think it's the flu virus either. That vaccine won't do you any good."

"I read online that if we expose ourselves to it, our bodies will be able to fight it off. Something to do with white blood cells," Mel said.

"You might get a cold once a year when the body adapts to it but this thing kills." Rebecca sounded exasperated.

"How are yous set for everything over there?" Fin asked.

Matthew looked up and down the street again to see if anybody else was listening. Fin saw the small window of the apartment next to theirs was open a little. Matthew stepped back out of view of everybody but Fin and Rebecca. "We haven't got anything here, few bags of rice and noodles. We're supposed to be heading to my family for Christmas." While he was saying that he was nodding his head, letting them know that they were okay for everything. "What about you guys?"

"Same," Rebecca said.

"Say, do you want something to garnish that rice with?" Fin asked. He threw the potted herbs to them.

"Cheers, buddy," Matthew said after catching the basil. "We'll chat to yous tomorrow. Stay safe."

They seemed reluctant to close their window and leave the comfort found in the company of others. They left their curtains open, and Fin saw them sit back down in front of the TV, holding hands and leaning against each other. He felt Solene's absence like a vital loss.

Rebecca closed the window and the blinds, not wanting the couple to see that they were packing to leave.

"Can you believe they're actually thinking of going to the quarantine zone?" Rebecca asked. She emptied the presses of what little dry food there was left, dropping everything on the sofa to sort out.

"Never mind the hospital, that talk about self-infecting to build immunity was madness. They're just worried. The army's there, people in charge that will tell them what to do. It's appealing. The alert messages on our phones just tell us to remain indoors. It's not really helpful if you're hungry with no food or sick with no medicine."

"We can't help everyone, Fin."

"I wasn't suggesting we do. I don't want to get sick and I don't want you to either. I want to get where we're going, lock the doors and wait for this whole thing to end."

"Let's get to it then."

* * *

When the cats ate their fill, Fin topped them up again.

"They're probably worried right now, wondering why I'm not chasing them with the brush."

With an absent smile on her face, Rebecca watched him vigorously pet Mooch. "Do you really chase them with a brush?"

"If you ever plonked your bare ass on my pillow, you'd get the brush too. They're cute, but they're nowhere near as cute as other people's cats." He sat on the floor and rubbed them while they ate. "Good luck, guys."

Before leaving, he opened a downstairs window for them to climb out, if they needed to.

"They might bring the infection back in with them," Rebecca said.

"Other than to feed them, I've no intention of coming back until this is over. If something happens to me, I don't want them trapped."

"All this time at work you've been giving out about the cats," Rebecca said.

"I've been annoying them since they were kittens. I got a little attached."

With the remainder of their food packed up, they went through the wardrobe for the warmest clothes. There were work shirts, pants and uniforms they could use in the hotel, along with a utility room full of washing machines and dryers to clean the clothes. "Are you sure she won't mind?" Rebecca asked.

"Given the circumstances, she can't."

"I like her," Rebecca said. She found one of the small notes Solene had left.

"What does it say?"

"Turn off the water heater."

Fin laughed. "That's not one for me, that's a daily

reminder she wrote for herself. I hope she's okay." He left the heater on for the cats.

They tied scarves over their faces and wore thick yellow cleaning gloves. They helped tape each other's closed at the wrist. When there was nothing left to do, they stood in the dark by the door, not wanting to turn any lights on at the front to draw attention to the house. Rebecca had a duffle bag over her shoulder, Fin had an old rucksack on his back, both carried a bag of spare clothes.

"You have the hotel key?" Rebecca asked.

He took it out of his pocket and made a show of zipping it back securely. A light drizzle fell. The wind barely rippled across the face of puddles. The car park beyond the court-yard was empty. Not even the local cats prowled.

Rebecca checked her watch. "It's two now, we can wait a bit longer if you want, but I've not seen anybody for a while. Should we go?"

Fin nodded and stepped out into the night, quietly closing the door behind them. He was careful with the bags, so the tins inside would not make noise. They were nearly through the courtyard when a window opened two apartments down from his. "Hey, where are yous going?"

They froze, worried others would be drawn by talking. Fin's hood was up, and it dawned on him too late that he should have pretended not to have heard his neighbour and just keep walking.

Rebecca broke the silence. "We've been infected. We're going to the quarantine zone in Castlebar for treatment."

It worked beautifully. The window slammed shut and the curtains closed so quickly that the hooks screeched across the rail. They stepped through the broken door into the empty streets. Apartments rested on top of dormant shops and restaurants. Every window was dark and lifeless.

There was no way of skirting the car park without being visible to dozens of homes.

"That was well done," Fin said in the middle of the field of tarmac.

"It just came to me, and now they won't think of looting your place."

"You think it will get that bad?"

"Maybe," she shrugged.

Without the storm, the world was eerily quiet. Their footsteps echoed around the amphitheatre of empty windows. When Rebecca unlocked the car, lights flashed. The road beyond the car park was blocked by empty vehicles; they would have to walk to the hotel with as much food from the boot as they could carry. Fin closed it quietly, leaving most of the supplies behind.

All day they watched the streets for infected, but it was impossible to tell them apart from healthy people. Not a soul wandered the roads so late. Rebecca gave his hand a squeeze on the bank of the main road. "We can do this."

Fin squeezed back, his courage bolstered by the knife in his fist. Confident that the way was clear, they turned left. Fin took a final look at his home. *She's right, we wouldn't last there.*

The only sign of life came from inside the Garda station. Light blared from an upstairs meeting room. Half the squad cars that usually idled in the lot were gone. *Out on patrol.* Fin remembered the car that flew by the crash the other morning, going so fast it nearly became a part of it. An officer watched them from the top floor of the station, his shirt dark with sweat. The fabric strained around the buttons across his belly, like he did not belong in it. Fin waved to show they were not infected. The officer spoke into a radio.

"They're earning their money," Rebecca said.

"If I was a cop or a nurse, I'd be calling in sick for the next while," Fin said. "What makes you go where others actively avoid?"

"They're cut from a different cloth. Nothing will have prepared them for this, but they're willing to try, suppose that's all it takes," Rebecca said.

"Best of luck to them."

"Stay where you are." They spun to face whoever called for them to stop. The young guard was too loud. Fin's heart was having difficulty getting back into a steady rhythm.

"I said, stop!"

Behind the approaching officer, a small group of people loitered at a side entrance to the station. They seemed ready to shut it at the slightest upset. The main entrance was completely barricaded. *Infected don't shout at you to stop. They don't carry guns.*

"Are you infected? Speak quickly or I will shoot," he kept checking the roads, the gun trembling in his hands.

"There's a good man," Rebecca said, her voice quavered.

What are you doing? Fin had never been so close to a firearm before, but he had a good idea how they worked.

"I have a live video feed going at the moment," Rebecca said. She held up her phone, Fin knew she could not have turned the camera on in time. "You and your badge number are currently starring. Now, we just need you to shoot us and this will go viral."

The officer seemed less sure of himself. "There's a curfew in place."

"And I see you're adhering to it inside your station, instead of enforcing it."

Don't push it.

He lowered his weapon. "Where are yous heading this late?"

"Leaving where the infected are," Fin said.

"Well you're heading straight towards them. They're everywhere."

"We came in along the Greenway from Newport earlier. Saw a few of them heading towards town," Fin said.

"We had barriers up, but what are we supposed to do, shoot everybody with a runny nose?"

Rebecca pointed the lens of her phone away from his face, in return for him holstering his weapon. "How bad is it?"

"Chaos. Of those that decided to stay here, half regret it. They want to break up supplies and part ways. The station is packed with family members, there's not a chance that place is free of infection. We're just waiting for the army to come through and set things straight. Stations across the country are going dark." His eyes wandered down to the bags they carried. "Is that food you have there?"

There was a brief, awkward silence before Fin started coughing. He lifted his bag-laden hand to cover his mouth. Rebecca flinched and drew away from him, giving weight to the lie. The officer stepped back, all familiarity gone. He looked to his superior officer, watching proceedings from the upstairs window. "Go, leave."

Rebecca kept her phone on the officer as he ran back inside and locked the door behind him. Once out of view of the station, they ran up the steep cycle path of the Greenway, leading straight to the quay and their hotel. Not stopping to see if they were followed, they walked briskly through a tunnel that would have seemed ominous before the outbreak.

"I wouldn't have thought to pretend recording him," Fin said.

"I had my phone out the minute I saw that guy go for his

radio. I've never seen him before. It's sickening that it was the fear of being watched that kept him civil. I've never had a gun pulled on me. The coughing was a nice bit of theatre."

"I learn from the best," Fin said.

Houses overlooked the path, but most of the windows were covered. The sound of distant weeping carried on the still air. They came out onto a ridge, high above the rooftops. The town was not sleeping, it was hiding.

Beyond the clustered housing estates, they were soon surrounded by fields and trees. Clouds hid the stars, but in the distance, they saw a solitary light slowly making its way up the side of Croagh Patrick.

"Do you think that's the mountain rescue?" Rebecca said.

"Say so. It must be horrible up there this time of year, but I imagine they feel a whole lot safer than we do."

Voices nearby forced them into silence until they passed. The tang of sea air as they approached the coast was a relief. They made it the rest of the way to the hotel without any further intrusion. They checked the locks and that none of the windows were broken. There were no signs of forced entry. To gain access to the hotel car park, somebody would have to climb down a four-storey drop from the estate above, down a slime-slick, sheer wall. Fin had to use both hands to get the key in the lock. He opened the door just wide enough for them to sneak through. Most of the built-up tension in his body evaporated once he turned the key, locking them in.

Rebecca sighed. "We're safe."

Instead of risking light and advertising their presence, they used the glow from their phone screens to move towards the kitchen behind the bar. Sound travelled far into the haunted shadows. Tinsel on the Christmas tree reflected light back at them. Before putting the food in the walk-in fridge, they rinsed everything, washed their gloves in bleach and put on fresh latex ones.

"We still have a lot of perishables," Rebecca said, doing a quick stocktake.

"It's a pity this didn't happen in July," Fin said. "In summer this place is stuffed to the gills with food for all the tourists."

"It's a pity it happened at all," Rebecca said.

"I meant there would have been enough food here to do the both of us for a long time."

"There's plenty. Tomorrow we'll do a list of what we have and when it goes off."

"Where do you think is safe in here?" Fin asked. "The advice was to stay as far from public places as possible. How many people do you think walked through these doors over the last week?"

"We don't need the whole hotel. What we should do is figure out where we'll sleep and the main places we'll use. We scour them clean with bleach and avoid the rest of the building."

"Sounds like a plan. We can check the system to see what rooms were used last. Find some new bedding and stay there," Fin said.

"I won't be able to sleep," Rebecca emptied the presses of bleach and sponges.

"How long do you think you can go without rest before you're a danger to yourself? Sleep now and you'll be more productive in the morning. We're safe. This place is a fortress. They're not getting in."

"Should we barricade the door?"

"The storm shields are on the windows. If we make a barricade people might wonder what's worth protecting.

Let's not invite curiosity. I'm having a pint. Will you join me?"

"How can you drink at a time like this?" Rebecca said.

"How can you not want a drink after today? I won't sleep either, so the sensible thing is to try and knock myself out."

Lost in the darkness, they followed the towering glow of the beer taps like ships orienting themselves by lighthouses. Fin took out the bottom row of pint glass trays. They were turned upside down to stop dust from falling in. He took two from the back; a reassuring film of dust rested on their bottoms. He filled the glasses and raised one to the camera, before taking a long drink and topping it up. He brought a few bottles of beer into the back office.

Rebecca had half her pint gone before the main computer booted up. "We've a suite on the top floor that hasn't been touched in two weeks. Loads of regular rooms with views of the parking garage that have been idle for a while too – Fin?"

"What? Sorry." His attention was drawn to the bank of security camera monitors on the wall. The screens were split into smaller tabs, displaying the video feeds from across the hotel. The hallways, kitchens, bar and lobby were all dark and empty. Night vision made it easy to make out details. Twice in the past he had caught drunken residents sneaking into the bar after hours, thinking they could get away with theft if the lights were off.

"What is it?" Rebecca asked.

"I thought I saw something on camera thirty-two." It was a dark hallway where nothing moved. "Right beneath it is the camera feed from outside. Raindrops keep falling in front of it. They shine brightly with the night filter. Probably saw that in the corner of my eye."

"Probably? Don't say that, this place gives me the creeps on a good day," Rebecca said.

They began a silent vigil. The foam of Fin's pint fizzled out, leaving it lifeless. *Please be nothing.* They relaxed, as much as was possible, given what was happening across the country.

"I'm glad I'm not here alone," Fin said.

"They asked me last year if I wanted the job of staying over the holidays to watch over the place. Turned them down, it's too creepy. Why did you take it?" Rebecca said.

"Wanted to bring Solene away on a long holiday. We had no idea what we were at, save for the future or emigrate. I'm terrible at saving – with money in general – otherwise we'd already be abroad. I hope she's..."

One of the security camera screens lit up.

"What the hell was that?" Rebecca closed the thick door of the office and locked it.

Fin used the computer to enlarge the view. "It's the basement," he said.

The door of the drinks fridge and the dry food store was on screen. Empty crates and gas cylinders clogged the hall, scattered across the floor. A cylinder stopped rolling and came to rest against the fridge.

"How did somebody..." Rebecca stopped as Fin cycled through cameras.

"They're all connected to motion sensors down there. A mouse could set them off, they're that sensitive. Relax, you're starting to make me anxious." He tried to sound confident to put her at ease.

"There's enough poison and traps set around this place to sanitise a plague ship," Rebecca said. "Will you minimise that screen please? I want to keep an eye on the others."

He did as she asked. Two more lights in the basement

had been activated. The small hairs on his body stood on end.

Rebecca pointed at the screen. "I saw something move in the edge of the frame. Can you play back the recording?"

Fin's hands shook. He clicked rewind and stopped. He saw it too. Somebody was in the basement.

9

LATE FRIENDS

"I'm not the only one with keys," Fin said. "All the managers have a set, the owners too."

He turned the cameras back to a live feed. One by one, the lights went off.

"We sneak out and head back to yours before the sun rises," Rebecca said. She started pacing and pulled her hair up under her hat.

"The apartment's empty, there's no food there and my neighbour thinks we're infected. We can't go back. There aren't any broken windows and the locks were fine when we came back. I'm telling you, we're overreacting." Fin opened the saved footage folder. "Camera only starts recording when it senses motion." There were only a few clips from the basement. He stopped when he saw Rebecca on screen, clocking in for her last day. The next clip was of a person leaving the women's changing room.

"It's a staff member," Fin said. "I don't even know the code to get in there."

"Oh my heart. I thought it was about to stop," Rebecca said, falling hard into her seat. "It's just Ciara."

Fin leaned back and let out a sigh of relief. "Do me a favour will you? Don't mention that I nearly curried my trousers because of her. George, her and I have this ongoing thing where we try and scare each other after hours. I think she just won." He sat up. "You know what, I might try and scare her."

"Now really isn't the time for messing," Rebecca said and he agreed, feeling foolish for even suggesting it.

"She must be sleeping down there," Fin said. "Not a bad spot when you think about it. Crisps and vending machine food, it's all kept down there. It's secure and who's actually going to go into the basement of an empty hotel? I always did what I had to do down there before the staff left."

"She's braver than I am," Rebecca said.

"That's one more on the team. Come on, we'll let her know she's not alone."

Knowing there was another familiar face around was nearly overwhelming. Fin took out his phone and rang her. Almost immediately one of the lights went on downstairs. He smiled. "Come on."

Rebecca unlocked the office door and they entered the stairwell just off the lobby. Fire doors throughout the building were closed for insurance purposes. Nothing stirred in the dark. There were no windows, so he turned the lights on without fear of drawing attention from the outside. They went down. Fin stopped before he reached the last step.

"What's the matter?"

"Her phone rang out." Fin dialled again.

"The lines are jammed." Rebecca went ahead and opened the heavy door into the basement. They heard Ciara's ringtone and something else, it was indistinguishable alongside the chime. Fin hung up. It was much clearer now. Crying. *No.* She was weeping. Fin crouched down and grabbed the bannister. Strength left him. He could hardly breathe. Heart racing, trying to outpace his thoughts.

It was too late to stop Rebecca. The sound of her friend in pain evoked more worry than terror. It was a sinister disease, using its host's humanity to lure more victims in. "Ciara." The weeping grew more intense, almost excited, but not so loud to mask the quickening footsteps coming towards them.

Rebecca let the door go. Metal hinges at the top made it close slowly to stop it from banging. Her hand automatically reached for a lock but there was none.

"Run!" Fin took the stairs two at a time, stumbling and tripping in his haste. Rebecca outpaced him. Instead of the gentle shush the fire door made when it closed properly, the metal handle smacked against the wall, pushed violently open by Ciara.

Rebecca hesitated by the door to the lobby. To get through she would have to stop and pull it towards her, losing ground to Ciara. Fin could almost feel her bloodied hands reaching for him. Her breathless weeping was deafeningly close, ringing in his ear. If he faltered, even for a moment, she would have him.

Rebecca continued up the stairs. Fin knocked over a decorative table on the first floor landing. He stopped on the second floor, turned and watched Ciara trip. She could have avoided the obstruction, but she was too focused on him. When she fell, her arms did not go out to protect her. It looked as if she had just passed out, her brain switched off and her body dropped. Carpet softened the blow to her head. Dazed, she lay there for a moment, her eyes never leaving Fin's. He did not run, desperately waiting to hear her speak.

"Ciara, stop, you've won, you've scared the shite out of me." Her skin was pale, the flesh beneath darkening like no heat would ever return. He knew, despite every instinct, that she was gone. She was still in her work uniform. *You never left.*

"Ciara. Would you stop it, please." His words were in vain.

Her lips moved, like a cat chirping when it has a bird in its sights. Still weeping, even though she was desperately short of breath. Each gasp she took, like a smoker's wheeze, seemed hard fought for. What chilled him most was the lack of expression on her face. It was void of anything resembling human emotion.

Dried vomit and yellow bile covered her shirt. She lunged at him, giving him a clear view of her ruined palms, which left copper stains on the carpet. There was no apparent malice to her actions.

Fin ran on. He could no longer see Rebecca, but he could hear her panicked breathing and cursing from a few floors above. Hundreds of doors in the hotel, and each room required a keycard specifically coded for it. There were also the locked doors on the staff side of the building, the ones that required physical keys to open. Those were currently on the desk in the office, right next to his master keycard. It was difficult to focus on a route ahead with her weeping.

Every floor he passed, he knocked over tables to obstruct her, giving them precious moments. He climbed until there was nowhere else to go. The top floor contained the function room, suites and a fine dining restaurant. Rebecca did not stop to turn the lights on and if she did not have the time for that, then Fin knew he certainly did not. Ciara was right behind him. He nearly ran straight into Rebecca outside the stairwell. She stood still near the little snug where they drank on the night of the storm and watched the news of the infection break.

He was about to yell for her to run, but choked on the words when he saw the moonlit silhouette of a man standing by the window. Ciara crashed over a table on the third floor landing. The sound made the man turn, but his movements were too slow, especially in the face of Ciara's unnatural anguish. He stumbled towards them. *Infected.*

In their panic, Rebecca went right and Fin turned left. There was no time for indecision, they had to commit to their paths. The man chased Rebecca into the function room, but that meant Ciara, having just made it to the top of the stairs, had only Fin to follow.

He sprinted for the restaurant. Just before his shoulder connected with the door, he wondered if was locked. His momentum sent the door flying into the cutlery table, sending knives and forks cascading everywhere. He stumbled and fell. Luckily the door swung back and knocked Ciara off her feet. Terrified of tripping over tables and chairs in the dark room, he had to move slowly. Countless nights wandering these halls over the course of his work meant he could walk the hotel with his eyes closed.

Ciara lacked that knowledge, but without fear, she was faster. She skidded on the cutlery and the noise stopped her until the door closed, leaving them in almost complete darkness. He had left the light in the wine fridge on the other night. Ciara made a beeline, struck the side of a four-seater table, careened off balance and disappeared from sight. Fin took one long breath and held it. There was enough light from the moon for her to make him out if she stopped to look.

Does she remember the layout? He weaved around several tables, careful not to make a sound. He pushed through the service doors into the kitchen. There were no motion sensors here, the only light coming from the emergency exit signs and the bulbs on the machines. There was not enough light to make out the edges of things. The door burst open behind him. If he lost focus he would not be able to orient in the darkness. He ran the length of the prep kitchen using his hand to feel his way. *Fridge, freezer, coffee station, baking tray rack, oven.* He turned into the bakery and dashed through the door into the staff room.

He had no clue how close she was. Falling to his knees, he crawled as far as he could beneath a large table. Feeling naked for the lack of anything to use as a weapon, he hesitated, wondering if he could bring himself to cause her harm. *She's just sick.*

Hands clasped over his mouth to muffle the sound of his heavy breathing. The door closed slowly, but he could still hear the manic weeping in the kitchen.

"Help." It sounded like Ciara.

Tears streamed down his face. Her weeping slowed but did not stop.

"Help."

Fin wanted to scream. The staff room door closed with a quiet click. She wept and ran straight into something, knocking the air out of her infected lungs. *If she can speak then she must remember the layout of the hotel.* It dawned on him that he could hide beneath the table in relative safety during the night, but when morning came, she would find him.

"Fin!"

Ciara was still winded from the fall. *Rebecca.* He felt something against his leg and imagined a hand on his trousers, the sudden sensation made him jump. He hit his head on the chewing gum-covered underside of the table.

His phone vibrated in his pocket. The screen light was blinding in the darkness. He put it under his sweater to hide the glow and pulled his head through the top.

Rebecca messaged him. 'Are you okay?'

Fin kept his phone on vibrate, but it hollowed him out to think, had Rebecca's message come through when it was set to loud, he would likely be in the process of dying right now. He had never passed out before, but he was pretty sure the lightheadedness he was experiencing was a warning. He turned the screen to standby and held it to his chest to muffle the light should she text again. *She's safe enough to text.*

He turned the phone back on. 'I'm in the staff room. Ciara's in the kitchen. Are you okay? Where are you?'

'In the function room bar. The shutters are down. Who was that man?'

'I don't know.'

Ciara knocked something over. She was hunting him. 'Are you okay?'

'Yes, the noise in the kitchen drew him away. He's heading to you. Can you make it to the function room? Please don't leave me here Fin.'

It never occurred to him to leave without her. He had not thought that far ahead yet. There was no lock on the staff room door, but there was another way out, through the bathrooms and out the other side of the kitchen.

'I have an idea.' The phone buzzed with every message he received. He feared Ciara was getting closer.

'What?'

'I'm going to put the volume on my phone up to the maximum. Then you call me. When it rings, I'll use the distraction to sneak through to you. Be ready with the door. If she's running after me and you don't open in time...'

'I'm ready. Just let me know and I'll let you in. Let me know when to ring you.'

'Don't text me again, my phone is now off silent. Make it five minutes, starting now.' Fin came out from beneath the table and approached the door. He wedged the side of his foot against it in case she tried to rush in. He slid his phone beneath a fridge. Ciara had wandered into the washup section.

Quietly, he went through the other door into utter darkness, suppressing the urge to lock himself in the bathroom and just stay there. He would have plenty of water, but without his phone he would have no way of contacting Rebecca, he would be trapped. Whether he wanted to or not, he was now committed to the plan.

At the end of the hallway he looked into the kitchen. Both of the infected were at the far end by the sink. The man was drawn by the sound of her weeping. Ciara tackled him to the ground. If she did the same to him, it would not matter if he got away, he would be infected, forced to hide in one of the many empty rooms and wait to turn. *Could I kill myself? Is there a cure?*

While they were distracted, Fin tiptoed to the dry food store. The hallway door slowly closed on well-oiled hinges, and hit the frame with a bang. Pots and pans clattered to the ground as Ciara rushed across the kitchen. Fin thought his own fear would give him away. He lay flat against the shelves, careful not to knock into anything. There was only one way in and out of the storeroom. No windows or lights, just the smell of spices and a touch of mould, likely from breakfast fruit that had hidden away beneath the shelves and festered. Ciara blocked the doorway. Her weeping was like standing next to a ringing church bell, every note struck, rang through him. Any longer and he would have been driven mad.

She stepped inside. He willed his heart to beat softer. He was convinced that she heard it hammering as loudly as he could. Had it been any earlier in the morning, the light would have betrayed him. The man walked in behind her, following her interest. All they had to do was to keep walking. Four feet. Three.

His phone rang. He flinched but neither Ciara or the man noticed. She knocked the stranger to the ground in her haste to reach the noise. Fin had to wait the infuriating seconds for him to stagger after her, before sneaking out, bent so low that he had to use his hands to balance. He only started breathing properly again when through the doors into the dining room. *How long before the call goes to voice-mail?* Standing up straight, he ran through the restaurant, only remembering the spilled cutlery by the moonlight glinting off them.

At the top of the stairs, he thought about going down, getting the keys and leaving, imagined the safety of his house, but he could not leave Rebecca. He had no way of contacting her. She would be trapped alone, imagining him dead. There would be no way of letting her know without his phone. Cursing, he entered the function room.

Black metal shutters closed off the bar to prevent residents from taking a night cap without emptying their wallets first.

"It's me, let me in."

The lock turned on the other side but the door remained closed.

"Are you infected?"

Fin pushed the door, knocking Rebecca back. "Are you serious?" He locked it behind him.

Rebecca crawled as far away from him as she could in the tight space, covering her mouth with her sleeve.

She shushed him harshly to a whisper. "How do you know you're not infected?"

"You were closer to that man than I was to her, are you infected?"

She answered with silence.

They sat on opposite ends of the bar and listened to the distant weeping of their friend. Fin felt pinned down by her stare – Rebecca watched him closely for signs of infection. She did not conceal the knife in her hand.

10

SILENT PRAYER

Despite the knife in Rebecca's hand, he was glad of her company. Aside from the latch and lock on the door, one of the few benefits of their hiding place was that it had not been used for months. It was unlikely that the pathogen that caused the infection was behind the shutters – unless they brought it in with them.

His head lolled against his chest as he struggled to stay awake. Every time he closed his eyes, he saw her gormless face. When he gave in, he found no comfort in sleep, regularly waking with a start, worried that Rebecca had succumbed to the disease. Heavy eyelids dipped slowly. The last thing he saw was her unwavering stare.

Before dawn, Fin was woken by a hand covering his mouth, muffling his frightened surprise. Rebecca pressed her lips close to his ear. She was shaking. "They're here," she said, in so soft a whisper that he barely heard it.

Fin got into a crouch, careful not to make a sound. He held his breath and looked through the shutters. The man wandered across the empty dance floor to the window overlooking the street. Fin wondered if it was the sound of the rain hitting the glass or the moonlight shadows that drew him there. Ciara followed him closely, watching everything he did. She stalked the room, agitated and uncomfortable standing still. She seemed more cognisant of her surroundings, like she was looking for them. Fin ducked out of sight.

Darkness dressed the infected with a primeval dread. By morning, the monstrous affectations of imagination were limited by light, and they became human again. Ciara wobbled when she walked. Her clothes were drenched, soiled and bloody. Noises from outside would cause her to weep. As the hours passed, she could barely manage a chesty wheeze. Seeing her in such a state and not being able to help was nearly worse than listening to her agonised weeping during the night, like a banshee keening her own death.

Fin kept sneaking glances at her, hoping to catch the eye of the person she once was. She just looked sick. He could so easily hear her voice and sarcastic jokes, but now her slack, expressionless face was like a funeral mask, a pale imitation.

Rebecca looked through the shutters. 'Look at him,' she mimed. Her breathing was more laboured. He could tell she was trying to keep her panic under control. Ciara attacked the man multiple times over the course of the night. His wounds were not something a person should be able to walk with.

They were trapped. Ciara only wept when she was riled out of a stupor by the man bumping into something. When that happened, her weeping became incessant until she was sure there was nothing to hunt. At times they were distracted by rattling radiator pipes in the walls. Fin's breath would catch whenever the refrigerator behind the bar knocked.

He held his hand against his forehead and did the same to Rebecca. Neither of them had a high temperature or showed any immediate signs of infection, but with two of those things in the room, it was only a matter of time.

Rebecca took out her phone and started typing a message. The brightness of the screen did not stand out as much as it did a few hours ago. She handed the phone to him. 'Will I ring your phone and when they go after it, we try for the stairs?'

He wrote beneath it. 'The keys are in the main office. If we get stuck in there with bars on the window, what will we do? There's no food in there. No water taps. How many more people are in the building?'

She typed quickly and passed the phone back to him. 'How am I supposed to know?'

'Did you check the passover report I made before leaving?'

'I was the only one here on the last day. There was a lot happening, people left. I don't know if they all went. I thought they did. I did not see Ciara.'

'We've food and drink here, let's wait and see what they do,' Fin typed.

Their conversation leached the phone's battery and they did not have a charger in the bar. He put it on standby and gave it back. Neither of them wanted to stay there but they had no choice but to wait in silence for something to happen, for one of them to wander off. Fin knelt and studied their behaviour: their movements were erratic, and sound drew their attention, but beyond that he could not guess what they were thinking. The man pawed at the window when the rain came again but, aside from that, he just watched Ciara with as keen an interest as she watched him. Deep scratch marks traced down his face and a mouthful of flesh had been bitten away from his neck. He appeared indifferent.

Rebecca opened a bottle of mineral, the escaping gas making a barely audible hiss, but the room echoed to the sound of Ciara running towards them, slamming into the bar counter. It knocked the wind out of her and she crumpled to the ground. The weeping became a choking, pained gasp. Fin sat with his back to an empty keg. Rebecca closed her eyes, her mouth moving in a wordless prayer.

Fin watched the reflection in the dark glass-fronted fridges. Ciara stood up. Her face spasmed and he saw the gaps in her mouth where she had lost teeth, two incisors jutting out from her lower lip at crooked angles. The full extent of the damage was not visible in the reflection. He remembered her braces only came off last summer. She had always been smiling since then – a smile that cost her six months' savings in dentistry bills. Watching her silhouette, he could hear her joking about spending all that money and smiling the whole time, until she had to stop because people either thought she was simple or coming on to them.

Her eyes lingered on his and he froze, but she kept scanning. Fin felt for Rebecca's hand and squeezed, hoping she would calm down. Eventually she lost interest and wandered off.

Rebecca mimed the words 'I'm sorry.'

Fin shook his head to let her know it was not a problem. He took the bottle from her and drank a few slow sips. He did not take too much, if he had to relieve himself in front of Rebecca he would, but preferred not to.

Time dragged by and slowly the day dimmed. Crisps and chocolate bars were the only things to eat, but they were not yet hungry enough to try open the crinkly wrappers.

Rebecca took her phone out and a few moments later

Fin vaguely heard his ringtone from across the hotel. Ciara ran and smacked into the function room door with a sickening crunch and collapsed. Through a gap in the hatch they could see her. Despite the damage and experience, she tried the door again, incensed, her fists thumped and slapped against the unyielding wood.

Fin made a slicing gesture with his hand across his throat and Rebecca hung up the phone. He gestured for it and wrote the words that just dawned on him. 'You have to pull the door from this side to open it.' Rebecca slumped against the kegs. She went back to ripping beer mats apart and building a little mound of broken pieces.

* * *

Fin and Rebecca were woken by the infected battering the window. A lot of noise came from the street below. Car headlights cast shadows that stretched across the walls. If he closed his eyes, the sound of so many people reminded him of summertime crowds, when people had a mind for music and drink.

"I'm calling the Garda station again," Rebecca said.

Fin did not object, with the infected on the far side of the room making a commotion, they could risk a whisper. He kept watch to let her know if they were coming back. Rebecca got straight through, she started talking, blurting to get everything out.

Ciara turned towards them, but then the man hit the window and she turned away.

"Oh, dear God. It's a recording, Fin." She pressed the phone to his ear. The voice on the line gave instructions on how to spot the infection, how to sure up your home and where to go in the following places that were being evacuated. Rebecca rang again. This time, there was no recorded message but a dial tone. She grabbed Fin's arm in relief. The phone rang out. On the third attempt she was greeted with the automated message. The national emergency number that the government provided played an audio clip on how to cope during the epidemic. *They're calling it that now.*

"What is it?" Fin asked.

"Tips on how to secure your home and how to deal with the infected."

"Perfect. They mentioned safe zones and evacuation plans..."

"Have you ever seen a horror movie? We go and join some evacuation and we die on the way. Why does nobody ever listen to the sound advice given in those films? Because it would be a boring one wherein everybody survives. I'm okay with boring."

They took it in turns to ring the local station until the battery bar dipped into the red and they turned it off to conserve it. Without his phone Fin had no way of knowing how his family were getting on, or if Solene had responded to his messages yet.

"Have you heard from your folks back on the island?" he said.

"I sent them messages about what we saw on the roads. Told them not to open their door to anybody. They'll be okay." She believed it, too.

The smell of ammonia from the ice bucket they were using as a toilet was barely noticeable now. Night crept in and broadened every hour, making it feel endless. The infected did not sleep.

Ciara ceased her weeping during the night. Fin and Rebecca jolted alert when one of the infected fell over. Ciara lay curled up on the floor. She was deathly still.

"Is she dead?" Rebecca asked.

"I don't know. Didn't the news mention infected going into a torpor and then getting back up? Maybe she fractured her skull running into the door."

The man left his vigil by the window and stumbled towards the noise, one foot tripping over the other. The toe of his shoes clipped and dragged along the ground. Rebecca went pale, pushing herself further under the counter.

"We need a plan," Fin said. He laid out everything useful that they had to hand. Glass bottles and a few fruit-cutting knives. A television remote and some kegs of beer. He could do proper damage with a keg if they could get the man to come through the hatch and drop it on his head – contaminating the area with his blood. He swallowed bile, hardly believing he could think of such a thing. The knives and glass bottle were not much better, too easy to cut yourself.

The man reached the shutters. The bar counter jutted out far enough that he could not easily put his weight against it. His fingers clumsily wove through the gaps. Mouth hanging wide open. His dishevelled suit was torn, creased and soiled with vomit and urine. All manner of smells oozed from him. Bloodshot eyes bulged from his head. He stared at Fin without any hint of recognition, his mouth feebly opening and closing soundlessly, bar the odd lip smack. The skin was pale and shrunken around the fat of his face. From news reports, they knew exactly what somebody as far gone as him could do without remorse.

Rebecca picked up a knife and pricked the sharp end into the creature's finger. He did not react.

Fin took the knife from her, careful not to touch the blade. "Sir, say something. I'm going to stab you. If you don't want me to, just nod your head."

He continued to stare back at him, unable to comprehend the words.

"What happens when he gets better or after all of this ends? I don't want to go to prison for stabbing somebody. I can't kill him just because he's sick," Fin said.

"You've seen zombie movies before, haven't you?"

"Will you listen to yourself? Those are movies, not instructional videos." He paced around their cramped confines.

"Look at him, there's no coming back from that," Rebecca said.

"What are you doing working here if you have a medical degree?" Fin said with more than a bit of scorn.

"Shut up. Likely, we're going to die. I don't want to be trapped in here. This feels too much like a coffin, I can't spend another night."

Fin put the tip of the blade through one of the man's fingers. He put force behind it and it slid through until it hit bone. No blood seeped out. Fin shouted at him to elicit any response, quickly glancing at Ciara to see if the noise roused her. She lay still. The man reacted to the sound, but it did nothing to vent Fin's unease. If anything, he felt worse. He ran to the sink, retched and threw up bile.

Rebecca moved away from him. "Are you infected?"

With his head in the sink, Fin took a few calming breaths, though the stale smell from the drain only further upset his stomach. He turned the tap on, washed his face and towelled off with a musty dish cloth. "I don't think I am, that was just the first time I ever stabbed a person. I wasn't prepared for that today."

Rebecca paced. The man followed her movement, but his swollen fingers were stuck in the shutters. The bones broke as he pulled away. Still no pain. Rebecca pointed the remote at the large television at the far end of the room. The sudden noise drew the thing's attention away from them. Fin dropped the knife in the sink and washed his hands. They hunkered out of sight. Eventually the man shambled off in the direction of the television.

"So, we don't know if all the guests have left the hotel?" Fin said.

"I don't know, I told you there was too much for one person to do on the last day. I thought it was empty."

"I'm not blaming you. I'm trying to come up with a plan. We can't draw the attention of people on the street because they've either already seen or will notice your man. We have to make a run for the office. We can't bring the packets of crisps with us and all the water is in glass bottles, so we can't carry too much or they'll clink together."

"What if all those people on the street are infected?" Rebecca said.

"That's something I did not want to imagine. That the uninfected are a minority."

Rebecca turned the volume up and put the news on. "... Never have I witnessed anything take effect so quickly with such impact."

"What advice do you have for people that might be worried by all of this?" the reporter asked.

"Don't panic."

The effect was made worse by the guest appearing so frazzled. He constantly wrung his hands together.

"Why did they put him in a lab coat?" Fin asked. "Did he come to the station dressed in normal clothes and they asked him to wear it?"

The interviewee filled the awkward silence. "Stay indoors. Have as little contact with other people as possible.

Cover your mouth and nose when outside. Avoid public spaces." He stood up mid-interview and walked off screen.

"I half expected him to suggest we pray," Rebecca said.

"While it's distracted by the sound of the television we sneak out and lock the doors, get the keys and get out of here," Fin said.

"Don't talk so loud, what if he understands you?"

Fin turned the volume on the TV up and they ducked back down. "How many more do you think are in the hotel?"

"No way of knowing."

"Right, no point in worrying about that now. Are you ready?" he asked.

"No, but if you gave me a week, I still wouldn't be."

They opened the hatch and crawled through to the function room. Ciara's unseeing eyes stared at the ceiling. They crept to the door and slowly pulled it towards them. Heart and thoughts racing. Sweat stung his eyes. Each time he looked away from the man he imagined him sprinting towards them.

When they were in the hall, Fin closed the door slowly behind them, watching the man through the window. Rebecca kept an eye on the restaurant. The only noise came from outside.

A blanket of grey cloud filled the sky, stretching to the horizon. The road beneath them was blocked with abandoned cars. Half the trawlers and ships that sheltered in the harbour during the storm were gone. He had never seen a crowd of people so widely dispersed. The largest groups were made up of five to eight people. Each bunch actively avoided the others. Some people further down the port were trying to get the sailing ships off their blocks and into the water. None of them were organised. Suitcases and backpacks littered the green. Horns beeped as people desperately urged the stalled traffic ahead of them to move.

They made their way down the empty stairway. In his imagination, behind every door they passed was a corridor full of infected. Silence was almost worse than the noise, it made them tense, expecting something terrible was about to happen.

They entered the lobby and Fin turned the lights off in the stairwell. Four floors of absolute darkness. Rebecca ran into the housekeeping storage and cut the cords off two hoovers with her knife. While Fin held the doors in place, she wrapped the cords tightly around the handles. Together they pushed a vending machine in front of the doors to make a barricade.

Rebecca nearly slipped on the tiles in her haste to get the keys from the office. She made for the main door of the hotel, and Fin fought back the thought that if he left the barricade, infected would spill out. He ran from one door to block another. "Hang on a minute will you? We can't just run out into the middle of a crowd of panicked people."

"Really? Because I think those are our kind of people right now."

"From the moment this happened the advice has been to avoid hotels. I can see why now. We can't just run out. If they think we're infected and could cause harm to them or their loved ones, who'd mourn the eradication of two potentially infected strangers? You were willing to let me stab that man upstairs. It's them and us now."

"Where are they all going?" Rebecca said. "Do they know something that we don't?"

"Just wait. Please. Or look, it's not my place to stop you. If you want to go out there, go, but I'm locking that door behind you."

"You're okay with staying here with those things upstairs? We've been together since the start of this, I don't want to split up now."

"I'm not going to follow you into danger just for the sake of it. We know what's in here. We have the cameras here and we can make it safe. The food is in the kitchen. We can check the recordings to see where the infected have been. We have water. We can control things here. You asked where all of those people are going. The right question would be to ask what are they running from? Charge your phone, we've the computer. We make it safe and then plan. If we must leave, then at least pack enough food and water. Look," he pointed to the camera. The man still stood in front of the television in the function room, oblivious to their absence. "We're better off here than we would be out there."

"Fine."

Together they heaped chairs and tables against the stairwell door. The next most pressing task was to ensure the bathroom was safe and take it in turns standing watch as the other used it. After they were sure there were no more of those things downstairs, Rebecca brought back a pint glass filled with ice, two glasses and a bottle of top-shelf whiskey from the bar. She poured liberally. The ice crackled as it rose.

"That's roughly two hundred quid's worth of booze," Fin said.

"I don't think that matters any more, do you?"

"I was thinking more about the hangover in the morning." He swirled the glass and sipped it. The coolness was more refreshing than the whiskey. He clenched an ice cube between his teeth and let it melt while he scanned the camera feed.

The whiskey was easier to drink after the first glass. It

made everything else easier too. Rebecca covered the floor of the office in towels and blankets from the utility room. She filled her glass and lay down with the light of her phone shining on her face.

Fin watched the recordings from the last few days. He swiveled the chair around to face her. "I just had a horrible thought. Somebody in the future could be watching back on the camera feed to see what happened to us before we..."

Rebecca turned onto her side away from him.

"It'll be okay." He finished the rest of his drink and lay down. "It'll be okay."

11

SUICIDE SUPPOSITORY

Most of the bottle was gone before Fin fell asleep. When his eyes closed for long enough, he had vivid dreams of men that did not tire and would not die, of running along the Greenway and getting nowhere. He vaguely remembered being woken by choked sobs. Head pounding from lack of sleep and an adrenaline hangover, his first thought was 'infected'. He opened his eyes wide enough to see he was still in the office, lying against the door to ensure nothing could sneak up on them. *She's infected.* He slowly reached for a knife he had taken from the kitchen.

Her ragged breathing gave way to words. "What are we going to do?"

That was a silence he could not break. He had no answer for her.

"I can't do this, I can't." She repeated the demoralising prayer. The anguish on her face looked grotesque by the light of her phone.

Fin moderated his breathing, pretending to still be sleeping, but she was too far gone on the drink to notice.

There was nothing he could say to comfort her, so he did not try. Not wanting to intrude upon her grief, he closed his eyes and left her stranded in the dark. His own tears fell silently. From what she was saying he assumed the infection had already reached Achill. *Why would it not? Survivors flee to areas without the disease, only to bring it with them. Why bother watching the news any more?* Whatever new horror had set Rebecca off was something he could do nothing about. Ignorance was the only balm now.

When he woke again he pinched the back of his hand. *Not so lucky*. He was almost sure she had nudged him awake.

"What do you think the rest of the staff are up to now?" Rebecca asked.

"Same as we're doing, hopefully." He sat up; his back ached because of how he slept. A cold draft coming from beneath the door had made it difficult to settle fully. Whiskey was a mistake, though he doubted he would have slept without it, knowing those things were in the hotel with them. "Any update on our guests upstairs?"

Rebecca handed him a bottle of water. "I've stopped watching. How's the head?"

He downed half the bottle to get rid of his cottonmouth. "I don't feel great."

"Well don't get sick in here. We'll head into the kitchen," Rebecca said.

"It's weird not having anything to do, or anywhere to be." Fin finished the bottle of water.

"Nothing to do? We have to get home, that's enough to keep us busy. What more do you want?"

"There's a country between here and where I need to be. Would you attempt to walk across Ireland with what's going on at the moment?"

"If I had to," Rebecca said, in a tone that stung for the implication that he was not trying hard enough to be with his family. "No point in wallowing. Let's get on with the day."

They raided the housekeeping storeroom for bottles of bleach and disinfectant. Both of them wore gloves and heavy aprons and covered their faces with cloth. Fin felt on the verge of tears for most of the morning. His thoughts raced uncomfortably, but the chores bled off some of his anxiety. At times he grieved for Solene and his family, only to admonish himself for losing hope. *If I'm still alive then they should have no bother.* In idle moments he heard the echo of her crying over the phone. No amount of labour could blunt the effect her anguish had on him. He would have cleaned the whole hotel if it meant keeping his mind active, but he was haunted by the thought that they were just wasting precious time.

* * *

Including the little bit of food they foraged from his apartment and what was left in the kitchen, there was just enough to see them through this mess, however long it took. *It will be over before we run out.* There were two vending machines on the ground floor. Fin emptied them of chocolate, sweets, soda and crisps. The freezers were mostly bare, but there was breakfast cereal and tinned food that would keep them fed into the new year. The bulk of the dry food that guests had for breakfast was stored upstairs, where the infected roamed.

The smell of bleach was unbearable. They opened the door into the private car park in the hope that fresh air would shake their headaches from fumes and hangovers. Susurrus conversation from people walking along the main-street carried through the tunnel to them. Roads were impassable in and around town.

"I don't know who is foolish," Rebecca said. "Them for leaving their homes, or us for staying here."

There seemed no end to the stream of refugees. Eventually, the cold forced them back inside the hotel. When they locked the door, the muffled, ghost-like voices vanished. With nothing left to do, they spent the rest of the day in their cell, only leaving to use the bathroom and make food. Fin was afraid to lose himself in drink. The temptation to slip from the world and slowly drown in false comfort was hard to ignore. Once that first glass was poured, he would not be able to stop.

To distract himself, he searched the camera archives to ensure there were no other surprises in the hotel. Using the guestbook, he found there were two rooms that had not checked out. One belonged to the dead man, David Brosnan; the other was occupied by a family of three. The thought of small and fast infected scuttling through dark halls made his skin crawl. It took an hour, but they found footage of the family. They had fled without checking out.

"You weren't messing when you said you were run off your feet," Fin said. "You're nearly in front of every camera."

"Told you." Her words came out slurred. She had started drinking before noon.

Fin loaded up the camera feeds from the day before the storm and let them run at normal speed. It was too easy to imagine he was watching live footage, that if he opened the door, he would see the day staff in their Christmas gear, happily whittling away the work hours until they could leave. *Maybe I need a drink.*

Eventually he gave in. Rebecca kept trying to show him news videos on her phone. Every time she did, he got angrier, as did she after each refusal. It was foolish to ignore things, but knowing did not help either. They drank to reinforce the walls that were shrinking around them.

Rebecca fell asleep while they were watching people walk by the building on the cameras. Soft snores let him know he was alone; only then did he open a new tab on the computer. Pressing the keys quietly, he logged into Facebook before fear of what he might find stopped him. The disease had even infected his feed – scrolling through it revealed nothing but images of the sick. There were more notifications and messages than he had ever received for any birthday. An Irish flag overlay covered most of the profile pictures in a display of solidarity. *I feel better already.*

People he had not spoken to for years reached out to him like old friends. *I suppose we are. Time has just made us strangers.* Nothing from Solene. Neither of his parents had an account on any platform. A digital display cooker was a technological step too far for them. A message from his sister Orla was dated a day ago.

'Dad said to let you know he's fine, did not catch anything while out. We're all okay. Doing as well as can be expected. Scared and thinking of you. When you can, let us know that you're safe. We can't reach your phone, but putting that down to the networks being jammed. We have not heard from Solene yet. Dad thinks she's still in Ireland, no way she made that flight out with the storm. Reporters are following up on the last planes to leave the country. If she was on one, they'll have her quarantined in France.

'It took me half an hour to finish this message. The last plane to leave Ireland, that's a horrifying thought, you know it will be made into a documentary or a tacky film when all this ends. I don't know why I'm worried about you, you spent most of your life playing video games with zombies in them. Aren't I the fool for thinking you were wasting your time?

'We turned the estate into a little fortress. Wait until you see it. They've built walkways across rooftops, it's ridiculous. This will be over soon and then you can see it for yourself. Mam is being her usual nosy self, she's having great fun breaking into houses to loot them and judge their decor.'

His sister rarely messaged him. They hardly spoke when they lived in the same house. There was no animosity between them, they were just a part of the furniture to each other. He nearly woke Rebecca to share the good news, but he felt that was unfair. He would not listen to her horror stories, so he had no right to share anything, not when the fate of her own family was still unknown. Instead he stifled his joy and used it to push the whiskey bottle away.

It took several hours to type a long response detailing everything that had happened since the outbreak. Reading over it felt surreal, like something that had happened to another. He wrote 'zombie' out several times, but had to delete it in favour of 'infected'.

Rebecca stirred. With enough drink in her system, she no longer needed him by her side to leave the office. The noise she made in the hall grated at his nerves and good cheer.

"Crowd's thinned," she said when she returned. She was unsteady on her feet and sat down on her blankets. "I don't feel good. I wonder if I have it. A weeping sickness they're calling it on the news. Like flu. Brain swells up making them stupid, then kills them. At least you're not you when you turn." She tried to pick up her empty glass and knocked it over. "Cruel disease. If I heard my mother weeping, it'd break me." Her face contorted in a grimace, but she held back tears. "Sympathy. They draw you in with it. That's horrible. Sympathy, that's how it spread so fast."

"Rebecca, stop."

"I should've left you and gone home. Have to look after myself." She looked at him with watery eyes. "I'm taking half the food. Leave you to rot."

"You're acting like I'm keeping you here. Take what you want and go, but you'll wait until you're sober. You can't leave in this state."

"I'm sick of waiting!"

Fin was on her in an instant. Hand covering her mouth. Rage making him enunciate every word. "Be quiet you idiot."

They listened, waiting to hear the weep of an infected. There was silence. Fin felt a warm dampness on the side of his hand. Tears fell from Rebecca's blazing eyes, dissolving Fin's anger, replacing it with shame.

"I won't be able to do it sober," she said. "How can the rest of the world just watch what's happening and do nothing?"

Fin shrugged. "Is it just in Ireland? Are we alone?"

"Just us. Watched a video of long lines of people outside blood banks across the world, ready to donate. Quite sweet actually. But what good is blood when your normal citizens turn into monsters?" Her laugh stopped with a scowl. "I hate feeling like we can't do anything. I want to kill them all."

The sound of her teeth grinding made Fin shudder. "You're a receptionist, I'm a nightporter. I can deal with rowdy drunks, one at a time. I've a bit of first aid training, do you? Does it even matter?"

"Can we watch the news, please?"

Thinking it would keep her mind off leaving, he agreed. "I don't want you to go," Fin said.

She buried her face in her hands. "As soon as this is over, I swear, I'm emigrating."

They laughed.

"What's that light for?" she asked, pointing to a large bank of bulbs, dials and switches above the duty manager's desk.

"Alarms." He stood up so quickly his chair fell over. "Those are for the emergency doors. One of them was opened."

"Where?"

Fin steadied himself against the desk. "Top floor." He brought up the function room camera feed. The room was empty, the TV was off. Fin pressed his fingers against his temples. "I wasn't thinking. The televisions are all set to standby. If left inactive long enough, they go off to conserve power." He scanned the cameras in the halls to try and locate the creatures. The eerie green glow of the night vision mode caught no movement.

Rebecca jammed a wooden wedge beneath the door to secure it. They had knives from the kitchen, sturdy cutlery that could tackle a steak, so long as it was not too well done. The useful tools were in the handyman's work room at the far end of the basement.

"Where's Ciara?" Rebecca asked.

"Off camera. We can't get caught in here."

"The door's locked, we're okay," she said.

"I can't find them." Fin frantically searched the hotel.

"Where do the emergency exits lead?" Rebecca said.

"The fire staircase opens on every floor. He could be anywhere."

Movement on the external camera drew his attention outside. People usually bowed their heads and covered their faces beneath hoods against the weather and to avoid eye contact with others. Now they gathered close to the car park gate. Fin changed to a different camera. He could make out David's silhouette in the tunnel. He was reaching through the metal railings trying to get at the refugees.

"While it's distracted, we should put it down, make this place safe." Her knife was rarely far from reach, the handle was slick with sweat. "You've seen what they do. If that thing gets us, we'll be wandering around just like Ciara. She looked like her last sensations in life were all painful. We'd be harmful to others. How many children have walked by the hotel? If you're worried about repercussions, we can destroy the camera recordings afterwards."

"Those videos could be a record of our last moments in this world. Solene, our families, they could be watching in the future."

"How do you want them to judge your actions?" Rebecca said. "The people getting sick now were not willing to do what they must."

"What if there's a vaccine?" he asked.

"Do you want to wait and find out?"

Panic rippled through the refugees. Fin was amazed at how quickly they gave in to fear. *How many people already have blood on their hands?*

"It's trapped in the tunnel – we sneak up and kill it," Rebecca said.

Fin's bowels churned at the thought of murder, especially in front of so many witnesses. "We can't leave the hotel now. Not when they know the infection is here."

"For now. Put your mask on carefully. There are a few

pairs of glasses in the lost and found box. Wear them in case of blood spatter," Rebecca said.

"What about Ciara's body upstairs?"

"We'll deal with her afterwards."

They checked each other's protective gear was tight and secure before Fin counted to three and opened the door. Fin turned the knife over in his hand, there was a good weight to it. *What if I hit bone? I suppose there isn't really an art to it.*

The people outside argued over whether to kill it or leave it be.

"We're idiots," Fin said. "They'll do it for us."

As he looked into the tunnel a child spotted him and shouted. "There are more zombies in there."

Rebecca stepped out and waved at them which caused confusion. She brandished the knife and the crowd caught on quick enough, they made more noise to keep its attention.

Fin was not entirely sure which side the heart was on. He took up a position on the left, Rebecca the right. They crept towards the man that had once been David Brosnan. When Fin met him in the basement, he never would have expected the hotel would be where he spent his last moments.

Without the corner to hide behind, Fin felt weak, exposed in the open. He kept in line with Rebecca, inexorably moving towards something he did not want to do. It heard their heavy breathing and started to turn. Without the sense to take its arms out from the gate first, it awkwardly fumbled. They charged into him with such force that the gates bulged outwards. The knives went into its back with little protest. Fin let go of his immediately. Silence washed over the crowd, leaving it so the only noise was the growing number of seagulls and crows.

A soft rasp escaped its mouth. Fin's knife nicked a rib upon entry but slid in nearly to the hilt. He was sure it had punctured a lung. What he found most sickening was how easy it was. With its arms stuck through the gate, the infected slumped, but did not fall over.

Rebecca swayed on her feet. She had drink to blame for that, Fin did not. Freckles stood out bold on her bloodless face.

"Is it done?" one young man asked. "Somebody go have a look." He had his phone out, recording the incident. Fin noticed several other phones.

"There are more of them in there, look at the bite marks on its neck."

"We're not infected," Rebecca said, the drink putting a slur on her voice that convinced those listening otherwise.

"Where are yous heading?" Fin asked. They looked at him with an expression that was barely softer than the one the dead man got. It said 'You're a murderer.' and 'There might be trouble to come.' Some of them offered sympathetic smiles, but would not go so far as to put words to those feelings.

"West..." The woman stopped speaking and as one the crowd moved back, their attention on David.

He started writhing. *How long does it take to die?* His feet kicked in what Fin thought was a death spasm, but the side of his shoe caught the tarmac, giving him purchase. He started rising back to his feet. The crowd dispersed, people pushed at each other to get away from the gate. Both knives were buried deep in its back. There was no way a human could survive that amount of damage.

Orders boomed above the din by a commanding voice. A woman wearing a full respirator roughly shouldered people out of her way, not afraid to hurry them on with the stock of her rifle. Framed by the gate, she raised her weapon to David's forehead and fired. The echo of the shot ricocheted in the tunnel. Fin and Rebecca threw their arms in the air and shouted over each other how they were not infected. David's head clanged against the gate. He did not move again. The creature crumpled, like a switch had been turned off, expression unchanged in death.

The woman aimed into the tunnel and fired. There was no time to get to cover. Fin flinched at the sound, expecting to feel it. *She shot Rebecca.* He turned to run, working on adrenalin and dread.

Behind him, Ciara's body lay motionless on the wet ground, only a few feet away.

The woman did not have to shout to be heard. When she spoke, others were silent. "You all know what you have to do." She moved aside so they could all see David, ignoring Rebecca and Fin. "It has to be the head or back of the neck, hit them hard enough to damage the spine. Pull the motor or cut the wires."

Before the epidemic the only time Fin had ever seen a gun in the Republic of Ireland was inside the American Embassy in Dublin when he was looking for a student visa.

"Are there any more in there?" the woman asked.

"Just us," Rebecca said. "But, we're not infected."

There were hushed conversations while other soldiers dispersed the crowd. It started to rain. Menacing white-capped waves out in the bay still carried a memory of the storm. The slow procession continued.

The woman approached the gate, but kept her mask on. It muffled her voice. She let her rifle rest ready against her front. "What are you doing in there? Looting has..."

"We work here," Rebecca said.

"I'm the nightporter and she's reception. We're watching the place over the holidays."

"The nine to five is on hold, or haven't you seen the news?" she said.

"We're just here to watch over the cameras." He made a point of mentioning those in case she was thinking of shooting them too, but it occurred to him that it would not matter what proof was on the cameras if he was dead.

"Have you come in contact with them? Cuts, bites? Been in a room with them?"

"No more than you have," Rebecca said.

"This mask is a little more hi-tech than your dishcloths. What's the food situation like in there?"

"Enough to get by for a few days. They cleaned out the stores before closing. The stock for New Year's Eve was due after Christmas," Rebecca said, telling only half-truths.

The refugees looked on with morbid curiosity, as if they assumed the killing was not finished. It was strange to see faces that would not look out of place in the local shop. What he saw on the news did not seem real, but the terror on those faces was inescapable.

Fin had no understanding of military insignia, but by the authority she commanded, he assumed she was a captain. His knowledge of ranks included 'captain' and 'not a captain'.

"How long have you been in here?"

"Since it started. We found him in the basement," Fin said. "On our last night of service. It was before Peggy hit. He was lucid and speaking. Well, mumbling. It's not uncommon for people after a night on the town to forget their room number and sometimes basic motor skills." Fin kept his mask up, but he wondered if them not being able to see his face would make it easier to kill him. "I had gloves on when helping him."

"What about her?" The captain nodded to Ciara.

Fin could not bring himself to look at the body. Thankfully, she had fallen forward, her face obscured by blood-matted hair. "She wasn't wearing gloves."

"I've good and bad news for you. That man there is the first advanced case that I've personally had to deal with this far west. Every person he came into contact with is likely infected. You are a risk until we know exactly what it is that we're dealing with. He came here by plane, train, bus, taxi? Walked through a crowd, coughed in a bar. How many people do you pass in a day?"

"This cannot be contained?" Rebecca looked to be on the point of collapse.

"Does not look that way. I can't let you out, not at the moment. The potential for further contamination is too great. Though, if we could trade places, I would in a heart-beat. You're in better shape in there than the rest of us. I'll leave a few ration packs behind, if they can be spared."

"I tried to get out to Achill Island," Rebecca blurted out.

"And you came back?"

Rebecca was crestfallen, obviously hoping for better news.

"We're moving survivors into the grounds of Westport House and the surrounding buildings. From there we are busing as many as we can to Achill Island. It's safer there. If you have people on the island, then they've just won the lottery." She took a small packet from a pocket and threw it through the gate. "Those aren't vitamins. Should either of you get sick, that'll make it quick and painless – relatively."

"This is being put out to the public?" Fin asked.

"I wish. Probably best to leave that body there. If others see it, well, there's no better deterrent."

"Is there anywhere else we can go?" Fin felt emboldened by the suicide pills, assuming it meant she was not going to shoot him.

"Achill is designated a safety zone, but we have no presence there yet. Camps are opening along the rail tracks to Dublin."

Home. I could walk the coast from Dublin.

"The news said to avoid public transport," Rebecca said.

"Those that can walk have been given directions to evacuation points."

A soldier ran up behind her and whispered something.

"If you decide to use those, would you do me a favour? Lock yourselves in a room and mark it. There have been reports saying weepers rise even after being poisoned. I can't validate that, but no harm ever came from caution. Good luck." She turned to the soldiers around her. "Quarantine this place." She left, listening to a report from the breathless soldier.

Fin picked up the poison and walked out of the tunnel with Rebecca. He ran aside, doubled over and vomited. Collapsing on the tarmac, he rolled onto his back, gulping air. *It got Ciara. There's no way that I'm not infected.* His teeth felt gritty. He wondered how many more times he could vomit without doing proper damage to his teeth.

Rebecca sat down beside him. Neither of them took much notice of the rain.

"There's no instructions on the packet," Rebecca said, turning it over carefully in her hand.

Fin closed his eyes, enjoying the cool rain falling on his face. "Well they don't really need 'warning choking hazard' written on the side, do they?" It felt like all the blood drained from his extremities and strength leaked away with it.

"They look fairly large, are they suicide suppositories? Imagine. What an undignified way to go," Rebecca said.

Fin managed a smile. "What a shitty end. I don't think I've ever fainted before."

Rebecca's reply sounded distant.

He passed out.

12

SOS

Fin barely remembered Rebecca helping him back inside. If not for a painfully full bladder, Fin would have stayed beneath the blankets in an embryo of warmth until sleep took him again. His dreams were muddled and melted away from memory, leaving only a residual feeling of terror. It took everything he had to get up.

Light seeped through gaps in the storm shield covering the lobby windows. By the colour of it, he guessed it was early morning. Only birds and joggers used to be out at this time. *Infected don't sleep.* The hotel never felt so empty. There had always been the promise of more guests. Regulars that came every year without fail. *Where are they now?* The Christmas decorations were still out, mocking what they should be celebrating. Dust motes fell slowly around the tree, the sweet smell of pine perfumed the air. *If I don't take it down, how long will it be up?*

The motion sensor in the bathroom turned the light on for him. The stranger reflected in the mirror gave him pause. Greasy hair and stubble shadowed his face and the bags beneath his eyes were black.

Bladder empty, he shuffled back through the lobby. Noise coming from the bar drew him to the door. *Rebecca would not make that much of a racket.* He stopped before entering. *What if she's infected?* He went in, fumbling with the packet of tablets the captain had given them in his pocket. *So easy. One swallow and then no more worries.* Solene, his family, all of those concerns were a dull ache. *Shame, regret and self-loathing, those would go too.* He took the tablets out of his pocket and left them on a table. *I have to get back to them. The soldiers never saw our faces. If I can get a train to Dublin, I'm as good as home.*

Rebecca stopped what she was doing and held her breath when he entered. *I must look like a zombie.* Silence stretched on and she relaxed.

"What the hell are you doing?" Fin asked.

The whole bar had been rearranged. Tables were upturned in front of doors; stools and chairs were stacked against the windows. Before answering his question she pulled off a blue knitted hat that had been sitting in the lost and found box for months. Her hair was butchered. It was hardly longer than his now and the sides were uneven.

"What do you think?" she asked.

Does she mean the hair or the bar? He thought the best answer in both cases was "Why?"

"The advice online is to not have anything they can grab easily. No hoods or long hair."

"It looks well on you. How long did I sleep?"

"You've been out for a while." She put a hand on his shoulder and guided him towards the coffee machine.

"What have you been up to here?"

"I can't sit still. There's only a lock and bolt securing the doors. If they put any effort into getting in, there's little stopping them." She put two coffee mugs under the tap. There were no chairs left standing to sit on.

"Is there any bleach left in the hotel?" he said, trying to breathe through his mouth.

Through the serving window into the kitchen, he saw all of their dry food organised into piles. "The stuff that'll go out of date first is closest to the door," Rebecca said, when she noticed he was appraising her work.

"Did you get the food from upstairs?"

"And the basement. Kept me busy. I'm going to spread it out around the hotel, in case of – just in case."

"You should have woken me."

"I tried to, but you wouldn't budge."

"How long was I out?"

"Two days. First, I thought you were sick, but you had no symptoms. Well, not of turning into one of those things. You held those poison pills so tightly that I thought you'd taken one. It could have been shock," Rebecca said.

"How are you okay?"

She spread her arms out wide, her fingers pointing to her head. "I'm clearly not."

"All I want to do is sleep. My thoughts feel like they're bubbling through tar," he said.

"You need to keep busy, keep moving." She handed him his coffee and loaded it with sugar.

He perked up suddenly. "Two days. Are things any better now?"

She hesitated and took a sip from her steaming mug. "It's not good."

The coffee tasted delicious; he savoured the warmth, a nice contrast to the feeling he got from Rebecca's statement. His stomach rumbled for something more substantial. "Much worse?" He wanted to search for his phone on the top floor, but he dared not touch it after using it as a lure for Ciara and David. The thought of Solene's voice on that phone was maddening.

Rebecca walked through to the kitchen. On the countertop was a categorised list of everything in the fridges and freezers. They made sandwiches. The bread was stale and hard. He picked off small circles of blue mould.

"We have enough food to last us weeks. So long as the power stays on, we'll have a decent variety of meals. As for tinned goods, we have fish, beans, pickled peppers, jalapeños, olives. Crisps and sweets. Water is not a problem. They ordered enough cases of it to see us through the New Year's party rush." She listed off the things she had taken from the drinks store and vending machines, and all the medicines and bandages from the offices and first aid kits. They were not in a bad situation, which made him feel guilty not knowing how his family were faring. "We've plenty of toothpaste and brushes too. More than enough body wash." She said that last part pointedly.

"Will the power go out?"

She ran her hand across her scalp. "This plague devastated the country. I assume it's only a matter of time."

They brought their food and coffee to the bar. Fin only now noticed how quiet it was outside. Rebecca held his arm before he could leave to look out the window. "The roads are not safe. People fell along the roadside to the camps, a trail of weak and sick to feed the weepers. Now they're all I see. Please don't draw their attention. We are trapped. On the plus side, it's mostly the slow ones like David."

Fin couldn't believe it. He stood out of view of the window, pulled back the blind and peered through the storm barrier. People walked the road in a slow melancholic shuffle, like a procession behind a hearse. *No, not people, not any more.* He stepped away from the glass.

"I've done what I can down here," Rebecca said. "I think we need to go through the hotel room by room and collect the complimentary bottled water and potted milk. There's a lot of food still upstairs too. I would like to move off the ground floor soon."

"How long are you're planning on staying here?"

"As long as we have to."

Fin pushed his sandwich away from him. "What are we going to do with the bodies?"

"Nothing, they're perfect where they are." Rebecca took his sandwich and put it in the refrigerator. "There's something you ought to see upstairs."

The stairwell was not a place to talk. Each door on every floor was tied shut with heavy rope that could only have come from the basement. She took him to the fine dining restaurant at the top of the hotel and pointed to the mountain, draped in diaphanous wisps of cloud. An SOS signal had been painted onto the side of the mountain. It had to be massive to be seen from such a distance.

"I've watched a light move down the mountain at dawn and climb it again just before nightfall. Somebody is living in the church at the top," Rebecca said.

"That's a cruel place when the wind picks up."

"Too many sick down here, too much panic. How many guns are there in Ireland? Now imagine soldiers that couldn't pull the trigger on ordinary people. Sure, look at you. I thought your head was gone when you stayed in bed for so long."

His cheeks burned. "I'm sorry. I –"

"Nothing to be ashamed of, how do you process this?"

Fin held a hand to his head as if he could physically

hold himself together. "Is this what it's like to have a break-down? Not knowing what's real?"

"Seeing this and not believing it is standard, I'd have thought," Rebecca said.

"So what are we supposed to do?"

"See this through. Survive, I suppose."

"Any word on a cure?"

"I don't think there's any coming back from that." She nodded towards the creatures on the street. "Some are calling this our extinction event, and they're not even the craziest ones with opinions and an internet connection."

Fin watched the movement of zombies until he was satisfied that it was aimless; visual and auditory stimuli attracted them, but they had no focus, constantly turning to the next thing.

"You wouldn't mistake one for human, would you?" Rebecca said. "They move as creepily as they look."

One bumped into a car and set the alarm off, drawing the others to it. A fast one weaved through the crowd and lunged at the infected, taking it to the ground. Fin was grateful the attack was blocked by the cars. Riled up, they mobbed the car, biting and clawing at one another, but after a while they parted without offence.

Something else was setting them off. Fin opened the window a little to let cold air and a fresh sea breeze invade the hotel. Mobile phone ringtones kept sounding, irritating the infected. One of the creatures, an old moustached man, fell over from the weight of his backpack. Those around swarmed him. He found it harder to rise with flesh torn from his legs. Another weeper in the crowd was quicker than the others. Unsteady and jittery on her feet, but so fast she had to crash into the side of a car to stop her momentum. Her weeping was raw and sharp, her voice broke and croaked, but the sound kept emanating from her slack-jawed mouth.

Is it she or it?

Rebecca yanked him back from the window. "I don't think those ones are fully dead yet."

The small hairs across his body rose on goosebumps. Adrenaline coursed through his system but he was developing a tolerance. "Not fully dead?"

"There are specialists across the world trying to figure this out before it has a chance to spread. Those fast ones are newly infected, some are still averse to pain, but that might have been a false report, there's so much fake news spread around this, that it's hard to know what's true. Weepers can be killed like a normal human, but unless you cripple them or destroy the brain, they will come back as those zombies – for want of a better word. That's what happened to Ciara, the infection killed her and she came back as that."

"This is only a few days old and already there are specialists. That strikes me as odd." Fin said.

"Really? I thought it necessary." She closed the window slowly, without making a sound. "It's fascinating stuff, really. The first stage of the disease is a fever. Think back to before the outbreak. It was national news that we were heading for the worst flu season in years. People have reported delirium and hallucinations. Maybe that's the point they stop being who they once were. The weeping at first drew sympathy from others, got them close enough to infect. Clever enough to begin with, but now it causes terror. Nobody has explained why they weep. The final stage happens when they die. Those slow, shambling things down there are by all scientific classifications, dead. Zombies."

Fin pinched his leg through his pocket. "We need to get out of Ireland then."

"I'm not going anywhere until those fast ones die. We're right on the coast. When rescue comes, this is where we need to be," Rebecca said.

A distant clatter made them go quiet. Fin rushed to the stairwell door on the balls of his feet and braced it closed. Rebecca had a hammer in her hand.

"You went down to the basement?"

She shushed him and passed him a knife.

He spent countless nights wandering the hotel alone. There were always unexplained sounds, but the knocking would have given him pause even before zombies had left the realm of science fiction. Glass broke. It sounded close. They were no longer alone.

13

FORGIVE ME

"I should have done more," Rebecca cursed.

The noise grew louder. "Whoever, or whatever it is, is not trying to be quiet," Fin said.

"That does not bode well. Come on." She bounded down the stairs two at a time, keeping close to the wall to avoid detection. The carpet muffled their steps.

Rebecca undid the knot of ropes sealing off the third floor corridor. Fin had turned the motion sensor lights off, so they would not accidentally alert the world to their presence. The fire door closed softly on well-oiled hinges, leaving them in a darkness that was total, two feet beyond the stairwell.

"What are we doing?" Fin asked, angry at himself for following her so readily.

"The hotel is empty, the halls are safe. I have the master key to get into any of the rooms. I just want to get a look at what we're dealing with."

"If they're not infected, won't they notice that this door is the only one that's not tied shut?"

Rebecca opened the door and pulled the rope in with

her. The noise was much closer. Fin felt hands primed to grab him in the shadows. A line of light cut through the darkness beneath the door, broken by the shadow of legs. Standing tight to the wall, they watched a man press his masked face against the small window and peer down the hall. His anxiety was clear from his heavy breathing. *Living.* He carried on, banging the railing with something heavy.

"I think there's only one," Rebecca said. "Go down the hall and when I start wailing, you run towards me as fast as you can. Make as much noise as possible. He's banging to scare out any infected. I want him outside and running from us."

Fin jogged down the corridor, breathing shallowly through his facemask in case the infection lingered in the hallway. Rebecca started wailing like a banshee. It was not far off the weepers. Fin sprinted towards her. The banging stopped instantly and a shadow darted past the door.

The man thundered down the stairs. From the sound of it he fell over on the second floor and yelled. "No, no, no!"

Rebecca pressed the chase, bolting from the corridor, weeping hysterically. She pulled a hammer from inside her jacket. She ran ahead of Fin, taking the stairs at a reckless pace, a convincing mimic of the infected. They slowed down on the second floor and stopped entirely before the entrance to the lobby. Whoever had come into the hotel would be under no doubt that the infected were inside, they would be terrified and dangerous, knowing they had to at least try and fight for their lives. Nobody would be stupid enough to go about unarmed these days.

"What now?" Rebecca asked.

"This is your plan." Fin crept to the door and peered out both ways. The lobby was empty. "Hello?" In answer, the door into the car park snapped shut and Fin lept back. The front door was still barricaded and he had the only set of keys on the premises.

Broken glass lay on the ground by the door to the car park. Rebecca opened it cautiously. Her whole demeanour changed and she started to laugh. "George! You bastard, I thought one of those things had gotten in."

The wall at the back of the car park was as tall as the hotel. With the gates and doors locked, it was the only way in. Beyond the wall, there was a line of old houses. A rope made from many different sources dangled above the tarmac. George, the bartender, clinging on for dear life, struggled only a quarter of the way up. He slipped on the moss and slime-slick, sheer wall, his face reddened from effort and Fin's barking laughter.

"You bastards, I thought I was dead." The laughter was infectious. When his feet touched the ground, he used his sleeve to wipe tears from his cheeks.

Fin could not imagine his friend would have easily pulled himself the whole way back up; he had a bit of weight on him and was only marginally fitter than he was.

"I saw the bodies and I thought you were dead." He shook his arms to bring feeling back into them before embracing Rebecca. "I'm so glad to see you both. Are there any more staff members ali... here?" He looked haggard since Fin last saw him.

"Just us," Rebecca said.

George approached Fin to hug him, but Fin stepped back. "Are you infected?"

"No." George stopped. "What about you?"

Chagrined by the awkwardness following his coldness, Fin held out his gloved hand. "No, but there were infected in here, I don't want to pass it on."

George shook his hand warmly. "Not to worry lad, you're

right. Was just habit that made me go in for the hug. Sorry, Rebecca. Reckon all physical contact is a no-go for the next while. Never realised how much I touched my face over the course of a day, until I couldn't."

"You'll get on grand now. Man like you is well practiced with no physical contact," Rebecca said with a good nature and a wicked grin.

George and Fin looked at each other, before George broke the silence. "Becca, gallows humour is all well and good at a time like this, but you're not supposed to send a man to the gallows with it. The hair was a good job, mine's probably a bit long too. I saw someone get nabbed because of a baggy jumper. Those people at the gate, were they guests?"

"So you saw the bodies and came in regardless. What madness made you make that climb? If we were infected, we'd only have to wait at the bottom of the rope for you to slide back down." Rebecca tugged on the rope to test how secure it was.

"Have yous been here since the beginning?" George said.

"For most of it."

Fin was quiet. He did not know how best to broach the topic of their friend lying face down with a gunshot wound.

George sucked in his bottom lip, his breathing still unsteady from the climb. "Madness is a good word for it, desperation probably closer. You can't imagine what it's like out there now. I didn't know where else to go. I haven't slept properly since the news broke and my family... I just need somewhere safe for a while. Stupidest idea I've ever had to climb down here. Halfway down I knew I wasn't going to be able to climb back up. Somebody I shared an attic with told me he read somewhere that they were going to start bombing cities. Stop those things leaving when they've finished feeding." He removed his gloves. His hands were red and raw where the rope had dug in. He took out a small bottle of green hand sanitiser and squirted half of it into his palm. He offered it to them like one would a piece of gum.

"I came here via the Greenway path, through a few fields and gardens."

"Is it really that bad out there now?" Rebecca asked.

"Weather isn't great, but sure you can't have everything go your way. Any of the soldiers I've spoken to told me to head to Westport House, but there's too many people. Those outside the cities want in, those left alive in them want out. People have ripped fences from gardens to block roads, creating safe cul-de-sacs but everyone is restless and food is becoming a concern. Half of those that I thought were infected turned out to be shell-shocked, panicked or just lost. The government doesn't seem to be doing anything."

"There's still a government?" Rebecca said.

"So far as I know, but it's not run from Ireland. Rebecca, what are you waiting around for? I've a mind to head out to Achill Island myself when I'm finished here."

"The infection is already out there."

"I'm sorry to hear that. Hope your parents are holding up well."

"It spread so fast, like a spark in kindling."

"The spread is much slower in the countryside, but people can't stay indoors much longer, who keeps more than a week's food at home? Sure I haven't cooked a meal at home in about a month. I just ordered out, so my cupboards are mostly decorative."

Fin could not think of anything other than Ciara's body behind him.

"You look white as a sheet," George said, taking a step back cautiously.

"I'm... I'm not taking this well."

George nodded. "Well hang in there, this can't go on forever. The trains have been going night and day. Supplies coming in and people going out. They'll get a hold on this soon enough."

"Why haven't you gone?" Rebecca asked.

"This is my home, where else have I to go? No countries are taking Irish refugees. Too many people are heading to ports, expecting rescue. I guarantee you, infected are among them. Crowds are dangerous. I stayed in an empty house overlooking the train station, I saw how easily fear can turn people into savages. Armed soldiers are stationed six to a carriage, back to back in the aisles. So many people crammed into them. All it would take is a spark of panic. Those guys with rifles are the same as us. They have families and worries. Only they've a brief solution a trigger pull away. I'll wait on good news and for the crowds to die down, if I go up at all."

"Crowds die down." Rebecca looked repulsed. "There's a saying that has become taboo."

"Ciara's dead." Fin blurted it out without any tact, not that it would have made the news easier.

George's face went slack and his shoulders sagged.

"You remember our last night here? The man we thought was drunk in the basement was infected. That's the other body by the gate. I don't know why she died and we didn't."

"And us giving out about her not joining us for a pint after work."

"She never left the hotel."

George lost all colour in his face. "I was down in the basement with him alone. That man was drenched in sweat, pissed himself too. Her hand was cut. I broke the glass." His eyes twitched. He stood close to her body. "Forgive me."

That silence could have continued indefinitely, but Fin ended it after a respectful amount of time had passed. "You did not do this."

George changed the topic immediately. "What's the food situation like here? I'm starving."

"Freezers are full. Chicken burger okay?" Rebecca asked.

"That'll do just fine." He followed them to the kitchens. Happy Christmas Eve by the way."

* * *

George washed his hands and put on a pair of disposable latex gloves. "Smell of bleach is giving me a pounding headache, but it's as sweet as freshly mown grass if it means this place is clean."

"How did you know it was safe here?" Fin said.

He started eating ageing, limp salad from the fridge. "I've been moving about from one empty house to another since this started. Trying to come up with a plan. I stole what I needed. Somebody got a drone for Christmas, so I set it up, moved a few houses down to hide and used it to scout out the town. After I sent it up, I was pinned down for a couple of days, sound draws them like flies to rot. I was stupid enough to land it in the garden of the house where I was staying. Luckily there was enough food there. The owners didn't bring supplies with them. Nearly everything was left as if they expected to be home again soon."

"If I had a car, I would have filled the tank and tried outrun the spread, do a lap of the country before going home," Fin said.

"That's probably how it spread so quickly in the first

place. I've the footage from the drone flight if you want to see. The town looks beautiful from above." He put his phone on the counter and brought up the video. There was no sound. Blades of grass obscured the picture, but danced when the rotors spun. The drone rose and hung awkwardly in the air while George learned the controls. Then it soared up above the house and estate and the camera looked over the rooftops of Westport, the bay and mountains visible in the bright morning.

It's so small. Fin's life and daily routine for the last year took place on that small stage. He saw the route he took to and from work. Most of the time he forgot there was more to the world than work and home. *There was Solene.* The peacefulness ended when he noticed how many cars were ditched with doors open. The whole Castlebar road was gridlocked.

People ran into their gardens and waved out of windows at the drone. Some had made SOS signs out of sheets laid out in the grass or on their roofs. It was painful to watch their dejection and despair when they realised rescue had not arrived.

Manned military checkpoints protected the train station. It was impossible to tell if the people roaming the streets were infected or not.

A tight line of soldiers walked down the main road, guns raised. He could not tell if the person hunched over the prone body they approached was a zombie or a mourner. Either way, they died. *Were the soldiers sure before shooting?* George flew the drone away from town.

The fields around Westport House were full of activity. There were too many people to count. Tents huddled together around campfires. A helicopter landed on the lawn close to the house, scattering sheep.

"They're fortifying the grounds," Rebecca said. "How old is this video?"

"Two days," George said.

"We need to go there. It has high walls, strong gates and soldiers with guns, it's perfect."

"I wouldn't. That last part sounded more like a deterrent to me," George said.

The drone flew above the coastline by the quay. In the distance, Fin could just about make out ships docked around the islands.

"That's where I'm going," George said, after a mouthful of raspberry yogurt. "The plan was to scope this place out and then fly the drone over the islands." The hotel was on screen. Hazardous material signs covered the entrance. 'Dead Inside' was spray-painted over the storm shields.

"You came in with that out front?" Fin said.

"I knew you were the only one staying here. Even then I assumed you would have gone."

"It was too late for that."

The drone scanned the windows, zoomed in on the gates and then returned to George's location.

"I was watching from the hill behind the hotel for a day until I was sure. Did you not hear me throwing stones down? I wasn't expecting to find either of you. Does me good seeing familiar faces. This gets any worse, finding people is going to be impossible."

Fin thought of Solene. Guilt and shame warmed him. *She cried for help and I've done nothing.*

"More staff might come here," Rebecca said. "This place is ideal – top of the line generators in case of electrical failure, beds, food and relative safety."

"Unlikely. First warning on the news was to avoid public spaces. The guy here on the last night that infected Ciara is a perfect example of why." George filled his mouth with crisps. He chopped up some onions and threw them on the tray with the chicken burgers and put it in the oven. "Yous got off easy in here."

"I still think we should consider Westport House." Rebecca threw a few soft tomatoes in after the chicken.

"If you go – and I don't think you should – they'll have you on work duties. Farms countrywide have been emptied. Temporary abattoirs set up to take strain off the traditional ones. It's the largest cull in Irish history, worse than the foot-and-mouth outbreak. Meat is one of the jobs they'll give you. There have been videos of lorries full of animals trapped in traffic, left to die of thirst. They were supposed to establish a fishery here with the port, but all the ships are out at the islands. A horrible job in this cold, but I'd sooner that than the butcher vans."

"Why shouldn't we help?" Rebecca said.

"No law that we have to, or at least if there is, there's nobody to enforce it. Personally, I think the less people around us the better. This here is the biggest crowd that I'm comfortable with. Are the fridges in the basement still running okay?"

Fin nodded.

"Then the beer kegs are still frosty. Lads, I'm getting hammered tonight."

14

NEVER WILL I EVER

"There's nothing like watching a zombie in a torn and bloodstained Christmas jumper to put you in a festive mood," George said. He came away from the large top floor window, washing his disgust away with a long swallow of beer.

Fin and Rebecca got up to investigate, but he put a hand up to stop them. "It's a small jumper."

"Why do you call them that?" Fin asked.

"Zombie?"

Fin nodded and took another swig of his whiskey. It went straight to his legs.

George walked over to the table to warm himself by the storage heater. The fake firelight crackled just right. "Dehumanise them. Call them demons, zombies, ticket inspectors, whatever does it for you. The only thing human about them now is the clothes they wear, those won't last long in this weather."

Fin stepped up to the window. He was hovering on the cusp of tipsy. A few zombies had stumbled into the pond across from the hotel during the night. Its fringes were rigid with ice, but it did not phase the undead. *That's what they are, stop denying it.* He could not any longer, not when the evidence was right in front of him. Heavy clothes weighed the infected down, keeping them below the surface of the water. They had been submerged for hours, but were still moving. *The current? In a pond? Trick of the light and wind rippling across the surface.*

"Can we have one day without thinking about this stuff, please?" Rebecca said.

"Yes!" Fin blurted out and left the window.

"I can understand that, even want it, but we can't," George said. "Right now we're safe, we have food, there's no way a zombie is getting in, they'll even protect us from other survivors. But acting as if nothing has happened is far too dangerous, maybe not immediately, but there'll come a time when we're no longer safe. We'll get hungry and if we're afraid to face the reality of what's out there, then we might find it as difficult to open the doors as the undead."

"We shouldn't forget that they are no longer human, but, by that logic, best remember to act like you're human," Fin said, giving George a weary look and nodding towards Rebecca.

He copped onto himself then. "Festive conversation, got it." He gave a wink that was so obvious it need not have existed. "What's your Christmas routine like?" he asked Rebecca. "Or what was it like before this?"

Fin took a long drink. He knew George meant no harm.

"I was after a different topic of conversation more than complete escapism," she said.

"Right now, I'd be jumping on my parents' bed to wake them up, so we could all go down and open presents," Fin said.

"I didn't mean what you did when you were a child, I meant now," George said.

"So did I."

"I'd be doing a Christmas Day swim with my cousins," Rebecca said.

"Normally I'd be out in my Nan's, she'd make us all go to mass. Hated it as a child, but I grew to like the ritual as I got older," George said. He cleared his throat. "What are the bets that that mad man living on the mountain carried a tree up to the church on the summit? Decorations and all. Forgot the star for the top of it and had to go all the way back down again."

"We can't be the only ones to have seen his light," Rebecca said. "People know somebody's up there. When rescue comes, whoever they are will be amongst the first saved. Kind of gives me hope, seeing that light each day, makes me feel like we're not alone."

* * *

To kill time they played the 'never have I ever' drinking game, but stopped when it started becoming a mood killer; there were a lot of things on their to-do lists that they might never get a chance at. *Never will I ever.*

"We don't need a game to drink. What do they have on the television?" George asked.

They brought a large one in from a suite that had been vacant for two weeks before the outbreak. Knowing how many people had called it home temporarily meant none of them wanted to linger long in its luxury. Some of the headlines could be taken as promising, if you squinted at them: 'Cases of suspected infection discovered in America' and 'Europe sterilised'. *So clinical a term for murder.* 'Dublin being fortified; renamed The Pale'. 'Humanitarian aid from around the globe flooding through capital'.

"Nobody wants to see it spread," George said. "They clear their conscience through their pockets."

Flicking through the channels, George paused on an American talk show. "So you're suggesting instead of air dropping proper guns for the Irish population, you want to manufacture faulty ones for them. How long will that take?"

"Built-in obsolescence as a safety feature, giving guns to people that feel hard done by, by the rest of the world – you stop one problem and cause two more. It is unconscionable to arm Ireland."

Another guest in the debate jumped in. "The majority of people feel the complete opposite. They're facing the most horrendous challenge of our time. What if the gun breaks at a critical moment? Not a month ago you were campaigning on the basis that you would not bring in gun reform in this country because 'they are just tools.' Well the Irish people are in desperate need of hardware. Somebody has deeper pockets than the gun lobbyists? Whose badge are you wearing now?"

"I refuse to listen to that from a person who wants to take away fundamental American rights from the people. You'd flood a country unaccustomed to guns with weapons that cannot be traced? There's no rule of law over there currently. You would only add to their troubles and ours. Don't forget, they know our warships are patrolling their coasts to keep us safe. You would risk American lives by arming a potential enemy?"

"An enemy? This country was built in part by the Irish. These are unprecedented times, historic events."

"I'll not see America come to harm because of those people."

Fin walked away from the television when he read the headline at the bottom of the screen: 'Christmas Day Death Toll'. George and Rebecca were wrapped up in the debate, giving out to the television as if they were watching a football match. They only looked away when Fin placed two durable shopping bags on the table. "Happy Christmas," he said.

"Ah, you big softy." George shook his. "Is it a pistol? You shouldn't have. Eh – I'm not into giving material things as presents."

"I bet you only ever tell people that after they've given you yours. If you don't want it, I'll take it back."

"I said I wasn't into giving them, but I'm all up for receiving them."

Inside each bag was a walkie talkie, with a little bow of tinsel stolen from the Christmas tree tied around the aerial, a selection box that Solene had gifted him and a nice bottle of merlot that the restaurant manager had left out.

"Not sure what the range is like on those radios," Fin said. "I know I'd feel more comfortable if we had them. George, if you want to stay..."

He stopped with a mouthful of chocolate. "Was there talk of me having to leave?"

"No, I'm just thinking, if there are three of us then we should start a watch. What if one of those things does get in, or people become desperate? Better to keep a lookout and be ready than not."

"What's going to happen when this is all over?" Rebecca asked.

"Let's stay around to find out," George said.

They raised their glasses in a toast to each other and to 'seeing this out.'

Dinner was a sombre affair as they used up the last of

the perishable vegetables. The eggs were gone too. Afterwards they lapsed into silence, only speaking to squabble over what movie to watch. In the end they chose one that they did not all agree on, but could not disagree too strongly against. They were comfortably drunk and happily full.

"We've worked together for over two years you and I," Rebecca said to George. "And coming on a year for us," she raised her glass to Fin. "But I know hardly anything about either of you."

"Well, I've just been sitting here thinking over the different choices I made that got me here," Fin said. "Like, if I chose to study a bit harder for a semester in college, or if I found something that interested me enough to follow as a passion, where would I be now?"

"Dead. You could have stayed in and studied a bit longer and then got hit by a bus crossing the road because you were there at the wrong time. The world ends and you get weepy over not finishing college?" George said. "Let me guess, once the last zombie falls you're going to dedicate a few evenings a week to a night course, get that degree to hang proudly on your shelter wall. Lad, I don't see this ending the way you think it will. Say they were all magically struck down as some Christmas miracle, how many people have already died? Nobody with access to a newspaper, radio or television across the world has not been affected by this. Sure there are tribes in Africa sending what aid they can to us. At any moment, a loved one could turn into something you can no longer reason with. Feelings, memories – all mean nothing to the undead. They have one goal and we are it. The world has changed. Hanging on to old ways is only going to make it harder to change with it."

"Here's a thing to think about," Rebecca said. "Christmas decorations are now going to be up in towns and houses across the country for months, if not longer. Imagine this plague did wipe us out –"

"Is it a plague or an epidemic, or is it a pandemic?" Fin interrupted.

"I think pandemic means its traveling around the world. Can you imagine what the economy will look like after this? Nobody's working, no taxes generated," George said.

"There's probably some poor soul in the arse end of Connemara, at work right now," Rebecca said.

George snickered. "Yeah, news will get out to sub-Saharan Africa long before it reaches deepest Connemara."

"Anyway, what I was getting at was," Rebecca continued, "imagine our collected knowledge is dissolved. Society fractures and a few generations pass. What will those people make of us? Us building shrines to trees that never need watering, never grow old or shed. Who was that fat man in the red suit they worshiped? Was he a benevolent God? I mean how freaky would that be? Imagine a religion starts up around it."

"Consumerism?" George said pointedly.

"Ah, it's just the whiskey wanderings of the mind," Rebecca said.

Fin tried not to imagine a world so far gone. *People always come back after disaster. The Irish could.*

"A lot of things will change," George said. "Priorities mostly. There are a lot of hungry people in hiding right now, with dwindling supplies. I can tell you, there will be a lot of money made by people writing gardening books."

"Somebody is profiteering," Rebecca put her drink aside and went onto water. "This seems too quick to be natural."

Fin ignored that. "I think that's what I want to do after all of this. Learn how to be self-sufficient, live off the land and teach others how to, too. Right now, I think I'd be dead by next week if I did not have a can opener."

After George's arrival they divided the food supply again. With an extra person, they watched solemnly as their time in safety was fractioned. They spent the night coming up with outlandish plans on how they would make the hotel safer. There was talk of having rappel ropes tied to wardrobes beside upstairs windows. That idea was scrapped when nobody offered to tie the lines and everybody agreed no matter who did, none of them would trust it.

George suggested a redoubt on the roof, should the zombies get inside the building, but considering the effort it would take, it was vetoed. "We'd be stuck on a four-storey building in the middle of winter, on the west coast of Ireland and you're after saying you wouldn't use ropes to climb down from the second floor," Rebecca said.

"Well what are we supposed to do then?" George's frustration was mounting.

"We make no noise and wait for this to end."

Before they could get into an argument, Fin called them over to the restaurant window. On the mountain, a lantern light shone in the darkness, the person living in the church was making the climb. They stood in reverent silence as the light rose slowly. George opened the window to let in the frigid night. He shook his head and returned to their table, unable to watch the man on the mountain. He held no magic for him.

By the end of the night, they had agreed that the best plan was to ensure the zombies never made it inside the building. Fin fell asleep listening to the snores of George and Rebecca. It was a comfort he thought could replace his growing dependence on alcohol.

He was woken by a loud squawk from his walkie talkie.

"Are ye up yet lads?" George asked over the radio. "I've finished a walk around the hotel, no windows are broken. I'm in the kitchen making breakfast, if yous care to join. Feel free to take your time, means more rashers for me. We've plenty of orange juice if yous want to mimosa up this fry."

"Can we kick him out?" Rebecca asked, as she sat up with a groan. All of them slept fully dressed with their shoes on. "We're coming down now," she said.

Fin noticed a thick book beside his pillow, 'Grow Through Your Garden'. He opened the front cover and written inside was 'It's mostly flowers, not much you can eat in it, but the principle has to be the same for vegetables. Happy Christmas – George.'

"I bet he forgot to write my name on it too," Rebecca said. "He get that from the library in the lobby?"

Fin smiled. "Yeah, if we're here long enough, we're going to have to start regifting some of the things we steal from the hotel."

15
THE FALL

George lay back in a comfy recliner that he had brought from the lobby into the bar. His breathing was laboured after a second helping of breakfast. Rebecca had mentioned rationing a few times during the meal, but they all agreed that they had to celebrate Christmas, if only a little.

She moved melting ice-cream across her plate. "I've had a look over the records again and the security cameras. I'm sure that we're alone. No more surprises."

"I still think we should sweep the hotel room by room," George said. "Each floor has a storeroom for the house-keeping staff, they keep everything there from tea bags and coffee to the little chocolates they put on the pillows. The suites have mini fridges, vacuum packed blocks of cheese, fancy meats and chocolate."

"If either of you suggest that we split up, then I'm out," Fin said.

"Have you been watching horror movies?" Rebecca passed her plate across to George, who had been eyeing up her dessert.

"Yeah, wonderful escapism."

George burped and put his hands behind his head. "You know, if we ignored the news and just forgot about the rest of the world, this wouldn't be half bad."

"What about survivor's guilt when this ends? We're just going to walk out of here when the all-clear sounds as if we were on holiday?" Rebecca pushed her chair away from the table, ready to get back to work. She seldom stayed still for long.

"None of us are getting out of this unscathed," George said. "We've all lost somebody, or some essential part of ourselves. You look back a few hundred years into history and think how brutal life was for them. We think we're far removed, but we're not. Take away our modern conveniences and add a new predator to the food chain and see how quickly we fall."

Before they started emptying the rooms of anything useful, they walked the ground floor with a clipboard and pen, making notes of all the potential weaknesses and problems. The glaring one was the rope that George had used to get into the car park.

"We can't just leave it there, it's too much of a temptation for others," Fin said.

George tugged on it and the line went taut. "I watched a video on how to tie one of those knots that you pull on and it comes loose, but I wasn't going to actually do it. I'm not stupid, I tied that thing so tight you'd need a knife to get it loose."

"If I was desperate and I saw the rope and the window you broke to get into the lobby, I'd try it. Somebody else already did the hard part and went first," Fin said.

"I'll go up and cut it free, just not today." George walked to the end of the car park where the smoking area, bins and generator were. "How long do you think it will last if the power goes?"

It hummed merrily, ignorant to the changes in the world. Metal railings protected the generator, it was as large as a small truck and cost more than the three of them would make in a lifetime on their current wages. "Honestly, I've never had to use it, power has never gone out here in my time," Fin said.

"Say we disconnected it from whole hotel, just used it for a few small things, that could last us a fair amount of time."

"George, they had to bring the engineers that designed it to install it and it wasn't done in a day," Fin said.

"We have nothing but time."

"Yeah, but not to get an education in engineering. Oh, and a bit of physics on the side for good measure. But you're not factoring in the time it would take me or Rebecca to learn how to resuscitate somebody that channeled a lightning storm through their body."

George exhaled and took a picture of the company brand on the side of the generator. "I'll check their website later."

David's body was still propped up by the gate. Ciara looked restless where she lay. Given what was going on with the dead in the country, it unsettled Fin to leave her there. Risk of contamination kept them from getting close enough to cover her body, though they all knew that – to cover her – would insinuate that there were others inside, living comfortably enough to respect the dead. Fin could not help but think that the natural rot of her corpse was far slower than the decay taking root in the minds of survivors. *How far will I go to live? How far will I have to go?*

The basement held the real prize. The deep, dark

warren was the last place they wanted to be, so they decided to get it over with before starting the easier tasks. Fin stopped on the stairwell. He knew Ciara was not down there but the fear he felt with her chasing him came rushing back. Rebecca put a hand on his shoulder.

"Are you okay?" George asked. He already had the fire door into the basement open.

Fin took a few breaths to settle himself. "It just hits me sometimes that this is real. It's like a panic attack, except with dread. She was down here for days, sick and dying."

"I've been down already, Fin. It's empty," Rebecca said. "The storeroom was locked, she couldn't have gotten into the fridges or workshop. If you don't want to come..."

He walked in, ahead of George, and turned on the flickering lights. Warm, exposed heating pipes kept the chill out of the naked concrete. Old broken furniture and empty crates lined the walls. The walk-in fridge that stored the kegs and drinks for the bar hummed and clicked. George opened the door and light flooded out. It was full of kegs, boxes of cider, racks of wine and boxes of craft beer. He laughed and mumbled something about how they were going to be fine.

Fin unlocked the dry storeroom. Four pallets of bottled water filled a corner, half sparkling and half still. Extra stock for the vending machine was kept here too, nothing of nutritional benefit, but food all the same. Fin checked the expiration date on a large box of chocolate bars. *Two years. Will this go on for that long?*

"That's one problem we won't have." George slapped a bale of toilet paper.

"I wasn't even thinking about that," Rebecca said.

"It's what we have to do now isn't it? Think about things we never had to," George said. "Take, for instance, the water in this room. It looks like we're never going to run out, but how much should we be drinking a day? Multiply that by three. Should we use this drinking water for cooking? Every room in this hotel has a kettle and most have bathtubs. I think we should fill them all. We don't know how the water system works. If it stops flowing, we're in trouble."

"That's a lot of work, filling these things and changing the water regularly." Rebecca said.

"Exactly. Right now, staying active is as necessary to our wellbeing as food."

They sprayed disinfectant on all the handles and light fixtures they passed. George scrubbed the clock-in machine before putting in his employee number. The machine beeped. "If we're going to be here looking after the hotel, we may as well get paid for it."

Rebecca clocked in after him. "This might offset all the drinks we're taking."

They emptied the laundry room of fresh bed sheets and staff uniforms. There were enough outfits that fit them so they would only have to do one wash a week. The window-less florist's room was carpeted with wilted petals and full of the remains of dessicated flowers, the ones that adorned the lobby before services ended.

The handyman never threw anything away. His work-shop was full of tools: hammers, crowbars, shovels, tape and nails. An arsenal. It held the contents of a small hardware store. George used a crowbar to pry open the lockers in the men's changing room. He found a little bag of white powder in the one belonging to the pastry chef. "He takes his work seriously, has a stash of baking powder at the ready."

"I always thought he was far too energetic in the morning," Fin said.

They found little of use. Rebecca knew the code into the

women's room – Ciara's final resting place – but they refused to enter. George scrawled 'DANGER' on the door with a marker. Then he placed a fistful of dead flowers in front of the changing room. They stayed there for a while in silence. They did not know what to say, except to comment on the unfairness of the situation, but that did not seem fitting.

It took them several hours to clear the basement, a daunting, but fruitful, task. Now he never needed to go down there again. After a quick lunch, they used a house-keeping cart to empty rooms on the first floor. Closets in the accommodation supply offices were stocked with shampoos, chocolates, bedsheets, toiletries and towels. There was enough sugar, coffee and tea to last them months. Fin flicked open a small bottle of conditioner and breathed in the strong smell of strawberries. *I wonder if it tastes like strawberries. Are there people out there already that desperate?*

Before they entered the first floor corridor, George shouted to draw attention. They kept their weapons drawn. There was no response. He shouted a few more times, just to be sure. They walked into the expectant silence, knocking on each door as they passed. Fin printed a master keycard for each of them. He slid his into the lock on the first room. The light went green. Inside, the bed was made, everything was clean and ready for guests in the new year. It took them less than five minutes to sweep the room and move on to the next one.

George disappeared long enough for Fin and Rebecca to start giving out that he was shirking work. When he returned to them, he had a fistful of printer ink cartridges. The palm of his gloved hand was magenta. Grinning, he held it against the window and dragged it down to make it look like a blood stain. "It might deter people from coming in."

"If they're colour blind. Or you'll have trick-or-treaters knocking at the front door," Rebecca said.

They repeated the process in a few rooms on every floor. Fin stopped outside David's room. "This is where it happened. We brought him here. Ciara..."

"Any clue how he was infected? Where did he come from?" George started writing a warning on the door.

"He didn't have an Irish accent," Fin said. "If you want to go in and check his passport, be my guest. Does it matter? There's nothing in there for us."

Rebecca sprayed the door handle with bleach and let it rest.

"I never knew there was a swimming pool up here," George started running down the hall, following signs to the spa. The smell of chlorine filled the air.

"Are you joking?" Fin hurried to keep up. "How long have you worked here?"

"You underestimate how little I care about this job." George started undressing. "Do me a favour and wipe the camera feed for me, will you? I don't have my swimming gear, so it's a dip in the nip."

"You could do with a wash too," Rebecca said to Fin as they entered the pool room. The water was still as glass and as blue as gravestones.

George lept from the edge, the backwash spattered the hem of their pants. He surfaced with a yelp and quickly swam to the edge. "It's freezing!"

Before Fin had time to counter, Rebecca barrelled into him, knocking them both into the pool. George was not exaggerating. Fin rose to the top and spluttered, wiping water from his eyes. She swam into the centre of the pool and floated on her back.

George acclimatised and started doing lengths. "I expected we would have found more in the rooms, but they hardly seem worth the effort."

"Wait until we get to the suites on the top floor," Fin said. "Those things are essentially self-contained houses."

"They don't put that chemical into the pool that changes colour when you pee, do they?" George asked.

"No, why?"

"No reason."

"You had to go and spoil it, didn't you?" Rebecca swam towards the ladder.

It felt odd to Fin, the three of them messing in the pool while the rest of the country fell apart.

They left a trail of wet carpet behind them as they went to the top floor to get changed. It was difficult to look at Rebecca in Solene's clothes.

There were fewer rooms on the top floor. All of them were larger than Fin's apartment. The first one was opulent. The fridge was fully stocked and there was a basket of nuts and dried fruits on the counter.

"Why are we not staying up here?" George said.

"I don't think I could stomach living like this now." Rebecca threw a few of the vestigial pillows off the bed and lay down.

"Well, I can, so keep your shoes off my bed," George said.

There was a wonderful vista of the bay and the islands beyond. "I wonder how people are coping out there," Fin said.

"They went out as soon as the storm would let them."

George chewed an expensive chocolate bar, weathering Rebecca's comments about rationing. "A few of them left before that. The islands are beautiful in summer. You'd think they'd make a perfect location to see this out, but they rely on food being brought from the mainland. They must be starving."

The chocolate in Fin's mouth soured. "They probably brought the infection out with them."

Rebecca kicked her shoes off and turned the television on. The good spirit they felt during the day seemed localised entirely to the hotel.

The video on screen was shot from a helicopter slowly flying above a small town. The streets were completely overrun; slow zombies followed fast weepers, all drawn by the sound of the helicopter. There was no chance of escape for survivors not already barricaded indoors. The helicopter hovered over a castle tower on top of a grassy hill. The camera zoomed in on people on the battlement, who waved the pilot away. They frantically tore down flags with 'HELP' written on them. The camera panned down to the base of the stone walls, where the recent dead converged, drawn by the helicopter and the sounds of the living from within.

"Those poor people," Rebecca said. "Are they idiots? Get the helicopter out of there!"

"This is live and exclusive on..." The broadcaster cut off as the gate, designed to keep out tourists, buckled under the weight and tireless force of the infected. The camera operator focused in on the zombies that poured into the caged civilians.

The uniformity of their deathmask expressions horrified Fin. It was their indifference he found so disturbing.

"Fly away," Rebecca stood up. "If they just flew away they could draw the infected off."

Zooming out, the camera panned up to the roof. Most of

the people had disappeared to find cover or defend themselves. They would find nothing of use within the cold stone skeleton. The lower windows had been barred for public safety. They would not escape.

A woman stood up on the parapet on quaking legs, held a hand out to somebody below the wall and screamed something at them. A hand reached up, trying to pull her to safety, but she backed away, closer to the edge. A man climbed up, holding his arms out to calm her. She walked into his embrace. Their foreheads pressed together. Both were crying. They kissed and spoke. There was no sound, they were given that small privacy at least, while the camera picked them apart.

Arms locked around each other, his hand cradled her head against his chest. He looked into the lens, eyes overflowing. He knew the noise, fear and danger were beyond them now. His stare a silent indictment to those watching from safety. 'How can you do nothing?'

He kissed her head, whispered a prayer into her hair and closed his eyes. As one, they stepped to the edge of the tower. Hands reached up and grabbed hold of him, more tore at his clothes. The woman held on to him, tried to pull him free. For a moment, it looked like she would, until she tugged too hard and lost her grip, tumbling backwards, to fall alone. The man was consumed by the mass of arms, slipping out of view.

The feed cut before she hit the ground, the video seemed frozen but the reporter in the studio pulled his earpiece out with shaking hands. He tried to speak but found no words.

* * *

"I hope they find the people in that helicopter and put them in front of cameras," Fin said.

"I don't think that fall would have killed her," George stared at the screen.

"Shut up." Rebecca changed the channel. The national broadcaster had calorific information graphics on how to ration what you have. She clicked again, to a different news channel that showed a fishing vessel burning, barely clinging to the surface of the sea.

"Infected were found onboard and the navy cleansed this ship before it could contaminate English shores. Volunteers have flocked to the coast to combat the threat of infected reaching land," the reporter said. "Panic grips the world, but nowhere more so than the island next to a ravaged Ireland. A reminder to our Irish viewers: all ships will be turned back. Aid vessels and cargo planes laden with support are inbound to Dublin. The newly formed Allied Nations Pandemic Defence has released a statement for the Irish people. You are not alone. Do not spread this disease. Do not break quarantine. Help is coming. The feeling in England is of complete panic. Behind me are members of the New Home Guard who have cordoned off the scene of a zombie wash-up during the night..."

The body above the tide line was surrounded by rocks and bricks.

"This comes ahead of the news just yesterday that brave people in Blackpool confronted a raft of zombies. Reports of refugees spreading the disease to the Isle of Man were confirmed by the British government earlier today. Rapid response units ensured containment. Emergency powers have been granted to the military in Britain, while the President of the United States has called a state of emergency.

Navy vessels from both countries have been tasked to the region to contain this natural disaster."

"Bollox to that," George said. "They expect us to believe that a boat of zombies sailed to Blackpool. It's propaganda. Look at those grinning, smiling bastards."

"I read online that there's a growing anti-Irish sentiment in some places, as if this is some race-specific plague," Rebecca said.

"I've not seen the zombies ask to see your passport before chowing down. The media has to be being censored," George struggled to open a bottle of water with shaking hands. It dribbled down his chin when he took a sip. "I don't begrudge them what they're doing. They're scared. If it had hit England before us, I'd be the first one on the east coast sands, with a rock in each hand. Right now, they have their loved ones. What I wouldn't do for the chance to have helped mine."

Gunfire outside made them jump. The three of them lay on the ground. Rebecca fumbled with the remote to turn the television off, but only managed to change the channel. Fin crawled to the edge of the window. A squad of soldiers swept through the street. Behind them, others used handguns to make sure the dead stayed down. Weepers sped towards them. Some of the soldiers faltered, but enough held the line to get them safely to the factory by the port.

Half an hour had passed from the time Rebecca thought to check, before they saw a speedboat come in from the bay. George cheered. "The cavalry's here."

Fin felt the knots in his chest loosen a little. Help was coming.

"They're going to make the port safe to start fishing," George said. "Actually, the job I want is to be set up on a pontoon in the middle of the river with ammunition, a rifle and a few beers."

"We have to help now," Rebecca said. "Imagine they find us living like royalty in here."

"Personally, I'm good until I run out of food and other options," George said.

"Guys..."

Fin followed Rebecca's gaze to the television. Dublin airport was burning; twisted metal, ballooning gouts of black smoke and tongues of flame lacerated the sky. Drone footage captured the explosions as fuel tankers caught and engines exploded.

George threw his chair against the wall. The noise was horrendous in this new world of silence. Rebecca took her phone out and went on the internet. "Belfast is gone too. There are pictures of small airfields destroyed across the county. This was an attack."

George ground his teeth. "I don't think we can stay here long," he said. "Maybe try those islands, or head out into the countryside. Survivors won't leave this place empty, not after seeing this news. There won't be an evacuation, we're stuck here and this place is too much of a good thing."

"We're safe," Fin said.

"They gave you suicide pills when they met you, let you do the hard work for them. Do you think they're going to take chances? They'll scorch this place."

Fin looked down at the crowd of weepers lining the quay. *I can't go out there with them.* "Maybe we'd be better off with the people in Westport House, with the soldiers. Hide enough food for the three of us. Or find a hiding place here, that's warm, with water."

George held his knuckles against his eyes and cursed. "We can't hide like that, without information about what's happening. I'll head out tonight and have a look around, now that the zombies are clear out the front. I'm not going with yous if yous decide to join Westport House camp. I know I sound paranoid, but I think we'd be safer on our own. Look what they did to the airports."

"A precaution," Rebecca said.

"No, I think we're on our own," Fin said. "Come here and have a look at this."

They gathered at the window and watched the speed-boat full of soldiers head off into the bay. They watched their hope shrink until it was completely out of sight.

16

MORTGAGE FREE

George left before dawn. The three of them stood in the light drizzle in the car park, looking up the long length of rope that George had left behind. He shook his arms and jogged on the spot, taking long breaths to psych himself up. All the cords on his rain jacket were taped down, or cut off. There was a bottle of cooking oil in his pack which he would lather on at the top of the climb, to "make the zombies work for their meal."

"Are you sure you want to do this?" Fin said. "If you fell and survived, that would be considered unlucky, given the circumstances."

Water ran down the sheer wall in little rivulets. George tugged on the rope, his knots held. "Stop talking." He put the rope between his legs, hooked it under one foot and pinched it to the side of the other. Grabbing the rope with his gloved hands, he brought his knees to his chest and locked his feet around the rope again. "Right, this is good. Send the stuff up after me."

"Be careful," Rebecca said. "I don't think it's worth going, not for us, we're good here."

"Your objection is noted, but as I said, I don't want to feel comfortable enough in a place to become trapped. This is my choice. Now, my arms are already getting sore. If I don't leave now, I'll be back much quicker than any of us are comfortable with." He started the climb.

He stopped halfway up the wall, lying into it to relieve the stress on his hands. "Do you think he's okay?" Rebecca whispered.

George looked down to them and seemed to be on the verge of speaking, but they were too far away, his voice would echo in the empty space. Both of them stuck their thumbs up to let him know he was making good progress. The last half of the climb was the hardest. His breaks were more frequent and lasted longer.

Near the top of the climb he was shaking. His sharp, wheezing breaths made Fin and Rebecca run to the base of the wall and sharply whisper encouragement up to him, regardless of who might hear. With one final push, he reached out for the top of the wall and slowly crawled to safety. The lump in Fin's throat shrunk a little as he watched George's feet wriggle out of sight. A few moments later, his head stuck out and he waved.

They tied a bag of supplies and a few tools to the end of the rope and watched as he pulled it up. Enough food and water to keep him for a few days, should he become trapped. There was so little strength in his arms that they expected the bag to fall back down.

"He's braver than I am," Fin said.

"It feels weird without him," Rebecca said. "Do you think he's right to leave?"

"Maybe. You saw how many people are in Westport House. It's just down the road. How long does it take for somebody that's infected to turn? Enough time for them to seek shelter amongst others?"

They did not wander far from the front door, taking their meals within a few feet of it, ready to open it should George need them. Fin lost track of the number of times he read over the same page of his new gardening book. By afternoon he stopped trying, and instead just counted the shadows of the infected walking past. Losing count of that was far more disheartening.

"Guys?" George's voice was little more than a whisper.

Fin and Rebecca huddled over one radio. "Are you okay?" Fin asked.

"Perfect. I feel like I've been out house hunting, except I bypassed the whole dread of getting a mortgage and wondering if I'll live long enough to pay it back."

"What did you find?" Rebecca said.

"A lovely little bungalow right on the waterfront, with a renovated attic. There's a massive, solid gate out front, with trees and bushes to hide it from the road. Granted we will have to do a bit of work, there are no walls around the back garden. If we are quiet though, it should be perfect."

"What about the owners?" Rebecca asked.

"They left a note," George's tone dulled. "I'm fairly certain they won't return before this ends. The roads are clearer than I had hoped. I'll head back now. Pack up as much food as the three of us can safely move and we'll bring it with us before it gets too bright."

Fin took his finger off the receiver so that George could not hear them speak. "What do you think?"

"We have to leave at some point, but I wasn't ready to leave now. I like the idea of having more options," Rebecca said. "But I can't shake the feeling that we are making a mistake."

"Sure we'd feel that way if we decided to stay."

"I suppose."

Fin held the receiver down. "Okay, George."

* * *

About twenty minutes after George ended the transmission, the infected outside the hotel started weeping and ran off. The slower ones took longer to leave; some were so slow that they forgot why they were moving and just stopped, stood still and wavered on their feet, or were drawn off by other natural noises.

When George radioed again he was out of breath. "Let me in!"

Just as they unlocked the door, he skidded on the path, trying to slow his momentum. He slammed the door behind him. Fin braced against it, while Rebecca fumbled with the lock. Doubled over, George was panting and laughing. "There's nothing following me, I just got it in my head that there was."

"Give us a bit of a warning. What would you have done if I was pinching a loaf?"

"Well, I'd probably pinch one too."

Fin laughed and clapped George on the shoulder. He imagined the reverence he felt for the man must have been akin to those who watched astronauts come back from the moon. They were already dressed and ready to leave. Their supplies were in bags that were stuffed with toilet paper to reduce noise.

"What's it like?" Rebecca asked. She leaned against the door and peered out of the side window. The night had a purple hue, meaning the day would soon start.

"Like a dream. One of those when everything seems

normal, but it's surreal enough that it couldn't be mistaken for anything other than a dream. They just stand there until something draws them. Gives me the creeps."

"Did you kill any?" Fin asked.

"Not a one and I'll avoid it like my life depends on it. Best way to survive this is to keep your head down. I set the alarm off on an empty house. If we leave soon, it should still keep them busy."

It felt real now. George had emptied his supply bags at the house and now filled them up again in the kitchen. "We stay quiet and we'll be there in fifteen minutes. It's beautiful. Guys, you're going to love it."

Fin left his chain of keys on the office desk and brought only two keys for the front door. He gave one to Rebecca. She put it in her pocket and clutched it through the fabric, not trusting the zip. George looked out first before stepping onto the street, hugging the side of the building. Fin had to steel himself before leaving, but it was the fear of being out in the open longer than necessary that got him moving. He locked the door quietly.

The morning air was sharp and cold, a nice contrast to the constant warmth of the lobby. A light fog hid the silhouettes of infected off towards Westport House. A few reassuring lights shone from its windows. They smelled woodfire and for a moment, Fin wondered if they might be better off heading in that direction. Hammer in hand, he followed George. There was barely a sound beyond the wind and the water. The bodies of infected that the soldiers had shot were glazed with winter frost.

They crouched along the sides of buildings as they followed the road. Apartment blocks gave way to houses, B&Bs and bars. No sign of life came from the buildings; if people were still inside, they hid behind closed curtains.

How many were drawn out by the march of the refugees, too afraid to be left behind? Only one building had boards haphazardly covering its windows. *So little time.*

The tide was high. Sea spray salted the air. They avoided the light from street lamps as much as possible. They stopped beyond the houses. Fin had a clear view of Croagh Patrick; snow speckled the peak. He could not not imagine the hardship those that lived up there faced. *If they can climb that every day, then I can't complain about this stroll.*

They jumped at the slightest sound, thinking it the first note of an infected's weep. Fin expected them to lurch out of every alley they passed. He imagined them behind bins and beneath cars. *Living on the mountain is a small price to pay for peace of mind.*

George stopped outside a bus yard. He walked around the rising arm barrier and snuck up to an old coach. Fin's skin crawled as he watched George pull the emergency door release. His face was scrunched up as if he expected an alarm to sound. When it did not, he looked to Fin and Rebecca, but hid his grin when he saw their angry faces. He came out moments later with a small, red-handled hammer, with a metal spike for shattering windows.

"You couldn't have gotten that when we weren't all carrying bags?" Rebecca said.

"Well, I didn't want to do it by myself. What if there were infected around?"

Beyond the town limits, old, rusted gates protected empty fields. After too long in the open, George turned right, down a small country lane. "This is a little peninsula, mostly houses and farms. If we combined our annual earnings, we might be able to afford the deposit of one of the houses along here."

A verge of brambles, hawthorn trees and blackberry

bushes pressed them close together. George gave his opinion on buildings he thought were still occupied as they passed them; those were few. The ones with open doors he avoided entirely, taking care to walk swiftly past them.

They stopped outside a large black, wooden gate. Overgrown bushes hid the entrance enough that Fin nearly walked past it in the gloom. "Welcome home," he whispered.

"How did you get in?" Fin asked.

"Hopped the fence." George climbed onto it and dropped his bags over. He took theirs and lowered them over the other side as quietly as possible. Noise in a nearby field made them stop, but it was moving away from them. *Fox or rabbit? Unlikely.*

Fin gave Rebecca a boost up and he took a running jump at it, making it on his second attempt. He felt a moment of self-loathing at his poor fitness. Before the epidemic, he could just suck in his gut until the bar closed and he was alone on the night shift. Now it endangered his life. Hiding indoors for the duration of the epidemic was not going to do anything to help things.

The property did seem ideal: a high wall and thick gate covered the front and a wooden fence and bushes separated them from the adjacent field on the left. *The infected could crawl beneath that.* To the right was a high bush with pathways worn through the base by passing animals. Brittle grass crunched as they walked across the manicured lawn. A few old autumn leaves littered the fringes of the gravel drive.

"Watch out for the pond," George said. "I've never heard of people eating koi fish, but if there are any in there, then we can give it a try."

Fin could hear the water in the bay behind the house. "Are you sure this place is empty?" he asked.

George nodded and took a key from his pocket.

"Where did you find that?"

"Under the flowerpot. It's getting too light out to risk another trip back to the hotel. We'll set up here. Come in and get settled. Wipe your feet."

Fin's breath caught when he saw the alarm box on the hall wall, but it was off. The blinds were all down and most of the doors were shut. It felt odd intruding on somebody's home without their knowing. They listened to the tick of a large clock. *When will that run out?* They dropped their bags and checked every room in the house, using the light of Rebecca's phone to shoo the shadows.

"This is the real prize," George said. He opened a door, revealing towels and bedsheets stacked on wooden shelves.

Fin thought it was a linen cupboard until George pulled the folded towels and sheets off the shelves. They were stairs. The space was so tight that the stairway doubled on itself and rose steeply. Fin looked into the dark hatch above that swallowed George. "You went up there by yourself?"

"I stuck my head up. When I banged on the wall and heard no movement or weeping, I was happy enough that the house was clear. Come up, this is brilliant."

They climbed the rickety stairs into the converted attic. Fin hit his head on the low roof. It slanted off either side. There was a bathroom with a cramped shower, two single beds, a futon and two roof windows for light and an office at the far end of the attic.

"This is perfect," Fin said.

Rebecca left without a word, taking the smiles off Fin and George's faces. Fin realised how disturbing it must look for them to revel in the misfortune of others. He wondered if the previous owners of the house were aimlessly wandering the streets now.

"Coffee, anyone?" Rebecca said up to them and they followed her down to the kitchen.

The light came on when she opened the fridge. "How is the power still on?"

"Saw on the news, the government has put every effort into ensuring we have light to die by," George said.

Rebecca started emptying the cupboards. The bubbling noise of the boiling kettle was sweet and foreign, like memories of a distant holiday. *Were kettles always so loud?* Fin rinsed three mugs, filled them with instant coffee granules and sugar. George dug out little packets of milk stolen from the hotel rooms.

"When do you think the next fresh milk will be?" Fin emptied a packet of milk into each coffee.

George sat on the counter and took a mug. "A few cows might survive, but just enjoy this, it's only going to get rarer."

Rebecca took a seat at the table, shifting the opened envelopes and stale newspapers out of the way. "I can't believe they attacked the airports."

George chewed his lip, tears formed and fell. He looked away out the window.

"That coffee's hot," Fin said.

George smiled, appreciating the weak joke. "I wanted to be a pilot once. Too expensive to learn, though." He wiped his eyes. "The outbreak was one thing, but to attack us, cripple our means of escape? I'm worried that if they think that's okay, what else will they do, to keep themselves safe? I understand the reason, stop the spread, contain it. I just don't like the feeling of dread that comes with thinking that they are more focused on mopping up the aftermath, than stepping in before we're all gone."

"If they send more people in, it's more fodder for the disease." Fin let out a sigh and held the scalding mug tight. Rebecca left the cupboards open and the aroma of spices that spilled out made him hungry. A shelf above the sink was full of cookbooks, from baking to vegan, savoury to sweet. There was a calendar stuck to the fridge with magnets collected from countries around the world. Fin lifted a few months up to see what the people that lived here had planned; dentist appointments, bills, weight loss goals. The feeling of unfairness was steadily becoming a numbing rage.

Festive fake snow frosted the edge of the window. George rummaged through the presses and found the can. With what remained inside, he sprayed 'Infected' on all the windows. The kitchen opened into the sitting room. He took the presents from beneath the Christmas tree and threw them onto the sofa. He started tearing open the wrapping. Fin and Rebecca watched the small desecration in silence.

"You wouldn't believe the amount of useless things people get as presents." George shook a large box. "In the handful of houses that I've broken into – after the infection – I've found mostly handbags, makeup sets and bath salts. The best ones for passing the time were computer games, Legos and books."

"Maybe we can camouflage ourselves from the infected," Rebecca said.

"Not with blusher and primer." George threw the makeup set towards the tree. "Where are all the mountaineers, cyclists and outdoor enthusiasts? I could do with some fishing gear or survival equipment. All the time we wasted in school, I can tell you about plant reproductive organs, but not how to use a map or do taxes, not that I'll have to worry about those for a while."

He emptied his backpack onto the table. Rebecca picked up her coffee as a compass rolled towards it. "Actually, I passed through a place not far away, with a great pair of women's hillwalking boots. Could be an idea for you, Rebecca."

"I don't want to wear the shoes of a dead woman, at least not until mine start letting in water."

George threw each of them a short flint and striker. "In case the power goes out."

Fin struck it a few times, but he did not produce sparks. "Let's hope the power stays on. You know lighters and matches still work, right?"

George ignored him and unfolded an ordnance survey map of the area onto the table. "We're here," he pointed to a peninsula, outside of town. Small cluttered islands hugged the coast up to Newport.

George poked Clare Island. "That right there looks ideal. Far from major towns, big enough community already."

"You're forgetting all the water between us and the island," Fin said. "The bay looks rough, can you imagine what it's like in the Atlantic? I don't know how to operate a boat in calm conditions. It's stormy out there."

"You're the very man that mentioned learning from books, we just need to find one on sailing."

"I still think Achill Island." Rebecca turned the map around to face her. "Fin and I tried to follow the Greenway, but the infected were on the road. There's one bridge onto the island, easily defensible. We have highland too, should the bridge fail."

George quickly looked to Fin. "The infected were on the road between you and Achill?"

"That does not mean they made it to the island," Rebecca said.

"What have your family said about conditions there?" It was a low shot, but it stalled Rebecca's enthusiasm for home.

"Say we managed to make it out to Clare Island, Achill wouldn't take much more effort. Or if we were able to get on the water, then we could stay close to the coast and sail to Achill. Scout out the islands in the bay along the way," Fin said.

"I still think we need a thorough plan," Rebecca said. "George, you mentioned you wanted high ground. The island provides that. I grew up there, I know every secret there is to know outside of closed doors. We need to be focused, have one destination and goal. I do think we need to consider it."

"I know you want to see your family," George said. "Maybe the infected haven't gotten there. Would the locals have thought to guard the bridge when this started? I certainly wouldn't have. Would they turn away strangers? Even if they thought they brought the infection with them, they would have no right to do so. We'd have difficulty doing that now without reprisal, let alone back then, when there was little information about the disease. I agree with you, we should go there. There's a lower population density, but I think we should go by water. It's the safest way."

"If the infection is there then it would be easier to avoid the weepers. The island is mostly fields and sparse homes. Keem Bay can only be reached by a long, windy road along cliffs."

"We need to prepare first," George said.

Fin put the kettle on again and made a second round of coffee for them. By the time they put the empty mugs in the sink, there was light enough to work by. Fin was jittery from the caffeine. He kept thinking of the train, he had heard it when the weepers were calm. *If I could get a lift to Dublin, I could walk along the coast to Drogheda.* "So the camp on the grounds of Westport House is out?"

"I think it would be madness to join them," George said. "We can't stay here because we're too close to town. That's not the army anymore. They're just people now, their uniform means less by the day. You want to try for home?"

"I want to be at home, I can't think of another way. Walking would be suicide."

"Well, lad, I'd be sorry to see you leave, mostly because I reckon you'll die not long after. It's your choice. As for joining the camp at Westport House, not a chance. Imagine the infection got inside their walls. All those people..." George was pale at the thought.

"Surely you agree we're better off knowing a bit more about what's happening. No harm can come from it."

George was silent for a moment. "Don't bring them back here, or let on that you have food. If you get a lift to Dublin, we might never meet again. That's mad. Are you sure you won't stay with us? Wait until the infected die off? For the moment, we have plenty of food. What we should do is stockpile more and look for a better place to hide. This is grand for now but I'd like a bit more security. Maybe a bigger telly."

Fin slumped into a chair and played with the spilled sugar on the table. "I'm just worried about my family. If I'm there, I could do something."

George ran a hand through his greasy hair. "The worst case scenario is not you dying. It's you becoming infected and living long enough to make it back to them. They won't turn you away and you'll kill them all. They've been around longer than you have. Stay where you are. Find them after."

An awkward silence followed. "Everybody will have thought of the islands," Rebecca said to diffuse it.

"Not at first," George said. "Nobody was expecting this. If you had the money, maybe you tried to leave the country. Otherwise you stayed put, listened to the government. There aren't enough boats to get many people to the islands. Besides, there's not enough shelter or food out there to support many. They won't share their supplies with us and if we brought enough to be self-sufficient, what's stopping them from taking that from us?"

"How did you become so cynical?" Fin asked, while secretly wishing that he could be as pragmatic.

"Working in a bar after two A.M. usually does it. I'm being a wet blanket, sorry. What I'm trying to say is, nowhere is safe. The more people that are around us, the less likely we are to survive."

"Right, enough talking, let's bring our stuff upstairs and see what they have of use in the house," Rebecca said.

They cleaned up after themselves and started carrying their gear to the attic. No matter what George said, it would not deter Fin's thoughts of home and family. Walking out of the hotel and making it to the house made him wonder if he could not make it home. *I made it this far and survived, the only difference between here and home is distance. And a country full of weepers*. Rebecca and George's conversation became pleasant background noise. The clock in the hall sounded faster.

17

HOT WATER BOTTLES ARE LIFE SAVERS

Once they brought everything of use upstairs, they had a quick breakfast of baked beans on hard, stale bread before checking the grounds. So long as they were quiet, they would be safe. The fields either side of the property were difficult to get into and the gate and wall at the front would act as a breakwater against infected stumbling down the road. At the back of the house, water from the bay lapped against boulders and a slim pebble beach.

It took them under an hour to empty the shed, bringing the spoils to the renovated attic. The stairs were too steep for uncoordinated zombies. It was difficult enough for them to climb. "We put the blankets and towels back and something heavy on the trap door and you'd never know we were here," George said.

"When you told us about this place on the radio, I was expecting spiders, rafters and cobwebs, thick as insulation," Fin said.

George put his bags on top of the hatch. "Feel that? Safety. I have not felt this calm in a while."

The bathroom had a shower and a toilet, though you

had to duck with the slant of the roof to use either. The press beneath the sink was full of toilet paper and wet wipes. Aside from the office and the bathroom, the loft was one long room. *World keeps shrinking.* A futon faced a large flatscreen television. Shelves were full of computer games, films and books.

George dove on one of the single beds. "Yous can fight over the other one."

"I'll take the futon," Fin said.

"Chivalry?"

"Oh, you know the word, George." Fin walked through to the office, it had the only wall-mounted window. Already the afternoon light was dimming. A lamp hung over a worn and battered armchair. A glass of wine and a book half-finished rested on a little table.

"This is a little slice of heaven," Rebecca said.

George plugged in extension cords and connected wires to four different brands of portable battery packs that he had salvaged. *When did it become salvage and not steal?* He charged multiple phones, torches and a laptop.

"I don't envy their electricity bill, if they're alive to see it," Rebecca said.

"We're fed, so the main rule is not to rush into anything," George said. "That's how we stay alive. We don't go out of our way to put down any infected. The only exception to engaging them is if somehow they get into the attic and are nibbling on your toes during the night. Aside from that, just let them walk by. There's electricity and internet here, let's use it. We'll make a nest in the attic. Salvage what's around. Mostly selection boxes and Christmas party foods. Which reminds me." He took out a fistful of toothbrushes and paste from his jacket pocket and handed them out.

Rebecca leaned on the windowsill and watched the

street. "This is a good spot. We have the water at our backs. I wonder why the owners left."

"Leanne was supposed to follow her parents when her college exams finished," George said. "They were going to spend Christmas in New York. I hope she made it."

"You knew these people?" Fin asked. He sat on the swiveling chair that had left deep dents in the carpet.

"I don't. From the moment we walked through the front door, I've been on edge, waiting to hear a key in the door and voices downstairs," George said.

Photos of family and friends hung on the wall above the desk. Personal mementos and exam schedules piled up to make it look messy, but somebody found order here. Fin turned the photo of a young woman on the desk around, to avoid her eyes.

"Leanne wrote a letter," George took a sheet of paper from the desk drawer.

"I don't want to read that," Fin said. "I feel bad enough being here as it is, without completely invading her privacy."

"This was written the day before flights stopped." Rebecca said.

"She made it," George delicately took the letter back and placed it on the desk, almost reverently.

"This is a beautiful house, Solene would love it."

"Have you heard back from her yet?" George asked.

Fin regretted mentioning her. He was able to ignore thoughts of her so long as he kept busy. He did not want to go to Westport House, but if the trains started bringing people to the capital, then he needed to be on one. "We haven't had much contact."

"There's something trending online, #I'mAlive. Maybe you want to post that before going out. When she manages to get online, it might bring her peace knowing you're okay," Rebecca said.

"Maybe the person living on the mountain should put a hashtag before the SOS. They might have been rescued by now."

"George!" Rebecca admonished him and laughed uneasily. "Probably safer up there than we are down here. It's all loose scree. From what I've seen, those things can't handle a steep incline well."

The chair squeaked when Fin leaned back, he stood up instead of risking more noise. "Can you imagine the amount of guns they have in America? You can get them in supermarkets. What have we got, hurling sticks?"

"My mam used to keep me in check with a wooden spoon, even the threat of it alone was enough to make me behave," Rebecca said. "Maybe the infected have retained a fear of it."

"We could get some wooden spoons and put some nails through them so," George said. "We could make some bows and arrows, used to do that as a child."

"Nonsense, waste of time," Rebecca said. "I assume neither of you are skilled archers. You get one shot. The skull is thick. Better a cinder block on a rope and drop it on one from the roof."

"I made it this long without having to kill one of those things," George said.

"It's mad how quickly we can talk about killing," Fin said. "I don't know what's going on in their heads, but something has to be. You think it's easy to stand, but it's a miracle of millions of years of evolution, all those muscles, tendons, the brain does it all. They can hear. Can they understand? All that movement requires energy and I doubt they're solar powered, not in Ireland at least. They become infected, they go manic and then slow down. There seems to be a natural decline. We might not need to kill at all, they might just die. We agree we can't fight them, that's ridiculous..."

"You don't think they're dead?" George said. "I've seen them moving with wounds no living thing could survive."

"I didn't say they're not zombie-like. Maybe their brain does not know when they've been wounded. Hormones all over the place. The movie zombie is illogical."

"Maybe it's a logic we have to come to terms with." George cupped his hands and blew hot hair into them. "It's bitter." He went downstairs to figure out the central heating system. The radiators started to hum.

"The kettle's on, I found a few hot water bottles, should be ready in a few minutes," George said, sticking his head through the attic hatch. He looked worried. "I don't know how long we will have it for. Need to find electrical heaters and maybe a place with solar panels or a wind turbine. The islands don't look too appealing now. There's a tank of heating oil in the garden, it's about a quarter full. If the gas and electricity go, then cold will get people before hunger does."

"We're just waiting for things to end," Fin said. "I need to leave."

Rebecca made to speak but lapsed into silence. Fin thought if he stayed he would eventually die, whereas there was hope in trying for home. *Maybe I couldn't live with myself if I didn't try.* He realised with loathing that he could stay hidden, hibernate away the worst of the plague. That was why he had to go, to prove himself wrong. *They probably think that if I leave I won't last long.* He was not one for hugs, so when Rebecca put her arms around him he flinched. Once his arms were around her, he found it hard to let go.

18

LAST WILL & TESTAMENT

The stress of leaving the safety of the loft to cook dinner hardly seemed worth the full belly. They destroyed down-stairs, pulling books from shelves, upending the kitchen table and emptying the contents of the cupboards onto the ground, to give the appearance of having already been ransacked. When they were finished, they filled the stairs to the loft with towels and bedding, so that on first glance the attic would go unnoticed. George took the lightbulb from the stairway. If you did not know the loft was there, it would remain hidden. They piled blankets on top of the trapdoor to muffle any sound they made. They felt safe in their little bubble.

The only thing the three of them could agree on was that they would look out for each other, which did not align with their separate plans. Rebecca wanted Achill Island. George wanted to disappear into the countryside – a lake island was his preference. Fin wanted to be with his family and Solene.

Rebecca regularly offered to ring her on his behalf. She

did not understand that if he called and she did not pick up, then he could be certain that she was gone. If he never rang, there was a chance that she was still alive. That chance was keeping him going.

Before leaving, Fin locked himself in the bathroom. The shower still worked, but after their efforts to conceal themselves, the noise of it would ruin their hard work. Hunkered because of the slanting roof, he undressed. He was not overweight by much – in his uniform he barely noticed it – but there was no hiding from the naked truth; he was in no shape for the trip ahead. He turned the hot water on and washed himself with a face cloth.

The skin beneath his eyes was purple. When he finished, he lay on the cold tiles and tried to do a few push-ups. He only managed eight before he sprawled on the ground, his arms shaking. *If I leave and they're dead or I can't find Solene, what then?* The anger that had welled up at the injustice of what was happening was gone, turned into anguish the moment he started wondering how Solene and his family were coping. *If she's alive, she must be terrified that I'm dead. I'm selfish.*

He tried to remember the last words they said to each other, but the echo of her terrified crying in the voice message permeated every precious memory he had. All he wanted was to curl up with her and fall asleep, warmed in the comfort of each other. *If something happens to me, she will never know how my last days were spent.*

He dressed quickly in stolen clothes and went back to the office. Rebecca and George were still sitting in front of the television.

"I'm sick of seeing 'breaking news'," George said. "I can't wait until they've nothing new to show."

Fin found a notepad with a few empty pages left and a

packet of plastic folder pockets. He took one out and put Leanne's note safely inside it, to protect it until the intended readers came home. It seemed so precious; if her family survived, this would give them closure. Solene deserved that, at the very least. He closed the door over to drown out the news report. Leaning over the page, staring at the pristine, blank space, he did not know what to say.

'What do I say to you?' He wrote that down to start with and then crossed it out and turned to a fresh page.

'This letter is frozen in a moment and in it I am thinking of you. For all the moments of my life to come, your memory will be with me, until I am with you again. I hope that this letter might bring you peace, if you read it. If I'm handing this letter to you in person, that last sentence probably seems a bit dramatic. Then again, after the ink dries, you might never know what follows. I'm afraid all the time and I feel guilty and ashamed, that I am here without you. I don't know how to explain it. I wish that I could though, to lie in our bed and just talk. I have no idea where you are or how you're getting on. You are my home and without you I'm lost.'

When he started writing down memories they shared, he did not stop until his hand cramped and many pages had been filled with fondness. Suddenly, the few remaining pages in the notebook seemed unfit to house all the memories he had of her.

George and Rebecca left him alone. When he finished, he tore the pages from the notepad and put them inside a plastic pocket for protection.

"Is there any ink in that pen left for us?" George asked, when he showed them what he was doing.

"What are you going to do with it?" Rebecca asked.

"Leave it in our apartment, if I can. Should I die, then at least she will have this."

"Never imagined I'd be writing a last will and testament while I still had hair and my own teeth," George said. "Why did you not just record a video and send it to her?"

"I didn't think of it. My words come off better when I write them down anyway, I feel like more of me comes across. It wasn't a pleasant experience. Mostly I was asking for posthumous forgiveness for throwing my slippers at the cats when they annoyed me."

"In all seriousness," George said, taking on a no-nonsense attitude that fit him poorly, "town is far too dangerous to walk through for the sake of a letter. You're safe now. If you go in just to leave that in your old apartment, then it may as well be a suicide note. Would you just email it to her?"

"Why didn't I think of that either?" He was glad he could still make them laugh. "What are yous going to do while I'm gone?"

"Write letters, try to find my people online," Rebecca said. "My friends list is like a virtual mortuary. So many of them have not been active in a while."

"If I get a chance to take the train, I will. I'll come and find you after this ends."

"Come back if you don't," Rebecca stood up to hug him.

"Thank you for everything, I wouldn't have made it this far without you."

George changed the TV channel back to the game feed. He took the remote and unpaused the game. "Don't tell them where we are."

* * *

They spent the night playing games. After George kept the remote for five missions, they stopped taking turns after each death, instead playing a mission each. Rebecca was the first to turn in. George suggested Fin have the bed. He thought he would not sleep, but he nodded off in the warmth of the blanket, listening to the sonorous sound of Rebecca's snores and the reassuring comfort of George playing games. He could understand why George was upset with him. *Why spoil this?*

In the morning Fin could not bring himself to eat anything. The three of them watched the road for twenty minutes before they were sure it was empty. Birds still chirped in their roosts.

"Are you sure?" George asked.

"No, but what's that saying, comfort is the death of progress, or something like that."

"Nah mate, zombies will be the death of you. A hot water bottle to keep your tootsies warm at night won't do you any harm."

"I'm a coward, George, to be honest with you. I want nothing more than to nail that door shut behind me. Live off our supplies and play games until the power fails, but I can't hide from myself. I have to try."

"There's no shame in living." He handed him a backpack that he had worked on during the night, taping the straps down. "Keep living."

Fin hopped over the gate, regretting that their last view of him was him struggling. There was no way of knowing what it was like in front of the hotel, but he kept the key to the lobby warm in his fist, should he need it. His pack was light: he had water, but little food. George insisted on it, in case they questioned him. He could say hunger drove him from his shelter.

Despite everything, it was a nice morning and he tried to enjoy that and not focus on the stares from Rebecca and George peeking over the gate, looking like they would never see him again. His heart felt lighter now that he carried it on a few pieces of paper, tucked away in his pocket.

19

THE BUTCHER VAN

Fin kept to the shadows where the sun had not yet reached and slipped on black ice. He fell to his knees before the unfamiliar weight of his gear brought him down on top of it. Water dampened his trousers, but he stayed still until he was certain nothing heard him. Satisfied, he opened his pack, dug out the kitchen knife he stole from the house and threw it into the ditch. If he fell on the hammer, he could survive a bruise.

The knife struck a stone in the ditch. The little noise it made was like a tuning fork setting the pitch of the weeping that started behind him. Turning sharply, Fin nearly slipped on the ice again. He saw the shadow of an adult weeper, sprinting down the drive of a house with an open door. The safehouse was too far away; the weeping was already picked up by others, like a pack of wolves. In that moment, he gave up. The knife was lost in the weeds.

Fin slipped his arms from the rucksack. The weight of the hammer seemed inconsequential in his hand. The weeper had been a woman. She barreled onto the road and searched both ways. Too late, he realised he could have hid in the ditch. In her haste to reach him, she lost her footing on the ice. Tearing at the frozen grass, she pulled herself up.

Run! With the ice he had a chance. His fist tightened around the hotel key. The weeping of the infected woman roused others around him. The countryside was suddenly alive with anguish. *I'm not going to make it, Solene.* Her letter was safe in his pocket with his bank cards. At least they could put a name on his grave. *If I make it to the pier I can swim to Westport House.* He was not sure if the cold would kill him, but he was certain the weepers would.

Back on the main road, she started gaining on him. These streets were better and less slippery. Fin slid over the bonnet of a car that had been abandoned behind a crash. He weaved between another one, trying to break line of sight. Daring a quick glance back he watched her feet fly out from under her. She slipped on the ice between the cars. Her head struck the ground with a sickening crunch. Her weeping stopped.

Stories about the banshee had haunted his childhood. The keening noise the infected made brought back that deep fear of facing something that could not be reasoned or bargained with.

Tall buildings kept the ice on the road, and it slowed him to a careful jog. He just had to stay ahead of them. Five emerged from alleyways and homes, racing each other to reach him. There was no time to get to the hotel and the road to the pier was full of them. *Get to Westport House.* If there were infected on the road between him and the gates to the camp – he did not want to think about it.

There was no way of knowing if the bodies sprawled on the road were thoroughly dead. Passing holiday homes and a block of apartments, it dawned on him that if there were sentries at Westport House, then they would likely be itching to shoot at anything running towards them.

"I'm not infected!"

The silence that returned was not reassuring. The closer he came to the gate, the less certain he was that anybody still lived beyond it. *Maybe they've all gone to Dublin.* Moments from reaching it, he was certain it was too high for him to climb. They would pull him down before he made it.

Cars were parked across the road to create a maze that the undead would have difficulty navigating. The morning light melted most of the ice here. They were quickly gaining on him. Fin tried calling out one last time. There was no movement on the walls or behind the gate. If he ran down the slipway into the water, they would have him in the shallows. He turned, fighting against every instinct not to. Hammer ready. More infected joined the ranks, coming down the hill from town. The slower ones did not seem to be much of an issue by themselves, but the sheer number would quickly overwhelm him. He could already imagine their teeth cutting into his flesh. Biting and beating him until their attacks elicited no more response.

Three cars away, two. Fin climbed onto the roof of an SUV. They would be able to swipe at his legs, but he hoped he could cave in a few skulls before the end.

"Come on!"

The closest zombie fell. The bark of the shot only registered as gunfire a few seconds later. He dropped to his knees on the roof of the SUV. "I'm not infected!"

"If you don't shut up, I'll leave you out there and you will be. Keep it down, you'll bring half the town down on us." A soldier lowered a metal ladder over the wall. Fin dropped off the roof and ran for it before the ladder touched the ground. He ducked when another shot was fired. Halfway up the ladder he looked behind him. A zombie was lying on the road twitching. Another one spun and fell. The bullet tore muscle and bone from its shoulder. The metal rungs of the ladder sang as he ran up them. He rolled across the top of the ivy covered wall, clutching vines to keep him in place.

"Right out of the frying pan, bucko," the soldier clapped him on the back and took an appreciative look at the crowd of infected. "Some shower of bastards, the lot of you."

Fin lay low on the top of the wall, gulping down air. "Thank you."

"You won't be thanking me if you're infected. No, actually, I take it back, the death we'd give you will be much cleaner than the one they had for you."

Fin helped the soldier pull the ladder back. Weepers tripped over their own feet, looking up at them while still running. Fin heard a jaw snap shut and the brittle porcelain click of teeth chomping together. A bit of dirt and grime was all that separated the people on one side of the wall from those on the other. Dim eyes stared at them. Most of the infected did not have the sense to reach up for them. With the weeping, they just looked desperate. The sight of them was maddening. *You can barely tell the desperate and the dead apart, not until you hear them weeping and by then it's likely too late.* The soldier spat at them, then set the ladder against the inside of the wall and began climbing down. Fin followed, but before he reached the bottom, he was pulled off. The ladder fell with a clatter and he was forced into the wet leaf litter.

"Are you infected?" Another soldier pushed his knee into Fin's back to stop him from rising.

"No."

"Take off the pants and jumper. I need to check for bites."

Fin complied without complaint. It gave him time to look around. The gatehouse was a hive of activity. Net curtains were pulled over so those inside could see what the commotion was all about. Most of the people there looked awkward holding knives, hammers, crowbars and axes. Uniforms were rare.

"Save the ammunition," said the man who pulled Fin from the ladder.

"Ah, come on, Burke. It's better in them than it is sitting idle here. There's only a few of them left." Fin followed the voice coming from the canopy. A woman lay on a wooden platform built on the branch of a tall tree. Her rifle aimed down the road.

"All you're doing is slowing them down for us," the soldier who dropped the ladder down said, raising good-natured laughter.

Weepers reached the gate. They tried to push them-selves through the gaps, distorting their faces grotesquely. Instructors in masks and protective clothing lined civilians up in front of the infected. Wood had been placed to neck height to stop them reaching through. The first zombie was downed by a woman in a long black jacket, frizzy hair and running makeup. It brought a cheer from the crowd and others joined in. Within minutes the sick were inhumanely hacked to second death.

The soldier called Burke took no interest in the slaugh-ter. "I told you to take off your clothes."

Fin stripped down until he was only wearing boxers and socks. He lifted his arms. His skin bubbled with goose-bumps, more from the chase than the cold. Burke ripped the mask from Fin's face. He held his breath, paranoid that the disease was in the air. Standing there with his face exposed seemed more taboo than wearing only underwear.

"Anybody know him?" Burke asked.

Buzzed from the slaughter of infected, the civilians barely paid any heed to him. All shook their heads. It just dawned on him that some of the regulars that drank in the hotel bar were sometimes sober enough to remember him. He saw no familiar faces. *Surely they wouldn't kill me for working there.* Two people checked every inch of his exposed skin and asked him to hold up his boxers.

Burke used his muddy boots to stamp on the pockets of his jacket to search it. It was over in a few moments and he could put his clothes back on. They were damp from the ground. The hostile atmosphere dissipated when the all-clear was sounded. "Are you from here?"

Fin's heart rate had yet to slow. "What does that matter?"

"Sorry for that welcome," the soldier from the wall nudged the human hemorrhoid away. "I'm Jason Lynch. Where are you from?"

"Drogheda."

"You're far from home."

"Feels like I've never been further. Thanks for the help. I thought it was over there."

"How did you know there were people here to ask not to shoot?"

Fin had just about gotten his breath back. "I've been up in the hills along the coast. I heard gunfire and saw the army working at the pier. Thought they might help."

"You didn't see them come back," Burke grumbled.

"Have you slept lately?"

"The world could be ending and I'd still try for my eight hours."

Lynch snorted. "Come in and get something to drink, the kettle's always on for people coming in. Do you take tea or coffee?"

"He'll need something stronger," somebody said, walking into the house without looking at Fin.

Sleeping bags covered the floor in the cramped building. He heard snoring behind closed doors. Boxes of tea were stacked on the counter, next to jars of instant coffee, more empty than full.

"How long have you been here?" Fin asked.

Lynch rinsed two cups in the sink and plopped two tea bags in each. A mound of used ones mouldered in the sink. The kettle still steamed from its last use. "We were deployed not long after it started. We were to quarantine Castlebar – didn't think there were enough rounds of ammunition in Ireland to purge that place. We were tasked with setting up safe zones to move survivors and stem the tide of infected. Like trying to get firewood to grow with nothing but wishful thinking. Town is still full of people in their homes but we let them know that when they run out of food, they are more than welcome to join us here."

"So long as they're not bitten," somebody in a sleeping bag beneath the table added. She shivered despite the heat.

"What's it like out there now?" a man asked. Fin was almost certain he worked in the supermarket.

Everyone went quiet, the sound of rustling sleeping bags stopped. Most of the survivors kept their face masks on.

"This is the most people I've seen in one place for a while. I can't see how it could get worse. Are we going to be evacuated?"

"Nowhere to go to. We're here until it's over, so settle in. We've started a quarantine for new arrivals. Had a few nasty incidents before that policy. Bites aren't the only way to become infected." Lynch downed his tea, rinsed his cup under the tap and left it upside down on the draining board. Fin left his tea untouched on the table.

"You said you slept last night, well you've a choice. Head out with the butcher vans. Saves one of the regulars doing it. When you come back, I'll make sure you're looked after."

George mentioned these were becoming work camps. "What's the other option?"

"You spend twenty four hours in a shipping container."

"So I'd be a prisoner?"

"Not at all. You're more than welcome to go back over the wall whenever you like. It sounds bad but we've a lot of children in here, this is a precaution to keep them safe. This whole operation is about keeping people alive. If you don't see the good in that, well, you'd not be welcome here."

"I only wanted to know what the other option was. I'll give a dig out in the vans, I don't mind."

"Drink up then, they'll be heading soon."

* * *

Lynch escorted him through the grounds. The land bridge separating the lake from the bay was barricaded with fences and parked cars. They walked through the woods along the shore. Felled trees littered the path.

Lynch followed his gaze. "It's to slow the infected if they get in."

"What if they get in and people have to run at night?"

"There's a curfew in camp, but to be honest with you, if they breach the walls, then that's it for us. There's nowhere else for us to go. We're all waiting on transport home."

"Any good news from my neck of the woods?"

"There is no good news."

Westport House was completely transformed: large generators stacked in rows outside the building, floodlights mounted on the roof, pointing in every direction. The grounds were alive with activity. In front of fences, heavy machines dug deep trenches and piled the dirt into steep embankments. Walkways were created using scaffolding, and soldiers patrolled, keeping constant watch over the civilians in the fields.

"They fortified a hotel in the woods. It's where most people sleep. We're planning on spreading out into the buildings on the quay. We can't ship people out fast enough, or bring enough supplies to keep us all. It'll be a modern-day castle by the time we're finished with it."

"Can you protect a space this large? What about the car park? It just has wire fence, the wall only goes so far."

"That's the truth of it and the worry is all of our efforts won't matter if we don't have enough people to defend the walls. We got fences up quick enough and are reinforcing them."

"What about the noise?"

"Necessary. We're racing against the infected coming from Galway and Dublin."

Fin searched the man's face, desperate to find any hint of joking. Throughout the wood he heard chainsaws chewing through living trees, the crack and snap of those that fell.

"Our recently qualified bricklayers used to be electricians, bakers and bankers. What were you before this?"

"Bartender," Fin lied. "What's going on in the house?"

"Command centre, infirmary and sleeping quarters."

"Infirmary, do you treat the infected too?"

"No, they get seen to elsewhere."

"There's a cure?" Fin sounded too optimistic even to his own ears.

"If you get sick, you have the option of a bullet before you start weeping or after."

Fin regretted ever leaving the loft. He imagined Rebecca and George watching movies on the futon.

Humvees, container lorries, trucks and oil tankers filled the gravel in front of the house. Cars, tents and people wore the grass of the gardens and fields into a muddy brown mess. Lynch slowed down. "You mentioned you're from Drogheda. Even if you didn't tell anybody, the accent is a dead giveaway that you're not from here. Try and keep that to yourself. If you can't hide the accent, speak as little as possible. Don't worry about standing out, a lot of people here have stopped talking."

"What happens if they find out that I'm not a local?"

"You'll be conscripted for a nasty job. Only difference between you and the soldiers will be training. Discipline, however, has no apprenticeship here. Welcome to the Irish Army."

"You're from Donegal?"

Lynch nodded. "I'll be heading home as soon as relief comes in from Dublin."

"You have family there?"

"Every last one of them."

The house was reflected in the lake. The imposing, impenetrable stone had weathered centuries; it only had to hold out a little longer. The swan-shaped pedalboats tethered to the jetty gently jostled. Hungry blackbirds tossed the leaf litter, before children collecting wood for the fires chased them away. *How will they remember this atrocity?*

The river feeding the lake was dark and dangerous, swollen from the storms. Hi-tech water wheels spun in the current, connected to generators on the shore. Dozens of large, refrigerated containers occupied the field. A helicopter sat idle in the gravel path, protected by an armed guard. *Just one.* It was less a symbol of hope and more a fear that somebody other than yourself was going to get a seat.

"Don't let them catch you eyeing that up," Lynch said. "A few idiots were overheard talking about borrowing it to get to Dublin. They're walking now."

The butcher's shop was a converted shipping container. Workers dressed in bloody aprons hefted carcasses off hooks from frozen food delivery vans to the chopping block. Frosty air billowed out from ones left open. Fin could see sheep and cow carcasses hanging inside. He no longer wondered where the sheep that usually populated the fields had gone. Sawdust lined the ground, but it was far from clean.

"Sean, I've a fresh pair of hands for you."

A man looked up from a half-butchered carcass. Bone peeked through the blushing flesh. It looked pale as marble cut right from the earth. Sean had a belt of scabbards for long, sharp knives. He nodded his head to them in welcome. "Do you know where milk comes from?"

"I've a good idea," Fin said.

"You'll do then. You're not going to enjoy what must be done today, but it must be done. If it's any comfort, you'll not have any bother sleeping tonight, that's a promise. There's two days' worth of work to be done before your head touches a pillow."

"I haven't cut meat before, but I'm a quick learner."

The butcher eyed Lynch. "You weren't told what you'd be doing, were you?"

"Helping out at the butcher's van."

"This here is the easy work, but it requires a bit of skill to save on waste. You'll be heading into town with a guard, a driver and others to scavenge. Your job is to find pets that have been left behind and, if they haven't had access to infected meat, kill them and bring them back to me."

Suddenly a day in a cold container seemed the better option.

"Appears cruel, I know, but it's quicker than leaving them without food or water. If we let them wander freely, they spread the virus."

"It hasn't come to eating them just yet," Lynch said. "But it's better to be looking at fresh meat than for it."

"It's your first time, so you'll be with one of our butchers. Mostly you're valuable as an extra pair of eyes," Sean said.

"If you don't think it's for you, then make an impression on the guard. Nobody will turn down another scavenger. There's plenty of work regardless of what you do," Lynch said. "I'll leave you to it. Good luck."

Fin had little time to process things while following Sean to the vans. A seemingly endless conveyor belt of trucks came in, were unloaded into refrigerated containers, turned around and went back out again. Nobody took a second look at the hammer Fin carried. Others had shovels, bloodied hurley sticks, hatchets and knives. *How quickly things change.* He could see the danger of idleness, those few he noticed sitting or standing still had a glazed look to them, like they escaped the horrors of the past few days, only to revisit them in memory. *Walls can protect against only so much.*

Sean introduced him to Frank, his driver, a bald man with a head full of freckles and a worn jumper. He started when greeted, while guzzling something from a traveling mug. Stifling a burp, he said hello. From the smell in the cab, Fin assumed it was not coffee in the mug. Sarah, the butcher, was a curly-haired, austere woman, who said little upon introduction. The scavengers Kayleigh and Emmet were a little younger than he was. He found their excitement at the prospect of breaking and entering a little disturbing.

Fin climbed into the back. Music played as soon as Frank turned the engine on. He had to shout over the noise to engage Fin in conversation. Remembering Lynch's advice, he kept his responses short, not letting his accent give him away. Frank lost interest and gave up before the first song ended. *What job could they possibly have me do, if they found out I was not local, that could be worse than killing pets?*

He pictured his three cats alone in the apartment. The thought of any harm coming to them made him shake. To lure them with a promise of food and then kill them. *Fair enough, if they would suffer, I understand it. The worst part is not being able to explain it to them.*

Since the soldier Burke stamped on his jacket, he wondered if his radio still worked. He imagined Rebecca and George in their redoubt, suring up its faults and exploring the area for supplies. *I don't feel safer yet. I'm here for information to send back to them before leaving. I can't do that if I stay quiet.*

They slowed to a stop in front of the main gate to town. The sheer number of people blocking their path was astounding. It was like the back end of a music festival. Frank held his hand above the car horn and caught himself before pressing it. "I tell you, you don't miss it until it's gone."

Not one person looked as if they had slept much. Gaunt, grief-stained faces scanned the new arrivals, hoping to see someone they knew. Heavy machinery dug trenches a few feet back from the walls, using the earth to reinforce the stone, any excess was poured into construction trucks.

"They fill dump trucks with soil and stone and empty them in front of the wire fences around the back of the grounds," Frank said, when he noticed what Fin was looking at.

"Is it enough, do you think?"

Frank glanced in the rear-view mirror. "It will have to be. Work goes on round the clock. If the infection stays out another while longer, then yeah, we'll be able to sleep a bit easier here at night."

The walls looked more decorative than defensive. Fortification around the main gate was more impressive: high fences and sharp wire manned by soldiers with rifles and high-beam lights.

"It feels like a warzone," Fin said.

Sarah finally broke her silence. "In war you might be awarded some quarter. There is no rest here."

"You're a ray of sunshine," Frank said.

A soldier approached the van and opened the door beside Fin. He moved over to make room for her. She stood her rifle between her boots. "Hello, New Face."

Fin nodded in response but did not have to worry about making further conversation. She turned and looked out the window. Two soldiers waved them through the gate. Outside, a line of people stood in their underwear, clutching their clothes for warmth. Inspectors in hazmat suits checked them for bites and scratches. They waded through a trough of disinfectant and were sprayed down with a strong smelling solution. The van jostled as it went through a bath for the tires. Vehicles entering the camp were washed.

They passed a few people down the street who were putting their clothes back on. A man was shaking so much that he could not button his shirt. One woman sat on the kerb, her head resting on her knees, she clung to her legs. Fin was staring at the bandage on her arm. He did not notice she was watching him until their eyes locked.

He turned in his seat to hold her gaze until she was out of sight. Her eyes were red from crying or the infection, he was not sure. *How can people just leave her there?* Nobody offered comfort or help. Other survivors left a wide berth between them and the living infected. He tried to catch the eye of the others in the van, but they pointedly ignored him. It was not their first time in town.

Fin put his hand over his mouth and bit into the side of it, putting every effort into holding back tears. He imagined a scene like that somewhere in the country, only it was Solene alone, invisible in a crowd, waiting to die.

20

CRUEL TO BE KIND

Snipers on the rooftops kept a constant vigil over the rejected refugees. The commotion made it seem like they were on a busy construction site, vehicles in a constant slow procession, leaving and entering the camp. When George had told him that they put you to work, he did not imagine the world had devolved so quickly, that survivors were now labourers. *Labourers are survivors.*

"They only give us enough fuel to get where we're going and back again," Frank said. "Sure, you could try siphon some out of other vehicles, but they only hire drivers with family inside the camp."

Fin looked over at the soldier from the corner of his eye. She took no offence to what Frank was saying. *Take the uniforms away, what do you see? The same despair as the rest of us.*

Abandoned cars were pushed onto the sidewalk and into the middle of the road in some streets. Traffic and people were all funneled one way. Shops, pubs and restaurants all had their Christmas opening hours displayed in windows. Most of the buildings showed signs of forced entry; one apartment had fingers of black scorch marks reaching from its burnt out husk. Looters had pried open all the shutters keeping them from food.

The pavement was littered with cigarette butts, a few used nappies, food wrappers, chewing gum and trash. Piles of rubbish bags mouldered in front of buildings. Excrement was mostly hidden by soiled tissue paper. Fin could not imagine relieving himself in front of others. *Then again, I'd rather that than being out of view and far from help.* A man sat on a bench overlooking the river, drinking cans of beer. He greeted passing refugees with a smile.

The moment they were beyond the gate, Frank turned the radio off. He continued the song by humming it from memory. His wedding ring clicked against the steering wheel as he nervously tapped out the beat. Fin had never felt the presence of silence so poignantly. He opened his window to let noise in. He smelled the smoke before he saw the pyre of burning bodies, a scaffolding of spent flesh. High fences hid the worst of it from view. Workers in sealed suits closed the gate after bags of clothing were tossed into the flames. It passed from view so quickly that he wondered if it even existed.

Bodies littered the streets outside town, the blood stains beneath them dark and old. Too many to be afforded immolation – they would drown the fire. Crows and other scavengers were doing their part. People had tried to cover them with tarps, tablecloths and bedding, but they were the first ones to die. Workers threw bodies onto the back of flatbed trucks. Armed soldiers escorted each group.

Frank pointed at a massive column of black smoke in the distance. "That's the first burning field they opened. It's like the plague. People wrap up their loved ones and leave the bodies on the side of the road to be collected. Ain't no way to treat the dead."

The comment made the soldier turn away from the window. "Frank, once the dead stop disrespecting us, we'll go back to respecting them. If they would voluntarily walk into their graves, I'd happily put wreaths on them all."

Fin watched the faces of the corpses with morbid fascination; all of these suffered head trauma, making them seem less real. *With so many gone, this will be a silent land.* Some survivors blessed themselves as they passed bodies and Fin found it difficult to understand how those that had faith before the outbreak managed to hold on to it now. Houses were emptied in an orderly fashion, everything of use was loaded into trucks and brought back to the camp. Fuel caps dangled open on every car they passed.

"That's not a job I'd fancy," Frank nodded at the groups collecting fuel. They had a much larger force protecting them. "Nobody is paying much attention to the fact the roads are mostly impassable, they only see the army taking away their means of escape."

"To go where?" Fin asked.

"Anywhere but here." Frank stopped at the entrance to a housing estate. As soon as they got out, he lit up a cigarette and locked the doors. "Pet food's in the boot," he said to Fin, through the window.

Sarah threw him a backpack and he filled it from crates of dog and cat food. She put a bandolier of canisters on and strapped a bolt gun to her waist.

"Are the injections not more humane?"

"Can't eat them then," she gave him a grim, sardonic grin.

"I don't want to do this."

Sarah put a gloved hand on his shoulder. "You and me both. I'm a veterinarian."

"How can you do it?"

"If I don't and somebody more eager and less skilled does, the animals suffer. Our job today is to ensure that none leave this world without a bit of kindness. All you need to concern yourself with is feeding them and giving them a little bit of love, before I do my job. You can do that."

The soldier brought them together. "My name is Muireann, shout and I'll be there. The estate has been swept for weepers, but we still have to approach every door with the belief that there is a hungry horde waiting behind it. Don't go far from each other. It's one house at a time. The quicker we get things done, the faster we'll be back behind the gate."

"You want us to shout?" Fin said.

"Yes. If there is trouble, the undead will be drawn to your shouting and I'll have an easier time of getting home. Let's go."

Across the street people lined up for a mini-bus, their shift over. Fin did a double-take: he recognised somebody, a middle-aged man with a well-defined paunch. Fin never saw him without his wife. They were regulars in the bar for a late Sunday lunch of pints. He was even wearing his usual weekend suit, though it was dirty and torn. He did not know their names, instead referring to them by their orders. *Your man who always asks "Have you pulled any Guinness today?" and his wife 'G&T with no ice'*. The man never looked up to answer Fin's stares. He was hunched over, chest rising noticeably, like all he could focus on was breathing.

They walked past an armed guard, his expression hidden behind the mask. "Are they stopping people from leaving?" Fin asked.

"They're here for your protection," Sarah's voice was so low that Fin was not sure if he imagined the scorn.

With the weight of the task ahead, all he heard was the sound of dogs barking across town. It was incessant, driven by the wailing weep of infected and the screams of those they hunted. Those noises were a distant but constant presence. *How many pets are there in town? In the country? Will the death toll after this ends be so high that it can only ever be an estimate?*

"There's a team of electricians ahead of us that deal with alarms," Sarah said.

Her voice shook him out of his secret thoughts of running away: sneaking off to use the bathroom and heading back to George and Rebecca. *No. I need to go home.*

The garden gate of the first house sighed shrilly on its hinges and the front door opened. An elderly man stood on the porch. Muireann pushed by Fin, rifle raised.

"Are you here to help? Is it over?" The relief on his face was painful to see.

"I'm afraid not, sir," Muireann lowered her weapon. "We're bringing survivors to Westport House, you'll be safe there."

A team across the road broke open the front door of a building and entered. The man's expression soured. "Bunch of thieves."

"Sir, we're not going to enter your property. All we're doing is taking food, medicine and the essentials from empty buildings and bringing it to those that need it. We've a bus at the entrance to the estate, please join us. You'll be given a room in the hotel," Muireann said.

"Leave me in peace, the radio said avoid crowds. Get off my property, please." He hesitated before closing the door, possibly afraid he was burning his last bridge.

"You know where we are." Muireann led them back out the garden path and closed the gate behind them. They went right next door. She rang the bell. The man from the first house watched them through his net curtains.

"You'd think he would jump at the chance," Fin whispered. People came out of houses further down the street with packed suitcases, running to catch the bus. Volunteers took their luggage and stacked it in trucks. Before they were out of view, scavengers were already entering their homes. Some of them had cat carrier cages and dogs on leashes. "What about those?"

"We let people bring them along. Killing family pets in front of children tends to hamper good relations," Muireann said.

They rang the doorbell again, but nobody answered. Emmet broke the lock with two swings of a sledgehammer. When the door flew open, they stood back, ready for one of the infected to rush out. The house was empty. Fin wiped his feet on the worn welcome mat.

Muireann checked each room before she let them in. Once they were sure it was clear, they separated into groups, two people per room. There were no pets, and Fin gladly helped search the house for anything they could use. Sarah emptied the press beneath the sink, bagging bottles of bleach and hand wash. The room smelled of stale smoke and potpourri. Fin filled a bag with tins of tuna in brine, boxes of cornflakes, porridge and pasta.

An orange in the fruit bowl was shrunken and green with mold.

"How long do you think it will be until we have lemons again?" Sarah asked.

"I can't remember the last time I used lemon when it wasn't for a drink," Kayleigh said.

"I was thinking more along the lines of lemon-zested pancakes."

"Next person that mentions food that does not come from a can will be shot," Muireann said.

It only took them a few minutes to bag everything of use from the house. Fin found an old biscuit tin full of money in the nightstand. He put it back with care. *The owner did not plan to leave, they might be dead then.* On a last sweep back through the house, he saw the tin open and empty, tossed on the bed. *Muireann carried ammunition and her weapon. Sarah was with me. It was Kayleigh or Emmet. Why take it? It's useless now.*

They left the spoils on the roadside to be collected by others. Fin brought the house plants he found and left them in sheltered places, out of the wind but where they would get a bit of rain. Most were too long without water, and he held them all under the tap to soak the soil.

"The cold will kill them," Muireann said.

"Then it'll be faster than dying of thirst inside."

They competed against the team across the road to see who could clear the most houses. Each subsequent home took less time to sack than the last. They came across their first animal in the fourth house: a small shaggy-haired mongrel, curled up in its basket, surrounded by squeaky toys. It was clear by the smell in the house that he was gone, but Sarah knelt to examine him, and stroked his head. Out of all the things he had seen, this scene would linger: the empty food bowl, the chewed boxes of food and desperate scratches on the door, the torn window curtains.

"Did nobody hear him barking?" Fin asked. "The street is full of people."

"It's not their fault," Sarah said. "They're terrified." When she turned around, she saw the consternation on

Fin's face and smiled. "You know what, I'm going to take great pleasure in firing you."

"I don't know how you do it."

"Necessity."

He found it much easier to empty this house. Any owner who could leave their pet trapped to starve did not deserve the respect of closing cupboards after he opened them.

Near the end of the estate there was a concentrated collection of corpses. Loud barking in the back garden had drawn the undead, but they had no way of reaching through the gate. Fin skipped a few houses to get a look at the dog. It growled when it first saw him, but quickly started whining and yapping. *Can it tell I'm not infected?* The massive labrador paced against the gate. Fin slowly approached, opening a can of food and holding it out.

The dog's tongue lolled and his tail wagged warily. He snarled his teeth when Fin came on too fast. There was a large kennel and a pond at the back of the building.

Before he could reach the dog, he was yanked backwards off his feet, the can of food falling to the ground. Muireann stood over him. "Can't touch that one, too dangerous. There are wounds on those bodies. We'll do it through the bars."

"Can I feed him at least?"

"Those are to distract them while we do the business. It won't matter."

"You think the headstone is for the one occupying the grave?" Sarah said to Muireann.

Muireann pulled a warning face, but relented with a nod and let Fin pick up the can. He threw a stick over the wall to get the dog to move away. It was emaciated and did not run, instead he shuffled after it in case it was food. Fin emptied the tin onto the ground inside the gate. The labrador dropped the stick when he saw the food and yapped. The pile of food was gone in a matter of bites.

"Head on to the next house," Muireann said. "You too, Sarah, the bolt is too short for this."

Emmet knocked and tried the door. It was unlocked. Muireann fired one shot which made them all jump. "Let's pick up the pace," Sarah said. "All this noise is bound to draw them."

Kayleigh took particular pleasure in opening Christmas presents. She found nothing of use, but she pocketed some of the finer jewellery and phones. Fin emptied presses in the kitchen, while Emmet sorted through the fridge for anything still edible. "Best part about this detail," he said with a mouthful of pudding.

A shout from upstairs caused Emmet to choke. Fin dropped a school report he was reading and fumbled for his hammer.

"Sarah!" Muireann ran through the front door and tore up the stairs. They knew by the scream that they were too late.

Emmet ran out the front door, quickly followed by Kayleigh. Fin followed after Muireann, she turned right into a bedroom. Fin tripped on the stairs when he heard the gunshot. Inside the room, the body of a teenage boy lay motionless on the ground. He was wearing headphones when he turned. They came off in the fall. Light shining through a crack in the curtains showed pillars of falling dust. Fin held his breath. Muireann examined the wound on Sarah's arm.

"Check the other rooms!" Muireann said when she noticed Fin gawking.

Sarah was transfixed by the wound on her arm and the small pricks of blood seeping through the sleeve of her jumper. He went through the rest of the house. There was nobody else.

"I'm so sorry, Sarah, I should have gone in first."

"It's okay, Muireann. Let's go," her voice skipped.

Fin stood awkwardly on the landing, unsure of what to say when he saw her. She held her bitten arm delicately. Muireann helped her down. She looked like a scolded child.

Sarah sat on the edge of a lorry trailer. She looked up into the sky, her teeth grinding. Every kind of emotion showed on her face. Fin tried to imagine what his last thoughts would be. Right now, all he could focus on was how cold it was.

"Fin, come here to me." She handed the belt for the bolt gun to him and showed him how to use it and reload the gas canisters. "You never want them to feel any pain, be quick. Always aim for the centre. Watch." She lifted it to the side of her skull and pulled the trigger. Gas hissed as the bolt shot out. Her eyes lost focus; one rolled back into her head. She collapsed, her back arched and her legs spasmed. She was still alive and making noise.

"Get out of the way," Muireann fired once from her handgun. Sarah stopped moving. "I would have done it for you."

Fin did not want to take the bolt gun. He made no promise to her, but Muireann handed it to him.

"Let's go, we've done enough for today," Muireann said.

"Are we just leaving her?" Fin asked.

"There's another group that deals with the bodies."

He was too numb to respond. Frank waited for Sarah to get back in the van. When she did not, he looked at their faces in the rear-view mirror, let out a sigh and started the engine.

21

MERCY

The trip back through town felt longer. Earlier, the sight of so many soldiers felt like a comfort of sorts. Now that he knew just how easily their weapons could be turned on him, they were a much more ominous presence. *Was the little haul of salvage worth a life?* He looked for somebody to blame. *Emmet did not wait long enough before entering. Kayleigh was too busy filling her pockets with useless trinkets. I was snooping.* With nowhere to put the anger, he internalised it.

Frank drove past the Garda station, the barricade by the front door was reinforced. Most of the upper windows had been broken by stones. Wooden boards blocked the guts of the building from view. People had graffitied slogans on the side of the station, things like 'Inhuman', 'Scum', 'Dead Inside'. Fin could see somebody standing in the shadows of an upstairs window. "Did you get the cops to come out?"

Frank rolled down his window and spat. "They never left. When we asked for help, they said the station was overrun with infected, that a few survivors were keeping the doors locked to hold them in. Lies. Then when we begged, they shot at us. That place is a fortress, but they're under siege by the living and the dead. They show their heads around town, they'll be shot on sight for what they've done. The real officers died protecting us, doing their jobs. Those in there are moral paupers in stolen clothes."

Fin was only half-listening. In a few moments they would pass the car park behind his apartment. A bubble of bile floated at the back of his throat when he considered abandoning the crew. Nobody spoke out of respect for the recently fallen member of the team. *I don't want there to be only silence that follows my death.* Solene's note weighed heavily in his pocket. As the car passed the entrance to the car park, Fin's mouth made up his mind before he could second-guess himself. "Stop!"

Frank slammed on the breaks, making the seatbelts cut into the passengers. Fin opened the door and ran, avoiding the few bodies he found on the road. He did not look back. Nobody shouted after him; nobody much cared for strangers these days.

He sprinted past cars, keeping low. Rebecca's car was still there, though her boot was open and the supplies they had left behind were gone. The door to his apartment complex courtyard was still broken. He stepped over the shattered glass and pile of tables and chairs, an ineffective barricade. He hid at the top of the stairs, out of view of the street, and waited. After a while something passed the door on the street below, a staggered shuffle, like somebody defeated by drink after a night on it.

Fin watched the apartments next to his for any sign of movement. After about half an hour, he opened the door to the courtyard wide enough to crawl through. He crept over the wet paving slabs beneath windows, keeping low and out of sight.

The key to his apartment was slippery from the sweat of

his palm. He stood, turned the lock, walked inside and slid down the wall to the floor. He locked the door while hiding on his knees. *Safe.* The smell of the litter box made him gag. A brief silence was broken by the patter of little paws across tile and wood. The three cats stopped at the top of the stairs, but when they saw him, they nearly tripped in their haste to be near him. They mewled incessantly.

Flo flopped onto her side for a rub. Poncho chomped as Fin scratched behind his chin, while Mooch dug his claws into Fin's trousers.

"I'm sorry, guys."

Fin fed them with the tins of wet food and the bag of kibble he had taken from the butcher's van. The cats were only quiet when their mouths were full. While they ate, he emptied their litter boxes and cleaned them out with bleach before refilling them. The downstairs window in the front bedroom was open, little pawprints muddied the floor. *They may have brought the infection in with them.* Fin kept his mask on.

He disinfected the counters and chairs and mopped the floor. Most of the kibble he had spilled onto the ground for them was gone. He rinsed out their bowls and filled them again.

The bolt gun felt like a toy in his hand. *No wonder Sarah was able to use it so flippantly on herself. If not for Muireann's bullet, how long would she have suffered?*

Fin filled the kettle and made a strong coffee. The cats went to their baskets, but kept an eye on him, for fear he might disappear. The washing machine was still full of clothes that he had forgotten to take out; he slammed its door closed after opening it and getting a noseful of the smell of mould. The fridge still hummed and the water heater had been on this whole time. It brought a smile to his face thinking that the electricity company would have a hard time finding him. More than likely they would manage to get a strongly worded warning letter to him. He put his letter for Solene on the kitchen table. It looked out of place, safe and crinkled in a plastic pocket. The surroundings were unchanged since she last stood here. Fin was tired beyond exhaustion. Body weary, he sat down in the shrine to the old world.

The coffee was cold when he woke. At one point he thought to put the games console on and disappear in a story, be the hero and defeat the enemies, earn the digital trophies and savour that momentary, artificial success: restart when he was overwhelmed, change the difficulty if it became too hard to handle.

Photos of him and Solene leered at him from the walls. Fin packed all of their photos into a plastic pocket and hid them at the bottom of his wardrobe. He kept one of Solene. *I wish I had taken more.*

While pouring his coffee down the drain, movement in the apartment across the alley caught his eye. He ducked out of sight, giving it a few minutes before standing enough to peek out the window. The couple in the apartment were long dead, the infection had robbed them of their humanity. They aimlessly wandered around the sitting room, not straying far from the light of the television.

What are their names again? If we had not been so selfish and just told them to join us, they might still be alive. They could be in the safehouse with George and Rebecca. No, they were a liability. He did not believe it. *If they were alive, would they be ransacking homes, culling the infected or killing animals? Are they better off?* He was not sure. *At least they were together in the end.*

The plants he had thrown across had been picked apart, not even the stems stuck out of the soil.

"Hey!" he roared at them. The cats bolted from their beds. The neighbours walked to the window, their milky, glazed, bloodshot eyes locked on his. Beneath the window, weepers stirred. He despised every last one of them. He shut the blinds, hoping he would soon be forgotten. Now he could pretend that the noise outside was from shoppers; maybe if he had something stronger than coffee in the house, he might have been able to numb himself enough to treat them with the indifference reserved for normalcy.

Mooch was first. Fin picked him up and set him on his lap. The cat had a little white stripe of fur down his front, contrasted against the black. He looked like a little gentleman in a tuxedo. When he meowed it sounded like a chirping bird. Those sweet, curious and full eyes always made him look like he was stoned, wired on the world. He nuzzled Fin's hand, nudging him for more scratches. Fin rested his forehead on the cat's. "I'm sorry for every slipper I ever threw at you and for those times when I accidentally stepped on your foot. I'm sorry I couldn't do more." Fin held a knife to Mooch's neck and carefully cut away the bell collar. "That's all I can do for you. Stay safe, I'll find you when this is over." He kissed the cat and set him down. He called Flo over next.

They looked strange without their red collars. The fresh food he put out for them should last a week. After that, they were on their own. They sometimes brought mice back to the house. *Would they know that was food? Even still, their life of relative luxury is over. If they did not eat the bodies clogging the streets, then the wave of rodents gorging on them would certainly be on their menu. There's something: if we survive this, then the rats, plague and diseases will finish the job.*

Fin emptied the water from the bath and put the stopper back in. He tied a towel to the faucet before turning the tap on. The stream of hot water ran down the towel, making no noise as it filled the tub. Steam fogged the window. When it was full, he dropped a bath bomb in to fizzle. Normally he would lower himself in over the course of a few agonising minutes, while his skin turned red. Now, he did not mind the heat. He felt numb to it. The water came up to his chin, his knees stuck out like pale, barren islands.

Rifling through his bunched-up trousers, he pulled the radio from his pocket. "Hey guys."

"We thought you were dead." George sounded jubilant. "Glad to hear from you. What happened? Where are you?"

"How is it?" Rebecca asked.

"I think the world is ending." He told them everything he saw in the camp: the forced work in order to eat, the implied threat of being sent out to walk to safety if you don't comply with rules. So many people crammed together, it was like tinder beside a spitting fire. Rebecca cursed at his retelling of the butcher van and what they did to the pets. There was a silence after he told them about Sarah. "It was the right idea to leave the hotel, there are so many people that have been infected and are yet to turn. There's nothing stopping them from going into the hotels to turn, they've nothing to lose now."

"Come back to us lad, that place sounds mad," George said.

"I don't think I can make it back the way I came. The lane to the house is too cramped. Sure I was only down the road from you when the first weeper came at me. Have you had any trouble?"

Rebecca took the radio. "We've watched a few of them pass by. They ignore the house completely."

"I don't know that you can stay there long. They have teams scavenging the houses around town. They'll run out of things to take in the more built up areas and will be out that way soon."

"We can't stay? Are you still thinking of trying for Dublin?" Fin could read the disapproval in her tone.

"I don't think it's safe to wander the streets with the military out, they aren't keen on taking chances. The safest option for me now is to head back through Westport House. If they tell me there's no train, I can head through the grounds and avoid the roads. If there is a train – I have to try."

"Do you think they'll let you back in after bailing on them?" George asked.

"Well they're a lot easier to reason with than the infected, I'll make something up."

"Fair enough."

"Good luck. Let us know what the plan is and we'll help in any way that we can," Rebecca said.

They had little to report on their end. They had spent the day searching for supplies and shoring up the house as best they could. Fin put the radio down and slipped deeper into the water. All that effort spent trying to get home and he only managed to get back to where he started. They were not letting people go easily – workers were too valuable for that – but they were mouths to feed too and infected to deal with down the line. *Not even the soldiers seemed like they wanted to be there.*

Fin soaked up the warmth of the bath, dried off and dressed in his dirty clothes. If they did have an issue with him running off, and he wore a change of clothes, they could say he was looting. He doubted they would, but just in case. He did not open the door of the bedroom he shared with Solene. He had never craved anything as much as to curl up in their bed and smell her ghost on the pillows. He would not be able to leave that room.

Upstairs the cats were sleeping, he stroked them while they purred. Solene's letter was safe on the table. At least she would know his last thoughts. Everything he wanted to say to her was there, and he did not know how much it had weighed upon him. There was a sense of relief. He was free now to make his way back home and be with his family.

With full bellies they did not care to get out of their baskets when he readied to leave. He pushed the spare bedroom window open further and moved the bed in front of the door to keep it open. They were afraid of strangers; if Muireann and the scavengers came here, at least they could escape. He quietly locked the door behind him while the cats dreamed.

22

TOURIST

It took ten minutes to get to the gates of Westport House from his apartment. It was the route he used to walk to work, but now he had to avoid corpses on the street and the aimless wandering of the shell-shocked. Fin was not the only one beyond the wall on work detail, and he melted into the crowd of downcast workers and refugees. So long as he acted as normal as could be expected of somebody these days, the soldiers ignored him.

When he started down the road towards the gates of Westport House, he felt like he could not shake the stares of the snipers on the rooftops, their intent hidden behind masks. Fin slowed his walk to look casual, but sweat poured from his face. *What if they think it's because I'm sick?* The thought made him sweat more. Screens had been brought out to hide the new arrivals' semi-naked bodies from view while they waited to be searched. Everybody seemed to have to go through the process to gain entry.

Fin was about to take his jumper off in the slow procession when he heard a familiar voice. "I didn't think I'd see you again, New Face," Muireann said from behind the gate.

Standing in the frigid water trough of disinfectant, he shivered; he imagined the only reason there was not a layer of ice on top was because of how many people walked through it. Muireann walked up to the line, ignoring questions from others looking for answers. "What was that about earlier?"

"I had family to take care of." He handed her the bolt gun with the belt of gas canisters. Before leaving the house, he had thrown two of them in the bin, just in case she questioned his story. If she noticed this, she did not seem to care. He wondered how she could function so well after Sarah's death. Before the epidemic he had not really known grief, it was something he knew he would eventually have to become accustomed to, now he was stepped in it beyond saturation.

"You back for work, or what's your plan? Frank thought you went a bit mad."

"Frank, the guy with the easiest job in the whole county?"

Muireann smiled. "We're down a vet, have you lost your taste for it?"

Fin thought about being honest – that his sole intention was to get a train to Dublin and leave this place behind him – but he doubted any of the soldiers stationed here would have much sympathy for him. "I don't want to kill animals."

"That's probably why Sarah gave you the bolt gun. Point to think on, though, they're just meat now, the weepers are just meat and we are just meat. You kept a level head when you heard the scream. The others ran away when you went towards it. You listened to my instructions in the face of... under stress. Burke told me you're on trial, so if you come back, it's either a metal container for a few hours, or more work. I've another job in mind for you. Interested?"

"No, not in the slightest, but I don't want to be trapped in one of those boxes."

She turned to a soldier coming in from town. "Donal, take over here for me."

"Ah here, I'm only finished sweeping the perimeter."

"How are you with digging latrines?"

He gritted his teeth. "I'm far better at watching gates."

She seemed calm and in control, but Fin noticed the flare of her nostrils and the muscles twitching along her jawline. The stress was getting to all of them, they were as fractured and broken as the rest of the country, but they had to hide behind a cool façade. There was no way the death of Sarah on her watch was not plaguing her. *Good. If they can't keep people alive, then they should at least carry their memories.* Fin lost his train of thought when he tried again to remember the names of the people in the apartment across from his.

"Are you okay?"

"Just thought about something from back home. Wondered if I could have done anything differently."

"Maybe you should have, but nothing to be done about it now, except learn from it. Walk with me, you don't need to be checked for bites, you won't be in long enough to turn," she said.

"Am I going to like it?"

"No, you really won't."

The people they passed barely looked up at them, those that did begged for answers. "How many do you think will turn to religion?" Muireann asked. "If people do survive this, they'll be in a new dark age."

Fin thought about it for a moment and it seemed to ring through. The future as a whole had seemed so certain, like a road heading into fog. There was a slow progression of technological advancement that could be relied on. The potential for new wonders, in a world so full of them that people hardly noticed any longer. Now everything was uncertain. If they did get beyond this, the world to come was so different that it was unimaginable in his mind.

"To be honest with you, I find it hard to think too far ahead."

"Good for mindfulness that is, being present in the moment."

While walking, Fin had more time to see the people inside the grounds. Many without tents curled up beneath the bald canopy of trees, for cover from sporadic rain. The last real sanctuary is the mind, but the walking dead had already claimed that. This was no haven, it was an asylum for the living.

"What I do is a job at the end of the day," Muireann said. "We're going to clock out soon, later than most, but that's what we signed up for. We have one goal and then we go home, once this safe zone is established."

"Are all these people going with you?" Fin could not help noticing the eyes watching him, the groups of people that hushed when the soldier walked past, like they were the enemy.

"There's nowhere better in the country for them than right here. They don't know it, they've not seen what Ireland has become. People two counties over will flock here once we broadcast it is safe. For now, this is all we have. Look at them, they think we are their jailers. Our relief is due in from Dublin on the train later. There are specialists among them, engineers, architects, builders, farmers and teachers. They will turn this place into a fortress and this sorry lot into survivors."

"Who wants to be that, when they still think they will be returning to their old lives soon?" Fin said.

"What's keeping you going, then?"

"Guilt."

Muireann did not pry and Fin wondered what was in her past to make her so observant of these new silences.

"I wasn't much use in the butcher's van, what help do you think I can be?"

"You'll be dealing with the infected. Don't worry, you won't be getting close enough to feel sympathy or fear. I can teach you how to use a rifle." She hefted hers. "Each body you put down is possibly one life saved. Think of it that way, it's the only thing that helps me. You handled yourself well out there and not knowing many people here is why you're perfect for this job."

"What gave it away?"

"Your accent."

"Where are you heading after here?" Fin asked.

"I'm going to see if I still have a home. If I find my family, I'll bring them back here. I wasn't talking shite when I said this place could be something special."

The prospect of having a gun and knowing how to use it was appealing, stopping the infected before they had a chance to touch you. With the hammer, he had to wait until they were close enough to know if their breath was warm or cold.

Muireann brought him straight through the commotion in front of the house and up the front steps. He held his head down as he passed the butcher vans, but with masks on, nobody was easily recognisable. He was just another body amidst the dwindling living. Thinking of his cats in those ice boxes made his fists tremble. *I did the right thing. Right?*

Windows on the ground level of the house were boarded up and reinforced. A flight of stone steps to the main entrance would unbalance most of the infected and it was narrow enough that they would not gain entry by sheer weight of numbers. At the back of the hall was a marble staircase that split in two beneath the feet of an angel statue. Most of the doors were barricaded, or blocked with a wall of sandbags, fronted with spools of barbed wire. The parquet floor shrieked from the sheer number of people rushing across it. At the top of the staircase, a heavy machine gun on a tripod watched over proceedings.

Fin had lived in Westport for over a year, but this was his first time inside the house. Electric bulbs on a chandelier lit the grand entrance. Sabres and swords that once decorated the walls now stood in the umbrella stand by the door. Military crates hid every inch of skirting board. Someone, with a macabre sense of festive cheer, had placed boxes of ammunition beneath the Christmas tree.

Muireann brought him through to a long room with portraits of regal figures. So many windows, it would be a nightmare to defend if the zombies could climb. They walked through a light shower of disinfectant set up outside a field office. It smelled like harsh chemicals and stung when it ran into his eyes.

Soldiers were gathered around a table laden with computers, radios, helmets, rifles and food. Surrounding them were banks of monitors and people typing into computers. His breath caught when he saw the woman that had shot Ciara back at the hotel, the one that had given him the suicide pills. She showed no sign of recognition when Muireann stood before her. The air felt hot and stale behind his mask. The chemical shower hid the sweat now beading his forehead.

EOIN BRADY

"I've got one for special duty, sir," Muireann said.

"Are you infected?" the captain asked.

Fin shook his head, afraid to speak for fear she would remember the sound of his voice.

"Take off your mask, I hate them. So long as you don't sneeze on anybody, you won't be shot."

Fin slowly took it off. She walked around the table and stood before him, a hand outstretched.

"I'm Denise, but this lot call me Reverend."

Fin stammered, unsure if he had already used his real name. He shook her hand and did not give his own. He was not pressed for it. He recognised the soldiers from the back gate: Lynch, who had helped him escape the weepers, and Burke, who had stripped him down, almost hoping to find a bite mark.

"What we are trying to do is to create a wave breaker. The disease is spreading faster than we can deal with it. There are a lot of untrained bodies here and more weapons than my people have hands to wield. It's no secret that those that left for Dublin in a panic were stalled in the blockades, stuck in crowds with the disease spreading. They ran from their homes thinking to escape, only to be chased back by it." She shuddered, though he expected that was theatrics. "We're in contact with a settlement out on Clare Island. If we fail here, that's our fallback, but they have about as much interest in having us as we do in being on an island in the Atlantic in winter. We can't fail here."

"I've seen people try paddle out there in crab and fish boxes," Muireann said.

"I'm recruiting survivors from outside the town to defend the walls. You'd be amazed how calm people can be when they see somebody else in uniform is making the difficult decisions. I need more bodies to keep order. It's just a

248

contingency plan, in case things get worse. Soldiers aren't going to continue working when there's no government or country to defend."

She offered Fin a cup of coffee in a polystyrene cup. "This is a safe zone, we want people trained up to keep it that way."

Fin did not like that she was telling him all of this. "If things go tits up, won't this place run out of supplies?" he said. "You want people like me to keep guard on food and things like that?"

"There are safe zones across the country that foreign governments will continue to drop aid to. We can no longer use the helicopter, draws too much attention. So we get ours from the train from Dublin. That won't stop. Too many eyes on it for that to happen."

Fin knew he would be leaving at the first opportunity, yet he still felt betrayed by these people in uniform who were sworn to protect. But they were just people, they had families like him and loved ones feared lost. If the government collapsed and people did not have to answer to it, then the only hope was that they would listen to their conscience. If he put on a uniform, then he would be their scapegoat when they left.

"Why not arm the locals?" From the expressions he had seen on people in the camp, he could guess why they were afraid to put weapons in their hands.

"It will come to that, but could you shoot your father to save your mother?"

Fin had no answer.

"Let's find a uniform that fits you, eh?"

Fin could do nothing but nod. He drank from the cup to let Reverend fill the silence. The only redeeming quality of the coffee was its warmth. They walked by rooms that had been turned into triage and medical centres. *I forgot this was a warzone.*

"Right now we need to be productive. Every effort must have a clear benefit –"

She was interrupted by screaming.

Fin jumped at the sound. "Was somebody bitten?"

"Not so much as a scratch, but they're as good as gone, for all the use they will be to us," Reverend said.

They walked down the stairs to the cool air of the basement. Fin felt trapped with Reverend in front, while the other soldiers followed behind, blocking the narrow corridor. The halls were filled with cots beneath iridescent lighting. People curled up with blankets covering their heads, some sleeping under their cots. Others were catatonic.

Fin tried to mask the deep breaths he took to calm himself. *This could have been me.*

"When this ends, the damage and death won't stop after the last infected body is burned," Reverend said. "I'm going to ask something of you and neither of us will know what the toll will be down the line. How's your head?"

"Not great if I'm honest. I keep thinking I'll wake up."

"Don't sleep until we see this through, and you just might. Do you have many friends in town?"

"No, just colleagues at work. The nature of the job meant I did not get to socialise much. Have you had any word from other countries, has it spread? What's it like in France?"

"A few occurrences outside of Ireland, but nothing substantial. That's what they're reporting. Wouldn't make sense to create panic, Ireland is a great example of what not to do. I've no leverage to hold over you, I can't ask if you want to give your all to keep the people here safe, but that's also why I could use your help in this."

"Why? What can I do that they can't?"

"I wouldn't ask them to kill their neighbours or be the defining, final moment to faces they've known all their lives. Some of the bodies walking around out there have relatives in here. Innocent people have been killed by accident. Keeners mourning over a loved one sounds and looks an awful lot like an infected feeding. I could put guns in their hands and train them to kill, but I would never be able to take enough humanity away from them to get rid of the hesitation, valuable seconds when they must shoot somebody they know. Look around this room. See what this has done to people." She opened a container of uniforms, eyed his measurements and passed him one that fit. "There are recruits coming down on the train from Dublin today to reinforce our presence here. Our aim is to teach people to defend this position, then I can go find my family."

"Technically they are my neighbours too." Fin let out a sigh. He did not know where to look. Behind him were those too broken by what had happened to function, they had closed themselves off to the world. In front of him was the uniform being offered and the knowledge that he would be taught how to kill. Rebecca cared for him when he stayed in bed for days after Ciara died; these people here were defenceless, those outside hardly better off. George would want to remain isolated, but from what he saw, there was no reason to fear this group. So many people working together. They were far safer here than out there alone.

"I'll do what I can." He was not sure if that was a complete lie or a partial one.

"Good. Burke, Lynch, Foley, take our tourist out with you. Bring him along for the train pickup. Cut his teeth."

Muireann and the two other soldiers nodded and

parted, leaving Fin to follow. Looking back, he saw Reverend stay behind, listening to the screams.

Lynch was burly with a shaved head and a wiry ginger beard. Tattoos of colourful cartoon characters on his arms were obscured by bristly hair, except for a well-done portrait of a little girl. He slowed down to walk beside Fin. "The vans didn't suit you then, no? Have you killed an infected yet?"

"Probably a stupid question, but when this is over, will there be jail time for killing them? I mean, aren't they just sick?"

Lynch ran his hand down his beard. "They're sicker than any human can be."

"There's your first mistake, they're no longer human," Burke said. Dark, lank hair covered his gaunt face. He looked like he belonged in one of the cots lining the room, not with an assault rifle hanging around his neck. "The train will be here in forty minutes. If I could have it unloaded before the wheels stop turning I would. Let's not waste time."

Muireann nodded. "Fin, you kill a human, you'll face sentence and punishment. Jail is a luxury for peace time. But every infected you put down is doing these people and this country a service. We do our job right and there might be a future to thank you."

"How will I know the difference between infected and somebody just panicking?"

She held a finger up and moved it in front of his following eyes to check his vision. "I don't think that will be a problem. Put your kit on. If they see a civilian going to the train, they might rush it."

He dressed quickly in military fatigues and slipped his boots back on without undoing the laces. They did not give him one of the earpiece radios they used, or a weapon. The walk to the main gate was spent listening to Lynch's instructions on firearm etiquette. Fin's ears felt like they were ringing, and nothing that he heard made sense, there was too much to take in.

"New Face?" Muireann said.

"Sorry."

"What was he saying?"

"Not to shoot any of you?"

"That's the gist of it. When we go out it's goggles and respirators. Any open wounds or scabs you seal them before we leave. Don't look so worried, we're doing the work, you're just a tourist. Noise attracts them, so when we get out there keep chatter to warnings."

Donal looked relieved to see Muireann approaching the gate. "Sure took your sweet time."

"I'm heading up to the train, you want to switch, while I watch the gate?" Muireann said.

"No, you're okay, I've nearly gotten the hang of this," Donal said.

"Now with the dead ones, you have to be extra careful," Lynch said to Fin. "They're slow and unsteady, though don't trust a headshot, that won't always keep them down. Famous case of a lad Gage who got a rail rod dynamited through his brain and all it did was change his personality."

"And the infected out there are already short on personality," Burke said.

"What's your excuse, Burke?" Lynch asked, winking at Fin.

Burke pretended not to notice.

"The weepers are a different story. Their bodies are fighting against the disease and losing. Those I've come across seem to want to avoid confrontation at the start, like there's still a bit of humanity left in them. Whatever it does to the brain, it turns them into beasts after a while, but these ones will go down with a body shot. Aim centre mass. Don't forget to destroy the brain when it's down, there have been reports of them still coming back."

The main gate into town was the most heavily fortified. Smoke drifted above the walls, acrid and alien in the winter sunlight.

Civilians in protective gear brought back their salvage. Trucks full of electronics, blankets and clothes lined up to gain entry. A mobile watchtower guarded the gate, a man in the nest had his rifle trained down the road. Workers were mixing cement to reinforce metal beams bracing the walls.

A group of people refusing to work banded together near the gate. They sat on their luggage, ready for the next train. Some demanded answers when they saw the uniforms approach.

"Let us on the train," an old man brandishing a golf club said.

"My child, my mother, my friend went on the train, I need to go."

After a while Fin could no longer match a voice to a face as the crowd grew. One man stood in front of Burke, who was far less intimidating than Lynch, and demanded to be let onto the train. He strangled the handle of a bloodied shovel.

"I can shoot you now, clean, or I can shoot you out there after you turn. Big boy like you, how many of your fellows will you slaughter? Have you got any family left to hurt?"

The man shrank away at the violent tone.

Fin had not noticed Burke raising his rifle until the crowd parted, muttering about their rights.

"Sheep," Burke said, loud enough for them all to hear. "Give them all pills and be done with it."

"They're just scared," Lynch said.

"Streets are swept and the roads are clear," a soldier coming through the gate said.

Fin put on the safety equipment they offered. With the tinted goggles, he scanned the crowd for familiar faces but Lynch tapped his shoulder before he could find any. "Take your phone out."

"I haven't got one."

"Come on, every toddler in the country gets a phone."

"I had to use the speaker to distract some of the infected. I didn't want to pick it up afterwards in case it had the pathogen on it."

"That's not a bad plan actually. Here, use mine before we head out. Go on your social media accounts and type #Alive. Whole country is doing it. Well, those that are still alive. Only thing that keeps me going is seeing my wife's been online. It'll give your folks peace."

He was either very sweet or quite clever. Fin would have to sign in under his own name. Not wanting to make a scene, he held the screen close to his face and logged on. His breath caught when he saw Solene's name. Tears ran down his face. He did not open the message. It was enough to see it there. He felt cruel for avoiding social media for so long. He typed #Alive and logged out.

"You okay?" Lynch watched him closely.

Fin could not wipe his eyes behind the mask. He smiled back at the soldier, which he realised, after seeing those that had lost their minds on the cots beneath Westport House, could mean anything. *She is alive and that is how I must remain.* "I'm good. Thank you for lending me your phone."

Lynch patted him on the back before putting his own respirator on. "No problem. Are you ready?"

"Not at all."

23

TICKETS PLEASE

The noticeboard outside the grounds still had holiday events and opening hours listed. Large diggers worked throughout the day. Next to their trenches lay mounds of rich umber-coloured soil. Barbed wire fences were rolled out and military engineers oversaw the creation of spiked defences. A tarp further down the grass by the playground covered bodies waiting for the pyre.

"At least we know they rot like humans," Burke said.

The smell of uncollected rubbish lingered around the town. Now that Burke brought his attention to the bodies, Fin could not ignore their putrid stench. *Imagine this happened in the heat of summer.* He swallowed the urge to vomit, it was not worth taking the mask off.

"We're not following the busy routes, try to keep the noise down. New Face, you stay between us, if contact is made then just keep out of the way," Muireann said.

They turned off the main road and followed the footpath along the shallow and slow river. If he needed to, he could just jump in and wade back to Westport House. The thought of being in the water reminded him of the infected he had met on the Greenway, the one that took too long to drown. He imagined bodies floating further upstream. *Is the water safe for drinking or cooking?*

They passed a small gated estate with a private court-yard. Cars were pushed against the locked gates and bed sheets and tablecloths kept most of the grounds from view. A top floor window opened and a flood of noise came from the living looking for help. A few people asked was it over yet. Each hopeful face broke Fin's heart a little.

One woman shouted after them when they ignored her. Burke grimaced and his gun was about to rise but Muireann picked up the pace and the woman's shouts dwindled to silence, broken by a nearby weeper. They hunkered low for a moment, until sure it was far enough away to be some-body else's problem.

Westport was a seasonal town, the population swelled in summer as people stopped off along the scenic Wild Atlantic Way. Some cafes closed in winter for lack of customers. Fin wondered what the outbreak would have been like with more people, longer days and more light to work with. He pulled his hands into his sleeves to keep them from the bitter chill. The streets were deserted. *Fewer people, fewer infected.* The only sound aside from their foot-steps was the river and the few birds that watched over the town. Smoke still rose from a few chimney stacks, those running out of coal and wood turning to burning furniture and rubbish, making the air noxious and waxy.

Passing the bank and credit union Fin imagined all the money sitting idle in there. Each week he took his wages from one to save in the other. It never failed to make him happy, that feeling of positive momentum, that he was doing something with his life. Regardless of how mind-numbing the work was, he was saving for something better with

Solene. What use was that now? *Money is just the physical representation of our time and we're all short on that now.*

The petrol station was shuttered, the pumps empty, most left lying on the ground. Abandoned cars filled the road, left by people trying to reach the train.

An old railtrack bridge crossed the road. Sentries were posted on both sides. Looking up, Fin could see they were on metal grates, not concrete. The stairway up to them was barricaded. As far as he could tell, they were safe from everything but the elements. The street ahead was lined with bodies; some had been moved to the kerb, but the more recent ones lay where they had dropped.

"You're late," one sentry said. "Everything okay?"

Lynch checked his watch and shared a discomforting look with Burke. "Training's over for today."

"We got no word over the radio that the train arrived early," Burke said. He made some hand signs to those posted on the bridge. The aloof yet watchful tone changed in an instant. They were alert. Weapons ready.

"You want to head back?" Burke asked Fin.

"No, I won't get in the way, I'll just watch. Extra set of eyes can't hurt." *The train is so close.*

"You make a noise and I'll shoot you in the gut to distract them," Burke said and turned away before Fin could say anything. He chose to pass it off as a joke, it was that or walk through town alone.

The road here had been cleared, all cars pushed onto the paths. The train was idle. "Burke, I'm getting nothing on the radio," Lynch said.

Burke continued on towards the train. "I told the captain I'd stay until this train came. If replacements and reinforcements aren't here, that's not my problem."

"Do you think she'd shoot you if you left?" Muireann asked.

"If I made a show of going in front of others, then I'd deserve to be shot. No, if I was going to do it, I'd go missing on patrol. Carry all I needed."

"You couldn't take much with you." Muireann stopped talking as they neared the small station.

They walked out from cover. The platform was empty. Whenever Fin went home to visit family, he would get this train and cut across the country to Heuston Station, get a coffee and a bun from the trolley and read. A tram and a bus would see him home an hour after he landed in Dublin.

He imagined sneaking onto one of the carriages and stowing away, the soldiers would not miss him. There was no plan beyond that, there was no knowing what he was heading towards. By all accounts, people were desperately trying to get away from the capital. George and Rebecca were safe. He could let them know that he was leaving over the radio when he boarded. Walking from Westport across the country was suicide, but following the coast from Dublin, that was manageable. He just needed to get there.

Crudely made metal railings like bull bars were fitted to the front of the train. Viscera clung to the joints. Blood streaked along the windshield of the engine, but the wipers kept a small partition clear for the driver to navigate by. Fin wanted to believe that an animal had gotten onto the tracks, but the shreds of clothing dispelled him of that lie. These were the remains of humans, a lot of them.

"That's fresh," Burke said.

Rifles raised, Lynch and Muireann jumped from the platform onto the tracks to check the other side of the train. "I don't see our replacements," Muireann said.

"Clear behind," Burke said. "I'm coming back. First carriage is empty."

The driver was still in the cab. Lynch waved to get his attention. The driver was slow to respond, shell-shock or terror, it seemed to take a great effort for him to talk. He refused to take his hands away from his ears. His face contorted, as if he were on the verge of crying or screaming, he could just not decide which.

Burke pulled the emergency escape handle, his rifle pointed squarely at the driver's chest. "What happened?"

The man started babbling, Lynch had to pull his hands down from his ears. He flinched back, covering them again. "The noise, please, I can't listen. Close the door, I beg you." The smell from the gore was like nothing Fin could have imagined; a fresh butcher's shop came close, though.

"So many of them. Every station overrun. I thought the train would come off the track. The line is not long enough, they'll follow. Close the door, please. They'll be here soon. Please."

"Where are the reinforcements?" Muireann asked.

Fin looked down the platform. All you had to do was stand behind the yellow line and you were safe. One window, two carriages down, was fogged up. The track behind the train was completely empty, so he went to investigate, staying on the safe side of the yellow line. The sound of the driver's infectious panic followed him.

"I don't want to hear them." The man rambled in a thick Dublin accent.

Every step forward was an exhausting effort against self-preservation, but he kept moving until he could see that the window was not fogged: it had shattered, frosted with spiderweb fractures. Sudden movement inside the carriage made him drop to a crouch, every muscle tensed.

A person ran down the carriage and stopped to listen to the driver's pleading. In the expectant silence, Fin heard them running and crying in the end carriages of the train. Weepers. Windows on carriages further from the engine were completely shattered and bullet holes peppered the metal, shards pointing outwards, fired from within.

Another person sprinted down the aisle, tripped and fell from view when it saw Fin. It crawled back up, leaning against an unbroken window. The infected slapped a hand against the glass so hard that Fin saw it ripple. The sound drew the attention of the others. Fin froze, bolted to the spot, while the creature watched him. The wedding ring on its hand clanged against the glass. Someone cut the engine. Without its low roar, the sound of weeping filled the silence.

Another weeper ran past, continuing on further down the carriage. Had the door been open, Fin would have died. *What use is a hammer against one of those? They don't flinch away from a blow to save themselves and you only have one shot, whereas their bloody fingers and ruined hands could reach me, while I'm fending off their teeth.*

The one that had him in its sights slid along the window getting closer to the brittle glass, delicate like spring puddle ice. It hit the window again, waking Fin from his stupor, and he fell back hard. Fin caught shadows moving towards them in the other carriages. A warm wetness blossomed in his crotch. Crawling into a stumble, he ran back to the others.

Muireann and Lynch immediately guessed what the situation was from the look on his face, their expressions sudden mirrors of his own.

"The train is full," he said. "All weepers."

The carriages rattled now that the creatures were riled. The train rang out with their horrid sounds. The driver pushed Burke out of the cabin, closed the door and started the engine back up.

Burke snarled and raised his rifle, but Lynch slapped it down. "Are you stupid? There are too many. With our luck you'd probably shoot an emergency open button and bring them all down on us at once." Lynch stepped back from the train.

"Come on, we'll take you with us," Muireann said.

A body tumbled out of a broken window onto the platform. It hit the ground hard. In the space of a breath, it stood up. More followed. The window in the first carriage shattered.

"Run," Lynch gave the order and led by example.

The sound of bodies hitting the platform put a speed in Fin that he never knew he possessed, nearly careening off balance as he sprinted to catch up to the soldiers.

"We can't go through town with those behind us," Burke said. He looked back and for a moment Fin wondered if he would make good on his promise of shooting him in the gut, so they could get away. When he turned his attention back to the road, Fin could breathe again. The soldiers pulled ahead. The respirator was choking him, not enough air reached his lungs. He pulled it off.

Fin heard Burke on his radio. "Compound go dark, no noise. Contact, contact." Burke's panting was out of pace with Fin's gasping. "Train is compromised."

The snipers on the bridge all came to the side facing the train. Four of them took aim. Whatever they saw made Fin go cold: all of them lost their composure, two attempted to get down to the road, but there was no time, all they could do was trust in their barricades. Fin, Muireann, Burke and Lynch ran beneath the bridge, none of them looking back now, there was no need to. Fin heard a crowd behind him.

Burke did not need to shoot him, they were all much fitter than he was.

The first shot from the sentries made him stumble. Weaving between the cars slowed their progress. A few seconds later he heard the infected crash into the vehicles. He gained a second wind knowing that the weepers could not navigate the traffic as well as he could.

"Up the Greenway," Burke said. "They'll overrun the gates if we bring them back."

They ran up the steep tarmac walkway. Fin's lungs burned, he tasted copper, the fringes of his vision blurred, but he was alive, stopping meant death.

Gunfire still rained down from the bridge. Lynch turned, took a knee, a breath, then fired. The noise was like nothing he experienced in the movies. He covered his ears, ducked and ran on, hoping they would not miss.

Lynch shouted something at him, but he did not hear it. Muireann and Burke were already gone.

At the top of the hill he did not get a moment to catch his breath. Bikes lined the fences. Burke pedalled ahead of the three of them. Lynch was kicking off the ground for speed. They looked ridiculous in full uniform, pedalling mountain bikes. Fin picked the first one he came to, a heavy city bike, and regretted it instantly. Kicking off, the pedal spun around and struck the back of his leg. The soldiers on the bridge were still shooting, but now they were joined by gunfire throughout town.

With the path steep enough that gravity kept most of his momentum going, Fin slowed down to catch his breath. They stopped in an estate at the end of the Greenway. Sweat pumped from his pores. Slumped over the handlebars, he rested his head for a moment, but fear of what he could not see brought him up again.

The path was clear behind them. The soldiers were in a much better state than he was.

"Where are we going? Camp or pier?" Burke asked. "Now's our chance to go missing on patrol. I've a stash in the factory by the boat yard. It's now or never."

"There are too many weepers," Muireann said. "If they started following us, we couldn't rely on help from the camp. By the sound of it, they're already busy. I think it's the wrong time to leave. Not now, we don't know enough. What happened to Dublin? We'll stay, clean up and then we can go on patrol."

Burke grit his teeth. "Fine, let's be done with it so."

They don't seem to care that I can hear them. That unsettled Fin as much as the infected. "Don't mind me, the only reason I came back to Westport House was to get a lift out of here on the train. You do what you have to, means nothing to me, but I don't want to stand around here. I have the keys for the hotel between here and Westport House."

They only noticed him now. "Those gates are sturdy, could draw them there and mow them down," Muireann said. "Relieve the stress on the camp. How much ammunition do we have?"

"One shot per person?" Burke mused. "Not nearly enough."

Muireann radioed it in to let command know. There was no response.

"That hotel was compromised with infected," Burke said. "That's why we ignored it."

"There were only two of them, both are dead," Fin said.

"There were two others in the tunnel. Probably dead, Rev gave them suicide tablets," Burke said.

It bothered Fin that this distasteful man would think he would opt out so quickly.

Weep

"Give me the key," Burke said. He ripped it from his hand. "If you're wrong, the last thing I do in this life will be to take yours."

Quietly, they crept along the road. Most of the weepers had been drawn off by the commotion in town. A few of the slower ones converged beneath a flagpole, lured by the sound of the rope slapping against the metal in the breeze. They were two buildings away from the gate of the hotel when the weepers that followed them along the Greenway spilled onto the street behind them. Their strangled weeping was made more inhuman by their wheezing.

The weep of so many brought infected already in the area down on them. There were too many between them and the camp, there was not enough time to reach the hotel. The only option that remained was the factory on the pier.

The passionless faces petrified Fin, blank as corpses. They moved like somebody had run an electrical current through a grave pit.

"It's your lucky day, Burke," Lynch said. "Get to the pier."

They cut across the grass, out of rank, only thinking of themselves now. Burke headed for the road for better purchase. It cost him time and allowed a weeper gain on him, but he ducked and weaved out of reach. *They can't handle sharp turns*. It careened face-first onto the road and was trampled by its kind.

Fin did not look back, he knew the fast and implacable weepers were aiming for him, the slowest of the group. He was not sure if the tide was in. If it was, he would jump into sucking mudflats. A horrible way to drown, if the infected did not reach him first. Lynch and Muireann sprinted ahead. He cried out for them to wait, but he knew he was wasting breath, when he should be running.

They turned left and ran past the shipyards towards an

265

abandoned factory ringed with high metal fences. He made to follow them but it was too far, he could already sense the infected about to reach out and barrel into him. Burke made it to the factory and closed the gates when Muireann and Lynch passed through. Muireann looked back, but only spared him a passing glance. They disappeared inside. The infected now only had Fin to devote their attention to.

The tide was out, so he ran for the sailing ships on stilts in the dry dock. He had never seen the place so empty. All of the seaworthy craft had been used by people trying to get out to the islands. Masts peeked out of the water beyond the pier wall, from ships that were not fit for use. He jumped for the railing of the first one he reached, but his foot slid off the side. Panicked, he ran to another. As he turned the corner, an infected slammed into the rudder he had just ducked under.

He weaved through three lines of boats before he found one high enough to be impossible for the infected to climb. Arms outstretched, he lunged for the railing. The wind was knocked out of him, but he kept his hold, his meagre, remaining strength bolstered by fear and adrenaline. His feet skidded along the hull, barely finding purchase on the slick side, but he managed to lift himself high enough to hook an elbow over the rim and fall onto the raised deck.

Weepers crashed into the ship and for a terrifying moment Fin thought they would cause it to fall from its perch, but the creatures had lost their momentum zig-zagging through the yard.

Fin lay still on his back, not bothering to quieten his desperate gasps. He could not be heard over the sound of so many weepers.

24

NOT LOST

The weeping stopped during the night. Morning was still hours away. The rigging on the boat next to his kept the infected from wandering far. Cold seeped deeper into his body, to the point that he wondered if he would ever feel warm again. A small pillar of moonlight, shining through the port window, illuminated his fogging breath.

There was no way of knowing if the soldiers were still alive. Throughout the night he heard distant gunfire, but it was too far off for it to come from the factory. *Surely those things need sleep, or is it the lack of it that drives them mad? Does the blistering cold even bother them?* Desperately thirsty, he tried to forget his lack of water by concentrating on how hungry he was.

The radio in his pocket crackled into life with a whispered voice. "Fin, are you okay?"

He held down the receiver. The battery was running low. "Rebecca? I'm glad you're okay." He begrudgingly took his finger off the receiver to let her speak but that caused noise. He turned the volume down lower.

Relief was audible in her voice. "Where are you? What's happening out there? It sounds like a warzone."

"I'm in the shipyard across from the hotel. In a boat called the 'Not Lost'."

"Don't leave us here," George said.

Fin laughed. "There's no fear of that happening, it's on blocks, there's no propeller and no sails. What have you been doing?"

George answered. "I was out walking the property. Can't sleep. The street lamps still work, I wish they didn't. We've seen a few infected walking past. None of them fast though. Are you safe where you are?"

"No, I don't think so. None of us are. The train from Dublin was riddled with infected. You should have seen it, the engine was painted with blood. Driver said every station he passed was full of them. They will follow the tracks and end up here. There are too many people in the camp, making too much noise. They will be overrun."

"How did you end up in the boatyard?" Rebecca asked.

"The soldiers here were relying on reinforcements coming from the capital. They were preparing to leave. Wanted to train me up, dress me in a uniform and put a gun in my hand."

They were silent on the other end of the line before Rebecca spoke. "We were thinking of heading out to the islands." There was no mistaking the cracking in her voice for static on the radio. "Tell us everything."

"George, you were right, I was put straight to work. So many people are still in their homes. How has the disease spread so fast?" He did not want to hear the answer to that.

"Were you inside the house? What are their medical supplies like?" George interrupted.

"They had people tied to beds and others that didn't

need the restraints. I was not paying much attention to be honest."

"George, what's wrong with you?" he heard Rebecca ask in the background.

The radio went dead and Fin could hear nothing. He called repeatedly, but stopped when he saw weepers turn in his direction.

"Sorry about that, Fin," Rebecca said. "The islands can't be much better, George was saying. They have food in Westport House and medicine."

"I'm stuck here," Fin said. "There's no getting to Dublin, not now. We need to check the islands out, get off the mainland and make a plan. The infection could be out there, but if it's zombies and not weepers, then we could try to handle it. Either way, we need to know. Our only other option is to wander the mainland. Can we survive it this time of year with the infected hunting us?"

"I agree," George said. "You and Rebecca head out to the islands, I'll scavenge from homes along the mainland. If we find a decent boat on the islands, we could make it out to Achill. Have you found a way to get away from the infected?"

"Not yet. How are we supposed to get out to the islands?"

Before she could elaborate, Fin held the button down on the radio to stop all noise. Hands slapped against the outside of the boat. "Guys, I have to go, they know I'm here." He turned the volume down nearly as far as it would go.

"Stay safe," Rebecca said.

"Conserve your battery, we'll come for you in the morning. Try and get some sleep," George added.

"Thank you." Fin turned the radio off. He believed that they would do everything they could to help him. He felt shame, knowing if the chance arose, he would have left them to get home. Now they were probably coming up with a plan to save him. The infected soon lost interest.

There was nothing of value to him inside the cabin. The mattress was made of cheap, stiff foam. He wrapped himself in blankets that were riddled with cobwebs and dead spiders, towels tucked around his legs for warmth. It wasn't much, but it made a difference. He watched clouds rush in front of the moon through the porthole and imagined that it was shining on Solene too. *Let it find her well. Baby, if you could only see me now.* She was alive, he knew it from the notifications on his social media. He just had to log on and read them.

Why did you leave me in silence for so long? He heard her voice, as well as his father's, and those of his family and friends. *Why did I? Fear? I can barely keep it together by myself, if I had to worry about others, I'd be lost. Selfish.*

* * *

Gunfire from Westport House drew the brunt of the infected away from him. Watching the weepers, he noticed some of them fall and lie still, and he knew from Ciara in the hotel that they had entered the next phase of the infection, they were dead and would rise soon, slower than before. He wondered whether their lack of interest in him was boredom, or had they no object permanence? That would mean they could be safe in their hideaway so long as they remained quiet and unseen. During the night he was woken from a weak sleep by splashes. *If only they would all walk off the end of the pier and into the water.*

If he moved too much, his blanket cocoon fractured and the cold got in. When sleep did take him, he dreamed of being on rough seas, the engine faltering and the ship floundering. He was sinking and he knew exactly what awaited him below the waves: dead that would not drown.

Morning light came late in winter, weak and brittle but as welcome as the spring thaw. Night gave the infected more power over the living; menace grows in the dark canvas of the imagination. During the day, it was hard not to pity them. He turned the radio on and waited. Parched with thirst, his head ached. The slower infected and the ones still lying on the ground were covered in a layer of hoarfrost.

"Fin?"

"Morning, Rebecca."

"Are you set?" The voice did not come from the radio. George was talking to him from outside the boat. The infected started weeping.

The morning air made him shiver when he stepped out on deck. Mist floated above the river. Only a few infected still wandered around the pier. They seemed unphased by the weather. He couldn't hope on an Irish winter to freeze them, whereas getting caught outdoors on a frosty night was as dangerous to him as the infected.

It was like he was on stage, or a busker trying to grab attention. Those shambling few still around the boat moved on him, arms raised. Most of them had wounds on their hands, necks and torsos. The faces looked terrifyingly serene for such affronts to the human condition. They were not surprised when Fin distracted them, they looked like a group of wide-eyed sleepwalkers. Fingers stretched and cracked, trying to reach him, he knew what harm they could cause. A lot of fingers no longer had nails.

These were the first infected that he had seen up close since Ciara. Some had grazed skin and torn jackets, and it only occured to Fin now that they could spread the disease by accidentally knocking into things, like cats spreading scent. A child amongst them had a cycle helmet on in a hope it would keep him safe. *That will make it harder to put him to rest.* Most wore winter jackets, gloves and scarves. They looked no different than those hiding in the woods of Westport House, reaching up at him like they were seeking salvation, their calm stares promising that if they could, they would turn him.

George and Rebecca were on the water, wearing wetsuits. George stood on a paddle board with a long oar. Rebecca sat at the back of an inflatable kayak. A second paddle sitting inside was waiting for Fin.

"Nice morning for it," Fin said. "Watch out, I heard a few of them fall over the edge in the night. If they haven't drowned, they could still be dangerous."

"I don't think they can drown," Rebecca said. "Let's hurry this up, I'm freezing."

George paddled further up away from them. After a few moments he let the current take him back, holding the paddle in the water only to guide his passage.

"There are a few soldiers in the factory, maybe we can help them out one at a time," Fin said.

"They left this morning, the zombies around your boat kept the factory clear of them," George said. "They snuck around the other side to get away. We waited for them to leave."

That stung more than it should have. If not for George and Rebecca he would have been trapped until thirst made him risk infection. *They abandoned me. How long did they deliberate over that?*

A rocket whistled into the sky, hissing as it gained altitude, a split second of silence before it erupted. Smaller explosions crackled as red and green light scarred the morning sky. It was a beautiful sight. The infected ran towards the noise and light, ignoring Fin completely. George held up his hand, signing for Fin to wait. Another rocket went up and then a third. Once there were a few feet of distance between Fin and the infected, George waved him on.

Fin dropped down quietly enough that none of the dead turned around. He sat on the edge of the pier and climbed down a long-rusted ladder. Some infected had fallen in, he had heard the splat as they hit the wet, sucking silt. The tide was in now and all he could see of them was torsos and legs sticking out. He could think of no greater horror than falling into that filth and becoming trapped in foul mud and darkness.

Rebecca brought the kayak in as close as she could and George knelt on his board to put pressure on the other side, so Fin's weight would not unsettle it. When he was safely onboard, Rebecca pushed off against the seaweed-covered pier wall. Fin grasped George's shoulder and hand. He took a few steadying breaths, tears of gratitude fell. "Thank you."

Fin lay down on the kayak. Rebecca rubbed his head, shushing him softly, telling him it would be okay. On the shore, Fin watched as a zombie went over into the water. It did nothing to stop its fall; no hands went up, no gasp of surprise. It hit the dark water with a splash, its back rose up and floated. Disgruntled gulls that had been displaced by the fireworks landed on street lights after the last shot fired.

At the end of the pier a car had crashed through a mound of crab boxes. They were too fragile to stop it from careening into the water. Fin sat up and took his paddle. They fell into an easy rhythm. "Where did you get the fireworks?"

"Nobody got to ring in the new year, so every fifth house

has a little arsenal of rockets," George said. "We found boards and the kayak in the shed at the bottom of the garden."

"You see the house up ahead, the one with clothes on the line?" Rebecca said. "The one to the right of it is ours."

It was easy for the eye to pass over it. The outline of the house was masked by bare tree branches and the weathered green coating made it wilt into the background.

"We're going to paddle around the headland a bit and get out of sight before we land," George said. "I don't like doing this in the morning and I certainly don't want anybody in Westport House knowing where we are. I don't trust a group that can so easily abandon their own."

They stayed close to the shore and scanned each field and house they passed. There was a large farm with plenty of machinery and a mound of silage. George was excited at the prospect of excavating the old world, as he put it. He had formed a new fondness for breaking into other people's homes. He never stole anything he could not use to survive, he just liked being there, in a building that somebody else had made into a personal sanctuary. For him it was spiritual; though the person may be gone, there was still a glimpse of a memory of what they were once like. Fin could not commit to that type of thinking, not yet. These were consecrated grounds, biding time until their owners returned.

They pulled up on a worn stone shore, sheltered by sand dunes. Behind them there was a large, new and well-built house. It was designed to stand out. A symbol asking to be seen and of no use to them during the epidemic. Fin's arms ached from paddling, and he shook them out before they dragged the kayak above the tideline. They hid it amongst bleached white driftwood. The kayak had deflated a little during the paddle, they could not safely go far in it if there was a puncture.

"Will you unzip me?" George asked, turning around so Fin could get at his back.

"We might have to let it out around the gut," Fin said, when the zip came down revealing white, freckle speckled skin.

"It's the only one we could find in such short notice." George raised his eyes when he looked at Fin's own gut. "You're telling me you'd be a striking model in this?"

"An upsetting one maybe. No, if you zipped me up in that I would have asphyxiated before making it five feet."

"Can you two stop comparing bra sizes and help me?" Rebecca said as she covered the colourful kayak with old seaweed.

The morning mist floating above the water melted as the sun rose higher. Searching for things to cover the craft with, Fin came across some beautiful shells and colourful stones, and he was brought back about two decades to wandering the strand near his home in Drogheda, asking his dad for the origin of every curiosity he found; his dad always had answers. *How could I be so cruel to not try and contact them?* Fin felt like he had put it off long enough. He pocketed a polished black stone with the intention of returning home and asking his father all about it.

George shouted out and danced backwards, wringing his hands and wiping them on the wetsuit as if he had unearthed a large and unexpected spider. Hidden amongst the seaweed and sand, invisible because of its silt-covered clothing, lay a body. Lank hair covered most of the face and its ears were filled with sediment. Its legs were broken and the eyes were gone. It had a dead crow clutched in its hands.

Rebecca poked it with the edge of the paddle and let out

a yell when it slowly pushed itself up. It was trapped, blind and deaf. Its head turned as if it were looking through empty eye sockets, like a badly made animatronic. With no further stimuli, the head stopped moving and it remained still.

"That shouldn't be alive," George said.

"Shut up." Rebecca held the paddle like a weapon.

"I don't think he can hear us," Fin said. "Let's just go."

They climbed up the stormbreaker boulders onto the land, through fields of coarse grass and weeds, lying flat from recent rain. They hopped over a wooden fence and a metal gate that they chose to climb because the hinges squeaked when they tried to open it. No more infected crossed their path. It was too easy to walk along the shore and gain access to the back garden of their sanctuary. As the undead near the kayak proved, they could just wash up on the beach.

After a quick sweep of the grounds and house to make sure they were clear, George put his paddle board back in the shed and turned the kettle on. Fin noticed they had strapped cloth to the bottom of the chair legs to stop them from scraping across the tiles. An extension cord meant they could boil the water on the table without having to get up and pour. Fin knew they would go through several mugs of coffee and tea before he was finished telling them all that had happened since they were together last. He downed a pint of water to quench his thirst.

"Are you bitten?" George asked as casually as if he wanted to know how many sugars Fin took.

"No, George, I spent the night in a freezer to avoid that. Are you bitten?"

"Only by your tone. Say you were bitten, what would you want us to do with you?"

The kettle boiled and clicked off. Fin sighed and filled three mugs with hot water. "If you're giving me the option then I'd choose that you went to find a cure for me."

George and Rebecca continued an argument they were having while he was away about how they wanted to go. Although the subject matter made Fin uncomfortable, the sound of their voices relaxed him.

25

ALIVE

The loft quickly started to feel like home. All the pictures of the previous owners were gathered up and respectfully placed in a desk drawer. Fin felt no guilt about staying in the house, but there was something unsettling about looking at pictures of strangers, not knowing if they were still alive. *We could stay here. If the power goes out, we can read during the day and talk until we fall asleep.* Fin knew it was not as easy as that. If he was guaranteed safety and a limitless supply of food and uncontaminated water, the nights would still take their toll; the long silences, the phantom sounds, the constant impending sense of dread. *Apart from that, it's fine.*

Fin downed a bottle of water and noticed how sparse their supply of safe drinking water had become. *We can't stay inside forever. We have to face them, or die in here.*

"I don't get it," George said. "Before all of this happened, I can't remember the last time I drank my daily recommended amount of water. By the statistics on the news, I shouldn't have lived this long. We have to be frugal with what we have."

"I don't trust the water in the taps," Fin said. "Is it safe to drink? Imagine infected got into the reservoir. I'm assuming, considering we're literally on the coast, we aren't getting our supply from a well."

"We'll just boil it." George filled the bath tub, every pot and unused cup in the house with water.

"What if you're only heating up the virus?" Rebecca said.

George scoffed. "Me there thinking the end of the world was going to have some excitement. A bit of bleach in each pot and let it set for a while, should kill off the nastiness."

Rebecca put her book down. "How far do you think we will fall as a species? Are we the new hunter-gatherers?"

"No," George said. "We are the hunted gatherers."

When Fin asked if there were any new developments in the ever 'breaking' news cycle, George and Rebecca shared an awkward silence and a look.

"To be honest with you," Rebecca said, "we've been watching too much of it lately."

"Yeah," George said. "What's that expression, a watched pot never boils?"

The kettle clipped off in the middle of the table and the silence endured. Fin did not have the imagination to wonder what had happened to make them act this way. After they ate a breakfast of porridge and nuts with honey and the last of the softening fruit, they hid away upstairs for the rest of the day. The cable at the back of the television that connected it to the satellite had been removed.

"We found a few games," George said, passing him a handful of cases to look at.

"There's Monopoly downstairs as well but considering what's going on, we thought it best to keep that from tearing us apart," Rebecca said.

Fin chose a game at random and they settled in to play.

The heating stayed on, and he relished the warmth after spending the night in unbearable cold.

After each death they passed the remote. Fin wondered how he wasted so much time on scripted paths and stories before the outbreak. *So much wasted time.* The pleasure, he knew, came from knowing there was going to be a happy ending, regardless of the difficulty. He could fail, learn and persevere, a pleasant fiction. Solene used to despair at the amount of time Fin wasted in front of the console, but that was what they needed now, a means of safely killing time.

"Oh, I almost forgot." Rebecca passed the remote to George, even though she had not died. She handed Fin a pilfered present; the wrapping had been torn open and badly taped back together again. "I know it's a bit late, but here's your Christmas gift. Latest model, no expenses spared – by whoever bought it originally."

Fin smiled and tore the wrapping apart, revealing a top-of-the-range smart phone, still in its plastic. Every laptop, computer and mobile phone in the country was either thumbprint or password protected. The code to access this one was inside the box.

"I thought you could try to get in touch with Solene and your family," Rebecca said.

Fin put the phone down to hug her. She pulled away first, taking the remote from George and wrestling with a smile that threatened to broaden across her face.

He retreated to the office and closed the door for some privacy. The phone was easy to set up; he put the new SIM card in, and let it charge while he thought about what he was going to say. The last time he felt this awkward about contacting his dad was when he was asking for a lend of money. *Not all that long ago.* He had no clue what he was going to say to Solene.

He could have spent the rest of the day preparing for the conversation. When the battery was charged enough, he turned the phone on. The moment he entered the default code to start the device the old government warnings flashed across the screen. *From now on everything new in this world will have scars from this event.* He connected to the Wi-Fi and logged into his Facebook account. Most of the new notifications were in response to his #Alive post. More than half of his friends list had not reacted to the post. *Either they're dead, or the algorithm has not shown it to them yet.*

Usually Solene's messages were terse, but he logged on to find a novel's worth of words from her. Shaking, he put the phone down, unable to read them. He pinched his leg, picked up the phone and dialled his Dad's number, it was the only one he knew by heart. The phone rang out for so long that he gasped for air after holding his breath.

"Hello?"

"Dad."

His father broke down on the other end of the phone. The only time Fin had witnessed his composure slip was when they had to put their dog down. He felt joy at the sound of a voice he thought gone from the world.

The crying stopped, became distant. "Is that Fin?" He knew her voice, it robbed him of his own.

"Solene?"

He could hear her breathing heavily over the phone. Fin laughed through his tears. "I thought you were dead." He slipped from the chair onto his knees, holding the phone to his ear with both hands. "I love you." He repeated it like a prayer.

There was too much commotion on the other end of the line for him to make out what was being said. Eventually his father took the phone. "Ah, that's lovely, I love you too son."

In the background Fin heard his sister and mother laughing, then other voices, his whole family was around the phone now.

"Hello everyone." Fin wiped his runny nose on his sleeve.

"Where are you?" his sister asked.

"Under the biggest rock that I could find. You're all okay?"

"As well as can be expected. What's it like where you are?" his dad asked.

"Overrun. The army has set up in Westport House, trying to make it safe. I'm with colleagues along the coast."

"Get away from the army if you can," Solene said.

Hearing her voice brought on a fresh wave of tears. Fin did not want to worry them. "I'm safe," he said. "What is it like back home?"

"We didn't fare so well," his mother said. "The hospital down the road was riddled with them. Then they started coming down the motorway from Dublin. Plenty of them bypassed us and continued on to Belfast, only to meet the infected coming from the north. We're okay now. We've blockaded the estate, but the town is still overrun."

Listening to the relief in their voices, he felt like a monster for letting them think he was dead for so long. "I'll try and get home."

"Don't." His father's tone changed. "It's not safe. Just – if you have food and shelter, then stay where you are. Of course we want you here with us, but we'll be together once this ends. Don't make any unnecessary journeys."

"Come on, give him and Solene some privacy," his mother said.

"I love you guys."

They returned the sentiment and left Solene and Fin to share silence.

"I thought you were –" They spoke at the same time, interrupting each other.

"You first," Solene said.

"I thought you were gone, Sol." Outside the office window, grey clouds drifted across the sky. "The last message I got from you was when you lost your phone. I thought..."

"That was in Dublin. My flight never left."

"How did you make it to Drogheda?"

"Walked. I got onto the motorway and followed it here. I thought I was being stupid at first. After I lost my mother, I didn't know where else to go. The bus never came and traffic backed up so much that I think I made it here before people on buses did."

"Your mother?"

"Lost her in the rush. I tried to find her, but it was impossible to know who was infected at the beginning. She would have gone to her brother's."

"Has she called yet?"

"No, but you're only reaching out now, so no reason why she won't do the same."

Fin was scared of facing the deaths of his loved ones. He did not try and contact them for selfish reasons. He knew her mother was a better person than he was. "I lost my phone, maybe she did too."

"You don't know my number off by heart?"

"This is the longest we've been apart for as long as I can remember. Do you remember mine?"

"How are our fur babies?"

"The cats are good actually, they miss you. They must have

thought it was Christmas, I poured weeks' worth of food out for them. Filled every bowl in the house with water. The windows are open for them to come and go as they please. Remember how they used to annoy me by leaving mice outside our bedroom door? We know they can hunt. They'll be fine."

"I hate thinking of them alone. I'm glad you were there to help them. I should be there with you. I can't stop thinking about you there alone and scared. Please don't die on me, please."

"I hadn't planned on it."

"Why did we never make a contingency plan in case the world ended? I saw your post online, but I was afraid to call you in case it caused too much noise," Solene said.

"I lost my phone."

"Oh, I hope nobody gets my nudes from it."

Fin laughed uncontrollably. When he was able to catch a breath he said, "I don't think zombies have much use for them, love."

"Don't call them that."

"Zombies?"

"They're people."

"Yes, dead ones."

"Anyway, I think your dad was right. If you are safe, then I want you to stay that way. As much as I want to hold you again," she said. "The country has gone mental. Drone strikes on cities. Outskirts of Dublin are being shelled by war ships in the Irish Sea. I can't believe what's going on. People are terrified. I am too. I don't think if this ended tomorrow the restrictions would stop. There's a lot of anti-Irish feeling in other countries."

"It's well for you then with a French accent."

"I know I'm fine, it's you with your bogger drawl that I'm worried about."

"How bad is it there, really?"

Solene started whispering. "People are clamouring for a cure, some in the camp have tried inoculating themselves with the flesh of recently deceased infected, thinking it would make them immune."

"That sounds stupid. Did it work?"

"It's one of the main reasons people here are still dying behind the defences. It's fine if they want to kill themselves, but they rarely die before they infect others. I miss you holding me."

That caught Fin off guard. "I know, I feel the same. Truth be told, I'm glad you're not here. I couldn't do this with you in danger. I don't sleep much now, but when I do, I dream of you. You are always with me."

"How many brownie points are you going for?" She laughed and sobbed. "I love you."

"I love you too."

They chatted until his arm went numb from holding the phone to his ear. His family came back and he told them most of what had happened to him since the outbreak.

When it came time to hang up, it felt like one of those nights when they stayed up talking until the sun rose. He felt satisfied, tired and spent.

Without her voice on the other end of the phone, he realised how quiet it was. He could hear the voices in the game that George and Rebecca played. He wiped his eyes and composed himself before returning to them.

"How is everyone?" Rebecca asked.

"Alive. Solene went to my parents in Drogheda after the outbreak. She's okay."

"Fin, that's great news."

"I have to get back there, somehow."

"Look at it this way, they're safe and you're safe. Why tempt bad luck by making rash decisions?" George said.

"I agree with you. If the infected from town start wandering out this way and get through the hedges, then we're trapped. The islands would be ideal for now," Fin said.

"We have a plan," George said.

"If that's the case then it's my turn on the game." George passed him the remote. "You can tell me while I play."

26

ISLANDS

The feeling of comfort beneath the warm, soft blanket was completely spoiled by George tickling the bottom of Fin's protruding feet. The rich aroma of coffee was a small concession to being woken so early. "Feels like I only just fell asleep."

"We let you stay there as long as we could." Rebecca handed him a steaming mug. She was already dressed in a wetsuit, a thick jumper and a puffy winter jacket.

"Sorry." Fin sat on the side of the bed. In the past, nothing in his life ever felt so bad that a good night's sleep could not, in some way, help. Now, he never woke feeling refreshed.

George left the other wetsuit on the bed. "No need to be sorry, we had to wait anyway and you needed the sleep."

Fin brought the wetsuit into the bathroom and struggled into it. When he returned to the bedroom he sucked his gut in until he could cover it with a jumper.

George had breakfast started in the kitchen. He made fluffy pancakes with coconut milk, drowned them in golden syrup and topped them with sizzling rashers, straight from the pan. "That, guys, is the last of the flour."

Fin's eyes rolled. "So good. Have you any idea how they make golden syrup?"

"Not a clue," George said. "We think we're so sophisticated, but individually, we're not. You take a baby from a thousand years ago and it'll flourish in our time. But it would no more know how to refine golden syrup than we would. I've never fixed anything that broke, I always just threw it out and bought another."

Fin swallowed a large mouthful of pancake. "Once things settle down, the libraries will be the new town halls."

"Put that out of your head for now." George pushed his plate away from him, no longer hungry. "We're a long way from that, Fin. We need to survive. We won't slip too far, but you have to wonder what the country will look like when this ends. If most of the medical staff were infected... The capital burned. We have already lost so much. I can't shed a tear for the culture, art and history now gone, not when so many homes across Ireland will sit silent in the wake of this plague."

"I'm probably eating better now than I ever did before this happened," Rebecca said, trying to change the topic and lift the mood.

Fin passed her his pancakes. "I'm not really hungry."

"You have to eat something," George said.

"Coffee will do just fine. You're like my mother before school," Fin said as George busied himself packing their bags. Each one was provisioned with two litres of water, a box of cereal bars and a flask of packet soup. Fin boiled the kettle twice and filled two hot water bottles. He gave one to Rebecca and put his beneath his wetsuit and jumper. She followed his example and both of them were sweating before they left the house.

They crept through the garden to the shore. Frost-crisp grass crackled underfoot. Small waves lapped against the sand in a slow, sleepy rhythm. George went into the shed and passed them out two paddle boards. Then he brought out two sun-weathered life vests. Fin's hot water bottle made it a tight fit.

"No prints on the sand." George was apprehensive about leaving any sign of habitation. Once he saw them to the water's edge, he brushed their passing off the sand. There was no sound beyond the waves lapping over the shore stones. "It's the quiet that gets me," George whispered. His breath clouded in the cold morning air. "I never imagined the end of the world would be so silent."

"Are you sure you'll be okay by yourself?" Rebecca asked.

"I'll be fine. Don't forget, I made it by myself before I joined you. Another day of it won't do me serious harm. I grew up here, I know most of the long forgotten pathways."

Fin hugged him. "Don't go getting morose on us."

"Says the very man who wrote his girlfriend a last will and testament."

Rebecca hugged him next. "You go handy on the drink."

"I need to sleep and it helps with the dreams. Besides, nothing aids sneaking like a hangover. You're tender on your feet when the head rings like a Sunday church bell with every step. Keep your radios handy in case of trouble."

The water in the bay was still, a ghostly reflection of the moon shimmered on the surface like slippery, molten mercury.

They lay the boards down, sending ripples echoing ahead of them. Fin walked into the shallows, the cold went straight through the rubbery material of his wetsuit. It took him a few attempts to gain his balance and keep it on the board. A light breeze forced him into deeper water and just like that, he was committed. Indifferent to the cold, George waded out to hand him a paddle. Reaching out for it nearly caused Fin to tumble into the water, but George steadied him.

"I surfed a bit when I was younger, but half the fun then was falling in," Fin said. "I'm terrified of doing that now." He could already feel the strain on his core as he tried to keep steady. "How are we meant to stand on these?"

"With proper training and knowledge of currents." George let go of his shoulder, but stayed close in case he needed help.

"We have neither of those things," Fin said.

"Well then, you best hope that the kayak is in good working order. Now guys, I'm going for a nap. Stay safe out there." George tied provisions to the back of their boards. His drone was wrapped in numerous protective layers to keep it dry. They had hammers easily accessible in the bags over their shoulders. There were knives there too. Taking into account the weight of his kit, Fin imagined falling in, his clothes absorbing water, weighing him down. Even the hot water bottle was a dead weight. If he went in, he would slip through the water and out of life.

They practiced in the shallows until they were confident enough to head out far enough that George became a silhouette on the shore, watching them paddle out of sight. When Fin got the hang of it, it felt almost meditative, ghosting beneath a glistening canopy of stars, marred only by a few scudding clouds. *Those clouds will drift over the country, what will they see?*

"Do you know what I need now?" Fin said.

"What?" Rebecca was too focused on keeping her balance to look at him.

"A good space documentary, there's nothing like it for making your big problems feel like nothing." His voice carried through the clear night.

Rebecca pulled her paddle from the water and looked up, her silhouette serene. "I've never seen a night sky like it before. Must be the lack of light pollution."

The implications made Fin wish he could keep paddling away from the horror behind. Wind struck them the moment they rounded the headland. Both of them went down to their knees to regain balance. They made for the shore, not daring to wade in the shallows; considering the infected body they had found, there was no telling how many of them were hidden in the silt.

Rebecca shined her torch along the beach. It took a few minutes, but they found the hidden kayak. Nothing came down from the fields and gardens. As far as they could see, the only infected was the one they had left there. Fin landed, while Rebecca kept him in light, his shadow elongated and gangly on the dunes.

The kayak was completely deflated. The dead man was motionless, a wedding band on his bloated fingers. Fin picked up a stone and threw it at him. The moment it touched the infected, it reacted, closing its arms in a sweeping motion, reminding him of a venus flytrap. Any sympathy he felt vanished. *That person is gone. This is a vector, a parasite.*

"How does it look?" she asked.

He did not answer. Instead, he hunkered over a large rock, bent his legs, back straight, and cradled it in his arms and hefted it up. Hunched by the weight, he quickly brought it near the infected and dropped it on its head. The zombie disappeared beneath the sand, its grasp loosening on the molting crow corpse in its hand.

Fin was left in darkness when Rebecca moved the beam of her torch off him and shined it up the beach. The light reflected off the eyes of multiple infected cresting the dune. Invigorated by their presence, some started weeping. The soft sand gave way beneath their feet and they tumbled down. Fin ran back to the water and the safety of his board.

"What the hell were you at?" Rebecca kept her light on the infected.

"The kayak is useless, there's not a bit of air in it."

"What you did was unnecessary and foolish. We agreed we wouldn't go out of our way to kill them. We don't allow ourselves to be provoked. We plan our moves."

"What if a child was wandering along that beach? How was I to know there were more in the field?"

"The only reason we're talking now is luck, if not for the sand, you'd be dead. Do you feel like a big man now? You act the fool on your own time, but if you ever bring a weeper's attention down on me by association again, we're done."

"You were on the water." Fin was not up for the argument, he knew she was right.

"You've alerted the whole shore of our presence. We're not far from George. Think before you act."

"I'm sorry."

Rebecca sat on her board and very carefully took her radio out of her bag. "George." She raked the land with her torch. More infected mounted the dunes, they did not blink away the light.

"How many are there?" Fin felt rather small as the crowd grew steadily larger on the beach. They were in deep water but he still worried he would feel the vice-like grip of their hands grab hold of him and drag him under.

George took a few moments before answering. "Are you okay, do you need me?"

"You weren't lying about going for a nap. We're at the kayak, it's useless. I'm staring at nearly a dozen infected. Only a few weepers though. The rest are slower zombies."

George did not respond.

"Are you there?"

"Yeah, sorry. I wasn't ready for them to be this far yet. I have to go, I'll block up the back fences while it's dark."

"We'll keep close to the shore and try to lure them away from you."

"No, don't. Are you mad? Think of the people that way in hiding. How many would you kill? Leave them be and head for the islands as planned. Be safe. I have to go."

Fin's one small act of vengeance seemed so peevish and inconsequential now. The howl of the weepers was taken up, infecting the silent night. *Most people move by night. How many have I endangered?* "Are you ready?"

Rebecca carefully put the radio away and slowly stood up on her board. He awkwardly regained his footing and paddled further away from the infected as they started wading into the bay. Weak waves unfooted the slower ones, the weepers only made it to chest height before the seabed fell away and they thrashed. They no longer needed the light to draw them, their own noises would lure the others out.

"They're only going to wash right back up," Rebecca said. "Hopefully they're in long enough to do damage to their eyes." Rebecca turned off her light, leaving them briefly nightblind. The infected sounded much closer than they were. "That's motivation enough for me to try for the islands. Still want to do it without the kayak?"

"Seems like our only option," Fin said. "Could you rest,

knowing these are our neighbours? I don't know about you, but my arms are in bits just from that little stretch of paddling. Will we make it that distance on the boards?"

"To Achill? No," Rebecca said. "We could hug the shoreline and keep an eye out for a boat instead, it wouldn't be impossible to find something, but we would have to contend with infected and the owners if they stayed at home. Alternatively, I've seen people kitesurfing in the bay. If we found the club's container along the shore, we could be out to the islands in no time. Downside would be getting wet."

"If we didn't drown, then we'd advertise our location to everybody, we'd literally be flying a giant flag," Fin said

"Remember you barely saw me this summer gone? I worked at a summer camp in Achill giving surf lessons. I'm confident on the board and I'm here to help you. I think we can do it. Nothing will happen while I'm here. We have life jackets and wetsuits. People would kill to be in this position. Let's go, before the hot water bottles get cold."

"Okay."

* * *

"Look at the mountain," Rebecca said, taking a rest from paddling.

They were far enough into the bay that they had a good view of Croagh Patrick. The lantern that had long been a feature of the epidemic in Westport was slowly descending the mountain, about a ten minute hike from the peak.

"What a horrible pilgrimage they've set themselves," Fin said. He could only imagine the cold at that altitude, with no shelter, in winter.

"It's probably one of the safest places to be right now," Rebecca said. "The infected don't seem so stable on their feet." She paddled close to him so that their whispers would not travel far.

His eyes had adjusted to the moonlight. The few shadows and noises they encountered turned out to be seagulls. When the wind picked up, they had to stay on their knees for fear of falling in. Aside from that and fatigue, the trip was pleasant.

"What was your plan before this happened?" Rebecca asked.

Fin heard a shiver in her voice. "How do you mean?"

"What were you aiming for? Any big ambitions?"

He was quiet for a moment. "Survive, I suppose, though that hardly seemed so noble a few weeks ago."

"I always knew you were a lazy sot."

"Ah, I'm only joking. I had some notions, but I never did much, there was always tomorrow and more likely the months after that. I was on autopilot, always seemed to be an endless stream of time ahead. Best thing I had going for me was the girlfriend. Each year I would write a letter to myself on January first. I'd open it again on the last day of that year."

"That sounds like a good idea. So like, things you wanted to achieve?"

"That's it."

"What was on the list for this year?"

He lifted the paddle out of the water to take a breather. It felt like the ocean absorbed all of his momentum and he soon came to a standstill. "If I'm being completely honest, it would have been the exact same stuff as I wrote last year. Likely would have just recycled the same letter for the next few years, with the addendum of 'do better.'"

"That's disappointing."

He looked at her and laughed. "I know. Well no, that's

an exaggeration. There's the disappointment when you read it that the big things were not achieved, but it makes you think of the small things that don't make any list. Solene has been on it for a while now, and I had planned for her to be on all the ones to come. It was an annual affirmation that I still had hopes and dreams left unachieved. If ever I opened the letter and did not feel down about it, I'd either reached my goals or stopped caring. Both cases would require serious thinking. What about you?"

"I don't want to die."

"To the point. I wouldn't mind living forever myself."

"With each passing day it's like I grow more numb to this world, like my mind knows that I'm already dead, my body just has not caught on yet. There are a lot of things I want to do that I'm only now realising. So much wasted time."

"I called George out for being morose and I'm not afraid to do it to you too," Fin said. "Take this upset and use it as motivation from now on." *I sound like my dad.*

"So how did you meet Solene?" Rebecca changed the subject.

"Online dating app."

"Ah here, I was expecting this magical romantic story. How did you introduce yourself? 'Hi Solene, do you have any STDs?'"

Fin could not help but laugh. Rebecca chuckled at his response. "Excuse you, we're a bit more cultured than that – we sent nudes first."

Rebecca laughed. "I could stay out here with you all day. It feels like the world hasn't ended."

"This right here is what you'd call a lovely moment. It's one of the first times my guts have not felt like an ice cream machine since this started."

"And the moment's over. Thanks for that image. Are you ready to continue?"

Fin nodded reluctantly. Long dormant muscles ached. Conversation lapsed as they focused on reaching the island. At one point, Fin lay down on the board to paddle with his hands, but ended up regretting it as the cool breeze chilled his wet sleeves.

"I definitely think I'll have a six pack after this," Fin said.

"We're still in sight of the shore. I doubt your muscles have started hardening already."

"That tense feeling in my gut is probably a hernia then."

Rebecca pointed towards a smaller island in the distance, it was more of a sandbar. "Remember the night of the storm? The pier was packed with boats. It wasn't much safer the next few days, but people went out anyway."

Fin tried to make out shapes in the dawn light. It was a wrecked trawler, lying on its side. "Maybe this was a bad idea."

"Better than waiting to die in an attic. There have got to be a few islands with boats, we can ask for a lend and go back for George, we could be on our own island before it gets dark."

Clare Island was as much a feature of the bay as Croagh Patrick, though it may as well have been a mirage for any hope they had of reaching it on paddle boards.

"Haven't seen any fires or lights on the islands," Fin said.

"We wouldn't from our house. If you don't get a good feeling for them, we can land on an empty one and just send the drone up. Save us checking them all."

"Do you want to find sanctuary here?" Fin asked.

"I won't, not when I know how close I am to home. I wouldn't be happy leaving either of you on the islands. Not when I know how good an option Achill is. I'm out here to find safe passage and a boat for the three of us. I don't see sanctuary, I see a slow death. That island with the house on it seems promising." She pointed off into the distance and turned her board to face it.

"Keep an eye out for boats," Rebecca said. "None of us know how to operate the big ones, one with oars and a propeller would be ideal. Don't even bother with the ones with sails, we might as well save time and just hang ourselves from the rigging, instead of heading out on open water in one of them."

Sun tinted the horizon to the east. The mountain was clear of cloud. When it was bright enough the climber's lantern went off and with it, the only visible man-made light in sight. They watched the climber's slow, careful progress as the sun brought the SOS daubed on the mountain into view. Fin gave a wave. From that distance the climber melted into the environment, but he was uneasy that Rebecca and him were the only people moving. They were targets for curiosity and worse. "Do you think they can see us up there?" he asked.

"They're not the only ones." Rebecca stared straight ahead.

To their left, a large ship had run aground in the storm. Dead walked the shore and gathered eagerly to watch them pass. There were no weepers amongst them. Impatient, they walked into the surf. Their faces so human, Fin wanted to roar at them to go back. Rebecca was not interested in them. Fin followed her line of sight; she was staring at the island with the house on it.

The silhouette of a man turned away from the shore and made his way slowly back to the building.

"Did he look infected?" Fin asked.

"Can't be sure, but he walked with purpose and we weren't it, which seems promising."

"If he was on watch and he saw us then we are his purpose."

They hoped to meet others, but that welcome had made them uncertain. The islands and sandbars protected the bay from the worst of the waves, boats wrecked on smaller islands, leaving the shore completely bare. Weary and wary, they proceeded.

Few of the islands were inhabited. Maps of the area did not show them in great detail, most of the larger ones were organised into separate fields by stone walls. The man walked up the beach at a leisurely pace and disappeared into a two-storey cottage.

Whoever he was, he made no attempt to signal for them to either land or leave. There were no other figures on the island, but much of it was out of view. The house was hidden in a dell, away from the worst of the wind.

"What do we do?" Fin spoke softly, so his voice would not travel.

"Stay close to the water, be ready to leave in an instant. I wish we had practiced codewords."

They stepped off their boards in the shallows and dragged them above the tideline. Fin was reluctant to leave the long paddle, but it would be of little use against the undead or the living.

"Hello," Rebecca called up to the house. Nothing came running at them, but nor was a verbal response forthcoming.

"No dead," Fin said.

"The living can cause us just as many problems."

They did not walk any closer to the house, keeping near

the water in case they needed to escape. "We're not infected," Rebecca said.

"Maybe they only speak Irish," Fin whispered.

"Nobody only speaks Irish, but I'll give it a go." She walked along the beach to get a better look at the front of the house. "Níl muid tinn."

The man stepped halfway through the door, ready to duck back inside. He covered his mouth with a finger, signing for them to be quiet and then beckoned them closer with the same hand. His other hand was concealed behind the door.

27

THE FIRST DEATH

They edged slowly up the beach.

"Try to keep your voices down. There aren't as many weepers as there were after the storm, but a few still linger on the other islands. That must have been a cold trip out, why start so early? Afraid of being seen?" By his accent, Fin thought him a local.

"Only a fool draws attention to themselves these days," Rebecca said. "We did not want to draw attention to our home. Those things don't seem to do too well in the dark."

"'Those things', that's an awful harsh way of talking about the sick," the man said. Fin was not sure if he was serious.

"I can think of worse," Rebecca said.

He took a long pause each time before he spoke, as if calculating the consequences of his words. "If you had a place to stay, why come all the way out here?"

"To find people. We weren't trying to sneak up on you, peek-a-boo is a bit taboo at the moment," Rebecca said.

The man's mouth turned up in a brief smile. If he had meant to disarm them with it, he failed. He stepped out of the house entirely and they could see his hands were empty. Fin relaxed. The man wore a knitted hat and a baggy green jumper that had been through the wash so often that it hung limp on him. "Do you know anything about the fireworks?"

"Diversion tactic," Rebecca said.

"Is your boyfriend mute?"

"No, sorry mate, I used to work nights in the hotel on the quay. This, right now, is usually my bedtime. Combine that with the trip out, which needed a level of fitness far beyond mine and a constant lack of sleep, I'm just trying to stay standing," Fin said.

"I'm starting to miss the eight hours myself. How are things on the mainland?"

"Do you have a television out here?" Rebecca took over again.

"I do, but I've a young one here too, so we mostly stick to cartoons and DVDs."

"Is it only the both of you?" Rebecca asked.

"That's not a question I feel comfortable answering." His demeanour changed. "I'll tell you what I tell everybody else that comes here. Clare Island has more space and more food, keep on paddling."

Fin did not know how to respond to the hostility. The expression on the man's face had not changed, but it suited his acerbic tone.

"Does it look like we're going hungry?" Rebecca asked. Fin looked down and wondered if his gut showed beneath the life vest and the hot water bottle. "We're not here for your food. Clare Island is our destination, we're just here to check out the islands with our drone. The battery would not see it out and back from the mainland. You do know that there's an army encampment in Westport House? Food is delivered and distributed to survivors. High walls, plenty of people and soldiers." She emphasised the last word.

"It's so safe and yet here you are."

Fin felt his anger boil away the last of his civility, but he reckoned he would be the same if he was alone on an island during an epidemic, with a child to care for.

"I'm from Achill," Rebecca said. "I'd sooner be back there. We tried the roads and walkways, but the infection spread too fast. The water seemed the safest route."

"We'll head on to the other islands," Fin said. "Maybe see if we can find something sturdier than a surfboard for getting us to Achill."

"You're heading out further and then returning to the camp?"

"Well, back for supplies really," Fin said. "And to pick up the rest of our group."

The man mulled that over for a moment.

"Have you any weapons for dealing with," he looked over his shoulder back into the house, "the trouble?"

"Honestly, we do our best to avoid it," Rebecca said. "We couldn't carry too much on the crossing."

"Will you have tea or coffee?"

The question threw them.

"We're just about to have breakfast. I can't give you our boat, you'll not likely get any of the living to part with theirs either, but there are plenty of spare ones around here. You're welcome to some breakfast before setting on."

"We won't take any of your food," Rebecca said "A mug of coffee would be great though. Thank you."

"Consider it a trade. A bit of grub in return for news about what's happening on the mainland." He leaned away from the door and whispered, "Just remember there's a child, don't go into too much detail, please."

The promise of warm food, a cup of coffee and a conversation went a long way to dispelling Fin's suspicions. The child had a lot to do with that. Anybody still trying to keep innocence alive was okay in his book.

"Leave your bags outside." He took one last look at the water behind them before going back inside the house.

"Fin, I don't know how I feel about this."

"It is odd meeting somebody that is not screaming their head off and trying to murder us, but I could get used to it. This is what we're here for. We'll go in, learn about the islands and hear if he can tell us anything about Clare. Then we'll send the drone up." The thought of heading back out on the water was not at all appealing to him.

"There are plenty of shipwrecks around here, he said so himself. Most weepers are gone too. We should find a boat and leave." Rebecca sounded like she was on the verge of pleading.

"I'm not stepping a foot on any island until I'm sure. Weepers don't just disintegrate, they turn into... zombies." It was still a difficult word to say seriously. "Relax, you're putting me on edge, that lad's probably worried you're thinking of eating him."

"Oh to live in your world for a time. He never asked us if we were infected."

Fin stopped. "If they've been out here the whole time watching movies, they might not know to ask." He continued on the rest of the way to the house alone. Glancing back, he could see that Rebecca was giving serious consideration to leaving without him.

He approached the front door from an angle, so he could see if anybody was waiting for him. *She has me paranoid now.* After stepping inside, it took a few tense seconds for his vision to adjust to the dimmer light. The man hunched over the sink in the kitchen, filling the kettle. Downstairs had an open plan layout and was decorated with enough tweed, throw pillows and spare blankets to be excessively homey. A child sat at the table glued to her phone.

"Take a seat," the man said.

"Mind if I join you?" Fin asked the child, but she completely ignored him. Conscious of how he looked in a wetsuit and life jacket, he took the sun-faded padded jacket off and left it by his chair. He took a jumper out of his pack; he was too self conscious to take off the wetsuit to remove the hot water bottle.

The child wore a baggy jumper that belonged to her father. The bags beneath her eyes looked out of place on one so young. She bore the vacant, hollowed out stare that so many wore on the mainland.

The man placed the kettle on the hob. It sparked a few times before the gas ignited. The rest of the cooker was full: a pot of beans, a frying pan of sizzling and crackling rashers. Fin could even see herb mixed sausages, so thick that they burst through their skin.

"You have a beautiful home..." Fin left a silence for the man to offer his name, but all he got in return was gratitude. "Property value out here is definitely on the rise, might even match Dublin by the time this is over."

"Oh, how so?"

Rebecca's shadow darkened the doorway. Fin looked to her for help. "I was only joking," he said.

"I know, I'm messing with you. We'd need a few more months of this and a mine of gold on the island for them to be a match for Dublin prices. Market value, there's something that will be a while in coming back. Right, who's for tea or coffee?"

"I'd love a cup of coffee, if you're making one for yourself," Fin said.

"Sit down," he said to Rebecca. "Don't let the heat out."

She wavered, clearly apprehensive about entering.

"You don't have to put food on for us," she said.

"Don't worry, we won't starve by filling two extra plates. I work online and you can imagine a weekly shop out here is a pain, especially if the weather turns. We do a monthly shop. We've enough to see us through this mess." He put a few more sausages into an already crowded pan and started slicing mushrooms.

The smell of sizzling, frying food made Fin aware of his ravenous appetite.

"I'd be pleased if you kept the information of our stores to yourselves. We're not setting up a diner out here."

"We will, of course," Fin said.

"I'm Dara, that socialite is Brian."

Rebecca and Fin introduced themselves. Fin would have sworn the child was a girl.

"Brian, will you listen to your music?" Dara asked.

The child put headphones on and continued to stare at his phone. Fin sat close enough beside him to notice that the screen was dark. *Clever.* He would eavesdrop on the conversation while keeping up the illusion of being oblivious, it almost seemed a tender act, so his father could pretend his innocence was intact.

When Dara disappeared into the pantry, Brian looked up so suddenly, it caused Rebecca to jump. "Don't eat the food."

Dara came back before Fin could say anything and set steaming mugs on the table. The child had gone rigid in a poor attempt at looking normal.

"Sit," the man said to Rebecca, forcing her to come

closer to the table or make her discomfort move beyond obvious and into obstructive.

"Eh, coffee is okay, you don't have to go to the trouble of putting on food for us," Fin said. "We don't want to leave you stuck down the road."

"Nonsense, I feel I was rude earlier. It's sad that that's necessary now."

Fin looked to Brian to see if he had assured him that they were not going to take all their supplies, but he continued to stare at his screen.

"Sugar's on the table, if you use it. I'll hang those life vests up for you."

Fin gave his over willingly, but Rebecca kept hers on. "We passed an island with infected on it, I was wondering about the ship on the shore. Do you think it still works? We could use that to get to Clare Island and then my home," Rebecca said. She moved her seat back against the wall, away from the table, before sitting down.

"I told you, none of the neighbours are going to part with their boats without a fight," Dara said. "There are over a dozen infected that I've counted and there are bound to be more in the fields."

Fin took his mug in both hands and held it beneath his nose. It was instant coffee, but the smell made him close his eyes and let it fill his lungs. He thawed a little with every breath.

Cartoons played on the television in the sitting room. The sofa was covered with blankets and empty sweet wrappers. It was a comfortable scene.

"Are you okay?" Dara asked while putting four plates on the table.

Fin wiped his eyes. "Sorry. It just seems so normal, you know."

"That bad back there?"

Fin nodded.

"From the little I know, it's just Ireland that has been hit. You don't think the rest of the world will watch on and do nothing, do you?" Dara filled their plates with slightly burned, bulging herb sausages, tomatoes, mushrooms, potato farls and eggs, with a dam of baked beans. "Dig in, guys."

Dara questioned them extensively on the army in Westport House. He wanted to know if they were talking about a cure yet. He was particularly interested in asking them about their own redoubt and what, if anything, the army knew about the islands.

"Do they even know what it is yet?" Rebecca asked. "They've hardly mentioned anything specific about that on the news. A cure is a long while away, I think."

Fin watched as she cut up her food and moved it around her plate, but did not eat. *Seeing this place must have brought back memories of her family. If mine were this close, I'd want to be with them too.*

Dara's plate was devoid of meat, he ate measured forkfuls. Fin noticed from the corner of his eye the look of disgust on his face, watching him while he ate. Brian's plate was untouched, grease droplets cooled, coagulated and turned milky white. Fin ate slower, using a napkin to wipe his mouth. "Sorry. I haven't had a meal this good in a long time."

"No harm, I'm happy to have somebody that appreciates my cooking." The look was gone.

Brian did not take the hint, continuing instead to stare blankly at the phone.

"When you get back, will you let the army know we're here?"

"If you want us to, we can," Fin said.

"Good people can do desperate things."

"Sorry?" Rebecca asked.

"I'm not sure I want them knowing. If you could keep quiet about us, I'd appreciate that."

"We won't say a word then," Fin said.

"Good, that's a relief."

The child started shaking. Fin corralled the last few beans and crumbs of white pudding onto his fork. The moment it was in his mouth Dara stood up with such speed that his chair fell back and clattered against the floor.

Caught off guard, Fin tried to kick away from the table, but his feet slipped on the slick tiles. He choked on his food, the breath driven from him by the force of Dara's fist. A blade hilt stuck out from his stomach. The child ducked beneath the table and ran. Books flew from a shelf as Rebecca reacted, her chair hitting the shelf with a bang. Fin felt a hot stream spill down his front. *Blood.* "What are you doing?"

Dara pulled the blade out, but never got the chance to answer. Rebecca dented the side of his skull with her hammer. She recoiled as human, hammer, and knife fell to the floor.

"Come on!" She pulled Fin up from the chair.

They skirted around the wailing man, his shrieks incoherent gibberish. They ran from the house. Fin stumbled and fell, throwing up his breakfast on the rocky shore. Steam rose from the vomit.

"No, no, no," he repeated it like a prayer, as if saying it could take back what just happened. Trembling hands fumbled at the zippers of his wetsuit, and with the initial shock passing, he was starting to feel pain. Rebecca yanked his jumper off and unzipped the wetsuit. His hot water bottle fell onto the sand, ruptured. Warm water spilled out from the gash caused by the knife.

There was blood on his belly, a steady stream of it pumped out of the puncture wound. It was not nearly as bad as he thought. Relief stemmed the flow of adrenaline that acted like cotton in his ears. Now he heard the screaming. Dara was alive and in agony.

Rebecca shrank in on herself. She flinched after every breath Dara took between screams. She turned to run for the paddle boards but stopped to face the house. It looked as if all strength had gone from her legs. Neither the screams nor Fin's voice reached her any longer. He never knew a human could make such noises. Pity was the only thing that made him return to the house.

Rebecca had acted instinctively. Dara lunged with such ferociousness that his chair was halfway across the kitchen. Muscles in his neck strained and spittle flecked his lips. Writhing on the floor, his kicking feet left black scuff marks.

Fin lunged for the hammer and jumped back out of his reach. Wringing the handle between his hands, Fin stepped closer. Dara did not seem to notice him. Fin dragged the cloth off the table; plates, cutlery and mugs crashed down on top of the prone man. Fin covered Dara in the coffee stained shroud.

"I'm sorry."

Fin brought the hammer up, but faltered. In his convulsions, Dara's hand hit the knife and sent it skittering away. Fin took a breath and brought the hammer down. He used all his strength for the next blow, terrified that Dara would feel any of it. The screaming stopped by the third impact. By the fourth the spasms ceased.

The hammer slipped from Fin's hand. Where Dara's face had been beneath the cloth was now misshapen and blood darkened. *What was the hammer used for last? Hanging Christmas decorations?* Fin could still hear the sickening thud the hammer made against a human head.

The air outside was fresh. Only by the contrast did he realise that Dara had soiled himself. Rebecca lay cross legged, looking out to the mainland. Her hands buried in the sand, making fists.

Fin walked past her and followed the backwash of a retreating wave. Barely noticing the cold, he waded out far enough that he could feel the suggestion of a current pulling at him. Water filled his open suit, making it a considerable weight, he let it take him down. Closing his eyes he screamed into the ocean. All he heard were cascading bubbles and the endless wash of the waves eroding the shore.

28

HOPE DIES WITH THOUGHTS AND PRAYERS

Fin crawled up the beach, coughing out harsh saltwater. Rolling over, he lay on his back. The waves lifted him a little, but not enough to drag him out. Just below the wash and gurgle of the ocean was the hollow ring of the hammer. He filled his lungs with air so crisp it felt like splintered shards of broken ice. Gulls and crows kept a watchful eye on him.

Rebecca came down to sit beside him. His eyes stung from the salt, hers were distant. "Let's go," she said in a voice so low it was barely a whisper.

Fin sat up, but could go no further. His head pounded, it felt like he was just coming out of a full body flu ache. *I killed a man.* The concept was so foreign that the thought barely registered. Rebecca did not give him time to think, she left him to drag their boards to the water's edge. He tried to stand up, but that increased the flow of blood seeping from the wound. He held his hand over it and lay down, knowing he could not trust his legs. Shivering, he said, "You saved my life."

Rebecca stood over him, blocking the sun. "Let's go."

Fin felt the familiar spasms in his stomach. He was about to retch, but fought it. "Wait."

She just looked out over the water.

"We have to send the drone up. We'll only have to come back if we don't."

"I'm never coming back. Is he... dead?"

Fin gave a single firm nod, it was all that was needed.

"I killed him," Rebecca said.

Fin clenched his jaw, the muscles in his face contorted from concentrating on ignoring the sound of the hammer. "You saved my life." The hammer strokes punctuated his words. Head in hands, he started laughing, it was the first time he truly feared for his mental health. "I think I'm losing my mind. It's like my sanity is an anchor on an old rusty chain and it's about to break."

"Oh my god, Fin! The child! Where's the child?"

Rebecca ran to the house. Fin got up and stumbled into a jog. He could not remember what happened to Brian during the struggle. They called his name from outside the house. Neither of them wanted to go in.

"We're not going to hurt you," Rebecca said.

"I don't think there's a convincing way of saying that." Fin said. He did not think it entirely true either. *The child knew what was going to happen. Why was he shaking moments before Dara attacked?* Together they combed the shoreline calling his name. Rounding the headland, they came across a pier. Brian was sitting low in the only boat. He was already too far out for more than their voices to reach him. His head snapped back when he heard them. Immediately, he pulled in the oars and started the engine.

"We have to go after him," Rebecca said.

"By the time we get the boards, he'll be out of sight. Stop and think. After what we did to his father, if we chase him, it would only force him into dangerous situations to avoid us. He heard us talk about the military camp. He'll go there, hopefully."

"He was petrified of us the moment we walked through that door," Rebecca said. "How did you not notice how odd Dara was acting? You just ate as if things were back to normal. People aren't normal now, Fin."

"What do you mean?" He was starting to feel the cold.

"How could you not tell he was acting strange from the moment he spotted us? You just went in as if the world wasn't ending. We should have just paddled away."

"He wasn't infected. Why would he do that? He had no reason for attacking us. We were no harm to anybody." He remembered the malice on Dara's face when he stabbed him. Fin pushed his thumbs against his eyes to shut the image out. He took shaky breaths to calm himself.

"The infection does not wipe out all the other bad in the world. It changes people. Survival is cruel." Rebecca knew Fin could not keep pace with her, but she did not slow down to accommodate him.

Fin walked in the husks of her footprints. The mountain seemed to be the only constant in this world of change. People turned into ravenous weepers. Survivors attacking survivors. The old world, bleak and empty. *When we are all dust, this won't even be a bad memory in the life of the mountain.* Rebecca paced the shore, running her hands across her bristly scalp. A radio in a pack on the back of one of their boards crackled into life, startling them to action. *Any diversion, keep busy, don't give the mind time to think.*

"If you leave that on when the infected are near, it'll get us killed," Fin said.

She threw the radio at him in frustration. "It's coming from your bag you idiot! It's a race between your stupidity and carelessness, over which will be the cause of our deaths."

"Well, guys, how was the paddle?" George asked in a tone that was alien in the moment.

Fin picked up the radio and wiped the sand off the plastic bag covering it. Once he pressed the receiver down, he realised that he did not have a clue what to say. He let it go.

"Just checking in," George said.

"It's not a good time." Dead air passed between them.

"Is everything okay?"

"Not really. There were people on the island. It's just us now."

"There were?"

Fin realised that, to satisfy George's questions, he would have to admit to murdering somebody. "We're all right now. Stay safe, we'll chat later."

"Okay. Listen to me now. There's a lot of movement here. I haven't been able to leave my position. If the island is safe now, then stay there."

"Thanks for the heads up, let us know if and when anything changes."

"Rebecca?" George asked.

"I'm here. Stay safe. We'll be thinking of you."

"That'll keep you warm," George said.

They were silent on the beach. "I'm with a pack of idiots." Her dim smile blunted her words a little.

Fin turned the radio off and stored it in his pack. Now they had a body to deal with. He went in first. Dara lay where he died. Blood soaked and spread across the sheet covering his head. Fin picked up the hammer and Rebecca took one of the knives that Dara had used to prepare breakfast out of the sink. Before they searched the house, Fin covered the hammer with washing up liquid and held it under the hot tap. When steam started coming out of the sink, he emptied the rest of the washing liquid into his cupped hand and used the metal pot scrub to cleanse the blood from his skin, gasping as the scalding stream burned him, a blinding and brief absolution through pain.

Rebecca kicked the knife that nearly killed him under the sofa, it was small enough that Dara was able to conceal it up his sleeve. "Those screams should have been my own. If not for the hot water bottle and your quick reaction. This time now was not supposed to be mine." He relished his next breath. "It's mad how quick life can leave a body. He's just meat now." He let his tongue loose, so he could keep a grip on his mind.

They searched every possible hiding place in the house. There were three bedrooms; the master, a guest room, and one decorated for a girl. 'Esme' was etched on a wooden plaque above a memory board of photos. Dara was in none of them.

"That's Brian," Rebecca said. "Dara must have cut her hair. Why call her Brian though?"

"I haven't seen a single photo with Dara in it throughout the house," Fin said. "I don't think it was us she was terrified of."

"Where are her parents?"

Their search of the house unearthed no answers. All that was left to do was to dispose of the body. They laid out a few bed sheets and rolled him on top of them. Fin unplugged the Christmas tree lights and wound the cord tightly around the body; he had seen too many corpses cause trouble in the last few days. The body was an incredible weight to lift, when no muscle worked with you.

"We need to bury him," Rebecca said.

Fin let go of a leg, it hit the floor without bouncing. "The dead are walking and you want to bury a body in soft soil. If I had a digger, I wouldn't feel like I could bury it deep enough. We'll throw it off the end of the pier. Tie it down with rocks."

Rebecca looked at him with horror, but she could not object.

Fin's stomach ached as he struggled to lift his part of Dara.

"Let me take a look at that."

"Not until this job's done."

Once they dragged the body to the door, they left it to search for a wheelbarrow. There was one full of sods of turf behind the house. The tyre was partially deflated, but it was better than carrying him across the sucking sand. Fin was sweating by the time they hoisted Dara into the barrow. Each breath brought less nourishment than the last, but he was determined to keep moving. If he stopped long enough to let what he was doing sink in, he would not be able to go through with it.

They managed to get onto the hard-packed, earthen road that led down to the pier. Fin found great distraction in weaving the barrow around potholes. The weight strained his shoulders, already sore from the paddle. Together, they filled reusable shopping bags they found beneath the sink with smooth shore stones. With two bike locks and a length of rope, they weighed down the body.

The water was clear enough that it was hard to judge the depth. Looking over the edge of the old pier, Fin saw something obscured by wind ripples. When there came a break in the breeze, he stumbled away from the edge. "Zombies in the water."

Rebecca dropped her bag and ran towards him, knife at

the ready. Her hand lowered after a few seconds watching the bodies. She took a stone out of the bag and dropped it with a loud plop, it struck one of the corpses and sank in front of it. "They're tied down, Fin. No wonder we couldn't find any decent rope, Dara already used it on them. It's a man and woman with the same colour hair as the people in the photos."

Fin did not look again, he did not need to. The image played vividly in his imagination. They finished preparing the body, checked that the bags were secure and pushed Dara into the water. Fin saw no justice in what they had done. He just felt sick that he had thought to do the exact same thing as Dara.

"Let's fix you up now," Rebecca said.

Fin agreed only because it was something to do. There was a first aid kit in the cupboard beneath the stairs. There were blue plasters as well as pink ones with drawings of rabbits. Rebecca poured antiseptic ointment over the wound and rubbed the dried blood away.

"I don't know if it needs stitches," she said, scrutinising the damage. "It does not seem all that bad. I mean the knife was small enough and the hot water bottle took most of it. This is good, I don't think he caused serious harm, just cut into the fat."

She lathered on half a tub of antibacterial cream before applying the gauze and glued it all down with plasters.

"If we were in the hotel right now, you can bet there wouldn't be a drop of the fine whiskey left," he said.

Rebecca threw him a looted tee-shirt from the laundry basket. "It's probably a good thing we're no longer there. We can't drink our way through this."

"Feels like the only ones that will see this through are

those that dig in and drink up. We'll have to stay here tonight," Fin said. "I might start cleaning."

They found a CD player and put Christmas music on as they mopped up Dara's blood and cleaned the broken plates and uneaten breakfast from the floor. The scent of pine bleach masked the fading smell of cooked sausages and crispy rashers. The thought of food made him queasy. Rebecca poured a whole bottle of bleach over the blood-stain that had seeped between the tiles. When the kettle boiled, she spilled it over the blood. Fin mopped. In the utility room they discovered fresh, folded, bloodstained towels above the dryer.

Rebecca threw the kettle in the sink. Fin emptied the rusty water from the bucket and put the mop outside to dry.

"This seems wrong, cleaning a crime scene," she said.

"He attacked us."

"I meant what he did to the owners. Did he know them? Why'd he do it? It'll be a crime that will never be solved. They'll just join the ranks of 'dead' when this is over. How many similar cases do you think have happened and will continue to happen before this ends?"

"There'll be plenty of work for those that come after."

When there was nothing left for them to do inside the house, they went through the wardrobes and borrowed clothes. Sitting in the shelter of a dune outside they sent the drone up. Rebecca wrapped a blanket around them. He could imagine staying here with her and George. Making a home, living a lie until it was safe to return to the truth, but Dara had tainted island life. They were exposed, people could land anywhere and they would not know they had guests until they knocked on the front door. The noise of the drone would have made it foolish to use on the mainland. How small the island looked from a few feet in the air. Fin pointed the camera towards the other islands and sent the drone over them.

Some ships were anchored in sheltered bays. Others were forced aground and washed onto rocks. One trawler was completely submerged. Most vessels were small engine ribs and fishing boats. Two islands away from them, there were fire pits, tents and infected.

After a while it was clear that there was no one left alive to dispute ownership over boats. A few trawlers had lights on in cabins. There was small hope that survivors were onboard, waiting for things to clear. Not many zombies moved quickly on the islands, the weepers had died off a while ago. Fin brought the drone home and put it back into the waterproof bag. Even with the sun well up, his breath was still visible in front of him. The footage was saved on his new phone. "What now?"

Rebecca shrugged. "Want to watch a movie?"

She helped Fin to his feet. "The view from out here is beautiful," he said. The mountain dominated the land. He thought of taking pictures and sending them to his family, to let them know where he was, but then he thought of talking to them. How could he keep what he had just done a secret? Was he not changed in some irrevocable way? *I just killed a man. Why don't I feel like I have?* "I want to try and get in contact with whoever is living on Croagh Patrick. Let them know about the camp. What if they're all alone?"

"Why? Look what happened when we tried the island," Rebecca said. "There are too many people that need help. We have to think about ourselves."

"We know the islands aren't safe. If one infected person reached Clare Island, then that's a graveyard too."

"Anybody unstable enough to climb that mountain

every day is somebody I want to avoid. We promised we wouldn't do anything unnecessary."

"How is it unnecessary? What if...""" His mind raced as he sought out a valid excuse. "What if we could live up there too?" He heard his voice and knew it sounded overexcited.

"I'm not going with you. I have to stay here in case that child comes back. Maybe I could charge the drone up and send a letter out to those trawlers. I'm so close to home."

They argued until it was too cold to stay outside. Once they were in the house, they locked the door and barricaded it. Neither wanted to put the animated movie off in favour of the news. Fin lost hope long ago that while he was away from the screen a cure was discovered and order was restored. Rebecca went through the DVD collection and took out a few for Fin to choose from.

The pantry was fully stocked. George had made the point that they should live off the supplies they scavenged before using their own. They ignored the healthy stuff and opened a box of sweets, hidden on the top shelf. There was a little post-it note stuck to the top that read 'Not to be opened until Christmas'. It came off easily. Rebecca found the remote and wrapped herself in blankets. Despite the heating being on, she still shivered.

"I just want to see if there's anything good on the news," she said.

Fin lay down on the other half of the couch. "In my house, sweets wouldn't last a day," he said through a mouthful of jellies. "The healthiest out of the lot of us is probably the sister, she was never quick enough to get any."

They did not recognise the newscaster. Images flashed across the screen of different cities in Ireland, people crying with their hands out, looking more like an advert for a charity collecting money to help a third world country.

"Operation Piper is being hailed as a success and the first step on the road to recovery."

That caught Fin's attention. Video showed military helicopters flying slow and low over Galway. Part of the city burned. Smoke furled into vortexes beneath the rotors. The recently infected filled the streets, knocking the slower ones down and trampling them underfoot. They followed the helicopters.

Fin remembered his favourite restaurants there, overlooking the cobbled Shop Street, the cold pints and warm evenings in the Latin Quarter listening to music. "If they can burn a city..."

"Earlier attempts at luring the infected from the city failed." They showed footage of a boat in the port blaring a horn. The zombies walked towards it and fell into the harbour, but there were too many of them. Fin just saw human lemmings.

It showed footage from all over the country; a military ship sounded sirens at sea and the camera caught the dead stumbling off cliffs.

"That's a great tourism clip," Fin said. "Zombies tumbling off the Cliffs of Moher."

Dublin was unrecognisable. Around the port were fortifications. Buildings had been collapsed to block off major roads. The only people visible were in hazmat suits. There was a shot of a line of massive ships pouring into the port. Aid from other countries. It gave Fin a little hope that this horror had run its course.

"Our thoughts and prayers are with the Irish people..."

"That's how hope dies, with thoughts and prayers," Rebecca said.

The president of the United States stood before a podium. "Countries around the globe have joined to fight the Irish Epidemic. We have sent a united front to combat the spread of this pestilence." There were cheers from the crowd, but it sounded to Fin like a recorded sound clip of cheering. "May we succeed so that our future is assured. Let those that are born into this new world have mercy on us, for if not for our actions, there will be no future generations."

"That sounded ominous," Fin said. "He's probably in a bunker somewhere."

"Let's watch a film now." Rebecca picked the closest one to her and put it on.

They finished off the box of sweets before they put the second movie on. Fin found it difficult to leave the comfort of the couch, and the only times he did was when Rebecca asked for something or his full bladder demanded it.

"Do you think I'll be put in prison for it?" he asked when he came back from the bathroom.

"No, Fin, I don't think that's likely. Will you put another film on?"

Light outside the house withered while they made their way through the library of movies.

29

___

PILGRIMAGE

The only alcohol they came across in the house was a sweet summer cider. They put it in the fridge for a few hours and took it out to watch the sunset. "What day is it? It's the new year, right?" Fin asked.

"I don't care."

Fin considered lighting a fire, but the prospect of drawing the attention of dead eyes on other islands was not worth the added warmth. He found a hot water bottle in the parents' bedroom. He filled it and wore it like armour and topped Rebecca's one up.

When the sun was only a purple hue on the horizon, the lamp of the climber on Croagh Patrick came on a little under halfway up. Fin held his finger over the speck of light for a few seconds to see if the climber was making any progress. He was, but only in tiny increments.

Stars filled the sky, ribbons of them unfurled in unimaginable expanses of space. "A lot of those stars are gone," Fin said. "They're so far away that the light we see could be coming from a long dead star."

"Fin, shush. I don't want to think of dead and dying things, just enjoy them," Rebecca said.

"People are scared to turn on the lights," Fin pointed to the lantern on the mountain. "It feels like us and whoever is living up there are the last people left in the world."

"So you're still set on going over?" Rebecca asked.

"I'd like to try."

"You're a fool." She left him alone and returned to the house. Fin downed the rest of his bottle and flung it as far as he could into the bay. He did not know Rebecca long. At the hotel he only ever saw her in passing really. He was more comfortable with the late night bar staff because the managers were never around and they could loosen their ties a bit. In a short time, circumstances brought them closer. She had helped him try to drown the weeper on the Greenway and she saved him from Dara. Though her words were said in anger and he knew that to be fleeting, it still hurt to think she thought him a fool. Then it dawned on him. *I might be all she has left of the old world. Her and George might be all that I have. I'd not be happy about her heading off with no real need.* Fin watched until the lantern reached the top of the mountain and went out. An arduous hike, but not even the sound of weepers would make it up there.

He locked the door behind himself and put their barricade back in place. Rebecca lay on the couch, nearly completely covered in blankets. Silent tears ran down her cheek into the cushions.

"What do you fancy watching now?" Fin asked.

"You choose."

He sat down beside her. "Me going isn't about atonement for what happened today, that's not necessary. I just need to do something. I think if I can keep my mind busy, I'll still have it when this ends."

"I wish you'd stay." Her breathing was hard; she wrapped her arms around him and laid her head on his shoulder.

Fin held her close, one hand rubbing her back, the other stroking her hair the way his mother did when he was sick as a child. "We'll be okay." *I hope she still has family left. After all that has happened, we're family. The three of us will see this through together.* He rested his head on top of hers. "Things will get better."

"I don't need you to lie to me."

They had brought their own toothbrushes but used the household's toothpaste and mouthwash, the latter so strong it made Fin's eyes water. The television was just company now. They did not care about the stories and it made them wonder if those wealthy actors were squirreled away in bunkers, hiding from this plague. He told her that he would stay up and keep watch and promised to wake her for her turn. He had no intention of doing that, he would find no peace here. While Rebecca snored softly on the couch, he crept over to the chair he sat at during breakfast, to question the spectre of Dara that haunted him.

* * *

Fin packed in the night. He left George's drone behind, using the space for more water and food. Had there been drink in the house to distract him, he might have stayed. When he changed the bandages, his wound opened and started bleeding again. With fresh ointment and a clean cloth, he scrubbed the area before dressing it. No death seemed preferable, but going out because of an avoidable infection seemed an ignominious end in a zombie apocalypse.

In the twilight before dawn, he wandered the upstairs bedrooms to see if he could get a feel for the previous owners. It still felt like trespassing, even though he knew their fate. He found a Polaroid camera in Esme's room. Her desk drawer was full of rolls of tape for hanging pictures up. There was hardly any wall space free of photos of friends, family and holidays. All her years of growth captured in mute memory. He had no idea who she really was when he left.

The unfamiliar stairs creaked, rousing Rebecca. "Fin, I trusted you to wake me. Did you sleep?" One look at his face was all the answer she needed.

He sat on the sofa and held Esme's camera in front of them. "Photo?"

"Sure."

They looked at the lens. Fin pressed the button and it hummed as a polaroid printed. They waited for the darkness to fade and their faces to show. Neither of them was smiling. "I think I'll call this one 'Shell-shock'."

"I feel better having slept," Rebecca said. "Do you want to lie down? I'll keep watch."

Fin put the photo in his pocket. "I'll sleep tonight. My mind is set, I want to try for the mountain. I'll be okay," he added.

Rebecca massaged her face with her hands. "You better go now then and not waste light."

* * *

Rebecca did not watch him leave. A blustering wind meant only the scorched skin around the hot water bottle was warm. Rebecca slammed the door to the house before he reached his board. The water was more lively today. He stood in the shallows, acclimatising to the chill, watching white-capped waves rise beyond the shelter of the islands. Undeterred, he set off. Like clockwork, the mountain climber's lamp turned on and it crawled down Croagh Patrick like a growing glacier.

The sight of it made Fin too hasty. Thinking he could be at the base of the mountain before the lantern wielder was, he put more energy into each paddle. Arms burning from the effort, he pushed on. The beaches of the islands he passed were lined with unmoving bodies; infected that had been lured by the song of the sea, only to be washed back up on shore. He dared not risk investigating the ships, not without George and his fireworks.

Overconfident in his limited experience from the previous day on the board, he lost his balance. A gust of wind unsettled him just as he struck a wave, tossing him into the bay. He experienced profound shock, gasping for air, inhaling water while the cold stunned him. He kept slipping from the surface. He was losing control of his breathing. In a matter of seconds, he became completely disoriented. His clothes and the backpack absorbed water, diminishing his mobility. The indifferent pull downwards filled him with terror, only worsening his situation. The straps of the lifevest were too loose. In his panic, he blindly struck the board and sent it out of reach.

Everything he needed was in the backpack, but he slipped the straps from his shoulders and let it sink into darkness without a care. He had a moment of vertigo, imagining how high he was hovering above the seabed. *Relax or die.* His numb hands shook, but he managed to pull the life vest tight and secure it. He lay on his back to wait out the cold water shock, remembering rudimentary lessons from the swimming pool. The waves around him rose and fell like a time lapse of mountain formation. He felt eons pass before he corralled his racing thoughts. Shouting for help would do nothing, the dark and impatient clouds above did not care, he was alone. If he did not act quickly, he would die, slipping from light into the dark, unfathomable bay.

"It's a bit chilly." He spat out a mouthful of brine. "Come on, you've seen old people swimming in the Atlantic during winter, nearly in the nip too, and you've a wetsuit, hot water bottle and a paddle board. Stop your complaining. Come on. Die somewhere else, around family. Someplace warm." Feeling more composed, he started threading water. Salt stung his eyes.

The board was nearly out of sight. He glimpsed a flash of colour in the brief valley of a wave and swam towards it. When he grabbed hold of it, he let out a shuddering laugh. *Dad used to say that on his deathbed, he'd say a prayer as insurance, just in case there was anything to the whole religion lark.* "I nearly did, Dad." Fin pulled his body onto the board and lay flat. His bare hands were grey, it felt like drying cement circulated through his veins. "You're not clear yet. Come on."

Panic became anxiety. Kneeling, he spotted the paddle and maneuvered the board towards it.

Caught out in the open with an unforgiving wind blowing across the bay, he knew how far he still was from the mainland. The island was barely closer, but the mountain lured him. Caught in its orbit, he had but one choice. The next hour was to be a bitter struggle, racked with cold and the fear of drowning. His progress was slow, taxing his aching body.

Hypothermia was another thing he knew existed, but had little knowledge of. There was always a specialist; if he got it, it would end up being somebody else's problem. *Hot water bottle saving my life again.* He feared the unknown and this whole experience showed him just how clueless he really was. In the distance, a great seam in the clouds ripped open. Black clouds solidified and fell as hail. The tear grew towards him. Freezing, he could still appreciate the wild beauty of it, watching as Clare Island disappeared in the misty veil.

Heavy pits of ice peppered his skin and unsettled the water around him. *It can't kill you.* Once he reached shallower waters, the land kept the wind from him. It had harassed him like a niggling doubt for most of the journey. Not even the sun brought warmth back to the world. "Good man yourself." He let the monotony of paddling occupy his body. His mind wandered and he found himself having a conversation with one of his best friends as if he were there with him. "I hope that was a figment of my imagination and not you haunting me," he said in the safety of the shallows.

Red buoys marked the location of oyster beds near the shore. "You know, I've never tried one of those. I don't understand how those slimy, gooey things are supposed to be an aphrodisiac." On that note, the phantom of his friend departed. Neal had left for America to pursue a career in the NYPD. *I'll look for your family when I'm home, I promise you.* He glided across stones that scratched the underside of the board. Fin collapsed, unsettling a few sheltering seabirds. There were no footprints near him. The only sounds were those made naturally by the world.

After he caught his breath, he dragged the board above the tideline, confident that he would never step on one again for as long as he lived. As good as naked and exposed on a beach in winter, he had to keep moving, or risk remaining still forever more. The knife wound throbbed and his hot water bottle was tepid.

There was not a soul in sight as he walked along the

fringe of the beach. Stairs led onto an exposed path to an empty car park, but he stayed in the overgrown swordgrass. There was a lifeguard prefab painted yellow and red. The door and window were covered with metal sheeting for the winter. There was no getting in. He told himself that he would find nothing of use inside anyway.

Sheep stood out in the nearby fields, the unfortunate white of their fleeces making them targets. In one field, Fin could see a ram walking backwards and then charge at an infected man. The zombie went down and immediately tried to rise. The ram started backing up again.

The most daunting aspect of the sparse buildings that he passed was their empty reflective windows. Abandoned by the desperate and likely infested by the dead. He was less sure about the strength of his conviction for leaving the island now that he was here.

Hunkered low, he walked along the verge of wet fields. Ready to drop at the first sign of movement. Grey clouds massed around the barren scree slopes of the mountain. The peak was obscured, blind to the world below. *Maybe that's why they sleep up there.*

It was easy to avoid the few houses between him and the base of the mountain by going through dry-stone walled fields. Twice he approached buildings, hoping to find warm clothes, only to run away at worrying noises. Eventually, he chanced upon a utility shed with no alarm and no lock. The cold room harboured spiders and the overpowering perfume of washing detergent. The clothes he found were ill fitting and old fashioned, but they were dry. He peeled off the wetsuit, used a pair of socks to dry himself, then donned three jumpers and a pair of slacks.

What am I doing? The day was much colder than the previous ones. He imagined that, without central heating,

George would be cocooned in blankets, waiting for dawn to end the blistering cold. *I can't go back to our house. George said there was too much activity and I'll not head out on water again anytime soon.*

He waited in the shed for the rain to pass. He was almost certain he saw something move in the house. It could have been a reflection from something outside, but he was not willing to gamble. Without pen or paper, he could not leave a note apologising to the people he was stealing from.

At a guess, he estimated that no more than two roads stood between him and his goal. When the rain became a drizzle and idleness chilled him to the core, he left the shed. Fin used trees and low hedges for cover. He had not felt such trepidation about crossing a road since he was a toddler. Movement on the bend left of his position made him melt into the long branches. Luckily his stolen clothes were neutral colours and did not stand out.

Whatever it was, living or dead, it was heading away from him, towards town. Fin bounded across the road and stopped to survey the next field. The living had to be quiet as the dead to avoid the attention of the damned. At a distance, it was nearly impossible to tell a weeper apart from an uninfected human. He worried somebody might take him for a zombie and sneak up on him. At least the weepers had the decency to give you a terrifying warning before hunting you.

Partway across the field, he heard a car tearing down the road, coming from Westport. It rushed past his position and moments later breathless weeping caught up with it.

Fin waited until he was stiff from the cold before coming out of the thicket. A few more fields and he made it to the pub at the base of the mountain. It was too tempting a prize for it to be empty. Windchimes sang in the light breeze, but there were no infected near. *Maybe they followed the climber.*

Not wanting to be trapped in the open, he took a long route around the pub, walking through a garden and an abandoned field full of briars. Once the land started rising, he felt safer. By now, he had certainly missed the climber. He was tempted to make the hike up the mountain himself, but after Dara, he was not willing to test his luck again by scaring them, or worse, provoke an attack.

A white statue of Saint Patrick stood over the path that all pilgrims took to reach the summit. It was the only company he could abide while waiting. The light in the alarm box on the café at the base of the mountain still worked, so he could not break in and wait out of the cold. The few houses on the path up the mountain were sealed up. At this point in the outbreak, nobody was welcoming of strangers. He waited. Far above him, the SOS signal appeared massive; it would have taken numerous tins of paint and multiple trips.

After sitting idle in isolation for too long, he decided to walk up the path a little higher. He hoped the exercise would keep him warm and exorcise his dark thoughts. He found a sheltered spot near a stream and started building a dam with rocks to pass the time. Most of the light was gone from the day when he started worrying about how he would spend the night. Staying there through the cold and fear was a type of penance.

He tried turning his phone on to message Solene, but water had gotten into the components and ruined it. The radio could still be sinking to the bottom of Clew Bay for all he knew of its depth. He had just given Rebecca and George undue cause to worry. *If they go out looking for me and get hurt, that's on me.*

From his position he watched people moving on the roads: refugees seeking sanctuary, or infected – he could not decide which. The question was answered when a helicopter disturbed the silence. Fin shielded his eyes and scanned the sky. A large military carrier flew high above the bay. The sound of its engine and rotors roused every infected within hearing distance.

Fin ran further up the side of the mountain to keep it in view. It was too far away for him to make out much detail in the dimming light. The helicopter hovered above what he assumed to be the grounds of Westport House. Dark shadows fell from an open door at its rear. A parachute blossomed above the small silhouette of a man, the last thing to leave the craft. They allowed themselves to fall much slower than the other cargo. They quickly disappeared from Fin's line of sight.

He ran back to his shelter, waving into the sky as the helicopter returned the way it had come. It paid no attention to him, but he did not stop waving until the world was quiet again.

"There's something you don't see everyday."

Fin fell off his perch, landing hard onto the sharp edge of a rock. He winced in pain, while trying to scramble away from the striking outline behind him. Dara's grimacing face was all he could see. Arms raised to protect himself, Fin cowered away. Letting out a roar. "Stop!"

The man put his hands up to disarm the situation. "I didn't mean to startle you, I prefer getting the jump on company, before it can be done to me. Are you okay?"

Fin lowered his hands slowly. He felt heat rising in his cheeks. "Sorry about that. I'm a bit on edge."

The man helped Fin back to his feet. "That's just a normal response to a horrible situation."

Once Fin was standing, the man stepped back, he seemed to be constantly alert, shading his eyes, always watching his surroundings. He wore high-end climbing gear. His head was covered with a hat and most of his face was obscured by a scarf. The bit of skin visible was lobster red from the wind. "What are you doing up here so late?"

"I saw the light."

The man nodded. "Curiosity?"

"Well, no." Fin realised how foolish coming here to offer help was. "I came about the SOS sign painted on the side of the mountain."

"So, you're the rescue, are you? Had I the patience and the paint, I would have added 'preferably by helicopter'. I can't walk my family off the mountain. Or, have you come from Westport House?"

"You know about the camp there?"

"Of course. What do you think I do with my time off the mountain?"

Fin did not know what to say or do, he had nearly died to come and offer help to the lantern man, but he was going to be sent off like a door-to-door salesman. "You're better off up there than down here, I suppose."

"You try hauling stuff up each day, I wouldn't do it if I had any other option." He stretched his back and looked towards Westport. "I don't envy them trying to sure that place up. The walls only go so far around the grounds. The rest is fence. Right now they're relying on the small population of the hinterland. If they were in Dublin, there'd be nothing left of them by now. Things must be looking up if they're brave enough to call in a helicopter drop off."

He took a packet of cereal bars from his jacket and threw one to Fin. "Remind them that we're here though. I don't want to linger longer than needs be. If something happened to me..." He bit away half of his bar and the rest of what he was going to say. "Where are you staying tonight?"

"I just came up to see if you needed help, I'll head back to Westport, I'm staying with a friend outside town."

"I riled a few of them up down there. Car alarms and radios – windchimes in a pinch. I wasn't expecting the fast, crying ones, but the place is overrun. They usually leave come morning, but it wouldn't be safe for you to try so close to nightfall. Especially not after the helicopter. That little stunt has undoubtedly cost lives."

"I was at the train station a few days ago. It was full of fresh infected."

The man was quiet while he thought about that. "Have you any weapons on you?"

"I don't. I fell in the bay on my way from the island. Lost my pack."

The man looked skeptical. "You said you were staying with a friend outside town."

"Never mentioned how far outside town. Nah, we're in a renovated attic. Too close to town though. We thought the islands would be better. They're not."

"Are they paying you to knock on doors and bring as many people as you can back with you to Westport House?"

"The last job they gave me was killing pets, so this would be a step up. But no, they don't know I'm here. I'm not part of that group."

"If you give me a hand bringing my gear up, then you're welcome to stay the night with us, so long as you let me search you. If you're uncomfortable with it, then I'll not keep you. Take your chances on the road."

"I don't want to impose."

The man looked at him blankly before laughing. "No imposition at all. I think I've either slipped something or gotten a nerve pinched in my back, so I'd be glad for the help."

Fin consented to a search for weapons and bite marks. He raced to come up with an excuse for the wound on his stomach, but could think of nothing but the truth. "That's a knife wound, not a bite or gouge."

"Why did that happen?"

Tears formed in Fin's eyes. "I wish I knew." He told the stranger about the situation on the island.

The man just nodded and peeled back the bandages to have a look at the wound. "It looks a bit red, but I don't think there's an infection. You're probably right, I am better off up here." He found the polaroid in the pocket of Fin's trousers. The one he took earlier with Rebecca. The man seemed less on edge when he saw that. "My name's Malachy."

"I'm Fin."

"We need to be quick, I'm not usually this low so late." Malachy walked on. He had left his gear a good distance away to sneak up on Fin. Wearily, he hefted the pack over his shoulders. His back bent under the strain. There was another large rucksack, he handed it to Fin. He had to lean forward to stop from tumbling back with its weight.

"You do this every day?"

"Have to." Malachy let Fin go first, but never gave out about his slow pace. He gave Fin a lantern in preparation for the night. "The houses around here are running out of food. Survivors are forced out of their homes with hunger. They either become fodder for the infection or live long enough to leave estates barren. If it were not for Christmas surplus, a lot more people would be dead right about now. I have to come down and salvage if we're to outlast those things."

"Why the mountain?"

Malachy handed Fin a bottle of water and refused it

when it was offered back. "After the outbreak happened, nobody knew if it was airborne or how it was transferred. I'm pretty sure you could be safe for a while in the upstairs of a two-storey building, so long as you knock out the stairs. I wish I knew that back then. My wife was against going up, but I insisted and that's why I do the runs every day, to ensure she's cared for."

"Does she know how bad it is?"

"No. If you wouldn't mind, I'd appreciate if you kept the news to yourself when she's in earshot."

"What about moving out to one of the islands then?"

"They're the first place people thought of heading to. The bay is unpredictable in winter, you can attest to that. What happens if a storm comes up and you're stuck out there with no food? We can't move. We went up the mountain when my wife was heavily pregnant. Now we have a little girl. She will sing for Ireland one day. With the set of lungs she has on her, half the country might have already heard her. I can't bring her down, she'd only draw the infected."

Fin did not know whether to offer congratulations or condolences. *I never thought about pregnant women. Giving birth must have been scary enough with the aid of modern medicine, but now there are no doctors, nurses or anesthesia.* "I see why you're holding out for a helicopter."

"I can't complain. Most days you wouldn't see the church on the mountain because it's shrouded by clouds. Nobody wants to make the climb, I've spoken with a few groups that set up camp around the base, but that's only to wait out the faster ones. Each evening it gets harder to leave. I keep thinking that we should be moving on, that our window of safety to leave is gone. It petrifies me to think that I should have left yesterday. I've been to the camp at Westport House.

They're friendly enough, but there are too many downsides. You could do me a favour though."

Fin was not overly keen on agreeing to favours. "What is it?"

"If there ever comes a time you don't see my light for a few days, would you come check on my family? Or let those in Westport House know? I'm going further out by the day to scrounge up what I can. It's only a matter of time before I'm nabbed. My wife is formidable, but it would put my mind at ease knowing that should my luck run out, they will be safe."

"Of course I will. I look forward to meeting them."

Malachy clapped him on the shoulder. "You're a good man, Fin. Right, the sooner we start, the sooner we finish. Break's over. It only gets tougher from here."

30

THE DEATH ZONE

One of the only things Fin remembered from his first climb up Croagh Patrick was that the photo he took at the top was one of his most liked profile pictures. He had forgotten how steep the incline was and how arduous the hike could be for one so unfit. *Come on, old people do this barefoot.* Before the outbreak, when he did summit, it was summer. Little crowds gathered in traffic jams, patiently waiting for those ahead to take pictures. The wind blew so fiercely that he thought it picked up the loose, jagged rocks to cut him, but it was only hail.

Cold air burned his throat and lungs. *Ireland's holy mountain, priests say mass in the church up here for Christ's sake.* Fin tightened the shoulder straps of the bag and stopped looking up. *You'll get there when you get there.* The hotel was a popular destination for stag and hen parties. There was usually always one member in each group that would stumble out of the bar and declare they would be climbing the mountain come morning. If they got up while he was still on duty, he would get great entertainment, watching as the first signs of a hangover on the horizon stripped away the paint and polish off their enthusiasm.

Not born to Westport, Fin assumed from all the stags and hens that the modern pilgrimage seemed to require climbers to attempt the summit while suffering from mild alcohol poisoning. "Pints put the pain in pilgrimage. Sure even Saint Patrick had his own personal brewer." They always enjoyed that fact. Had he known how bitter the walk was when not in top form, he would have advised them to have a lie-on instead.

A quarter of the way up he had to stop to catch his breath, he slipped on rock and overstretched his leg to keep balance. "Does it get easier?"

"The climb? No. After doing it regularly? No. On the plus side, I'm steadily losing my gut. Just focus on your footing. We need to move, Fin. I'm sorry to rush you."

Malachy looked behind them at their progress and cursed. A great curtain of rain was closing over the land, encroaching on the mountain. The island and Rebecca were already buried beneath it. Malachy went ahead and set a quicker pace. Already the stones of the path were slick and slippery. The temperature was plummeting. Water would freeze during the night, and he would be their guest until it was safe to descend.

To his right was a steep drop off; he could see nothing but rocks, briars and a few sheep in the distance. It did not do to dwell on what would happen if he injured himself here. Malachy might help him, but if doing so put his own life in jeopardy and the lives of his family, he would forgive the man for leaving him – in theory. The thought of being a permanent feature on the walk up the mountain, his body the halfway marker, made him hunker lower to the stones, so the wind could not get a better purchase on him. Using both hands, he climbed.

"Malachy, do you know at what point above sea level the death zone on Mount Everest starts at?"

He laughed. "Are you that unfit? This mountain is not nearly so bad, it's the baby toe of Everest, if even."

"I've let the fitness go without even noticing. This holy hill is battering me, but that wasn't why I mentioned the death zone. I just thought that it has lowered considerably. When you're in it, people can only care for themselves. To tend to others just adds another to the body count."

Malachy stopped at that. "Due to oxygen deprivation, not zombies. I get what you're getting at, though. I reckon it's at sea-level now then so. The death zone – I'm surprised they haven't started calling Ireland that on the news. You should try and steer your thoughts away from such dark places. Don't let the horror seep in too deep, it'll rot right through you. All there is to living now is switching off and letting your body get on with surviving. I've come across plenty of people that fed their dark thoughts. Most of them are swinging in their attics now."

"How do you do it? Not let them in?" Fin asked.

"I run from them, up and down the mountain every day. Just about keep ahead of them."

They followed the path set by thousands of pilgrims. The cold penetrated Fin's resolve to climb higher, but below him, the dead roamed and the guilt over murdering Dara washed against the base of the mountain, tidal, creeping. He did not know if he could ever rise high enough above it. *I've killed a man.* His hands shook. Malachy passed him and put a reassuring hand on his shoulder. "Not long now."

What if Rebecca's blow was not fatal? What if he was just

stunned and I murdered a prone man? No. Too much blood. Dara, if that was his name, had to die. He did away with the previous occupants. Tried to stab me in the gut. That man could well have been normal before the epidemic. He was unwell. A month ago he could have found help. Pop a pill and there wouldn't be a bother on him after that.

What am I doing? He turned around and looked at the land. Westport was a small patch on the Mayo quilt. It never would have occurred to him before to wonder about the lives of so many others. The cluster of houses that were home to communities, where so many hopes were sown and healthy doses of failings experienced innumerable times. Now they would be barren, scavenged by hungry survivors and dressed in bones once the weepers were through. Before this, there was always time. His life had only been about time, he never experienced the slow awareness that comes with age, that each day brings you closer to your last. It was all he felt lately.

"You want to help, but all you end up doing is running," Fin said. The wind kept it from Malachy's ears.

"What are you saying, lad?"

They were granted a brief reprieve from the wind by a rocky outcrop. "Just that it does not make sense. A disease that turns the host into something so close to a zombie, that there's no point in arguing over the difference. It seems an impossibility, and on the west coast of Ireland, of all places. There has to be a decent chunk of the rural population that are unaffected by what's happening."

"A few, yes. They won't know until their milk spoils and they head into town for more. Out here, people in farms and small villages, they will endure. Scavenge enough food to see them through until planting season."

"Planting season! It won't come to that. Surely." The wind passed through him. Leaving their brief shelter, they were exposed to strong gusts that nearly tore them from the rock. Above them, the summit was soaked in impenetrable cloud.

The ground eventually levelled out, which was all the break Malachy's pace would allow. He was always conscious of the ever-dimming light. With a grimace, he made for a bare stone building, bathrooms for tourists.

"We'll leave the bags here and collect them in the morning, we need to hurry up," Malachy said.

The urinal was a trough in the ground. The fresh air had not removed the smell. Fin longed to hide behind those walls, let the wind howl harmlessly through the night. Malachy started to jog. Without the weight of the pack, Fin thought he would be blown from the side of the mountain. The barrenness of the land on the other side of Croagh Patrick was an inviting prospect. *We could ignore the islands and just go where people aren't.* A dip in the hillside had stones arranged to spell out names. Harmless graffiti before the epidemic, now he took his hat off while passing the mausoleum of memory. He remembered his hike in summer, beautiful picturesque clouds, smiling people and cameras everywhere. In winter, it was more primal.

Before rising into the clouds, he took one last look at the land. Mostly fields and empty space. *I can make it home, I can get through all of that. It's just one foot at a time.* On the other side of the mountain there was bogland and the loneliest homes he had ever seen. Ravens flew beneath him. Cultivated forests and fields stretched out to the distant mountains that he could not name. Wrecked ships and islands in the bay were completely hidden by a fresh wave of rain. They would not outpace it.

Malachy became a silhouette, his features lost in the darkness. Fin scrambled up the loose stone, chasing the light, its edges muffled in the cloud. Every step and breath took him away from the pain below. He had heard that every face in your dreams is supposed to be somebody you've seen before. *Where are they now? Am I one of those inconsequential glances?* He felt like a stray comma in the story of another.

Fin climbed beyond his capacity, the wound in his stomach caused him pain, his arms were still weak from paddling to and from the island.

The ground levelled. There was little light to cut through the oppressive cloud cover. "Malachy!" It was a hard thing to not notice a church on top of a mountain, but fear of missing it and falling off, kept him from moving fast. Piercing cold made his arms retract into his core, like a dead spider.

"Fin!" Malachy's voice was barely audible, but his lantern guided him.

Fin crawled towards it. He hid in the shade of a low wall, while Malachy unlocked the door. There were no lights shining through the windows.

"I wouldn't wish that climb on the dead," Fin said. He followed Malachy in.

"Coming here wasn't my finest idea, but we're alive and a lot of people I knew are not. Some nights, it gets so cold you would wonder why they never made an icy version of hell. That would scare me. More than once it was too cold to sleep, so I waited for the windows to shatter and my blood to freeze. Never happened and sleep always came in the end. Once I've enough supplies up here, I might look into catching one of the sheep on the mountain. I have no clue how to butcher the carcass and treat the meat though. Stocking up gives me time to learn."

"Has it come to that yet?" Fin asked.

"Did it bother you when you bought the well-designed packets of meat in the supermarket?"

"Not really." Fin blew into his cupped hands. "My girl-friend could work more magic with vegetables than I could with meat. That said, I'd do terrible things for a cheese-burger right now. Few slices of tomato, onions and throw on a bit of coleslaw for good measure."

"None of that. Any mention of burgers, pizza or steak and I'll ask you to leave." Malachy turned more lanterns on inside the church. There was no movement or welcoming call from his wife. Bags full of clothes, food and tins lined the walls. A tower of neatly stacked, folded blankets was wedged between packs of bottled water.

"You collected all of this?"

"Yep, my back has paid the price for it."

"What did you do before all of this, Malachy?"

"Wife owns a café in town. I helped out there during weekends. The rest of the time, I make and fit blinds. I have this lovely little workshop out the back garden where I made them. Coffee machine, radio and the smell from the flower beds in spring and summer. I don't reckon blinds will be the first thing on people's minds after this is fixed. One of the unforeseen benefits is knowing what houses have the best pantries. What about yourself?"

"Nightporter in the hotel by the quay."

Malachy inhaled appreciatively. "That's not a bad spot to hold up, I bet. I'd thought about it, people would be too afraid to go there, but I saw lights on at night. You, obviously."

"Ha, I spent my nights there looking at your light and thinking you were better off than me. Infected were inside.

We came across two. The military in Westport House have their eye on it now."

Malachy took off his sweaty clothes and told Fin to pick something dry and warm from his collection. "Not such a bad climb right?"

"Let's just say, I never want to meet one of the people that did it barefoot, if they're infected. They're a different breed entirely."

Malachy zipped up a padded jacket over his fleece. "That's exactly what they are. I've two of them trapped in houses down below. I'm studying them." He said the last part with a hint of embarrassment.

Fin pulled a hoodie that was too large over his head. He struggled with the zip around the neck. When his head came through the top, Malachy was laughing. "Do you hear her? Making fun of me for thinking I'm a scientist," he said loudly, towards the room behind the altar. "Didn't you put me through my study, making me watch all those daft medical shows?" He shook his head. There was no answer back. He made a face as if to say he was in trouble.

"How are you studying them?"

"Just watch and learn from their behaviour. The more you know about them, the less terror they exert on your imagination. One of their best weapons is our own fear, makes us as stupid as them. I've a fella down there that was infected recently. Didn't take him long to turn. Wasn't quick enough for him though. I stayed with him through the change. He talked me through what it felt like. Until he lost the use of his words. I don't think there's anything left of them in the manic phase. I'm sure they're gone by the time they come back. He was my best friend."

"I'm sorry."

Malachy cleared his throat and put on a smile. "We're not taking flower offerings for him, but if you wanted to do away with one of the infected, that'll do nicely. Every one you kill, is a life saved. Those people you save will never know to thank you."

"How do you kill something that has no fear?"

"With great pleasure. Now get comfortable, make yourself at home. I'll do us up some food. After dinner, I want to ask you a few things about the infected you've come across, see if it supports my notes."

Fin stuffed his hands in his armpits and looked around. The humble structure did not keep out the cold. Night had fully set outside. The windows were single panes of glass. "I can see the appeal of living up here, calm and quiet. If only you could get your groceries delivered."

In a break in the clouds, stars were already out, appearing like the first specks of frost on a winter window. "I wonder how many satellites they have tasked above Ireland right now?" Fin said.

"There's probably a few. The world is watching the historic modern fall of a nation."

Despite being safe for the night and knowing that a flood of zombies could not break upon them, Fin still felt uneasy.

Malachy gently knocked on the door behind the altar. "Just me, love. I've found a helper, don't get up." Malachy lit a few candles on the altar and turned the lamps off. The light cast shadows on the statue of Saint Patrick. *If this plague wipes us out, those that come after will have some time trying to understand our idols.*

"It's bitter cold out there, love, and I'll not send him down in the dark."

Fin's anxiety spiked.

"We have to get the bags from the bathroom in the

348

morning. What? No, no, not a bite or scratch on him."
Malachy threw him a box of pills and spoke in a low voice so
his wife would not hear. "Antibiotics. I think they're general,
but if your cut starts acting up then try them. There are no
more hospitals now, buddy. Try to avoid the sharp end of
knives. Right, I think a drink is in order."

Malachy set up a stove on the altar. Fin took a glass of
whiskey and wandered through the other rooms in the
church. The room to the right of the entrance was the
confessional. It was in the middle of a renovation, most of
the tools were still there. Malachy had barricaded the
windows with wood and nailed blankets around the
corners, in an attempt to conserve heat. Fin was amazed at
the amount of supplies Malachy managed to squirrel away.
There was more here than they had in the hotel.

Malachy carefully measured out water and poured a
bag of pasta into a pot over a gas flame. "One thing I'll have
to bring up is a rain barrel. Good clean water is too
precious to waste like this." He tossed Fin a tin opener. "I
bring one back with me with every trip. Nothing is as
annoying as being hungry while you've a tin you can't
open."

Fin was starting to feel awkward that he had not introduced himself to Malachy's wife. When Malachy topped up
his whiskey, Fin asked, "Will I bring one in for your missus?
What's her name?"

"Liz. She wouldn't be mad on drink at the minute, with
the baby. I swear I've read more books in the last nine
months than I have in ten years, all about babies." He fished
a bar of chocolate from his jacket pocket. "This now, will put
you in her good books. Don't be shy, she won't bite... I
reckon that turn of phrase won't transfer well to the new
world."

Malachy drank his glass down in one gulp. Fin did too; anything for a bit of heat.

The back room would have been where the priests prepared to say mass. All the walls were painted white, but the one separating the room from the rest of the church was only a panel that did not reach up to the roof. Fin brought a candle with him, and walked slowly to keep it from going out. The windows here were barricaded too. The thick colourful fabrics gave it a cozy feeling. He was greeted by a ripe and pungent smell.

Liz was huddled beneath a mound of blankets in the corner, leaning against the wall. The baby swaddled in a jacket, rested in her lap.

"Hi Liz, I'm Fin. I come bearing chocolate."

As he approached, the candlelight illuminated their features. For a second he thought they were statues, a modern Pieta, but they were just dead. Her skin was pale and waxen, gaunt and black beneath the eyes. Her empty stare fixed on the bundle.

He pulled his jumper up over his mouth and nose. *There's no way Malachy does not know.* It was too dark and dangerous to make the climb down the mountain. Even with the torch, he was not sure Malachy would let him go. He left the chocolate bar on the ground before the bodies as an offering.

One of Fin's first thoughts was to find a weapon, but he knew Malachy would have a knife at the ready. He was bigger, stronger and possibly mad. *He said his back was giving out, I could use that. Unless he said that to make me think he was less of a threat.* Unable to remain in the room much longer without raising suspicion, Fin returned to the main chamber.

Malachy was in the middle of setting up blankets for his

guest, and he had topped up their glasses with more whiskey. Fin kept to the shadows when he returned, not wanting to give away his fear and revulsion. Unused nappies and boxes of baby formula were stacked by the door of the refectory.

"Tea?"

Fin nodded in the dark. Malachy stopped what he was doing to look at him. "A bit more whiskey if you have it. If you don't mind."

"Not at all. I used to think it was the one pleasure I allowed myself in my pack, but it's more of a necessity." Malachy spoke as he made dinner, talking about the houses he had cleared and the horrible things he witnessed.

When the pasta was finished, he strained the water from the pot into a hot water bottle. He mixed in herbs, a jar of sauce and a tin of tuna. Fin was terrible company during dinner. His mind was in the back room. He wished he had stayed longer to observe the bodies. Were they bitten? Had he murdered them? He tried yawning a few times to pass his behaviour off as tiredness.

Before going to bed, Malachy applied muscle pain pads and creams to his back. "One good thing about that climb is it helps me sleep. That and the drink. Help yourself to more. There's plenty. Goodnight." He picked up the cold bowl of pasta for Liz. "The blankets are set up there for you. Sorry I don't have any more hot water bottles, this is for Liz and the baby."

Maybe he does not know. "What you've given me is more than enough."

"Thanks for the help today." He went into the back room with the bodies, only slightly closing the door behind him.

Fin listened to his hushed voice while he settled down. "Don't stay up too late, love," he heard Malachy say.

Fin wrapped himself in a couple of blankets and slid down the wall beside the door. He opened a naggin of whiskey and lost the cap in the folds of his bedding. He did not need it.

Malachy returned. "I'm just going to put the candles out now. Are you set for bed? Can't really waste much these days."

"Goodnight."

Malachy stopped walking in the darkness. "It's our first child. I read about the sleepless nights parents suffer. I had my fingers crossed the whole nine months that ours would be one of the quiet ones. But you can't be lucky in all things. The last time that I was not woken by her crying was when I was trapped by infected. The whiskey was sorely missed then, I can tell you."

The thought that this insane man heard the crying of a dead baby made Fin's blood run cold. *Maybe reality manages to reach him in his dreams, so he drinks to stop those.* Fin raised the bottle to his mouth, but stopped. He would have swallowed the whole thing to feel numb, but he feared being senseless around this man. With reduced inhibition he would likely try to walk down the mountain in the dark. Malachy seemed harmless, but so had Dara.

Considering he had not slept the previous night, Fin hoped that exhaustion would be enough, but he could not switch off. The wind picked up and whistled around the church. It sounded like the wailing of the banshee. Fin's body rippled with goosebumps as he heard Malachy shushing his child back to sleep.

Wondering if a few blankets wrapped around him would be enough, Fin stumbled through the void towards the door. He opened it as quietly as he could, stepping out into the crisp clear night. The stars were astounding, but the cold robbed them of their appeal. Beyond the shelter of the church, the cold nearly brought him to his knees. He knew without doubt that leaving now would be his end. Over his shoulder he saw the silhouette of Malachy standing in the doorway. Fin fought against the wind and his fear, back to the church.

31

NO SLEEP FOR THE LIVING

"Some stars, eh?" Fin said.

Malachy was silent for a moment, before moving out of the doorway. "You must be daft heading out there. I should have said, if you need to piss, there's a bucket in the confessional." Malachy returned to the back room and left the door slightly ajar.

Fin found his naggin, the raw whiskey burned as it went down. After a quarter of the bottle, it started to warm him. Once it took the edge off the fear, he put it aside. While Malachy snored, Fin stayed awake and wondered how the infection spread. *Was she bitten? No, there was a lot of blood, she gave birth up here. Do the dead rise like in movies? It takes a lot to walk, never mind run. They weep when they see others, severe brain damage then.*

Eventually, exhaustion overcame him and the darkness diffused into his mind, blanketing his worries. He passed out with the disturbingly comforting thought that if they did turn, then Malachy would be attacked first. His screams would give Fin enough time to sneak out. He would have to fumble blindly for the lock and latch, then hope that the night and cold would not kill him.

Fin was woken by Malachy opening the zipper of his sleeping bag. The squeal of the metal made him tense. Malachy quietly closed the door to the room where his wife and child lay, as if trying not to wake them. He stretched; Fin heard his back crack from the other side of the room. He shuffled to the stove on the altar. Fin rubbed at his face to shake the tiredness off, but exhaustion hung on him like a second skin. Already fully dressed, he got out of his bundle of blankets.

"How did you sleep?" Malachy asked. His breath frosted in the air.

"Like the dead."

Malachy gave him a weird look but made no remark. "Would you like tea, coffee or a dissolvable multivitamin? It's tropical flavour."

"Vitamin tablet, cheers."

"So what's your plan?"

"There's not a hope that I'm going back to the island on the board."

"What about your friend?"

"She has it in her head that the child will come back. Do you know anything about the people that lived out there?"

"Nothing, I'm afraid. Though common sense would tell you, that child will never return."

"I'll go back to our safehouse and wait for George, use his radio to let her know that I'm alive."

"You could always use the spare paint I have lying around and write it beside my SOS signal."

"Tempting." Fin smiled at the thought of Rebecca waking up to read a message from him on the side of a mountain. *How can you act so normal? I'm sorry for you.* At

355

times, Fin wondered if he saw the strain of reality age Malachy's face. "I saw on the news that the military used helicopters to lure infected away. If they're dropping supplies into Westport House, we might see the end of this soon."

"Don't be so flippant," Malachy said. "There won't be an end to this, not for our generation. In decades to come, they will have articles on the old survivors of the epidemic. I tell you, what a time to be a practicing psychologist, they'll be capitalising on this trauma to be sure."

He might be mad, but he's not bad. No grieving. Maybe he's forestalling his grief until he can indulge in it afterwards.

"We'll have two torches on as we descend, at least that way your friend Rebecca can assume you made it and have joined this odd little constellation that everyone puts so much stock in."

"Mock it all you want, but seeing your lantern on the mountain gives people hope. At the very least they are not alone – others will live on. To some, that's all the hope they need to make dying easier."

"It shouldn't be easy. You fight for the morning after, for a glimpse of sun, a free breath. Fight for the sake of fighting. Find something worth dying over and then strive to live for it."

"What have you found?"

"Them in there. My wife is the soul of every moment I have worth remembering and our girl will be at the heart of every good feeling I have from now on. Life should not be something to give up easy, it's all we have."

"Do you want me to mark out where we are staying on your map?" Fin said. "Just so we don't hear you rifling through our bins."

"Fire ahead, map's on the altar." He pointed at a cylinder

of rolled up paper beside the stove. "I've spare gear in the other room, take a scarf, gloves and hat. A jacket could just save your life."

The cords on the jacket were all taped down. "I've a friend you'd get on well with," Fin said, thinking of George's meticulous attention to detail.

Malachy poured out three cups of water and popped an effervescent tablet in each.

"Thank you." Fin drank his in two gulps.

Malachy unfurled the map. "Anywhere with a strike to it, I've been to." He opened a marker and crossed off a few more houses. "That was yesterday." He was compulsive and thorough in his search. Fin tried to memorise it for George's own map, so they would not waste time.

All those black crosses over houses and estates gave Fin pause. *So many lives altered.* "This is us here." Their peninsula was still untouched by him. Fin took the pen and circled the general area where their hideout was. "If we're going to be neighbours, we could pool our efforts."

"Sounds like a crowd," Malachy said. His tone was jovial, but his meaning was not lost. "Back at it again." Malachy let go of the map and let it curl in on itself. He put two empty bags on his back. "We'll have a few cereal bars for breakfast on the way – I like to get down as fast as possible. Can't waste what little light there is in the day. Here," he threw Fin a hiking stick, "you'll need it for going down."

Fin dressed gratefully in the offered winter gear and opened the front door. It was like stepping through a portal to another planet. Clouds completely obscured the land below. He could only see the ground a few feet in front of him. It was serene and beautiful. He stood and watched while Malachy got ready. The cold woke him up more than coffee would have. His nerves felt like fuses, a night in the church had shortened them.

Fin's head swam from lack of sleep, dulling his senses like a hangover. While waiting outside for Malachy to say his farewells to his family, he remembered a dream that woke him during the night. Liz staring down at him, her expressionless face like that of a weeper. Each time Fin moved, she matched and countered. All he could do was remain still and stare into those dead eyes. Even though he knew the infected could not easily make the climb, he imagined walking into a group of them in the low visibility. Each breath was crisp and damp, submerged in clouds, so thick he could only see the church as a silhouette after walking a few feet from it.

Fin sought shelter at the side of the building. He checked on the suicide pills the captain had given him back at the hotel. One for him, the other for Rebecca. Carefully, he broke the perforated edge and pulled them apart and put one back in his pocket. Fin bit his lip to stop it from quivering. During the bleakest parts of the night he fumbled with the idea of the pills. Had it not been for the phone calls with his family and knowing they were safe with Solene, he would have considered taking one. They were dangerous to have; a quick and – he hoped – painless solution. One with a swallow of whiskey and that darkness would become permanent, minus the cold.

The temptation was incredible, the thoughts invasive and starting to make sense. It was like a craving he knew he would likely indulge. *I don't want to die and I don't want my family to find out that I just let myself go out.* Nothingness did not scare him as much as thinking about what it would do to his loved ones. *It must be too easy to do it in countries with*

access to guns. Put a bit of pressure on a trigger and it's over.
Leaves little time for consideration.

The church door closed and Fin heard it lock. Malachy came out with two lamps, their light considerably tarnished now that he knew what was inside the church. "Have you ever just wanted to scream?" Fin asked.

"I've done it a few times."

"Did it help?"

"No."

"I have something for you." Fin held out the small silver plastic packet. "It's for taking if something bad happens. It'll make it quick."

Malachy made to give it back, his expression stern. "No."

"It's a gift. You're the man up here collecting everything just in case it might have a use. This might. Keep it."

Malachy's hand stayed awkwardly out with the tablet resting on his palm. He closed his fist around it. "There are only a few moments when this feels real," he said. He let out a long breath. "That was one of them."

There was no talking as they descended. Once moving, Fin could focus on his footing. It did not matter what they were going into, walking did wonders for his mind. Loose rock went from beneath his feet and he fell on his back a few times. Now he understood why Malachy had so much pain relief medication.

The silence was ruptured by the distant sound of an explosion that rolled across the land. They stopped to listen. There was nothing for a few moments and then the growing hum of a heavy machine.

"That's a helicopter," Malachy said. He set off quickly down the mountain. He slipped a few times, but used the momentum of the skid to move faster down the scree. Fin tried to keep pace, but his self-preservation would not allow it. Malachy vanished in the cloud.

The residing thought with the helicopter coming closer was that this might all be over. He nearly ran into Malachy. Beneath the clouds he could see just how ugly the sky looked; broody grey, with the promise of a wet day ahead. It was the search and rescue helicopter from Westport House. It kept low over Clew Bay, heading towards the Atlantic. Malachy was not looking at it, his gaze was on the town. Fire and smoke rose from somewhere close to the quay. It could only be the survivors' camp. "What the hell is going on?" Malachy said.

All hope at seeing the helicopter disappeared. "What could have caused that explosion?"

"Sabotage. Mutiny." Malachy shrugged. "Only thing keeping those soldiers in line was habit. That was no fire, sure, we heard the blast all the way out here."

Another smaller explosion tore through the air, black smoke curled up from the grounds.

"Should we help?" Fin knew the answer before he asked.

"Not a chance. What are we to do? How far do you think that sound travelled? Every infected within earshot will be riled up and heading that way."

The sound of the helicopter dwindled as it passed from sight. Not all of the soldiers could fit on it, if they were even the ones on board. He wanted to know what happened but was starting to believe that ignorance would keep him alive much longer than satisfying his curiosity.

"I'll not be heading down today," Malachy said. "You're welcome to stay above with us."

Fin had no intention of ever returning to that place. "I need to go back to my friends. We made a promise to look out for each other."

"Well at least you know we're here. Remember, if you don't see the light for a few nights, will you try to get people up to help my girls?"

"I promise, I'll take care of them," Fin said.

"Good luck." It did not seem like the handshake of a mad man. Though he did not like to use that label. *How sane can anyone be these days?*

"I hope you're not up here too long." Fin said.

"We'll have a pint when this is over." Malachy walked back up the slope, disappearing in the low cloud. Fin wanted to take the hike slowly, but he knew the roads would now be filled with the infected. He could see a few bodies moving on the road below already.

* * *

Near the base of the mountain, Fin stooped to wash the sweat from his face in a marshy stream, before putting his mask on and trying for the coast. There were too many places to hide near the houses, he did not want to surprise a group of the infected. Instead he hopped the walls of gardens and moved hunched and slow through them. He watched the zombies shuffle past the roads, all heading towards Westport. Cold morning dew soaked his trousers, but he was sweating from the climb and close proximity to death.

He made it to the coast without incident. The only prints in the sand were his old ones that led back to his board. Cold water drove the breath from him. He waded out to his waist before kneeling shakily on the board. He paddled a few feet from the shore before standing up. The fear of falling in again robbed him of all confidence, and he made slow progress. Looking back at the mountain, he knew he would not risk his life to return, should the light stop. *When this mess ends, if you are gone, I will bury those bodies. If I survive.*

He watched a few infected trapped in wet mud. Cows had lured them, but they did not have the sense to find their way out of the field. Weepers, hearing the sound, rushed those standing at the gate. They fell in a mass of biting, clawing bodies to be caught by the mud. *Maybe they'll destroy themselves.* He thought of some of them being preserved in bogs and coming out in a few decades. *Our myths, lore and legends will be changed.*

Hiding out of sight until he was sure they forgot about him, Fin continued towards their peninsula. By the time he reached the back of their safehouse, he was wrecked. He hauled the board above the wave breaker stones and left it in the garden. They had no way of barricading the grounds of the house without making too much noise. Their only hope was that infected would be drawn to Westport and just stumble past their lane. The gate would be enough, so long as they made no noise. A disturbing thought was that they might stay idle, like anemones, waiting for food to come to them.

George had outdone himself. The safehouse looked so imposing it gave Fin pause before approaching. The windows were marked with rusty handprints that smeared and dragged across the glass. The 'Dead Inside', written with Christmas snow spray, which would have looked cartoonish as Halloween decorations, seemed fitting now.

He had no way of letting Rebecca or George know he was coming in, if he knocked and there was something on the road, it would only attract it. The key was where George had left it. Inside, the kitchen was destroyed. The fridge door hung open, food inside left to rot, a putrefied smell perfumed the lower house. He wished he was not so accustomed to the smell of death to know that this was not it, but it might turn away a wary looter, if the warnings were not enough.

The loft was empty. He replaced the board over the entrance and tucked blankets and folded bed sheets over the edges to muffle any sound he made and to block the smell from downstairs.

He threw his new clothes in a pile. A drop of blood darkened the bandage on his stomach. The skin underneath it was red, and warm to the touch. He washed the wound out at the sink and swallowed a few of the antibiotics Malachy had given him. Going through the cupboard he found ointment and smeared it on the scab that had torn either from overreaching when he slipped on the mountain, or while on the water.

Collapsing into bed, he pulled the blanket over his head. His breathing slowed and he sank into the growing warmth. He slept, or at least did not think for a few hours, until startled by a blaring alarm. Fin fell out of bed and fumbled beneath the pillow for the hammer he placed there.

They've broken in downstairs. Heart thumping, he remembered that George had found the code for the alarm box while searching the house. He had disabled everything.

Through the roof window he saw nothing on the road, but that would not last long if the alarm kept sounding. He pulled a chair beneath the window and climbed out onto the roof. Crawling on his stomach so as not to move the tiles, he felt the scab tear. Lying flat on the edge of the roof, he used the gutter to support his weight. The alarm box was a foot below him. His ears rang with the sound. He smashed it with the hammer, confident the noise he made was hidden by its wailing. It whined, quietened and died.

Fin lay back in relief, his heart racing. What he first thought to be the echo of the alarm ringing in his ear was actually alarms going off in the surrounding houses. All of them. *The power's failing.* He heard distant voices, other survivors coming out of hiding to deal with their alarms. They mingled with the shrieking weep of infected.

32
─────

LONG OUT OF LUCK

Fin raced to finish reading a chapter of a book before it became too dark. He was tempted to light a candle, but being alone with those monsters in his thoughts was better than actually having them for company.

Just after nightfall, Fin heard the door to the loft stairway open and a moment later a mass of brown, dried grasses and branches pushed opened the hatch. Fin reached for the hammer just as George took off the cloak. He was flushed and sweaty and momentarily terrified to find somebody else unexpectedly in his loft. "Where the hell have you been?"

"The church on top of Croagh Patrick. What the hell are you wearing?"

"It's a ghillie suit, or at least it will be, when I finish it." He bundled it into his arms and brought it into the bathroom, to hang on the shower railing. "I think it will work, wear the scenery, those things don't seem interested in smelling the roses."

"So become a rose?"

"Well, more mouldering leaves and damp moss. It works

though. I set up on the roadside and just stood there while a few of them walked right past me. Then that helicopter showed up and I was nearly carried away in the crowd of weepers." George kicked his boots off and put on a pair he kept for the house. They had all agreed not to wear outdoor shoes inside, to prevent the infection from coming in, if that was even how it could be transmitted. George's feet were only bare for the length of time it took to put another pair of shoes on. He had new shoes he wore to bed, so he was always ready to run.

"Have you heard from Rebecca? My radio got destroyed in the crossing, Fin said."

"She's fine. Why did you leave her there alone? That was bad form."

Fin could hear the derision in his voice and did not deny he had earned it. "I wanted to go, she wanted to stay."

"She told me what you found. I think I'd want to put the place behind me as quickly as possible, if I nearly died there. How's the wound?"

"I don't know if it's red because it's healing or because it's infected. Not that kind of infected."

"Well, when you're planning to stab somebody, I doubt the first thing that crosses your mind is having the courtesy to clean the knife beforehand. I mean, my first reaction to being stabbed would not be 'How rude, your knife's dirty.'"

"Did you see the explosion this morning? And the helicopter yesterday? What's happening?" Fin asked.

George's expression darkened. "I didn't go near town. The explosion and gunfire is drawing the infected from every direction, they're gathering a horde. That was a good job you did with the alarm box outside. It's happening all over the place. Power outages. I've found another survivor."

"Me too."

George was taken aback for a second. "How many people are on the mountain?"

"One living. Two dead."

"Infected?"

"No. What about yourself?"

"An elderly woman. Near gave me a heart attack when I broke into her house and found her. When I learned what her situation was, I wished I had encountered a zombie instead." He grimaced at the thought. "I don't mean that."

"Is it safe where she is?"

"From the dead? Maybe. For now. She did not have an alarm. I disabled the ones on the houses around her."

"What's the issue?"

"She has problems with her lungs and needs oxygen. Her tanks are dry and all she is going off is a condenser that's plugged into the mains."

Fin let out a long breath while thinking about something to say. "What can we do?"

A scornful look crossed George's face. "Everything we can. They have things in the camp that might be able to help."

"The first helicopter dropped stuff into the grounds. The other one was the sea rescue. When I was there, they told me that people had tried to steal it. Whatever happened there, I don't think it was good."

George rubbed the stubble on his face. He was always clean shaven at work. Taking off his jacket, he revealed an old jumper beneath, far too small for him. Thinking he had been caught out somewhere and wore what he could find, Fin offered him one of his jumpers.

"No thanks, this is mine. I'm comfortable in it."

"Does not leave much to the imagination."

"Saving people time then. You're right, we can't just

bring her there blindly, I have to go and see what's going on, I promised I would help her. All I need is a few extra hands."

Optimism seemed so foreign now to Fin, but he would not stop George's, if it helped.

"I'll go with you." As much as he hated the thought of leaving the safety of their shelter, he felt keeping his mind active was key. "Can you make a ghillie suit for me and the woman?"

"Can't do that, she gets coughing fits. As daft as the zombies are, I bet even they would be curious about a coughing bush. Tell me about the survivor you found on the mountain."

"I don't know that I'd classify him as a survivor." Fin recounted his time with Malachy.

George lay on the futon looking through the skylight. "So many people are in trouble and nobody is coming to help them."

"Yeah and we don't even know what happened at the camp yet."

"What was it like to kill a man?"

Fin was not expecting the question. "Worst thing I've ever had to do in my life."

"You mean you didn't have to study Irish in school for sixteen years?"

"Second worst thing I've been forced to do."

George snorted air through his nose. Humour helped, but it was a weak medicine. "Don't let it trouble you, you're alive because of it and he can do no more harm. We can get help for Malachy at the camp, maybe they can do something for him."

"I don't think there's anything that can help that. I hope I'm wrong," Fin said.

"Me too, or there's no hope for any of us."

* * *

Rebecca took so long to pick up her radio that Fin and George started devising a plan on getting out to the island. When she answered, her voice was dull and apathetic, she used as few words as possible to answer. Listening to her speak only increased their concern for her wellbeing. Fin let go of the receiver. "Don't say a word about Malachy, I don't think she's in a good space, let's not give her more bad news."

"Sure then we'll have nothing to talk about." George told her about the old woman he came across, how they were going to Westport House to find help for her. Fin mentioned meeting the man on the mountain. She did not seem to care.

"Are you guys coming out here afterwards? Can we go to Achill then?"

"One thing at a time," George took the radio. "Fin got into bother on the water on his way to the mountain. I'm not convinced it's the safest route. We'll have to talk it out later. Might be that heading into the countryside would be best. Follow a river far up its course to where there are no roads or people."

"I'll go by myself."

"Rebecca, come on, we don't rush things."

"A body washed up on the far end of the island here. It didn't move, but I made sure it wouldn't. Makes me wonder how safe these places are. What if a live one – well, a walking one – makes it here? Maybe you're right. But I don't have the luxury of time."

"You could be right," George said. "We'll have a look for a boat when we go help this woman. What have you been up to?" George asked to change the subject.

"Not much. It feels like I'm just waiting."

"We're all waiting for good news. We'll all be a while waiting for that," George said.

"Did you notice the person parachute into the camp at Westport House yesterday?"

"Surprised they didn't drop like a stone with the weight of the balls on them," George said. "Parachuting over a zombie infested land."

"Any sign of the child?" Fin asked.

"None. I don't think she'll ever come back."

"You should consider coming back," George said. "Those islands are a beacon for the desperate."

"I found a shotgun here, but there's no ammunition for it, a few empty casings though," Rebecca said. "I reckon he was using it on anybody that approached until he ran out of ammo. No point taking it out if he had no shells left. If we had known his actions were hostile and called his bluff, then he would have had two of us to deal with."

"Now that you mention it, I found a gun too," George said. He opened a small hatch into the crawl space of the loft. Their stores of dry food had increased substantially.

"You've been busy," Fin said.

"We have to be, just look at the guy on the mountain. All he does every day is gather things like a jumped-up hamster. He's not the only one. It's not as if people are going out to replenish what is taken. Nobody grows anything for themselves, towns are supplied by trucks. People have already started to starve." George took out a long-barrelled rifle. It would not have looked out of place in a museum.

"Found it in a farmhouse. The gun locker was closed so I don't have much ammunition for it."

"Rebecca, it looks like something out of a War of Independence movie. It's bolt action," Fin said.

"Those are more trouble than they're worth, you'll only attract the zombies," she said.

George poured a few bullets into Fin's hand. "I've had to swallow vitamin tablets that looked more intimidating than those," Fin said. "Have you tried it yet?"

"Not a chance. Rebecca's right. The sound of that against those things – no benefit outweighs the drawback. On a boat now, picking them off on the shore, that would be ideal."

"I think you've just created the new national pastime," Fin said. "The previous owner just left it behind?"

George licked his lips, smirked and snorted. When he put the ammunition carefully back into the box it rattled about loosely. A few rounds were missing. "It was a cleaner end than they would have gotten at the hands of the infected," George said.

"It's a good find. Let's hope we won't need it," Fin said.

George locked the gun away. "We're going to head in, Rebecca. Stay safe."

* * *

With sharpshooters posted at the entry points to Westport House and light seeping from the world, they opted for the paddle board. Both of them knelt on one. Fin realised George's aversion to water was far greater than he first assumed.

"Are you taking the mick?" Fin asked George, who flinched whenever a wave mounted the board.

"No, I'd deal with a zombie sooner than I would water."

"But sure, you came for me in the kayak."

"You needed help."

Fin considered just how terrified George was of the water. "Thank you." It did not seem like enough to say it.

"Got it when I was younger. Family and I were in this small boat doing a crossing into Northern Ireland. I asked the owner how deep the water was. Him thinking he was putting my mind at rest said, 'You could stand up in it, it's that shallow.' And sure of course didn't I try."

"He was lying, I take it?"

"We were on the deepest lough in Ireland."

Fin paddled closer to the shore. "There you are, you can near stand up in that."

"So can the zombies."

They stayed close to the shore and travelled up the river. Hidden by the pier wall, they were unable to see what was happening outside the hotel.

"What the hell is making all that noise?" George asked. "It sounds like an army."

"Can you imagine if they were all infected?"

George spat into the water. "I didn't until you said it."

Fin grabbed a rusted ladder and pulled them close to the wall. George held it so tightly that his knuckles were white. "Hurry up," he said through clenched teeth.

Fin climbed the rungs and peaked over the wall. There were no infected in sight; people streamed out of the camp in orderly lines, entering the Quay Hotel. Most of the lights in the rooms were on. *So much for silence.* With all the food Fin, George and Rebecca had taken from the place, there would not be enough for more than half a mouthful for each of those people.

"What's going on?" George asked as Fin steadied himself back on the board.

"They're moving people into our hotel."

"Any zombies?"

"No, just people and a few soldiers."

They paddled around a hilly island, out of view from

prying eyes, and hid the board and paddle. Their clothes were destroyed by the sucking mud, but at least they found no other footprints. With torches on, they moved quickly through the woods towards the main road of the camp, completely bypassing the gate. Plenty of people noticed them, but nothing was said. They turned the torches off and walked against the crowd fleeing the camp. The looks they got from strangers were unkind and they decided against asking what happened, they could judge well enough by the faces.

Moving through the crowd was an unnerving experience; so many people crying, moving erratically. The only discerning difference between them and the infected was that they were not attacking them.

"Last time I was here the place was a maze of tents," Fin said. Most of those had been trampled. A new fence installed in front of the house cut the manor off from the fields. It was reinforced with camper vans parked end to end. Sharpshooters fired into the field from scaffolding nests and the baskets of two electrical maintenance trucks. Floodlights and gas generators hummed so loudly that they almost muffled out the weeping and wheezing. Runners ferried ammunition from the house to the shooters.

"How many are there?" George said. He walked as close to the fence as he dared. The lights were strong but half the field was still in darkness. It would take too long to count the bodies of the dead, a task made especially difficult with so many infected trampling them.

Putting down the faster ones seemed to be the priority. Fin and George watched as a slower one nearly made it to the fence. A soldier unloaded an entire clip into it. The inner lining puffed out from its jacket like blooming white roses. Bones broke and it slumped down, unable to bare its dead weight. Sinews torn, muscles ruined, but it did not die. It rose up unsteadily, a terrible gash above its right eye, unrecognisable as human. Another soldier put a carefully placed bullet through its skull. It went down and stayed motionless. The soldier that had fruitlessly wasted so much ammunition was quickly relieved.

"So long as they keep their heads, this place will be safe," George said.

"That's asking a lot. Imagine being up there in one of those nests and thinking about what would happen if the zombies got through or came up from behind."

One of the soldiers on the roof of a camper looked down on them with wide eyes.

"Sorry," Fin said.

The remains of a fire by the main gate filled the air with smoke. Some trees still burned, their smouldering red glow made it look like the dead were coming straight from hell. Fin did not want to say it to George but he knew they would not find any help here for the old woman. She was out of time and long out of luck.

"They're evacuating," George said.

Soldiers manned the barricades, while others were still in the process of reinforcing them. Fin turned away from the light and the field of moving death. *So many people.* George was slower to look away. His face was pale, his stare distant.

The house was a hive of activity, mostly people taking whatever was not nailed down to reinforce the walls. A few took things and joined the crowd leaving. *Looters should be shot. The efforts of others keep them safe and they use that time to steal.*

"This is our chance," George said. "Let's see if we can nick an oxygen tank."

None of the soldiers cared to stop them entering; they only had time for the infected now.

Gunfire deeper inside the house made them stop. "Let's come back in the morning," George said. "We'll only get in the way. I know a place that's close and secure enough to last the night."

Before they made it to the door they were forced into cover when more gunfire came from inside the house.

A soldier ran into the atrium, sweating and out of breath. "They're coming through the woods." He pushed through the stationary crowd. When he slammed part of the door to the house closed, the others sprang into action. Half of the soldiers abandoned their posts and fled. The rest remained with the ammunition.

Fin and George joined the rush to get out. Those behind pushed into them, clogging up the exit. In the brief breaks of gunfire, Fin could hear the screaming much closer now. The last part of the door was forcefully closed against the swell of people trying to get back in. Bullets ripped through the wood. People screamed at the front of the throng. Chaos erupted, but Fin felt through the crowd and pulled George to him. Together they shouldered, kicked and elbowed their way out. Fin caught the expression on one man's face change from frantic panic to serene indifference. He unholstered his pistol and was swallowed by the crowd, which parted after the gunshot. He was gone. Some quick thinkers filled the space he left, desperate to find his weapon. The soldier manning the heavy machine gun on top of the stairs roared for people to move. None could hear him. They ran deeper into the house. Fin succeeded in swallowing his panic, until he remembered the castle on the news, swarmed by infected. *We're trapped.*

Another shot from ahead stopped people in their tracks,

but these were slow and methodical, against the chaos out front.

George pulled Fin into one of the side corridors. "Not upstairs. If we go up, we're done for. Get to the back of the house, we'll break through a window before the infected swarm the building."

So many ran up the grand staircase, without the where-withal to know they were doomed. Shutters barred all the downstairs windows. They passed beneath pictures and paintings of the house and town as it had been in the past. People hid in the library and cowered beneath the long table in the dining room. Fin stopped at a doorway where a soldier was choking down pills. He had a sickening suspicion they were the same ones the captain had given to him.

As soon as the soldier realised he was being watched, he scrambled for his weapon. Fin dashed away. There was no way to easily discern the living from the infected. He heard hurried footsteps behind him, but after a deafening spray of bullets, the patter of feet stopped, replaced by anguished screams.

The next room had been converted into a hospital wing. There were not enough bunks for all of them, so most lay on the floor. The weight of what they ran into slowed them considerably. There was no way to help these people. There was nothing with which they could barricade the entrance in time. *Most of these people will be weeping before the end of the day.* Reverend was at the far end of the room, standing vigil over a sickbed. She raised her pistol and fired one shot into the forehead of a frail woman. She pulled the blanket over the body which still spasmed. A squad of soldiers followed her lead, moving up the beds as quickly as they could.

They're killing their own. Fin wanted to turn George away, but it was better he saw this. There was nothing anybody could do to prolong the life of the old woman George had promised to help.

A soldier pushed past them, but aside from that, he did not say a word or make a sound to give himself away. He walked up close to the captain, but excitement got the better of him. He raised his weapon too soon.

Sensing the motion, she turned and reacted instinctively. She dove to the side and fired. George and Fin fell back out of the room, hiding until the shooting stopped. The sound of the infected against the main door pushed them on. Somebody started using the heavy machine gun on the stairs. It sounded like a thunderstorm raging in the lobby.

The captain shakily got to her feet. Her face pale, sweat beaded on her brow. She clamped her hand against her bloody side. Standing over the soldier, she shot him in the head before collapsing onto the bed occupied by the corpse she just made. She let out an anguished roar which drew soldiers faster than the gunfire had.

George sprinted ahead, inefficiently searching for oxygen tanks.

"You!" the captain said through shuddering breaths.

Fin froze.

"I told you if I caught you around here again I'd shoot you."

Weepers were inside the house.

"Sounds like I won't have to go to the bother."

She was talking to George, who paid her little attention. "Where are the oxygen tanks?"

People started running through the ward and did not slow when the soldiers aimed their weapons after them. *I can't tell the difference between somebody crying and a weeper.* Not wanting to try guess them apart, Fin ran ahead of them.

George cursed and joined him. Together they tried every

window they passed. The shutters were solid, but could be broken with time, something they had little of. They ran through a tight corridor into a reading room at the back of the house. One long window was not boarded up. George picked up a chair by its back and swung it against the glass. It shattered. He raked the chair legs against the bottom of the window to remove the few shards that stuck to the frame.

There was little time to gauge the scene outside, but from a glance they knew there was room to evade and a chance to escape, neither of which they had inside.

George turned and held Fin's face so he knew he was listening. "Don't break your ankle, we land and go fast. Head for the shore of the lake. Keep the water on one side. Stay on me until we get out of this. I know a place to hide."

Fin followed George. He landed hard, letting the dangerous momentum carry over into a graceless fall. Scratched, bruised and sore, he picked George up and ran.

Despite the burning pain running up his leg, Fin sprinted through the garden. The shots coming from inside the house were drawing most of the infected. There were others lured by the crowds leaving the grounds that ran towards them. Weepers abandoned the house to hunt the living.

Fin chanced a momentary glance behind. Others had tried to follow them out of the window, but they were overwhelmed. A horde of weepers swept around the building. Once they reached the woods they left the main trail and kept to the shore. They could lose the weepers amongst the trees.

George nearly ran straight into a tall man that stood still in the middle of the escapees. "What are you doing? The weepers are coming!"

The man barely looked at him, his eyes were constantly scanning for somebody. He looked past them to continue his search.

They left him. They did not have to say anything when they cut through the larger crowd. Their sheer panic became instantly infectious. The sound of gunfire and death followed them off the grounds. Flickering street lights marked the way to the hotel. People were crying and panicking, not able to trust those close to them. The enemy could be working its way through the veins of their loved ones.

Soldiers shouted to be heard, telling people to hurry towards the Quay Hotel. Fin saw more than a few military personnel join the crowd. George grabbed hold of Fin's jumper and dragged him up the road.

The hill was littered with bodies. The sound of weeping was close and came from every direction. The small hairs stood up across Fin's body. George looked through the ground floor windows of an abandoned three-storey building. By the look of it, it had long been derelict.

"Seems clear," George said. He hopped over a crumbling wooden fence at the side of the house, kept standing by a wild growth of briars pushing against it in the overgrown yard. A few small trees had taken root. Only cats and other small animals had forged trails through the mess. Fin kept his arms raised. His fear of spiders now seemed ridiculous.

The lock was broken and the back door held shut with a length of rope tied to the handle and weighed down with a cement block. George shined his torch through the kitchen window. A fine coating of dust blanketed everything. Broken panes let damp in. *How long before all the houses in Ireland look like this?*

The staircase had been destroyed. "Didn't take as long as you'd think to do that," George said. "Those things aren't able to climb from what I've seen. We'll be safe upstairs." He took an improvised grappling hook from his bag and tied it to a length of rope. It clipped around the banister. He threw his backpack up and awkwardly climbed after it. He did a quick sweep of the upper floor before giving Fin the all-clear.

Fin passed his bag up and made the climb. There was little difference in temperature between upstairs and outside. A few pigeons kept them company. The floor was covered with their filth and feathers.

Long forgotten construction gear lay covered in grime and unfulfilled promise. They used it as a barricade at the top of the stairs. When there was nothing left to do, George paced by the window overlooking the street. Fin could not catch his breath and put it down to a panic attack. Staying seemed like a terrible idea. He doubted the infected had the brains to spot them; it was the living that worried him now. Light outside made George fall in against the wall. Fin crept to the opposite side. In the house across from them, lamps in the sitting room went on. Shadows danced.

"At least we still have power," George said. The sight of others calmed him. The cold glow created gaunt shadows in the street.

"Do you think she's dead?" Fin asked.

"I'm no doctor, but getting shot can't be good for your health."

"She knew you."

George, pointedly, stared out the window. "I thought she was talking to you. Woman got shot. Mind might have gone. I say we wait here until it's light enough to see what's left of the camp."

"We are not risking our lives to go back for an oxygen tank."

"I was thinking about what we could do for the survivors – if there are any," George said.

The sound of gunfire and minor explosive ordnance was incessant. There could only have been so much ammunition shipped in before the walls failed, but more than enough to deal with the infected this far away from major cities. The soldiers just needed to survive long enough to use all of the bullets.

"It was a stupid place to try to fortify," George said. "Too much land to guard. Too few people and so many weak points. Sure, if the same amount of military were trying to keep people from breaking into a concert there, they'd still have bother. What happened? Was it the infected on the train from Dublin? All those weepers, they didn't all come from the capital, those are locals. Can you imagine the terror they must have felt? Trapped behind the walls they thought would protect them?" He wiped his eyes. "I grew up with them."

"We'll do what we can," Fin said.

"I've been studying the maps. The islands would be brilliant if nobody else knew about them. I say we head down to Connemara, disappear into the highlands there. Loughs for fish, shellfish and salmon farms in Killary Fjord. Find a house and renovate the attic. Me, you and Rebecca. We could get a car going and head out the old roads into the countryside. We just need to look out for each other. After we do something for that old woman. I gave my word and it's the last time I ever will, so I may as well honour it."

"I need to get home, George. Why not come with me? We wait out the worst of it and then head east. You're more than welcome there. More food, more people."

"You'll never make it, mate. There's too many people to eat the food and then too many people to try to eat you.

Your family is safe where they are. Getting yourself killed to see them is insane. All we can do is survive. We have to be selfish. Don't go yet. Just wait it out here."

A momentary dip in the light drew their attention to the house across the road. Infected mauled the windows. They were drawn to the light like moths. The residents put out the lamps too late. The house was old, and the window broke. The door gave under the weight of so many.

"They'll go upstairs and wait them out," Fin said.

"You're talking about them as if they had any sense. If that were the case, they wouldn't have turned the light on in the first place. Nobody can easily stomach the dark at the moment, but we have to change if we are to survive."

"How can we beat such a thing?" Fin asked.

"Time, I suppose. We just give them time to rot away to nothing."

They moved away from the window. "Right, should we come up with a plan then so?" Fin said.

Defeated, George agreed.

33

SMILE

The gunfire stopped in the early morning. Its absence left an unsettling silence. Neither Fin nor George thought it was because the soldiers had euthanised all of the infected.

"Do you think they were overrun?" Fin drank sparingly from his bottle of water. He had not felt the urge to eat for days now, but each morning he chewed and swallowed enough to keep his energy up. He was living off vitamin tablets, caffeine and adrenaline.

George did not answer. Weepers inside the house across the road were still active, their voices low and hoarse from overuse. *That must mean the survivors got upstairs to safety.* The disturbance kept infected on the street. Fin suggested luring them into their house and using the height advantage to smash in their skulls. George vetoed the plan, saying they did not have the time or the resources for something like that. Especially not if the camp had fallen.

They emptied their packs of all but the bare essentials. The hammers they kept in their hands. Before leaving the house, George covered the sleeves of his jacket in two layers of duct tape, only leaving the joint at his elbows clear for maneuverability. "If it comes to it, let them gnaw on this while you teach them some manners with the hammer."

Fin took the roll from George and started taping his own sleeves. "Does it stop their teeth?"

"I haven't tested it. Show me your arm." George knelt and bit into Fins sleeve.

Fin winced. Despite George's best efforts, when Fin rolled up his sleeve, there was not even an indent of teeth on his skin.

George spat on the floor. "That's a decent jacket. It's thick enough alone to keep them from breaking the skin. People are prone to forgetting that these are just humans. Not monsters."

They practiced some rudimentary emergency hand signals. Neither of them wanted to speak once they were out in the open.

"What are you laughing at?" George asked.

"Seems a bit redundant," Fin said. "If you see me running, you can probably guess that it's likely a good idea if you start running too."

"What if I want you to run a different way to distract them from me?" George winked.

They checked everything twice. Fin added a few extra knots to his shoe laces to ensure they would not come undone. Nerves soured his stomach, what little he had eaten gurgled uneasily. Eventually, there was nothing left to do but leave. Thinking this may be their last moment of peace for a while, Fin wondered what to say. George stopped any possible conversation by dropping a stone over the bannister.

They waited for noise, but no infected had gotten inside. Before George could descend, Fin grabbed him awkwardly and hugged him. George went rigid.

"Would you ever go away." George relaxed and did not step out of the embrace. "Don't start acting soft. You had plenty of time to hug me in the loft, don't start just before we do something stupid. Makes me doubt it." When they parted, George squeezed Fin's shoulder. "We'll be okay."

Fin went down first. Trying to open the front door would make too much noise, so they went out through the overrun garden. There was only light enough to make out silhouettes. None of the infected on the street were focused on their house. George pulled a dead plant out of a small ceramic flower pot. Old, bone-white roots clung to barren soil. George took a few long slow breaths before covering his face with his mask. Fin did the same. George reached his arm back and threw the pot far over the wall, down the road towards town.

The shattered pot drew fresh laments from the infected. Weepers poured out from the house across the road. In the gloom, there was no discernable target. They barrelled into a zombie, piling on top of it. Fin doubted even one of those creatures could get up again after such a vicious attack. Chaos erupted. Now only the slower shuffling ones blocked their path to the pier. They waited a few moments more for those to pass.

Together, they clambered over the mouldering fence. There was little time for doubt on the street. They ran as quietly as possible down the hill. The gates to Westport House were locked. As soon as they walked by a coffee shop, the sound of agitated weeping started up behind them. The infected tripped over broken class, rousing others.

Caution forsaken, they sprinted towards the river. Bodies lay on the road. It all seemed like a horrible prank to Fin, as if these people were trying to stifle laughter. It did not seem real. *How could so many die in Ireland?* There was no sign of the living. The doors to the hotel were closed tight. The gates held and none of the windows were broken. *There are survivors.* Other weepers joined the chorus, dashing out from a block of apartments.

Not knowing whether the tide was in or out, they reached the pier's edge and launched themselves into the air. The mudflats were covered with enough water to soften the landing. George splashed down ahead of him. The shock of the cold was like a vice, squeezing the air from Fin's lungs. While under the water, he heard the thunderous explosion of bubbles, the impact of several other bodies entering the river. He kicked out, trying to gain purchase. Something touched him and he lashed out viciously, not knowing whether it was George or a zombie.

"Come on!" George called to him the moment he surfaced.

Fin heard more bodies splashing into the river. All along the quay, dozens of them just ran to the edge and fell in. His waterlogged shoes made it difficult to swim, but he made for the deep middle of the river.

"Did they get you?" George spluttered.

Fin had no clue whether he had been infected, he was so on edge that he could have been bitten and not know it. He shook his head, giving a best estimate.

George's teeth chattered. "Let's get the board and get out of here."

Fin sank knee-deep into the silt on the opposite shore. He slid the board out to George and joined him in deep water. A single gunshot echoed from the grounds of Westport House. Weeping eerily filled the woods and steadily died away.

Passing the hotel, they saw lights on in several rooms.

* * *

Back at their safehouse, they did a quick sweep of the grounds for infected. In the loft, George's legs went out from under him. He lay on the ground gasping. His clothes squelched, wetting the carpet. Fin checked his arms and legs for bites. He was covered with dark bruises, but the skin was not broken.

"Any chance of that hug now?" George asked.

Fin smiled. "The moment's gone. There are people still alive in the camp. You heard the shot." Fin said.

"Yeah, one. I'd choose that way out over being mauled to death." George covered his face with his hands. "We're done. The army can't hold them off. All those newly infected."

Fin took the radio out and called Rebecca. She did not take the news that the camp had fallen well. Time alone had made her more reclusive and less responsive. Talking to her was like trying to coax words from somebody that was already half asleep. "I'm going to make the crossing. Wait for me."

"The water in the bay isn't calm."

"I'm coming back."

Her radio was silent, she did not pick up again. There was nothing for them to do now but wait for her return. George could not sit still. He packed and unpacked his bag twice. Then he started working on his ghillie suit, adding branches, leaves, and pieces of neutral coloured cloth.

Fin knew the islands were out of the question now; anybody surviving the camp would think of heading there next. They were running out of options. The weather was too unpredictable to make supply runs safe. George was set on the empty highlands. Rebecca was bound for Achill.

With every passing day, Fin felt further from home. *There's no outrunning this plague. Nowhere to hide.*

Fin went out to the shed to see if he could find anything of use. He found turf, coal and plenty of sleeping spiders. *That's what we need to do, hibernate and sleep through this. I wonder what advice my parents would have for me now.* His mind lingered on them hiding in fear, or worse. He was not sure when he had started smashing things with a garden rake. It was only when he became aware of George's presence that his swing faltered. His chest ached.

"Find anything useful?" George asked.

Fin walked out and leaned the rake against the side of the shed. There was no weeping. *They're probably all in town now.* "Petrol can is full." The corners between his thumbs and forefingers were rubbed raw. "Has me thinking, we'll find something similar in most gardens in the country."

"Are you thinking boat?"

"Car, maybe. We could siphon out enough to fill a tank and a few spare cans for the boot from the houses around here."

"Nobody cuts their lawns in winter, how long can fuel sit still before it goes off?" George asked.

"It's another question to add to the ever-growing list that I cannot answer," Fin said. "Can you drive a car? I can't."

"No. We need Rebecca, but she'll try drive us to Achill," George said.

"What harm? She knows the land. Plenty of hills to run up, if need be."

"I'm afraid of going hungry. We need to stay close enough to large towns for the sake of food. Honestly though, lad, I don't know why you're asking me my opinion on this. I've no notion what to be at. I was serving pints not long ago."

"And you weren't even doing that well." Fin went to the water's edge and sat down. Unable to remain still for long, George periodically brought cups of tea down to him and would stay until their mugs were empty.

When he saw Rebecca coming around the headland, Fin felt a massive release of pent-up stress. He waded out to meet her. Pale and shaking, she dropped the paddle and used Fin as a support. She felt like a wisp in his arms. Her clothes were damp, she had fallen in on her journey. George had a steaming cup of tea and a blanket ready for her.

"I'm sorry..."

"I'm sorry."

Rebecca and Fin interrupted each other.

"I should not have left you there by yourself. That was wrong of me," Fin said.

"I'm sorry I didn't go with you."

"Let's just say we'll not do it again."

"How is the wound?" She pointed to his stomach.

"Hasn't killed me yet."

They sat around the table to listen to her bleak account of the other islands. George filled a pot with water and put it over a gas burner. *How many warm cups of tea have we left?*

"Most of the ships were destroyed in the storms," she said. "Weepers, hunger and the elements whittled away at the survivors. Scavengers were thick as flies when I flew the drone over boats. Remember, Fin, we saw lights on? They stayed on during the day. Solar or battery operated, I couldn't get close enough to check with the infected on board."

She charged her phone from one of their few remaining portable chargers. Her expression hardened when a message she was waiting for did not appear. *When will we have a conversation about her family passing?* Sensing her growing unease, George gave her a moment of privacy and analysed the drone footage, his cup of tea untouched. He slouched in the chair. "There's nothing out there for us."

"Let me see," Fin said.

George turned the phone off. "No. I wish I didn't look at it. No sense both of us having nightmares."

Fin did not argue. "We're running out of options."

"What are we going to do about Westport House?" Rebecca asked.

George stared off into the distance, lost in thought.

Rebecca went on, almost excited. "They've got the largest cache of supplies we know about outside of Dublin. From what you've told me, people just wanted to get away from there in a hurry. When things calm down, survivors will pick that place bare. We're so close. Imagine we took the risk of going in. It would be the last time we'd need to leave the attic. We could nail down the trapdoor here. Bring up some books and nest until this ends."

"It's some risk," George said. "We'd be taking from all those holding up in the hotel."

That did not deter Rebecca. "Like you said, we look after ourselves. Let them head off and find food elsewhere. Every building we go into means taking a greater risk. We use the paddle boards to get into the lough at Westport House. Scope out what's going on and try to get as much as we can out of there. I've no interest in dying."

Fin looked to George, but found he was already won over by the idea. "They were firing throughout the night. Every weeper within hearing distance will be there."

"It's worth a look," George said. "If it's too dangerous, we go out with the tide."

"Do you think the infected called for a ceasefire?" Fin

said. "They didn't stop shooting because they ran out of bullets."

"Is it a bad idea?" Rebecca said.

George drank his tea to give himself time to think. "With the New Year on the horizon and even though fireworks are illegal, I've managed to accumulate an arsenal of rockets."

Rebecca let out a long breath. "What are you thinking?"

"Nothing good," George said.

"Will we take a photo?" Rebecca took out the Polaroid camera.

"I haven't washed in days," George said.

"I'm not looking to record your smell."

"Yeah, but I must look like I reek."

"The picture isn't for us. I want to keep a record of our lives while we wait this out. Something to look back on."

George tried to brush his hair with his fingers. "Rebecca, why would you want to remember this?"

"Because pictures are all I have left of some people. I'm worried that I'm going to forget faces."

Fin did not like her reason for taking the photo.

The three of them gathered close.

"Smile," Rebecca said.

Fin could not muster up the energy to. "Why lie?"

34

SWAN SONG

While scouting the bank across from the hotel, a few inquisitive zombies on the shore approached and were swept away by the current. *It's only a matter of time before one of them washes up in our back garden.* The shore was clear of infected. They brought the boards onto the land and climbed up the sheep grazed hill. There was not much activity visible from the hotel – it was still early – and Fin thought, if they had any sense, the new tenants would occupy the back rooms.

"I wonder what they make of your finger paintings on the windows, George," Fin said. He could just make out the faded printer ink handprints.

He shrugged it off.

"I've always wondered what was over the other side of this hill," Rebecca said.

"Prepare to be disappointed. It's fields," George said.

They crested on their bellies. Cold morning dew soaked through their clothes. Some zombies occupied the land in the distance, stragglers drawn by noise.

"I don't think they ever planned on using that helicopter," Fin said. "The sound of it undermines all their work."

"If they did not mean for it to fly, then it wouldn't have left the ground." George planted a line of fireworks in the hard earth and handed Rebecca a fistful of lighters. "I've no idea how long the fuse lasts." He checked their radios were working. "I'll call and let you know when to start."

"Why am I left out here?" Rebecca put her hands up to forestall an answer. "Now, I'm not saying that I'd rather be going in there, but still."

"You've already paddled in from the island. I barely trust you have enough strength to start the lighter," George said.

"Fair enough. This is going to grab attention for kilometres. What about the people in the hotel? We're not doing them any favours."

"If we can do this without lighting them, we will. It's a last resort," George said. "I don't want to use them, but it could be the difference between life and death. If we have to go out, might as well be with a bang. It might just give some people out there a bit of breathing room too."

"Be careful," Rebecca hugged them both.

Fin and George returned to the boards to paddle the rest of the way. Fin used a small child's board they had found in the back of the shed, leaving George with the steadier adult one. They only encountered one of the recently turned, a man hunkering on a slipway. He stood over the water's edge, listening to the sound it made, or – more horrifying – looking at his own reflection. When it spotted them, the creature stumbled in its haste to reach them. It waded into the water, fell over and did not rise again.

"When you see how pathetic they are up close, you wonder how they brought the whole country to its knees," Fin said.

George lifted his feet out of the water. "Because the whole country is like that."

"Still want to do this?" Fin asked.

"Not at all, but if people were infected during the attack and managed to hide, then we don't have long before they become mindless weepers. We need that food."

"You mean you need an oxygen tank. There's no guarantee there is one there."

"Let's focus on getting in safely first."

"If we find more of the pills they gave us, would you consider giving the old woman one?"

George looked like he was about to punch him, but in the end he shrugged and went back to paddling.

The lough on the grounds spilled over a small weir. A body lay halfway over the falls. The water had pulled off most of its clothes and kept its arms flailing in the current. The noise it made swallowed the sound of their movements. A few bodies clogged the shallower parts of the river, and a few of them still moved. George took out his hammer and ensured they were all still. Fin rested the board against the moss-covered wall and joined in the slow execution. None of the infected could stand on the slippery riverbed stones. George hunkered low, resting his elbows on his legs. He retched, but kept himself from vomiting. Fin saw his eyes watering before he staved in the skull of a small infected.

One zombie was grotesquely bloated, its eyes were opaque and saw nothing. In his nervousness to be done with the deed, Fin went in too quickly and nearly slipped. The zombie's hand shot out and gripped his leg with horrifying pressure. Fin brought the hammer down twice. The first strike only glanced off the skull. The second one connected with such force that the ghost went straight out of the corpse. He feared that if the gloves broke then the open blisters on his hands could become infected.

The last one Fin killed by letting out a ferocious volley of blows. The zombie's face distorted into a bloody pulp. It did nothing to dull his growing rage. He held the gore-slick hammer under the weir water to rinse it clean. George startled him by putting a hand on his back. "Are you okay?"

Fin nodded. "It reminded me of Dara. I've never had something haunt me so much. I dream of hitting him. I hear the hammering like I'm just below church bells and no matter how often I strike him, the screams never stop."

"Maybe you need to work on your swing. Do you need a hug?" George said.

"You're a bad man, George," Fin smiled.

"Are you good to go?"

In answer, Fin picked up his paddle board and slid it onto the grass near the falls. He checked the coast was clear and tried to climb up, but slipped. The sweat of his hands made the gloves cumbersome. Taking them off would risk infection. *Trapped in small ways.*

George went up instead and bent to give Fin a hand. They heard weeping from the woods. Wide-eyed, George let go of Fin and disappeared to deal with the weeper. Fin landed hard among corpses. He rallied and tried to climb up again, grabbing hold of a fistful of grass and dragging himself up.

George swung the pack from his back and threw it at the zombie's legs. It paid no attention to the bag and tripped. Its momentum carried it to the edge. Fin rolled out of the way just as the weeper careened into the shallows, meeting bedrock face-first, stopping its weep.

The sound coming from the woods was a horrendous harmony of countless dead and dying. "And we've just gone and ruined the surprise," George said. Before he could pick up his pack, two infected ran from the road. Fin threw his board into the lough and jumped in after it. He glided over the shallows to deeper water. The densely wooded banks were full of movement. Bodies bobbed on the surface. The smell of smoke was strong, muffling the stench of death. George joined him and together they gazed in muted terror at the sheer size of the horde.

No birds sang, but the carrion gulls, ravens, and crows gathered in the leaf-barren trees.

"They can't hold a tune worth a damn," George said.

"If they could harmonise, then you'd have packs of barbershop quartets laying melodic traps in the woods."

"Fin, it's no wonder we get on. You talk as much shite as I do. Right, we've just started and our plan has failed. What now?"

"This was your idea," Fin said.

Despite the clear danger they were in, George still seemed undeterred. He brought out his ancient, scavenged rifle from his back and carefully took it out of its plastic covering. "Still dry," he said after a quick check. He carefully set the box of ammunition on the board between his legs.

"Don't stand up to shoot that," Fin said.

"I'm not that daft." George angled the paddle board point towards the manor.

"Go for the fast ones first," Fin said. "A shot anywhere on the body will incapacitate them, otherwise the slow ones need headshots."

"I know as much about guns as you do, if I hit anything I'll be doing well."

The grounds were ruined. During the night the barricade had come down under the sheer weight and effort of so many bodies.

"See how they crouch down, the ones by the house?" Fin said in a whisper.

"It looks like they're in prayer." George aimed down the sights of the rifle. "I don't want to know what goes through their heads." Many of the creatures were kneeling, others lay against the walls in a torpor that looked like death.

"Do you think they remember the people they used to be?" Fin asked.

George let out a long breath and a laugh. "Shut up with that nonsense. I bet you wondered if the cow your burgers came from had a name like Daisy."

"It was Mootilda, actually."

George scoffed. "If there's anything left of who they once were, then I reckon they'd crave a well-placed bullet."

"Well, their luck is unchanged, considering you're the one trying to place that bullet. They can only hope for a ricochet. Zombie rights activists will hunt you down if word of this ever gets out."

"You know, I bet there will and all, be zombie rights activists."

"All life is sacrosanct. Hallelujah, brother." Fin held his hands aloft and bowed his head reverently. "I'd say there's a Satanist somewhere sweating and pulling at their collar right now, wondering if they lit the wrong end of a candle in a pentagram."

"You're some man for messing, it's time to work."

Fin's smile fell away. He would not admit the truth to George, but joking and rambling was like a release valve on a build-up of pressure. His lips quivered and he shook. He knew it was not due to the cold, but he hoped George believed so. Surrounded by such horror, he felt like weeping himself. There were too many zombies to count. To stop his mind from racing, Fin studied them. *There's little sense to their movements. The slower ones are being targeted by the faster ones. They eat each other.*

"Have you noticed that there aren't many old weepers?" George said. "I think whatever pathogen is causing this kills a sick host. They skip the weeping phase and go straight to zombie."

They showed no signs of communal bonds or communication. All of them were slaves to stimuli, often attacking their own. George squinted down the length of the barrel, tested both eyes before choosing one. "It's how they walk that gets me. It's like they're wearing a human suit they learned how to pilot by watching a drunk stumbling home after the pub."

"Think of it this way, every one of them you stop, is potentially a life saved. If we could kill all of these here, how many lives do you think would be spared?"

"Alright, okay, feck off. You're putting too much pressure on me. I'm only practicing. I can make out a bit of movement in some of the windows of the house," George said. "We'll know if they're alive when the fireworks start."

"You good? Fin asked.

"Absolutely not, but sure, it's a bit late to worry about that now. Focus on all the supplies in there. It's worth taking one big risk, instead of a load of small ones."

"It's not a gamble if we know we're going to lose," Fin said. "There are too many of them."

"True, but the bridge across the river was full of them. They would have followed the people through the woods. They know we're here. We can't go back, not for a while yet. I'm not saying we rush anything, just scope out a plan."

"No rush, only the risk of hypothermia."

"There has to be people still alive in the house or stuck up a tree," George said.

"I'm not ringing the doorbell to find out."

Swan-shaped pedal boats were moored to a stone jetty. During the summer, families rented them out for a few minutes on the lough. "We'll have an easier time of it, sitting in one of those," Fin said. "Better than lying on the boards in the open."

"Okay. I'll distract them and you untie them. We'll pedal around the shore and search for survivors." George carefully took his radio out of his pocket. "How are you keeping, Rebecca?"

"How many are there? I can hear them from out here. It's like you're at a concert-sized silent disco."

"Whole town is here."

"Do you want me to light these?"

"No, not yet."

"Well hurry up. I'm too exposed out here and there's a lot of movement in the hotel."

"Do you want us to come back?" George asked.

"No. We're committed now."

Fin lay on the board and slowly paddled to the last swan boat on the tethered line, keeping low. The infected soon lost sight of him. Using a steak knife stolen from their safe-house, Fin sawed into rope. It caught several times before he had a good rhythm going. The wind jostled the boats against each other, and the sound drew infected. They watched from the jetty with dispassion. Every movement that crossed his field of vision made him freeze.

He expected hands to reach out from the dark water and drag him off the board to be torn apart while he drowned. Even after heavy rainfall the lough was usually clear, but now it was churned and murky. A string of bubbles rising nearly made him paddle back to deeper water. The boats bobbed together and jostled gently. The swan he was trying to free moved. Something blotted out the light, putting him in shadow. Just as Fin looked up, an undead lunged out of the boat.

The zombie hit the water, narrowly missing him. It swiped out and scraped at his wetsuit. Fin saw it happen in slow motion. The hand found no purchase on the rubbery material. One of the only remaining fingernails bent back and hung loose.

Unbalanced, Fin came off the board. He let out an involuntary yelp and got a mouth full of water. In his panic, he lost the knife and it disappeared into the rising cloud of silt. He caused too much noise trying to swim away from the blindly reaching weeper. He pulled himself into the last boat and checked himself for bites and scratches. His chest ached from his heart's frantic pace.

Infected along the shore moved towards him. His board had drifted into the shallows, too close to danger. Zombies spilled from the woods. They started wading out towards him. Hands and fingers of submerged zombies ruffled the surface of the water. Distorted sound and refracted light confused them. Fin thought back to the infected he tried to drown on the Greenway with Rebecca. He wondered how long it would take for the body to break down.

Lying on the bottom of the boat, out of view of those unnatural things, he caught his breath. *That zombie in the swan must have been bitten, tried for the boats and stayed there until turned by the infection.* Without his knife he could do nothing. Fin sat up quickly from the contaminated bilge water. He felt it run down his back like acid. *The disease!*

A shot echoed and a body hit the dock. Fin looked to George, but he held the rifle in the air in a non-threatening manner, shielding the sun from his eyes while he searched the building for the shooter. Somebody waved from a top floor window. The dead swarmed around the building again.

A firework let off a high-pitched shriek as it shot into the sky on a column of smoke. It erupted in a spectacular blaze of light. Infected were silenced by the deafening boom. Several others followed in quick succession.

"Did you ask her to light them?" Fin said, but he could see George was desperately trying to get his radio out to call off the rockets.

He roared into the radio, but got no reply. "There's about ten minutes worth of rockets to go off, before the infected come back."

Those still alive in the house must have thought there was a plan in place. Fin saw the shooter rush back inside and others filled the upstairs windows to get a look at the fireworks. They cheered, their hope renewed.

Fin could see them moving through the house, trying to get downstairs and out. Windows shattered on the lower floors, infected fell out in their thoughtless efforts to reach the noise. Those upstairs would not be able to know the full extent of the infestation. *How did anybody survive?*

George screamed at them not to leave, but Fin could barely hear him above the sound of the horde and explosions. Soon the survivors would be outside, thinking they were saved.

"There's no plan. Stay inside! Please!" George shouted.

There is no plan.

35

___

EXPRESS ROUTE TO HELL

When George fired the rifle, dust rose up from where the shot struck the building, a good foot above the tallest zombie. He loaded another round and took aim again. The house took another beating, but he was getting closer. He looked to Fin with an awkward, near-apologetic desperation. It did not matter if he managed a kill with every shot, there were too many infected. The only observable benefit was drawing the undead into the lough. They were incapacitated in the water. So many nameless faces disappearing beneath the surface was a nightmarish sight. Some floated, their backs barely warmed by the winter sun. Beholden to the breeze, like mines, harmless until you came upon one.

The boards are useless. Fin could imagine the surface of the lough hardening over with ice-like human flesh.

The hammer. Fin's hand went for his belt. Relief flooded through him when he felt its hilt. He rammed the claw hammer between the metal tether and the hard white plastic of the swan and pulled with all his strength. The plastic cracked and shattered. He stopped before the boat came free. *How many people are in the house? One boat won't be enough – if they manage to get out.*

Trapped at the end of the tethered swans, he could not risk swimming to the dock. A crowd of undead watched him from the shore, held back from the water by a low stone wall.

"Where are they coming from?" George reloaded with shaking fingers. "Most of these are weepers."

"Maybe all the survivors didn't make it to the hotel. They could have followed the train from Dublin," Fin said.

They heard gunshots from inside the house. George's hands were shaking so badly that he dropped a rifle round. It fell into the water with a plonk.

Fin pulled on the rope connecting the boats, dragging himself alongside the others. They were all empty. Leaving a space of less than two boats between him and the dock kept him far enough out of reach from the weepers. His presence invigorated them. They jostled, some fell in. Most were unable to manage in the deep silt, but one kept its balance and started wading out towards him.

Fin hurried. In his haste he found it difficult to get the claw beneath the metal ring. The zombie was nearly on him. Cursing, Fin turned his attention to it, waiting for it to get closer so he could crush its skull. Its skin was ashen. Wounds on its face had left one eye ruined. Its hands reached out to strangle the neck of the swan. Before it got closer, a bullet destroyed its brain. Bone, brain and blood splashed into the water. The zombie fell backwards, to stare blankly into the sky.

A soldier on the top floor of the building waved at Fin to hurry up. Then he took aim at the other zombies by the boats. He fired twice and two zombies dropped from their standing with a wet, fleshy sound. Fin struck the metal ring with the blunt end of the hammer. The plastic casing cracked and the mooring came free. Pedalling as hard as he could, he barely managed to pull the rest of the boats away from the jetty. George paddled over, climbed in and set his own feet to the pedals.

"Hit anything yet?" Fin asked.

"Keep that talk up and I guarantee I will."

"From two feet? I like those odds."

The slack and drag from the other boats made it awkward to maneuver, but the shore below the house was not far.

The fireworks and gunfire caused enough confusion that the infected no longer paid any attention to them. Faces crowded around windows throughout the house. Glass shattered as the dead inside reacted to the shrieking explosions. On the ground floor, fingers wriggled through the boards barring the windows.

"That could have been us in there," Fin said.

"None of those people probably thought that this was how they would end."

Weepers toppled out of the higher floors, indifferent to the fall, others were pushed. Hardly any of the bodies stayed down. Grotesque marionettes rose up with broken limbs and deformed faces.

"There's nothing else we can do," George said. "We wait. Want to try out the rifle?"

Fin took it from him, pulled the bolt back and loaded a round. Aiming down the sight, he tried to ignore the faces. It was hard to think of them as anything other than human; when he looked at those faces, ravaged by sickness, they were still human. It was easy to dismiss them as people, once they stopped acting as such. Now that he was trying to put a bullet in their skulls, his hatred for them only just surpassed his empathy. There was a bit of a kick once he pulled the trigger. The shot went wide.

"Harder than it looks, right?"

"I was trying to save your pride," Fin said.

"In the movies they always say to take a breath and let it out slowly and you'll get a perfect shot. Maybe the sight's off."

Fin rested the rifle on the swan's head and reloaded. This time he was more careful, aiming squarely for the body of a man wearing pyjamas and a dressing gown. The movement of the water, though minute, was enough to put him off again. He could not tell how far off he was. Fin put the rifle down. "I don't want to waste any more ammunition."

George laughed. "You know what? I think these must all be blanks."

There was no further sign of survivors in the building. They heard automatic gunfire and a percussive bang that shattered a quarter of the remaining windows on the second floor.

Fin's heart raced. He felt like he was trapped inside with the survivors. "How do you think they got in? How could the walls have fallen so quickly? None of this should have happened. The infected don't have any wits."

"Fear makes people stupid. Look at me for instance. I'm in the middle of a freezing lough, surrounded by zombies because I'm afraid to be alone."

That caught Fin off guard. "You'll not be alone. We're with you."

"You were nearly gutted. Rebecca... she becomes more frayed by the day. I lost most of my people. I think I'm the last of my line, that's such a weird thing to say. Think of all the generations, all the chance meetings. The history of the world and I'm the forefront of it. I'm one of the last Synotts."

Trying to reassure him about family was dangerous territory; there was no way to soften the truth, not while surrounded by so many broken homes, shattered dreams and ended lives. *How many mourn for these?* "Well, stay alive then, put more Synotts in the world. Though I'm not sure anybody will thank you for that. I think Rebecca is dealing with things better than most. Before you came along, I was in a dark place, she took care of me. That's what we are now, a family of necessity. And I wouldn't go commenting on her sanity, giving that you only wear a jumper that you outgrew years ago."

George smiled, lifted the hem of his jumper up to his nose and sniffed. It brought him some comfort, like a talisman. "My family went on to Dublin, I stayed behind to look after those that could not. Going through my belongings, it was easy to leave all my possessions behind. They're just things after all. I found this in the back of the wardrobe. It was a gift from an ex. I'd say it's two – no, three – years since we broke up. I've had the jumper longer than that. She became a stranger to me after the split. I just forgot to throw this out. I've tried, but I can't. Throwing it away would be like throwing the last bit of her away. I can't stop wondering if she is already gone. I'm talking out my arse though. I keep it because it means that, at one point, somebody cared enough about me to dress me."

"As soon as we're finished here, I'll get you a jacket that fits."

"It's a memento of good memories, anything I get from you will just remind me of late nights behind the bar." George pointed to a first floor window. "Look there."

A zombie turned away from the glass and moments later was violently pushed out backwards; a soldier stood in its place, gauging the ground beneath him. Bags were thrown down, while shooting increased behind him. They could not go any lower, the windows on the ground floor were all welded shut to keep out the dead. Ropes were dropped out. The soldier rappelled down so quickly that Fin thought he had fallen, until he slowed just before hitting the ground.

George and Fin were shocked into action when terrified, crying children started clambering over the windowsill. Makeshift rope harnesses were looped around them. Soldiers inside the building lowered them with little more care than they showed the bags. The fireworks cleared a path between the building and the shore where the swan boats floated. The survivors would have to swim out a little bit, but it was better than their only vessels becoming swamped by infected. Once on the ground, the soldier took a knee and started shooting with restraint. A single bullet per target. The fireworks kept most of the attention off them. As the children reached the ground, they lay low until everybody was ready to run for the lough.

The sniper that aided Fin still remained on the top floor. He took careful aim and helped thin the numbers of the curious infected. A string of people went out the window, many of them children. A wounded soldier was lowered down.

"That's the captain," Fin said, incredulous that she should still be alive.

Eight escaped. Just as the ninth was about to leave, he was pulled back into the building. There was a short period of yelling, a spray of bullets and after a brief relative silence, a loud blast warped the building. Splinters, stone and debris rained down on the survivors.

"So few," George said.

The blast broke the spell of the fireworks for many of the infected. The children ran in the middle of two protective lines of soldiers. Their combined effort kept the captain standing. They were slowed by the water. As they waded out, the dead and dying behind them closed off all other means of escape. George used a paddle to push infected off balance.

Fin dragged two children into their swan and helped steady the other. The captain roared as she was hoisted in. One soldier lifted the children on board. Fin saw him go rigid and gasp. All colour drained from his face. Unsheathing a tactical knife, he kept it close to his body so those behind could not see it. In one swift motion, he plunged it into the water. When he lifted it out, there was blood on it. Fin could just about make out the outline of a body sinking further into the mirk. The soldier froze when he saw Fin watching him. The man's shoulders slumped. He let out a long, shuddering breath and seemed to relax to the chaos around him. Snapping out of it, he went back to lift the few remaining children out of the water. He protected the rear so his comrades could get to the boats. He was the last one to leave the water.

Only three swan boats were needed. The soldiers carried thick duffle bags on their shoulders. The muzzles of several rifles peaked through the top. Once all the survivors were on board, they pedalled and paddled to be free of the shore. Most of the weepers had long followed the sound of the fireworks, leaving the slow and injured ones behind. They made easy targets for the soldiers. Without a word, they set to thinning the infestation. With each loud abrasive shot, a body crumpled.

The zombies became disoriented, frenzied by so much stimulation. They started attacking their own kind. One bit down on the neck of another and, using its body weight, dropped to the ground, ripping flesh from bone. When the assault ended, both got up and parted as if nothing had happened. They were creatures of base instinct, soulless. Fin wished he was a marksman. With grim satisfaction, he watched the soldiers ending them.

"What about your man on the top floor?" George asked. "Should we draw the zombies off and come back for him?"

"No," was all the captain said. She was ghoulishly pale, her breathing shallow and ragged.

After a while, they just gave up shooting. There were too many infected for them to have much impact, like trying to cut a lawn one blade of grass at a time. They pedalled into the middle of the lough. Rebecca was still sending up fire-works. A soldier cut through the rope tethering the boats to each other.

"I can't say I've said this much lately, but I'm glad I didn't shoot you," the captain said to George. A pistol rested on her lap.

"You would have made my life a whole lot easier if you had," George said. "Are you okay?"

"All considered, no. It's a gunshot, not a bite. As luck goes, it's not the worst. What's the plan now?"

"The weepers will be blocking our escape. So we wait for the tide to rise and pedal these over the waterfall and get you to the hotel on the quay."

"How long away is that?" the captain asked.

"Two hours, I think," George said. "Are you in a rush?"

Blood darkened the front of her uniform. "I'll happily be late for my own funeral."

Fin tightened his grip on the hammer when the first soldier out of the building pulled off his mask. Leaning back in his seat he wiped sweat from his face. *Burke.* He recognised the soldier he followed to the train, the very one that threatened to shoot him and then abandoned him in the boatyard. The presence of his rifle was no longer a relief.

"Thanks for that," Burke said. "I didn't think we were going to get out of there."

"Well, you prick, remember me?" Fin said.

Burke had already caught his breath. He scrutinised Fin and simply said, "No."

"What happened?" George asked.

"Mutiny," the captain said. "People got sick, too many for it to be a coincidence."

"This was a crime against humanity. Mutiny is too soft a term. They never even tried to make it look like an accident," Burke said. He was exhausted.

Despite his dislike for the man, Fin's anger burned itself out in the face of the few people that the soldier did manage to save. He wondered if Burke kept scanning the shore to look for those he lost.

"They poisoned the camp's rations. Likely laced it with biological waste. Country's full of infected meat," Burke clenched his teeth.

Fin went cold at the thought of somebody cutting up bodies and feeding it to a camp of survivors.

"So many of them started turning. Then they blew the front gates wide open while we were dealing with the infected. They came pouring out of the hotel in the woods and overran us. Some bastard in a van, the thing was packed with explosives."

"Survivors made it to the hotel on the quay," George said. "We can drop you off there. You could see about getting a helicopter to winch people out of the car park or from the roof. Get them to one of the ships off the coast."

The captain's laugh was brief, the action causing her immense pain. "They're not here for our protection."

The soldier that Fin assumed had been bitten in the lough was stoic and contemplative. His duffle bag covered his injured leg. Fin did not know what to do. *How fast does it take to become infectious?*

"Are there any oxygen tanks in Westport House?" George asked.

Reverend injected herself with something. The tension in her body subsided. The creases in her face ironed out a little, the cross-hatching at the corners of her eyes less pronounced. "No. We moved everything to the hotel." She turned to Burke. "We're far enough now. Get rid of it."

"Hold on." Burke grimaced and took out a radio. "Michael, you set?"

The radio chirped before a voice came back. "As good as I'll ever be. All make it?"

"All except Ronan," Burke said.

The sniper came to an upstairs window, leaned out and waved at them. "Give me five, then do it. Once you've your own seen to, will you check on my family?"

"I'll make it my mission," Burke said.

"Thank you." The man stayed at the window for a while, watching the swan boats bob on the water.

Nobody on the swans broke the five minutes' silence. The soldiers frantically pedalled the boats until they were nearly out of sight of the manor. Burke took out a device from his front pocket. He held his radio to his face, wet his lips. "Cover your ears and get down low," he said to the survivors. He pressed the radio receiver in and said, "Safe travels, brother." Before his friend could respond, Burke pressed something on the device. A second passed before every window still intact in the building was shattered. Part of the back wall was blown out by a massive explosion. Shattering stone and warping metal. A shockwave rippled across the surface of the water. Fire engulfed the lower rooms, incinerating the infected still inside. Flames blossomed up caressing the barren stone. The fire caught and raged, driven on by man-made ordinance.

Blocks of stone and debris rained down on the manicured garden and splashed in the lough. One brick struck a zombie in the gut, pinning it to the ground.

"Why did you do that?" George yelled. "There could have been people still inside."

"There were," Burke said. The light of the fire showed how gaunt he looked. "I could hear them all night. I couldn't get to them."

"I didn't hear a thing." Another soldier took off her mask and marvelled at the blaze.

Even from this distance Fin shied away from the heat.

"It had to be done," Reverend said. "Hopefully it's enough. If not, then at least we've bought ourselves some time."

The comment was cryptic, but before Fin could ask after it, a soldier alone on the swan boat with most of the bags started retching. It went mostly unnoticed until he went into a fit of uncontrollable sneezing. The mask covered his mouth. He held his left arm close to his body. The last of the fireworks stopped.

"Sweeney, please tell me you cut yourself on the window," Burke said.

Everyone pedalled away from the infected man.

"Have you any messages you want me to pass on?" Burke readied his rifle.

"Nah, I sent my emails a few days ago. This place is kind of nice." He started crying.

"Have you any prayers to say?" Burke's voice was starting to crack.

"What's the point?"

"Short and sweet, I like it." Burke never got a chance to pull the trigger.

The shot came from behind him and brought silence over the water. Reverend let her smoking pistol fall back into her lap. "Infected are not human. The longer it's left untreated, the more chance it has of spreading."

Burke's lips curled in a snarl. He fought against himself to lower his weapon and sat down hard. The soldier Fin knew to be bitten was breathing heavily and staring at him intensely. He shook his head so slowly that only Fin could see it.

"Get us upwind of it," Reverend said.

* * *

Without the fireworks to draw them, the fire mesmerised the infected. They walked into the inferno. Fin watched in horror as those closest to the origin of the explosion burst into flames. Their clothes smoked and ignited first. Most dropped before they got inside the building. *Express route to hell.*

George steered them towards his board. He took his radio out and tried to call Rebecca. "Are you okay?"

Her response was quick. "I'm on the water. The place is crawling with weepers. I heard the gunfire and the explosion, did you kill them all?"

George put down the receiver and laughed. An eerie sound to hear while steeped in despair.

The mountain no longer seemed so bad to Fin, once you got over the smell, the cold and Malachy's madness. He wondered if he would take the three of them on as apprentice scavengers.

After a few moments without a response, Rebecca's voice came back over the radio. "There's something wrong with the hotel, it's riddled with walking corpses."

The soldiers shared looks. Reverend went even paler.

"How many people were in the hotel?" George asked the captain.

"Every living soul that left these grounds went there," she said. She was deathly weary. "Hundreds." She shrugged and wrapped her jacket tighter around herself.

"What's the point?" Burke echoed the last words and sentiment of his friend.

Fin felt his anxiety rising under the scrutiny of the infected on the shore. Their faces were caricatures of their former selves: exaggerated expressions, grotesque grimaces as their mouths hung wide open. He stopped trying to count them. He had not seen so many in one place since the news footage from Dublin and Galway.

"Won't the current take them down to the falls?" a teenager asked. "They'll clog up our only escape."

"Don't worry," George said, but gave no reason for reassurance.

There was nothing they could do but wait. Weepers, returning from the fireworks display, churned the lough water to froth in their haste to reach the roaring furnace. *At least the dead don't swim.*

"What are you after oxygen tanks for, anyway?" Burke asked.

"I found a survivor with bad lungs, she's run out of tanks," George said.

"Wouldn't be a kindness. You'd only draw it out," Reverend said with her eyes closed. Her voice sounded distant and dreamy.

Burke was agitated. He looked to her, but she had lost

interest in them. "There won't be any more deliveries. No more tanks. She's not a survivor. I'm sorry – for what it's worth."

Now that the fireworks had cleared, they heard cries for help coming from high in the trees around the lough. Suddenly, it felt like the tide was going to change too soon. They started paddling towards the closest caller, but there was nothing they could do. Fin finally noticed the cold as screams of the desperate and despairing haunted them. There was no plan; they just gave in to instinct and tried to help.

36

SAFEHOUSE

They stayed on the lough long after the tide turned. Nobody wanted to abandon survivors that might still be trapped in the trees, too scared to call out. "We'll be back!" Burke shouted. He wanted to stay behind, but the boats were crammed with those they had already rescued. "Avoid the hotel!" They stopped pedalling at every sound, fearing that calls for help might be drowned out by the noise of their wake.

The few they had saved were exhausted from a frosty night spent clinging to branches. They barely had the strength to tread water long enough to be dragged into the swans. One person screamed for them to wait and not to leave without him. Despite their reassurances, he rushed his attempted escape. He screamed as he dropped from the canopy and ran towards the water. He screamed when the infected caught him. Burke erratically aimed at the shore, arching the rifle to try and find a shot. "Come on." The man died, but Burke would not let them continue until he made a shot. In the end, he settled for methodically emptying a clip into the heads of undead. With shaking hands, he took a fresh one from his vest and reloaded. He lowered the rifle and sat down, trying to affect a look of disinterest.

The river gurgled over the short falls. Fin, George and a few of the survivors lifted the boats through the shallows. River stones scraped against the slippery plastic bottoms. The children went ahead into deeper water, carrying the captain with them. The soldiers protected the rear.

"I'm not going with you," said the soldier that had been bitten by a submerged zombie. The roosts were still full of the cries of survivors.

"You're no good to them, Mark, we can't give you a boat. You won't get them out," Burke said.

"None of us are getting out of here."

Burke looked almost relieved that somebody was staying behind. He took a magazine from his belt and gave it to Mark, clapped his shoulder and followed the swans. Mark drew his knife, crouched low and entered the woods. *Either the infected will finish him off, or he will turn slowly and join them.*

They tilted the swans, bowing their heads low to fit beneath the bridge. Bodies that washed down the stream choked the channel. They were no longer menacing, reclaiming their humanity in true death.

Fin nearly jumped when George lay a hand on his shoulder. He did not say anything, but Fin was now conscious of how quick and loud his own breathing had become.

The island from which Rebecca had set the fireworks off was crawling with weepers. The smell of gunpowder hung heavily in the air. Rebecca shone her torch to alert them of her position. She paddled out from the shelter of a river marker. She was shivering. Fin thought it was from the cold at first, but when she drew close, he saw her red eyes. "The hotel..."

Most of the windows were broken. Fin looked away, but he could not hide from the melodious cry of hundreds of infected. The mudflats were filled with them, indifferent to the rising tide. *How long will they reach for the light from the darkness before they rot away, like a primordial dread?* Each day that passed, the numbers of unfeeling killers grew. *There's no reasoning or bargaining with them. They won't bend against threat of harm.* It was enough to turn his guts to water.

"These boats will be swamped far from shore," Burke said. "We need to find shelter for the night, somewhere safe."

"I know a place," George said.

The swans were cumbersome and without a keel they were unsteady. Most of the children were too cold and miserable to make much noise, but one child mustered up the enthusiasm to cry. She was slapped by another child. "We don't cry, they do. Are you one of them?"

Her eyes darted to the rifles and she shook her head vigorously.

George stopped outside their safehouse, but Burke passed over it after a brief assessment. "It's too close to town."

Despite George's best efforts, the soldier would not be won over. The survivors deferred to his judgement. Beneath the roof tiles, rafters and insulation was their safehouse; two single beds, a futon and enough food to see three people through the worst of the outbreak. *There is no seeing this through.*

"There's a solid gate at the front," George said. "Only a small road cutting off from the main one. If we could put a few cars together, we could block it up, we'd only have to worry about possible infected in the houses around here."

"No. Still too close to town. I want to get as far from the camp as we can with the light we have left."

"We have food there. Your mate looks like she's dead already. Give us time to make a plan."

Burke looked as if he was about to snap, like he was being hunted by something other than the infected. "We need to find a boat and get as far away as possible. Something that can get us out to Clare Island. If you want to stay here, we'll not keep you. This place will be overrun. Think about all the people in the hotel, once they turn, they can't go through town because we've blocked the roads. The noise will have drawn all those in town that weren't already inside the camp. There's only one direction for them to go." Burke started pedalling without another glance at the building. "If you think you can do better than us, piss off and try."

Fin kept glancing behind him, trying to catch the phantom that caused his hair to rise. "It feels like we're being watched."

Burke shaded his eyes against the sun. "When an animal's sick, it'll find a quiet place to die. People aren't much different. If they could, they went home. It was the last bit of comfort they could hope for. Most houses will have infected inside, too stupid to get out. We'll not find anywhere safe to sleep tonight."

"There are survivors in some of those houses," George said.

"You think those aren't just as dangerous? Remember, they still have their wits. As I said, we won't find anywhere safe to sleep on the mainland."

"There's a man on the mountain," Fin said. "He lives in

the church. He has plenty of supplies, mentioned he was looking for help."

"Mad Malachy?" Burke said with a grim grin. "You were up with him? Is it true what people say about his family?"

"If it's that they're dead, then yes," Fin said. "Maybe he needs to pretend that they're alive, so that he gets through until he finds something worth living for."

Wind rocked the boats beyond the headland. Burke set the pace, while another soldier landed and scouted ahead. It was incredibly disheartening to watch him jog out of sight ahead of them.

Reverend noticed the children watching the infected on the shore. "The trouble is in not knowing how much intelligence they retain. You look at their faces and you see people. There's nothing supernatural. Inside those skulls is a defunct human brain. I haven't gotten much sleep since this started, but when I do nod off, what haunts my dreams are intelligent infected."

"You must know what's going on," Rebecca said.

Reverend did not look away from the children. She did not answer.

When the scout returned to them, he directed the swans to a farmhouse further along the coast. They would have made better time walking, but nobody wanted to leave the relative safety of the swans. Light rainfall made the cold worse, but nobody mentioned it. Reverend was used as a control by which to gauge their own discomfort. No matter how horrible they felt, she was going through it too, with a gunshot wound.

The crowd of infected that followed them were quickly left behind; they could not manage the cluttered waste ground, field hedges and boundary walls. They watched the farm for a long time before Burke gave his approval. It was getting too dark for them to look elsewhere. They brought the swans into a sheltered natural harbour. Fin jumped off the boat into clear water. He dragged the boat closer to the black rocks to keep it from drifting. The children remained behind. This place was completely new to him. With George and Rebecca, they would have moved silently and trusted each other to watch out for the group. These were strangers.

"Have we passed the house with the old woman in it?" he asked George when they had a bit of privacy.

"No, she's still on further."

"Why did you head out this far by yourself?" Rebecca asked.

"Scouting for a better place. Your man was right, our place is too close to town."

"Maybe we can convince them to bring her with us to Clare Island," Rebecca said.

"We both know what their mercy is," George said. "I don't know that I'd put her through that. Yous have already been to the islands in the bay. Why should Clare be any different?"

The sky was tinged a dark velveteen by the setting sun. Black clouds obscured the moon and stars. They promised a wet and miserable night for any caught outdoors. The place was too quiet. A sign of what the rest of the country would be like if Ireland did not get the help it so desperately needed. With soldiers watching the entrances, Fin shined the weak beam of his torch through a window. It glinted off the glass. Undead faces stared back at them.

They were back on the boats as the last light left the world.

* * *

"I've been along the coast, there are no boats just lying around," George said. All of them were on edge. Burke kept pushing for them to keep moving. Everything was silhouette, all detail lost in the darkness. Their fear populated the fields with inquisitive infected.

"We'll have to search the grounds. In garages. Look for slipways. We'll not find any in the dark, though," Rebecca said. "We can go back to the house."

"We're not turning back." It seemed fear was Burke's guiding drive now.

"Rev needs a place to hold up," Rebecca said. "At least for the night. We need a plan and we can't come up with one out here. If you want to continue on, then away with you, but the rest of us are stopping at the next decent-looking house." Rebecca paddled away from the group. Fin and George followed.

"Those are graves, not houses." Reverend's words had a chilling effect on all of them. "Now, I'm likely already dead from this wound," she said. "So I'd sooner spend my last night on earth somewhere warm. Failing that, at least out of this poxy rain. Where's this woman on oxygen you were trying to help?"

"A bit further on," George said. "When I came out, I went across land, cut through fields and familiar paths. These swans are a joke."

"How far gone is she? What chance does she have off the machines?"

"I'm not a doctor, but I'd say unless we get her on an aid ship, she has none."

"No country will take her," Reverend said. "Asylum seekers are openly shot down when they don't turn away. How do you even get her across the country to Dublin? Galway is gone. Belfast is in ruins."

Belfast too.

"What about the ships patrolling the coastline?" George asked. "Surely they would have the equipment and the means to look after her."

"You didn't strike me as stupid. The risk of bringing a potentially infected, mortally sick old woman onboard, is not worth jeopardising the wellbeing of every person on those ships. They have a duty to protect others. They do that now by ensuring this plague stays in Ireland. One life cannot be weighed against that of a nation, or the health of others beyond our borders. If this woman is on the way out, I'll put her to rest."

"Why are you worth the bother of keeping alive then? What's keeping you up?" George said.

"Spite. If I'm going to die, then there's one last thing I've left to do. Find those who brought death to our camp. How many children and elderly do you think were under my charge? Do you imagine this will be the last time the perpetrators commit an atrocity to benefit themselves? They won't stop. They must be stopped." The effort of prolonged speech took its toll. Her breathing was much heavier.

"Revenge. That has nothing to do with us," Fin said. "Where's the benefit? All the supplies in the camp are now surrounded by infected."

"I understand the need to adapt to survive. Whoever poisoned the food in the camp did what they thought was needed. I'm going to kill them for that." Reverend leaned back in her seat and took a drink from a flask. She winced when she put her hand back over the wound. "There's not as much in there now as you'd imagine. Whatever aid came in went through Dublin first. The Pale they're calling it now. We only received a fraction of the provisions promised to us. Until the end, when our shipments dried up nearly completely. They had to keep filling the carriages when the cameras were rolling."

"You think the infected on the train were put there intentionally?" Fin asked.

"We were promised food, we got a bioweapon."

Rebecca laughed. "What a sight that will be. A group of children, a few soldiers and a dying woman, valiantly pedalling swan boats on a revenge mission. They have a helicopter and could be anywhere. I thought those foreign warships were shooting down planes leaving Ireland."

"Not all of them. If you leave our borders you're a target. I know where Lynch is going."

"You don't just adapt to do such a thing," George said. "There's something there that has festered for years, if not a lifetime."

Burke broke his silence. "There are a few reasons for committing such a crime against humanity. One of them is that they have none left, the other reasons are just subcategories of that one. There were enough rations there to support those people for weeks, if we kept the freezers running. Now there's enough to support a small number of people for a few years, and the only hungry mouths there no longer have an interest in it."

"We need to get to the islands," Reverend said. "There are survivors there."

"They're not too welcoming," Rebecca said.

"Only the stupid ones would be. We lose the uniforms. They're meaningless now anyway. The kids should get us entry, nothing screams harmless like a flotilla of pedal-powered swans."

They pulled into a sheltered cove. Fin and George shone their torches low, seeing nothing but tall grass moving. Burke took point. The three of them pushed the swans out to deeper water before moving up the beach to find shelter for the night. Frost was already forming. By morning the infected would glisten like Halloween decorations left out until Christmas.

Weeds pushed up through slabs on an old stone path. They followed it in single file. Burke's rifle was useless now, it would only draw the infected down on them, but it still felt comforting to have it. Rebecca remained behind, keeping the swan boats from drifting too close to the shore. Fin noticed how she scrutinised their faces and he guessed she was looking for the child from the island. Rev was of little use to anybody, unless they were to use her as bait.

"Any idea of what caused this?" George asked Burke. "You'd be in the know."

"If I were, do you honestly think I'd be here?"

"Fair point. My money was on a biological weapon. Why Ireland though? A test gone wrong?"

"Could it have been natural?" Fin asked.

"Does any of this seem natural? You're talking to a soldier sent to the arse end of nowhere to babysit. You see the uniform and think we're in charge. I thought I could get more use out of the uniform before I had to dump it." He stopped. "If this wasn't a weapon to begin with, it is now. If we live long enough, we'll learn what this is. Somebody already knows, I'd swear to that."

"Do you have a silencer for your rifle?" Fin asked as they approached farm buildings. It would freeze tonight. The windows were already glazed.

"Those are suppressors and they don't cancel noise entirely." Burke checked the buildings surrounding the house. They were locked. Something moved beneath a hedge, Fin thought it a fox, but it had the dimensions of a small human. *Infected.* "Burke!" Fin shined his torch on it and briefly blinded the soldier when he turned.

Burke whistled to keep the zombie's attention on him. He butted the stock of the rifle into its face and kicked its legs from under it. Burke's face looked demonic in the unnatural light. He turned the zombie onto its front and buried his knee on its spine. With both hands on its forehead, he pulled back as hard as he could until they heard a snap.

George got sick.

"It barely made a sound," Fin said. *If it had come for me, I would have died.*

"The slower ones don't weep, that's how they'll catch you off guard. Would have got me if not for the warning. Cheers."

The house was empty. They did not encounter any more infected. *Why was it out here by itself? Did he die alone?* George found a ladder and destroyed the alarm box. It squealed briefly. The noise of his hammering did not draw anything from the adjacent fields. It was safe for the time being. Burke went back for the others, while Fin and George barricaded the doors and windows.

"This crap about hunting down whoever stole their helicopter has nothing to do with us," George said. He tore boards off the stairs with more force than was necessary and more noise than was wise.

"You saw what he did to that zombie outside. You sure he wouldn't be a decent one to have along with us?" Fin said.

"Don't forget, he left you to die when there was no benefit to helping you."

"Yeah, I remember. What about the children?"

George nodded. "I know. Do you really think we can't go

back to the safehouse and stay there? He could just be saying that to keep us with him."

"Somebody poisoned all those people," Fin said. "Maybe we should stay with this lot. Might get out to Clare, then Achill. We can't go back now."

"The storm barriers should keep them inside," George said, but he did not even convince himself.

* * *

Rebecca helped the children upstairs, while the soldiers carried Rev and their gear inside. Once they were secured, they finished barricading the front door.

"When the sun comes up, we need to find a proper boat," Burke said. "We'll head out to Clare Island. Maybe find you a doctor, Rev, though I still think a multivitamin will have you back on your feet."

Reverend was in for one hell of a night. She self-medicated until she was barely able to speak. Now she was unconscious; if she stopped breathing in the night, Fin would not be surprised. *A bullet would be kinder, but it would only be a death sentence for the rest of us.*

Burke gave each of them a ration bar. They all stayed in one room. All the mattresses in the building were piled together in the master bedroom. The children curled up together, buried beneath thick blankets and spare clothes from the wardrobes. Few slept, the cold was too bitter for that. One soldier tried the heating system, but the electricity was out.

Burke patrolled the windows. "Do you want to rest?" Fin asked.

"I'm all right."

"I don't need any special training to look out the window."

"I won't be able to sleep," Burke said.

"Why? Are you kept up by the thought that you should have been on the helicopter with Lynch?"

"So that's why you were asking if I had a suppressor." Burke said. "To make sure I wouldn't shoot you. Didn't recognise you without the look of terror on your face, but it came back to me in the garden when you spotted the infected."

Fin gripped the hilt of the hammer so hard his fingers hurt. "They left without you?"

"Lad, you watch yourself. I don't need this gun to kill you."

"There's three of us watching you and you already look like you're dead on your feet," Fin said.

Burke let out a breath. "That's one way of putting it. I'm not going to apologise for leaving you. Maybe if you added a bit of cardio into your routine before this happened, you would have kept up."

Fin bristled at that, but knew to take an olive branch when one was offered. He did not bother with the fake smile, it was too dark to see it.

"I was leaving, you heard well enough. I had a car, enough food and fuel to get me home. Never got the chance though. I kept saying to myself, I'll do it tomorrow. But each morning I thought, somebody like me has a loved one under my protection. If I stay at my post and do my job, maybe whoever's looking after my family will do the same too. We all have people caught up in this. It was Lynch that told me that."

"Do you wish you went with them?" There was no accusation in Fin's tone.

"I don't think they thought about what they would leave behind. The explosion at the gate was only a diversion. They're good people, at least they were. I wish I was away from here, but I wouldn't pay that price. And those things out there don't scare me half as much as Rev does. Lynch, Muireann, and the others that left with them know something. They were some of my best friends. I'd begrudge it, but I'd have died for them and I would have thought they would do the same for me. Whatever they know changed that. Rev knows too, but we haven't had a chance to have a heart to heart. You want to know why I'm pushing so hard? There's something that made good soldiers do terrible things to escape." He paused. "You know what? I will take you up on the offer. Wake me if any of them get inside the house."

The scout stepped out of the shadows at the door. Rain had soaked his jacket. Fin imagined he could easily melt into the vegetation. "Found a boat big enough for the lot of us."

"Aidan! Is it far?"

The soldier opened out a map and showed Burke. "An hour or two at our pace. Couple of days on the swans."

"Is it safe to go now?" Burke asked.

"Not with this lot. The infected are spreading out from the town. Give them a few hours and they'll disperse."

"We have until morning," Burke said.

Aidan shook his head, but said nothing.

In the silence that followed, they listened to the house and car alarms set off by the horde. The sound was distant, but nobody could fool themselves by thinking it was not getting closer. There were fewer of them as the days dragged on. The land was slowly shutting off. Heavy raindrops tapped at the window before it started lashing, drowning out the noise outside.

"Goodnight," Burke said.

When he left the room, Rebecca whispered in Fin's ear. "There are no soldiers any more. There are only mercenaries."

* * *

One of the children woke up screaming. It set everybody on edge. Weapons were drawn, but another child was on him instantly, covering his mouth. Burke turned his torch on low. Nobody intervened. The child seemed indignant; held down by a stranger, he tried to fight, thinking he had brought his nightmare into the waking world.

They heard weeping outside. The torches went off. The child kept struggling. His friends begged him to stop. They started crying.

"It's coming from the garden," Rebecca whispered.

"We can't get back to the boats," one of the children said, her voice rising in panic.

"We're safe here, we're not going anywhere. So long as we remain quiet, they won't know we're here," Burke said.

Other weepers joined those already in the garden, drawing more to the area. The sound circled the house. Burke lifted the child from the floor and pushed him hard against the wall, holding him up by the collar. "Shut up." His voice was just above a growl, incensed, just like the infected outside.

The blow winded the child, he tried to catch his breath. Either he had come to his senses or fear of further pain cowered him.

"The weather is throwing them off," Rebecca said. She

stood by the window. Fin joined her and instantly wished he had not. The rain fell heavily. The gutter on the roof was clogged and could not deal with the volume. Water spilled out and splattered loudly on the ground around the house. It was that noise which was drawing the curiosity of the infected.

"We're stuck here until it stops raining," Fin said.

Glass smashed downstairs. The weeping was louder now.

37

FOG

Lightning briefly illuminated the room. The crack of thunder was barely audible above the pounding, freezing rain. It frenzied the weepers, they now seemed intent on razing the house to the ground with their bare hands. The scared faces of the children shone like ghosts in the dark. Fin realised, too late, that he did not know any of their names. Reverend was still breathing and Burke had a thousand-yard stare. Though the light was brief, it gave him a glimpse into the terror experienced by the others.

By the sound downstairs, one weeper had made it inside the building and was blindly knocking things over in the dark. More were drawn to it. Most of the windows downstairs were strong enough to withstand the infected, except for the frosted glass set into the front door. It cracked and threatened to shatter. The bitter cold and incessant rain was no deterrent to them.

"They don't know we're here. So long as we're quiet, they'll tire themselves out. We saw it happen in Westport House, remember?" Burke said.

A few heads nodded silently in answer. He conducted

the children, keeping them busy by ordering them to get everything they could use to barricade the stairs and then move up to the attic. Spiders and ghosts were now a familiar comfort to them, as opposed to the ravenous infected.

Fin and the others stood at the top of the ruined staircase, waiting for the infected to enter their field of view.

"Those things are blind down there," Burke said. He took a knee and steadied his rifle. "We have to put them down before they bring all of them inside. The rain will give me some cover, but we need to be quick."

"How much ammunition do you have?" George asked.

"Enough. It's the food and water I'm worried about. We can't get caught up here, we don't have the rations, or the time."

Suddenly a night on the boats did not seem like such a chore.

"Be ready with hammers and shovels." When everybody was in place he yelled to the weepers in the house. "Hey!"

The weeping intensified. Fin shined his torch down the ruined stairs to guide them. The light glared off the glass of the picture frames on the walls. More made it inside. Others slammed against the doors, but they held. Faces pressed against the windows were distorted.

The shoes of one squelched on the hall tiles as it shuffled into view. Water ran off its muddy, torn clothes. The first one rounded the bannister. Cat-like, it did not follow the path of the beam up the stairs, instead it tracked its movement across the wall. Burke had to shout again for its attention. It turned slowly; the growing number of infected outside held its dull fascination. When it caught sight of them upstairs, its mouth opened and it started to weep, before it was interrupted by a bullet. Its head snapped back and it fell with a sopping thud.

A body pushed against the glass of the front door and a brittle crack cut through it like a bolt of lightning. A head pushed through the shards, flesh peeling away from bone. Glass opened the face, ruining an eye.

Burke aimed and fired. The zombie fell slack, but the sheer number of bodies behind it kept the body up. Three entered the hall from the kitchen. Burke put them down with ease. One weeper ran up the ruined steps and fell through the missing boards. Its teeth chomped together with a jarring crack and the tip of its tongue fell from its mouth.

We're safe, Fin kept telling himself. If the undead made it halfway up the stairs, they would tumble through the broken steps. George left them to get his bolt action rifle.

"Keep that in reserve," Burke said. "If not for the weather I wouldn't risk any shots. Just leave it to me."

Rebecca emptied their packs and stacked the ammunition and Reverend's pistol near Burke.

"How does it look out there?" Burke asked.

"I've lost count of them," Rebecca said.

Had we just gone to the house we would have enough food and water to wait them out.

"They must have gotten out of the hotel. We can't stop now. We'll thin the herd and leave in the morning," Burke said.

Fin looked at the dwindling pile of ammunition and realised that they would eventually have to fight their way out with hammers, knives and hands.

"Why not just stop firing now?" George pushed an oncoming infected back down with the end of a sweeping brush. "Stay quiet and wait them out."

"I would if we had the time, but we don't. I've seen them lie down and wait in place for days until stirred. The thunder might draw them off but we can't chance it. If we clear enough of them and keep the rest in the house, we could try for the bay. The swans will capsize in this weather. How far is this boat you mentioned, Aidan?"

"Too far with so many of them and I've no idea if it works or not," the soldier said.

It did not take long for them to discover they were thoroughly trapped. There was no easy way to get out of the house, besides the stairs. The torch batteries failed just before morning. The soldiers took it in turns to guard the stairs.

Burke's head lolled on his chest. It was a cold, miserable night and the morning held little promise of improvement. The rain was light and feathery. Reverend coughed and winced at the pain it caused. The noise made the others flinch. "Where's my pistol?" Her voice was hoarse.

Burke handed it to her. "If you're thinking about using it on yourself, you may want to wait, we're surrounded."

She inspected the magazine. "What are we down to now?"

"Running on fumes, curses, knives and a hammer," Burke said.

"Just make sure to leave me a bullet."

The children shaded the windows with sheets. Mattresses slouched against walls, they hid behind them. Many of the thicker blankets were on Reverend. Fin found a few bath towels that would keep the worst of the chill off him. Infected had not made an attempt on the stairs for nearly an hour. He lay down in the bathtub. When he closed his eyes, he saw infected faces made horrid by torchlight. The hallway beneath him was choked with bodies.

Fin gripped the side of the tub and grit his teeth. The house was contaminated by the weeping virus. They had enough food for another day, but not enough that any of them would feel full. It felt like he barely closed his eyes before he was roused by Rebecca.

"We're leaving," she said. "There's a fog so thick you'd swear we were buried by an avalanche."

"Infected?"

"I can't see to count, but they don't disappear when the sun comes up, so assume so. If we can't see them, they'll have the same difficulty."

"What about the children? There's no way the lot of us can get to the coast without attracting attention," Fin said.

"They're staying with Reverend. We'll get the boat and come back for them."

Fin could only imagine the fear they would experience when they heard they would be left behind. *What if something happens to us? They'll starve in a dark attic, surrounded by infected.*

"How has George been?" Fin asked.

"He hasn't slept. He's talking about going out to that sick woman's house when we get the boat on the water. Forgive me for saying it, but I kind of hope she didn't make it."

"We can't let him go by himself." Fin rubbed his eyes, he wasn't asleep long enough for crust to form.

Everyone was on edge. Rev went paler still when she saw the sheer number of infected that had been put down during the night.

"If I had the time I'd set fire to the place," Burke said.

"That sentiment is probably shared by most countries about Ireland right now," Reverend said.

The children did not react as Fin thought they would. They were quiet and despondent, nearly catatonic, when left alone.

Burke went down first to secure the ground floor. There

was the sound of a brief struggle in the kitchen before he returned. He wiped his knife on the shirt of a dead infected. "Too many out the back," he whispered to Aidan. "Use the front door."

Fin carefully stepped over the gore and the lifeless limbs, half expecting those sightless eyes to turn on him. He could hear his heart beating in his ears as he tried to make as little noise as possible. Aidan opened the door slowly, it creaked. He had to use both hands to stop the weight of a body leaning on the other side from pushing it open too fast. The body slid against the window, dislodging what little glass remained. A large bloody shard wobbled like a loose tooth and fell towards the tiles. Instinctively, Aidan put the side of his foot against the door to stop it from opening further and snatched the shard before it shattered. He let out a sharp hiss and put the glass down gently. Fresh drops of blood fell to the ground below his hand.

Fin just had enough time to see the small cut on the side of Aidan's finger, before the other soldiers were on him. One held him tightly, while Burke took a small, clean knife out of his jacket.

"Don't worry, I haven't used this yet," he said before he removed Aidan's finger near the knuckle. The cut was clean and smooth, like he was chopping a vegetable.

Aidan grimaced and shook. He barely made a sound. Another soldier readied a medkit.

"Bring him back upstairs and deal with him," Burke said.

Outside, visibility was reduced to a few feet in front of the house. Fin, George and Rebecca walked closely behind Burke. He set the pace. Unable to see, the infected just stood still, waiting for purpose. Fin felt like a ship at sea without a lighttower. From here on out, there was no talking. He put his hand on Rebecca's shoulder. She did the same to George. They made for the cove in silence. Behind them, the house was swallowed by the fog.

The morning was crisp and cold. Tall grass lay flat, beaten down by the heavy rain. Infected made noise as they stumbled blindly through the fog. Some of the bodies they passed had been mauled by weepers. *If we live long enough, they might just kill themselves off.*

Burke stopped abruptly. Fin nearly bumped into Rebecca. A weeper walked across their path, head leaning to one side, almost resting on its shoulder. It was hard not to think it was listening. Something knocked into the side of the building and it hurried towards the sound. A rain-soaked jumper hung limp down to its knees. Stale makeup ran down its face.

They continued, passing infected on either side. The undead stood still, swaying in the breeze. Twice they had to detour around one that was lying down, though Fin expected those were weepers that were entering the slower stage of the infection. They appeared as dark shadows maring the dull white fog, like a growing stain. Burke took them over rocks to avoid what turned out to be a tree. The growing sound of waves made them careless.

George stepped on a plastic bottle. The crunch drew an immediate response. One of the shadows closest to him lunged blindly. George stepped back, grabbed its arm and swung it in an arc. The infected lost balance and landed hard. Weeping started and others around them converged on the noise. Burke turned on a battery operated radio and threw it as far from their position as he could. Then he ran without saying a word.

The crackling sound of the government warning and advice over the radio seemed too loud in the field of undead. They swarmed the radio from every direction. Burke ducked and weaved between them. Fin lost him in the fog, unable to tell which outline belonged to him amongst the weepers. He lost his grip on Rebecca's shoulder. Fin thought she had stopped ahead for him, but it was a weeper. He skirted around it, its features becoming crisp enough for him to see its eyes suddenly swivel and lock onto him, all while the radio gave advice on how best to avoid the sick.

The shoreline was overrun. Fin raced down the sand and barged through a group of them. *They're drawn by the sound of the waves.* They followed him out into the painfully cold water.

The swans had survived the night. Fin pulled himself on board with numb hands. He started bailing out the rainwater that had collected in the bilge. The infected lined the shore, chasing seabirds. It was rare to see one alone. Burke was the first to emerge from the vapour; he climbed over the slippery rocks that the infected were unable to traverse. Rebecca followed behind him. George had run straight into the bay, as Fin had.

"Anyone infected?" George asked when everyone had gotten onboard.

Rebecca and Fin vigorously shook their heads, conscious of Burke's knife that was still wet with Aidan's blood. Burke ignored them and started working the pedals. They used one boat, a paddle board in tow.

* * *

The sun had passed its zenith by the time they pulled in close to the shore where the scout had marked the boat.

It was a large fishing boat on a trailer with deflated tyres.

It was covered in a protective tarp that was dotted with mouldering autumn leaves. Nestled at the back of the house, it would have been invisible from the road, which was little more than a country lane. A quick sweep of the house brought up nothing. George and Fin searched for dry clothes and food. Fin took a sharp kitchen knife from the drawer; a scabbard protected the narrow, bendy blade. He preferred the crudeness of the hammer. With a knife he could not let his anger control him, precision was required.

George tore up the staircase, ripping out the worn carpet. Fin watched for signs of infected, while Burke checked out the boat. "Good walls around the property. We can block up the road no problem," Fin said. He wore stolen clothes from the house, they smelled of disuse, but he was happy to be out of his wet gear.

"Do you need me for anything else?" George asked Burke. "Noreen does not live far from here. If that wave of infected have not reached her yet, then it won't be long."

Burke handed him his pistol. "I've work to do on this before I put it on the water. Do what you have to do and get back fast. I won't wait for any of you."

"Will you be okay on your own?" Fin asked.

"Jeep in the garage still works. The gates will hold long enough for me to get it into the bay."

"You don't have to come," George said as Rebecca put her backpack on.

"Shut up, let's go."

Fin clasped the suicide pill packet in his pocket. *Last one.*

38

SLEEP SOFTLY AND DREAM OF NOTHING

The wind picked up, churning the sea and pitching high waves against the rocky shore. Falling hailstones went from a small annoyance to a brutal, bruising hindrance, landing with little thuds against the frozen earth. Happy to leave the swan behind, they continued by foot to save time. Fin put his hood up without thinking. The crackle of the fabric as he moved, and the sound of hail against it, muffled the other sounds in his surroundings. He pulled it off and looked behind. In his imagination, infected had flanked them. The biting hail was preferable to the alternative.

It felt good to be back to just the three of them. Fin wondered how their lives would be had they ignored the rest of the world. Hold up in their safehouse, conserve their food and leave only when they needed to. Living in close confinement with George and Rebecca was an easy thing, though he imagined they would all wear on each others nerves in time. Such thoughts no longer warmed him. Until recently he could have ignored the world, but not any longer, not when he experienced firsthand the suffering endured by survivors. *The world abandoned us, we cannot abandon each other.*

They walked through fields that were old and long forgotten. They passed the bones of a few old buildings. Trees and briars grew strong in the shelter of their walls, rain nourished their roots without roofs. "You never consider how hard people had it in the past until you see how they lived," Rebecca said.

"What are you talking about?" George said. "That right there would go for a quarter of a million on the Dublin property market. We're not far now."

Two fields and a small stream later, George carefully climbed over a crumbling, dry-stone wall into a messy garden. At the back of the house, flower pots were stacked like school chairs over summer, waiting for new pupils. Bags of compost were heaped alongside turf and logs in the coal bunker. A small cottage stood near the shore. Ancient, leafless trees sheltered it from the worst of the wind. An old glasshouse had been turned into a conservatory at the side of the building. The panels were glazed with aged moss. Nothing grew there now, pots and trays of patient soil slumbered until spring. A well-cushioned armchair was placed where it would receive the most sun and the occupant could watch over a verdant kingdom.

The road to the house was barricaded with cars and an old coal truck parked sideways. Sandbags were placed beneath it to block the gap. The dead would be funnelled along another road.

Somebody took great care before leaving this woman. "George, did she say what happened to her family?" Fin asked.

"They left her with food and what comfort they could. Blocked the road and went looking for help – an ambulance or oxygen tanks from hospitals. Nobody came back. I don't expect they will, either."

"Not by choice," Rebecca said. "Look at the effort they went to, to protect her."

George nodded and turned away to check for infected. "I'd love to know what happened to them. Are they wandering around as weepers? Have they died? Or did they manage to get out somehow?

"No point in worrying about it now," Fin said softly. "When this is over, we can search for the lost."

"Easy for you to say. Your family are alive and well. Rebecca and I..." He seemed to deflate. "I'm sorry."

"No need to be," Fin said. "The only thing keeping me going right now is knowing that they're okay. I want to be back with them more than I've ever wanted anything in my life. If I didn't know..."

"To do all this and not come back. Why leave in the first place? It seems sound enough here. Better even than our safehouse," Rebecca said.

George shrugged. "I bet you anything there were people on the islands that left the safety there, everybody thinks sanctuary is where they're not. They left because they were scared and wanted to do something to soothe that anxious feeling. You know how a funeral is for the living and not the dead. Perhaps this small gesture was for them, rather than her. Made it easier for them to leave."

"What are we supposed to do?" Rebecca asked, making them all stop. So far none of them had spoken about what was to be done now that they would get no help from the camp.

"What we can. What they couldn't," Fin said. He let go of the tablet in his pocket in case heat from his hand denatured it. George knocked on the back door before entering.

He wiped his feet on a bristly welcome mat. Empty milk bottles on the doorstep waited for a milkman who would never come. Fin had a surreal feeling when he cleaned the muck from his own boots. *We're here to kill her and he's worried about threading dirt into her home.*

The smell hit him immediately; it was stale, made up from the smoke of hundreds of cigarettes and countless meals prepared so regularly over the years that they held the bricks of the building together. It smelled like the home of a grandparent. A clock that would give the hearing-abled a migraine kept a doleful count of things. It stood sentinel over the kitchen, keeping time to the way things were before.

A sugar bowl on the table was left open for easy access during tea chats. The bread bin was full of biscuit packets, nourishment should the chats run into dinnertime. That is how it was in his own grandmother's house, before she was moved to the retirement home. *I can't do this.* The fridge was covered in magnets from around the world, souvenirs from children and grandchildren. The crayon drawings were on crisp white paper, possibly from great-grandchildren. Photographs covered every inch of wall space, depicting little moments. Most were inconsequential, given worth and cherished for the memories they held. Family gatherings where she and her husband were at the centre. There were plenty of newer ones wherein they were slowly pushed to the edge, their run done now, to watch others take the torch. *Crazy how life works.* From family weddings to christenings, they moved further down the line. Eventually there were pictures without her husband. Deceased, Fin guessed by how young she looked in the ones when he was around.

Memories, fragments of community during times of isolation. *I should have visited my family more when I had the chance. It feels like it's too late. Why does it feel like that?* Never one to give much heed to premonitions or odd feelings, he still found it difficult to shake this one. He put it down to a general sense of dread with the situation.

George went through to the sitting room. Floor-to-ceiling brown curtains stretched most of the way across one wall, hiding the world outside. A transparent tube snaked across the luscious cream carpet and disappeared beneath a door to the bedrooms. A low machine hum could be heard, like a fridge on its last legs. Two fangs opened out from the tube and were stuck in the old woman's nose.

Cocooned in a quilted blanket, she lay comfortably in an ancient chair. The cushions were dimpled from use and propped her up. Her legs rested on a poof. A book lay open on her lap. She was only a quarter of the way through it. *How many books can we read in a lifetime?* Fin could not imagine having to choose a last one. Then again, when do people ever pick up toothpaste at the store and think that it will not be finished? *Is that what shopping after eighty is like?*

Purple veins stood out on her blotchy skin. *It's not a bad place to die, in a room full of memories, in the comfort of your home. Many without the choice would envy her.*

George knelt and placed a hand tenderly on her arm. "Noreen?"

For a moment, Fin was hopeful that she had passed, but her yellowing, red-rimmed eyes opened behind thick glasses. She stirred with an "Oh", followed by a fit of coughing.

"I'll get you some water," George said and quickly left the room.

"You startled the life out of me," she said.

If only it were that easy. He rebuked himself for that.

445

"I'm Rebecca and this is Fin. George mentioned you're having difficulty."

She took one look at their appearance and gave them a queer look. They had not bothered to take off their packs. Only now did Fin notice how odd they must look to her; shell-shocked and dishevelled, in clothes that did not fit them.

Despite that, she offered them a welcoming smile. Fin could not bear to match it. He turned away and saw the dirt they had walked into the formerly pristine carpet. "Sorry about that." How fast old etiquette was forgotten. She did not seem to care. "I'll clean that up." He left the sitting room, wet a cloth at the sink and brought it back to clean the mess.

"I'm afraid I can't be moved," she said. "Not without oxygen or an ambulance. Haven't gotten a delivery of fresh tanks in ages."

"What's the matter?" Rebecca asked.

"Pulmonary fibrosis, caused by smoking, I think, but could have been a hundred little things. You know you always think you'll be fine, but then you end up old and get stuck with the bill. Well, no, you wouldn't know yet. Bit of advice, run that bill sky high, let future you worry about it."

"That's terrible advice," Rebecca said.

Noreen laughed, a sound like somebody trying to clear stubborn phlegm from their throat. "I know."

"Is there anything we can do for you?"

"A new set of lungs would do the trick, but sure, while you're at it, I'll take a twenty-year-old body." She winked at Fin.

Rebecca laughed along with her when Fin's face started glowing hot with a blush.

"Will you settle for a cup of tea?" Fin asked.

She nodded and he went to join George. The kitchen

was empty. He found him out back, sitting on an old swing. The rusted joints squeaked when moved, so he sat still. Fin took the swing beside him. They watched her rain-saturated clothes weigh down the washing line, barely moving in the wind. Apart from fear and the infected, the only other constant seemed to be the mountain in the distance behind the house, veiled in clouds. *How many scenes like this one have played out within view of Croagh Patrick?* He felt a reverence knowing these were Noreen's last moments.

By the time Rebecca came out to see what was keeping them, they still had not said a word to each other. George tore tufts of grass from the lawn.

"She doesn't really know what's going on," Rebecca said. It sounded like an accusation.

Fin thought it was a gift to keep her in the dark. "What harm? If she knew, she would just panic. What good would knowing do her? If you had to leave this world, wouldn't you rather go imagining it was only getting better for those that follow?"

His enthusiasm left him when he heard an inquisitive mewling from beneath the shed. A jingling bell announced a proud little cat as it sauntered towards them. Fin crouched down to entice it over and scratched behind its ginger ears. It arched its back and went straight for George, wrapping its body around his legs.

"I used to think that I'd love to live forever," Fin said. "To see what new discoveries and inventions were sure to come. Imagine how sickened you'd be if you died just before they could upload consciousness to the cloud, or something? But you'd also have to live through unforeseen horrors."

Neither of the others spoke, so he continued. "We have the chance to send Noreen off without worry. Her family are likely dead."

George pushed the cat away from him with the toe of his boot.

"Let her dream of finishing that book in the morning. Worry about her washing and look forward to giving out about the oxygen tank delivery being late."

"She has a right to know," Rebecca said. "Are you suggesting we just kill her?"

"She's dead already. No?"

"Then tell her, give her a choice. Let her make the decision whether or not to take the tablet," Rebecca said.

"And what if she says no? You're asking a person to end their life on the basis of what a couple of strangers are saying. Could you leave here knowing her oxygen machine will fail and she'll be left gasping for air until she dies? We can only hope that she will be alone and the infected don't make it to her beforehand." Fin stopped speaking when he noticed that George was crying.

"Who are we to decide how her life ends? We're not the final full stop, or grim reaper," Rebecca said.

"Tell me I'm wrong. Give me a solution. There is nobody we can take her to. There are no more hospitals. Galway's gone. Dublin is far worse off than we are here. What help can we provide other than mercy? If we risk anything else, then we all die. The electricity is failing. Is she religious? If so, she won't be too keen on killing herself."

Rebecca paced. "This isn't fair. It shouldn't be up to us."

"We have more of a right than the infected. They'll do it without remorse, compassion or kindness. Then she'll be up walking and could take another life. You're right. It's not fair, we shouldn't have to. But we must," Fin said.

"Guys. I can't do this." George stood up slowly as if testing the strength of his legs, to see if they would carry his weight. "I'm going home." He handed Fin the pistol Burke had given him. "I'll just say goodbye. Give me a minute. Please."

Fin had not thought that he would be the one left to kill Noreen. When it had been the three of them, it felt easier somehow. Not like killing at all. Just helping. Same as making a cup of tea.

The tea! He jogged back to the house and was about to turn the stove on when he heard sobbing coming from the sitting room.

"I tried, I'm so sorry, I tried. I tried."

Fin crept from the house. The last thing he heard was Noreen's comforting shush. Fin grasped the suicide pill in his other hand. Giving her the tablet felt like a kindness, the gun was a wicked weight in his other hand. There would be guilt if he pulled the trigger. *Is it cowardice that I'd sneak her the pill instead of using the gun?*

"This is yours, Rebecca," he said. He handed her the suicide pill. "I gave mine to the man on the mountain. I wish we had one each just in case. Maybe somebody in my family or Solene might need it. I'd sooner this than a bullet, and those are as rare as these tablets." He knew he was making her culpable, spreading the blame. It was her choice now, the pill or a bullet.

She knew it too, her face contorted in disgust. George came out of the house and left them with a wave.

"Wait!" Fin called. He ran to catch up with him and handed him Burke's pistol. George took it without a word and then followed the path along the coast back to the boat.

"Helping others just ends up taking from us," Rebecca said. "This is the last time. Give her the pill. I still think she should know though." Rebecca did not protest further.

"I say let her go in peace," Fin said. "I'll kill her but you can tell her."

449

She took her hat off and rubbed the short bristles of her hair. She sat down on the swing beside him. "I hated my job. Having to put on a fake smile every day and pretend to give a shit if somebody didn't get enough jam for their toast in the morning. I remember acting like the world had ended when a woman told me that her room didn't have enough of a sea view. I thought I was going to get fired, I was clearly taking the piss out of her. But no, she was happy that somebody saw things her way. I have a calendar in my bedroom with the number of days I had left before I handed in my notice. I'd work that job every day for the rest of my life over this. I hate what we've become. We're only really getting to know each other now, but we're not who we used to be."

The cat stood over its food bowl. Fin went in search of something to feed it. He emptied the whole tin of meaty chunks in gravy out for her. While she ate, he removed her bell collar. *That's all I can do for you. I hope my cats are okay. What must they be thinking? Do they wait at the top of the stairs for Solene or me to return? Are they hungry? Are they scared?*

Rebecca went in to talk with Noreen while Fin set about making tea on the gas stove. Once back in the sitting room, all need for haste disappeared. They spent the day there. Fin and Rebecca made dinner in silence. Most of the food in the fridge had spoiled and needed to be thrown out. There was a large freezer in the shed, but once the power went out, that food would be useless. Whenever the cat wanted inside it would scratch at the door. Fin checked for infected before letting her in.

They tried several times to tell Noreen about what was going on in the country, to ease into mentioning the suicide pill. They did not know where to begin. Remembering the radio in the kitchen, Fin nearly tripped over her oxygen tube to bring it in and turn it on. *Let her find out that way.*

He twirled the dial looking for a station to listen to while the three of them ate in silence. It was mostly static. She did not seem perturbed by the warnings that played on a loop. Fin kept scrolling through the FM and AM bands. Nobody was broadcasting live.

"I think I have it easier than yous," Noreen said, when she put her plate aside.

"Are you religious?" Fin asked.

"I was when I was younger. Not so much now, but I'll pray the odd time as insurance."

Fin smiled. "My dad used to say that. I knew he didn't come up with it himself. Would you pray for us?" Fin asked awkwardly.

Rebecca drew the curtains back to let in the dying light of the day.

"Do you want to finish your book?" Rebecca asked.

"No dear, I've had better. I'm ready to sleep."

"I'll make you a cup of tea," Fin said.

Fin and Rebecca stood shoulder to shoulder while they waited for the water to boil. "I'm not sure if crushing the tablet up and putting it in the tea will ruin the poison," Fin said.

Rebecca turned to him and smiled; her cheeks were wet with tears. "Poison is poison, no? It's not going to get any better for her."

Fin poured water in and they watched the tea diffuse into the mug. He left the pill in its packet. Rebecca took his hand in hers. "Did you think we'd be doing this when we watched the news break in the hotel?"

"Honestly, all this time, I've been hoping you slipped a little something into my drink on your last night."

"We'll have a drink after this, I promise."

Fin set the cup of tea on the coffee table beside Noreen.

The tablet, still in its wrapper, lay on his sweaty palm. "This will help. It's –"

"I'm ready to go. I'm sorry to put you both out like this. I couldn't do it by myself." She took the pill, peeled back the foil and let it rest in her hand. It absorbed all of her attention. Fin offered her the cup of tea. She took a mouthful. "Oh, that's very sweet. I won't forgive you for that." She laughed and coughed.

Rebecca sat on the arm of the chair and put her hand on Noreen's. Fin knelt on the floor by her, ready with a bottle of water should she need it. The oxygen machine whirred in the far room.

"Look after George will you? I know he tries to not let it show, but he's soft-hearted and all of this will weigh heavily on him."

"You know him well?" Rebecca asked.

Noreen looked surprised. "He's my grandson."

"He never said a word," Fin said. He turned pale remembering the conversation they had on the swings, as he tried to strong-arm them into agreeing to kill her.

"My family knew the risks in leaving. They were down for Christmas. Most of them call elsewhere home. They wanted to go, but I told them it was stupid. They weren't going to let anybody leave, didn't matter if they had foreign passports, they were here and that's where the rest of the world wanted to keep them. Honestly I thought I was being overcautious. Only George stayed. He knows this land. He knows where to find food, especially when the weather turns favourable."

"Does he know you know?" Fin asked.

"Oh, he probably thinks I'm a doddery old woman. If that was the role I needed to play to keep him here, then I wouldn't have had qualms with blowing bubbles to sell it. I knew I was done when the news stopped playing. Do look out for each other. I'm sorry this happened on your watch. I am glad he has friends like you." She lapsed into a fit of coughing.

"What's it like?" Fin asked. Curiosity got the better of him. "Knowing you're going to die."

"We all know our days are numbered. I could ask you the same question. You'd have as easy a time answering it as I do. Beneath the wrinkles I'm still in my mid-twenties." She rolled the pill between her thumb and forefinger before quickly popping it in her mouth. She swallowed with a grimace.

After Noreen fell asleep, Fin took the book from her lap and closed it. The bookmark fell out, but it did not matter. "Sleep softly and dream of nothing," he whispered.

Rebecca finished his little prayer. "Be at peace."

39

WEEP

The return walk to Burke and the boat seemed to take much longer. Before leaving Noreen's house, they wrapped her in blankets, closed the heavy curtains and locked the sitting room door. A temporary tomb, until sense returned to the land. She would rest surrounded by photographs of her family. Fin only noticed Rebecca's absence when he climbed over a metal gate and she was not behind him. He ran back, fearing what he would find. She just stood in the middle of the field. Every step lost returning to her was agonising. They were exposed, a target in the open. It would only take one weeper to cry out and they would have nowhere but the frigid water of the bay to escape to. When Fin reached her, she shook her head, answering a question he had not asked. He took her in his arms and hugged her until she was ready to continue.

"I want to go home, Fin. Can we just go? I'm finished."

"Yes. We'll get George and go to Achill." He held her hand and started walking. At first he had to pull her along. "Burke and the others are taking the children to Clare Island. We'll continue from there to Achill. We'll be at your place soon. I picture your bedroom covered in dolls and horrible shades of pink." He joked, even though he felt sick.

Rebecca shivered violently. She threw up, hunkering down on her knees. When she was finished vomiting, she collapsed onto her side. "I can't do it, I can't. I don't want to." Her eyes were glassy, tears streamed down her face.

Fin used the sleeve of his jumper to wipe vomit from her chin. He placed his hands on her cheeks, forcing her to look at him. "We can do this, Rebecca. Take a few deep breaths."

She grabbed a fistful of grass in one hand and Fin's jumper in the other. "My family are dead." Saying it, she let out a silent anguished cry and curled up.

Not here. Fin scanned the perimeter of the field. It was steep, there was no road frontage, so the infected would have difficulty reaching them. He lay down in the wet grass beside her, becoming invisible to any onlookers. He stroked her short hair while she sobbed.

It started snowing. Large flakes fell from yellow-grey clouds. "I just need a minute," she said.

"Take as long as you need." He was not sure if he was doing the right thing. *In situations like this, are you supposed to rush them, keep them moving and their minds occupied?* He did not want to force her beyond her limits.

"I don't think Solene would be too pleased with you rubbing my head."

Fin's touch faltered and Rebecca laughed. "Given the circumstances, I don't think she'd mind. Now if I started popping your spots or blackheads, then the dead wouldn't cause me as much dread as Solene would. Whenever I was sick, my mother used to rub my head, it was better than any medicine. Head rubs are literally the only way I know how to deal with other people's emotions. Did well in a test?

That's a head rub. Lose a loved one, hard luck, have a head rub."

"I can't wait to meet Solene." Rebecca tried a smile, her lip quivered and she closed her eyes. Fin listened to her breathing slow to a calmer speed. "I'm sorry, I feel stupid."

"Don't. You were due a breakdown, I've already had one. I'll have another when we get to the island. When you're ready, we'll go."

She got to her feet. "If that were the case we'd never leave this field."

The cold got deep into his body, making his movements slow. He just wanted to sleep, fall into unconsciousness and be oblivious to everything. *Would that be a bad death? Letting the snow form drifts around you. Letting its slow, numbing bite take your life as it masks the horror beneath a pristine white veil. There are no good ways.* Fin was working off of fumes. He could have stayed there and watched the snowfall until dark, but, numb and listless, they continued.

"I can't remember the last time snow stuck and didn't turn to slush," Fin said.

"Before the epidemic it would have been a rare treat if it stayed. Now, it'll only make our situation worse."

Already the peak of Croagh Patrick was white. Malachy would not be able to leave until it passed.

Climbing over gates and walls took more effort than it should have, as if his body was telling him that it was done. Noise on the road made them duck down and move towards the hedges for cover. With fear came a wave of adrenaline, which made him lithe and nimble. It did not sound like survivors, but he was not willing to check. They hid until the noise went off in the direction of Noreen's house. It was little solace knowing they could not harm her now. They moved further off road, it was much safer, but doubled the time it took to get back.

"So we go to Achill and then what?" Rebecca asked.

"I think we hibernate. As much as I want to go home, I don't think I'd make it out of County Mayo. Solene and my family are beyond me now. You guys are all I have at the moment. Go or stay. Nothing seems like the right choice. If you will have us, me and George could live with you."

"Of course. I don't want you to leave. Why do you think he did not tell us that Noreen was his granny?"

"I don't know, but we have to find him. If she was his last living relative... Well, I don't want to think of him alone right now."

"Had I known, I wouldn't have let him leave. Back there I just thought he didn't have the stomach for it and I resented him because he had the good sense to walk away before I could."

"He'll be okay. We'll make sure of it." Fin said.

Back at the house, Burke had the tarp off the boat and was working on the engine. A few bodies littered the garden.

"It's us," Fin said.

Burke stood up on the deck, lowering his rifle. "It's functional, just in need of a bit of paint. How did you get on? Where's George?" He scrutinised their faces and jumped from the deck. "What happened?"

"What do you mean? Did he not come back?" Rebecca asked.

"I haven't moved from here since you left." Burke cautiously looked over their shoulders to the bodies of the infected he shot. He did not hide his relief.

Rebecca took the radio from her pack and turned it on. Her calls went unanswered. "We would have passed him on our way back. He said he was going home." Rebecca turned on Fin. "Home – he's going back to the safehouse."

"Idiot," Burke said. "I found drums of fuel here for the boat. Enough to get us out to the island. It will take us a while to get it on the water. I haven't tried the engines yet, too much noise. I'll wait until we're ready to leave. Do you want to wait and help us get it operational? We get Rev and the others, then collect George?"

Fin thought about it for a moment. It made the most sense, but George was not exactly acting rationally. "I can get to our house in half an hour on the board," Fin said. "I don't want to leave him by himself right now. We just killed his granny."

"There's only one board," Rebecca said.

"You're not long back from the island, I'm fresher. Do you mind if I borrow one of your radios, Burke?"

"Here," he handed it over. "We'll head to the cove and get the others out of the house. Don't dawdle, I want to leave with enough light to reach Clare Island."

Fin ran to the shore and untied the paddle board from the swan. He had no wetsuit and the wind beyond the shelter of the shore whipped the crest of high waves to spray, drenching him. Despite his loss, Fin cursed George for doing this. His shoes did not give him good grip on the board, he had to kneel and use his hands to paddle.

Infected along the shore walked in a motivated manner, possibly following George. It gave Fin hope and a time limit. Thick flurries of snow started falling. So many weepers clogged the roads that it made him think there was nothing left for them in town. Fin ignored the numb pain and paddled faster, no longer looking at the coast as it passed by slowly, giving the illusion that he was not making any headway.

* * *

He landed on the beach behind their safehouse, kneeling on the shore, clenching his blue-hued fists to urge some feeling back into them. He just needed enough for a tight grip on the hammer. There was no light coming from the skylight above the loft, but the back door was open. He could not tell if the footsteps in the dark brown sand were fresh. He watched and waited until he was as sure as he could be that the building was empty. From what he knew of the infected, they did not tire of idleness, they only had to wait for something to come to them. Fin did not have the luxury of patience.

He checked that the kitchen was clear before entering. He remembered fondly the fun they had destroying the downstairs rooms. It looked like the infected had been inside and could still be there, a deterrent for other desperate survivors. They had done their job well, it was working on Fin: he moved trepidatiously through the kitchen, not daring to call out to George.

The door to the loft was open. Before he reached it, a noise from the sitting room made him pause. If he went up hoping to find George and infected were downstairs, then he would be trapped. It was impossible to tell if it was his friend making the sounds. *He still has the rifle and the pistol.* Fin could call out, but if he did and it was a weeper, then he would have to make it to the water before it reached him. On the other hand, if he said nothing and approached the door, George might attack him.

Edging closer to the sitting room with his hammer drawn, he peered in. The curtains were torn off the railing, they covered a body lying on the floor. Fin watched it long enough to notice it move, not much, but enough that he knew that whatever was beneath it, living or undead, was a threat.

Maybe George threw the blanket over it and knocked it to the floor. Without sound or movement to entice it into action, it just lay there. *Why leave it though? Why not kill it and be done? What if that's George, his only means of hiding in short notice?* Fin's mind raced.

Movement to his left drew his attention away from the body beneath the curtain. Somebody was looking right at him, leaning against the double glazed window. Not somebody. It looked him straight in the eye like a nosy neighbour, but without the shame of being caught snooping. There was no mistaking it for human. It struck the window, its hand bouncing back, leaving a dirty wet smudge. The body on the ground flinched. The noise drew others that were in the garden. Weepers. They ignored the gate and walked straight through the hedges. So many had already passed through that only the strongest trees still stood.

A woman with an empty baby carrier strapped to her back made slow progress towards the window. The sleeve of her ripped jacket covered the fleshy remains of a ravaged arm. Many of the infected had lacerations and bite marks. What was once a man wore a knitted jumper. The fabric around his shoulders was a bright yellow, the rest was a sickly brown from dried blood.

Weeping started from the garden, so close it felt as if it were right behind him. The thing beneath the curtain scrambled and made to rise. Fin bolted from the room towards the stairs to the loft, but if the curtain in the sitting room covered a weeper, then he would not have time to get to safety before it had him.

Running into a wall in his haste to be free of the cramped hallway, he nearly slipped on the kitchen tiles.

Once outside, it would be a short sprint to the water and safety. Something ran past the back window towards the open door. He could only see a shadow behind the closed blind. *Hide.* He considered sliding beneath the kitchen table, but with its flimsy cloth covering, he would be too exposed in a house of weepers. An infected child would be of a height to easily spot him. He had seconds before they were on him. To go back would mean facing the one in the sitting room. He was trapped.

I can deal with one. Then get to the loft. Fin reached the door moments before the infected. He slammed into it with his full weight, but there were too many of them. They forced their way inside. Fin was trapped between the crook of the door and the wall. The handle caught him in the gut, knocking the wind out of his lungs. Muscles spasmed in his abdomen. He went red in the face, trying to stop himself from coughing and gasping for breath.

Three weepers ran into the kitchen. One fell and others trampled it in their haste, ignorance or indifference. If one of them turned around, he was dead. He could not tell how many, if any, were left in the garden. They smelled musty, foul and stale. Infected around the front of the house knocked against the sitting room window again, drawing the weepers deeper into the house. They sounded like mourners at a funeral. When they disappeared down the hall, Fin pulled himself around the door by the handle, catching his breath as he bolted for the bay.

Fresh weeping started up on his right. He did not dare look. Running for the water felt like a dream where no matter how hard he pushed, he barely made any ground.

"No!" The scream that followed was shrill and full of rage. It came from inside the house.

George! Fin stumbled, but could not stop, not with

infected behind him. He could imagine their bloody and ruined fingers swiping at his back. There was no time to grab his board. He ran straight into the water. It dragged and slowed him the deeper he went. He could not guess how many followed him by the sound of bodies entering the water behind him. Thrashing his legs to get purchase, he swam until he was treading above inky darkness. The troubled water rose up, blocking his view of the house. He roared at the top of his lungs to draw more infected to him. A mouthful of brine caused him to cough and splutter while he dangled high above the seabed, hanging from the surface.

The dead can't swim. Alone, Fin watched a swarm of them rushing from the adjacent field into the house. Weepers knocked the slower zombies to the ground, following George's shouts and cries. Fin felt a spite so strong it became a physical pain. *It was George beneath the curtain. Had I just checked, we could be upstairs in the loft right now.*

Fin kicked out in the dark water at invisible hands that reached out from his imagination to pull him down.

There was a final roar from inside. Brief and quick, filled with grief and anguish. After the sound of the single gunshot, Fin's own cries joined the keening of the weepers. He shouted until he lost his voice. Infected were drawn towards him, some came out from the house and followed him into the bay. Weepers were silenced as they sank. Some were pushed back on shore by the wash of the waves.

"George! I'm sorry." His fury was replaced with shame. His calls went unanswered. But for the dead, the house was silent.

* * *

Fin treaded water, unthinking, unsure, in a state of shock, until fireworks erupted further along the coast. *Rebecca!*

The infected turned towards the explosions and colours, ignoring Fin. *She has no idea how many she's bringing down on her.* He unstrapped the hammer from his belt and swam towards the shore, keeping low in the water. His hatred for the infected was unbearable and he knew of only one way to rid himself of it.

He swam perpendicular to the shore until the infected lost sight of him amidst the waves. When the stragglers turned their attention to the fireworks, Fin swam towards the land and dragged himself across the shore on his belly. He grabbed the leash of the paddle board and pulled it into the bay, avoiding the thrashing bodies of waterlogged weepers. *Escape route sorted.* The first infected he crept behind wore an old beanie cap. It did nothing to protect its skull, only muffling the sound of Fin's hammer. It collapsed, air hissing from its lungs.

Fin used the claw edge on the next one, a hunched-over middle-aged man. It parted his coarse grey hair and went right through the bone. He had to hold the head down with his heel to pull his weapon free. It took him a while to realise that the fireworks had stopped. Most of the weepers were gone. There was only the slow zombies to deal with now. So he thought. Burke's radio had survived the water inside its protective case. Rebecca's voice came from his side like a spectre, calling the undead to him.

They filled the garden like grotesque, gothic statues. He almost felt awkward standing before them with the bloody hammer and two dead zombies behind him. They could not weep, their lungs were too congested with that foul phlegm that slowly choked the weepers. Four had mortal wounds. One well-muscled man had his throat gored, the blood that oozed out was thick and clotted like stale cream. All those dead fish-like eyes were concentrated on Fin.

An infected child peaked its head from behind a young female zombie's legs. The child's mouth worried tough muscle and flesh. Pus and blood seeped down her chin. She moved with startling speed, frantically rushing ahead of the others, her weep muffled by the human meat she choked on. Bloody, ruined fingers tore at the air between them.

Repulsed, Fin stumbled back with a new lease on life, with its end trundling towards him. He returned to the water. He felt shells and stones underfoot, testing each step for fear of falling. The waves breaking around her legs made the weeper cautious. Fin thought her actions almost human. "Come on! Prime Irish beef! Get a cutlet." Despite his hatred for them, this was still a child. At least it had been recently. She wore a good rain jacket and warm clothes, somebody had cared deeply for her.

Fin ran his hand across the surface of the water, spraying the child, coaxing her out further. When she was waist deep, a wave unbalanced her. Fin rushed forward, shouldered her ruined hands out of the way and knocked her off her feet. Her weeping was drowned out. He grabbed the front of her jacket to keep her steady, then caved her skull in.

An animal wail escaped his mouth. Fin faced the blame-less eyes of the zombies. "George, I'm coming!"

He dragged the limp body of the child onto the shore with him. He could not in good conscience let her disappear completely from the world. *Somebody will look for you after this. You will be remembered.* Keeping the bay close at his back, he made slow progress towards the first zombie. He swung with the hammer and jumped back, but too soon, just landing a glancing blow. The nose crumpled with a snick. Unbalanced, the zombie toppled backwards. Fin rushed in and sideswiped the prone zombie's temple. Its eyes rolled back. The second swift blow broke its jaw.

Fin dashed away from the remaining zombies. There were only six, but even one could overwhelm him if he was not careful. He had an idea. He ran to the side of the shed and picked up the rusty rake leaning against it. Still shaking, he advanced on the next zombie. Standing as far from it as he could, he violently struck the end of the rake into the zombie's head. It stumbled back, held its balance until it leaned forward and fell on its face.

Fin let out a laugh of success and finished the zombie with a hammer blow to the back of the head. "Goodnight you prick! George!"

With the next zombie he turned the rake vertical, wedged it between its legs and then turned it so the rake was against the back of the zombie's knees. When he pulled, the zombie went down. This time when the hammer destroyed its brain, it lodged in the skull and would not come free. Forced to abandon it, he unsheathed his knife.

The remaining zombies forced him back into the water. He let the waves knock them down, before moving in with the knife. It was a horrible weapon, slicing flesh but getting stuck in bone. He nearly cut his hand when a zombie's skull stopped it. The blade quickly lost its edge. He had to get in close and personal. His weapon was too broad to pass fully through an eye socket. The damage he caused them was horrendous, but most of them rose without the faintest sign that they were aware they were missing eyes or savagely scarred.

Whenever they had the upper hand, he waded out further into the bay to draw them out and incapacitate them. He had to push the knife in under the chin and jigger it about to destroy the brain. The knife made a sucking sound when he pulled it out. Fin collapsed into the water, pushing away from bodies. Already the shallows were thick with human remains. He went out further lying on his back to catch his breath. His limbs throbbed from the brief engagement. He looked up into the thickening clouds, eyes stinging from the salt. His stomach cramped and he turned over to vomit.

"George!" Fin lost his breath roaring his friend's name. An answer came in the form of weeping in the fields close to town. Rebecca's rockets had drawn the horde. The ambling plague and ravenous blight moved towards their safehouse. There was nothing he could do to stop them. "Sit tight, George. I'll think of something."

* * *

No matter how many went into the bay, their numbers only seemed to swell. His throat ached and his voice was hoarse from shouting. Gurgled weeps were silenced by the bay, but it did not seem deep enough to quieten them all. Exhausted, he retreated to the paddle board. His energy was spent, but his rage remained. The garden was filled with infected. Without the rockets to lure them off, they remained focused on Fin. There was only one he owed a death to now. Kneeling on his board, he waited for George to come out of the house and join his kind.

Rebecca's voice came from Burke's radio. Words were beyond Fin. He clicked the receiver down a few times to let her know that he was listening. The effort proved difficult. Snow started to fall in thick flurries.

"Fin, there's a boat coming from the island. The Clare

Island ferry. They saw our fireworks! We're safe! Have you found George yet?"

Slouching on the board, Fin clicked the receiver again in response. Then he turned the radio off. There was nothing left to say. *She's safe.* The thought brought him no peace. *There is no safety left in this world.* He continued his vigil for George. His blade was bent, blunt and badly damaged, but it was good enough for a few more uses. *Sleep softly and dream of nothing.*

* * *

A large wave rocked the paddle board, nearly knocking Fin into the bay. It curled closer to the shore and wet rocks that had dried since the tide went out. It was the wake of a large ferry, its old engines roused the weepers. A searchlight blossomed in the dark, its beam traced across the shore. It stopped on Fin in the freezing water.

Blood and gore covered his upper body. His arms were caked in it to the wrist. Paddling had kept his hands clean.

"He's infected. Look at him. Shoot him and let's head home."

There was a scuffle and a rifle shot that went wide. "Get off me!"

It was difficult to hear them over the whipped up weepers. "Give the lad a chance."

Was that Burke?

"Fin!" Rebecca called out. "Where's George?"

Infected. He looked directly into the brilliant light that scalded his retinas, sending darts of pain into his brain. His earlier anger was numbed by the cold. He no longer had the strength to lift the knife.

Fin turned away from salvation to look back at the house. The light left him and scanned the shore. Infected gathered in such numbers that it was impossible to count them accurately. Fin studied each one, looking for his friend's face amongst them. They fed upon each other. All aboard the ferry were silent. Somebody started praying. Another started firing into the mass of bodies, at least he had some results. The light cast Fin's shadow far ahead of him across the dead, gaunt and brittle. The house was overrun.

Fin wept.

THE SURVIVORS CLUB

**The story continues in
Feast & Famine
Book 2 of the Weep Series**

Don't miss Weep 2. Join my Survivors Club.

Survivors get access to:

LATEST NEWS AND UPDATES
EXCLUSIVE CONTENT
SPECIAL OFFERS
FREE STORIES

All delivered straight to your inbox.

For more information check out
www.facebook.com/EoinBradyAuthor

PLEASE LEAVE A REVIEW!

You can make a massive difference to the series by leaving an honest review. If you enjoyed Weep, you can support it by simply giving it a star rating on Amazon. Or, if you have a spare moment, writing a review. It can be as short as you like.

Your effort helps other readers find Weep. If nothing else, it will make my day.

Thank you.

ALSO BY EOIN BRADY

HAVE YOU READ THEM ALL?

I'm Not Saying It

Romance

Travel blogger Shade Watts never stays in one place for long, or lets herself get too close to anyone. Romance just complicates things, so she travels alone, editing her life along with the articles she posts. Then, on an Irish island, she meets Diarmuid, a shy but charming musician who's as reluctant to open up as she is. One week is all it could take to change everything.

Somniloquent The First Dreamer

Fantasy

The First Dreamer is Waking...

Pre-Order Now!

Releasing June 1st 2020

ABOUT THE AUTHOR

Eoin Brady is the author of apocalyptic horror, epic fantasy and contemporary romance novels. Most of which are set in Ireland, where he lives and writes. Weep, his most recent story begins on the west coast of Ireland, as the country is ravaged by a horrifying disease.

He is currently writing three series; **Weep** (Post-apocalyptic horror), **Somniloquent** (Epic fantasy) and **I'm Not Saying It** (Contemporary Romance).

You can follow Eoin Brady on the platforms below.

ACKNOWLEDGMENTS

There would be no Weep without Manon Nagy. Her enthusiasm, belief and help has bolstered me from first idea to published book. My favourite part about writing this story has been sitting down to read it with her. *I cannot thank you enough, but I won't stop trying.*

I'm enormously grateful to my editor Gheorghe Rusu, without whose many talents, the book you read would be quite different. May he take the knowledge of my terrible grammar to the grave.

My thanks to friends and family, great inspiration for post-apocalyptic horror.

Finally, but by no means least of all, thank you for reading.

COPYRIGHT

Published by Eoin Brady
Cover Design by Damonza
Copy-Edited by Gheorghe Rusu
Proofread by Manon Nagy

Made in the USA
Columbia, SC
03 October 2024

43569090R00290